THE
FRAILTY
OF THINGS

TAMSEN SCHULTZ

EverAfter Romance
A Division of Diversion Publishing Corp.
443 Park Avenue South, Suite 1008
New York, New York 10016
www.EverAfterRomance.com

Cover Design by Sian Foulkes
Edited by Julie Molinari

This is a work of fiction. Names, characters, places and incidents either are the
product of the author's imagination or are used fictitiously. Any resemblance to
actual persons, living or dead, events or locales is entirely coincidental.

For more information, email info@everafterromance.com

First EverAfter Romance edition March 2017.
Print ISBN: 978-1-63576-037-8

CHAPTER 1

KIT FORRESTER TOOK A SIP of her beer and eyed the man sitting across from her. Drew Carmichael looked every inch the business tycoon he was. At over six feet of lean muscle, his blond hair, blue eyes, and strong chin gave him a hint of New England aristocracy. And she knew that, truth be told, Drew *could* trace his family back to the Mayflower. But it was his presence more than his appearance that conveyed an inherent sense of authority.

And authority was good, considering what Kit knew his *other* job to be.

She set her glass down and leaned forward. "Drew, in all the years I've known you, you've never, and I repeat *never*, asked me for a personal favor."

Her eyes stayed on his face even as he flicked a look out the window. Under normal circumstances, she might think he was just taking in the view of the beautiful winter night through the front picture window of the small restaurant in which they sat. But as charming as the Hudson Valley of New York, and particularly Old Windsor, was this time of year, she suspected Drew was being vigilant rather than appreciative.

His eyes came back to hers. "I know, Kit. Believe me, I know. And you can say 'no.'"

"But you'd rather I say 'yes,'" she said, finishing his thought, if not his statement. Drew gave very little away, but she'd known him long enough, nearly fourteen years now, that she could see in the shadows of his expression the unease she heard in his voice. "Tell me what you need," she said.

She watched some of the tension leave his eyes, but he paused before answering as a couple came through the door, followed by a gust of cold wind, and headed toward the bar. Once the new patrons were well away, Drew set his elbows on the table and moved closer to her.

"Jonathon Parker is an agent with MI6, which, as you know, is the British version of the CIA."

Kit nodded. She traveled a lot for her job, met a lot of interesting people, knew a lot of interesting things—especially considering the fact that for the past eight years, she'd helped out Drew and his employer more than a few times.

His position as one of the board members for his family's multi-national conglomerate was a perfect foil for his real job with the CIA. And Kit, well, she was the high-flying daughter of a very wealthy, and very deceased, businessman. That, coupled with her own international success as an award-winning writer of modern literature, gave her easy access to people and places.

"Jonathon was placed on probationary leave several days ago," Drew continued. "They're investigating his potential involvement in the release of information that compromised several key MI6 assets in the Middle East."

"That's not good," Kit said, leaning even closer to Drew. She knew what she did for him, for the agency, was potentially dangerous, but she never really gave it much thought. She knew Drew well, trusted him, and trusted that if he asked her for help, it was for a good reason. Still, she didn't like the idea of anyone else knowing what she did on the side.

Drew let out a little huff of air that could almost, but not quite, be called a sardonic laugh. "No kidding. It's not good for anyone involved. Not Parker; not the assets."

"So, what do you want me to do?" she asked. "This sounds professional, but you said you needed a personal favor."

Drew took a sip of his own beer, set it down, and took a deep breath. "You're already going to Rome later this week. I was hoping you could stop by London on your way through and hand off some information for me."

"Drop it to Parker?" she asked.

Drew gave a single, sharp nod.

Kit stared at her companion as her mind went through the logic. She didn't know all the ins and outs of the CIA, but she was pretty sure that passing information from an active agent to an agent being investigated wouldn't be looked upon kindly. Especially considering that the agent being investigated was foreign. She also didn't know what would happen to Drew if he were caught, but she was certain it wouldn't be good.

"Drew," she said, concern lacing her tone.

"You don't have to do it, Kit. And if you choose not to, I won't hold it against you."

"But?" she prompted. Drew wasn't the most straight and narrow guy she knew—she figured, in his job, he couldn't be—but he *was* one of the most principled. If he wanted to involve himself with an agent under suspicion, he had to have a reason.

Again, his gaze traveled out the window before returning to her. She could see he was debating whether or not to answer. Finally his eyes slid closed, and for a moment, he looked older than his forty years.

"Drew?" She leaned forward and laid her hand on his arm. He opened his eyes.

"I'm not going to lie, Kit. It got bad. Three of the four assets were killed within days of the information leak. Whoever did this deserves whatever justice the British decide to mete out. But it wasn't Parker. He's being framed."

"Framed?" She couldn't help the single eyebrow that shot up. When spooks started framing each other, it was bound to get messy.

One side of Drew's mouth ticked up into a smile. "I know, it's like a bad version of *Who's On First* when spies start playing these games. If it ever gets unraveled, it will be a miracle."

"But you know Parker wasn't involved?" she pressed, tucking a strand of auburn hair behind her ear.

"He wasn't," Drew answered with certainty.

"And why can't this go through official channels?"

Drew let out a sigh. "Because the information I have isn't information that we, the Agency, want to share with MI6. And before you ask," he said, raising a hand to stave off her question, "the official Agency answer is still 'no,' even when we know that it will likely ruin the life of a great agent."

Kit sat back in her chair and, for a moment, regretted getting into this conversation in the first place. There wasn't any doubt in her mind that she would help Drew, she'd just been so stunned when he'd asked for a personal favor that she'd started asking questions. And, not surprisingly, she didn't like what she'd ended up hearing. She didn't like that her own government seemed to value life so little. She wasn't naïve and knew that there might be a very good reason why the CIA didn't want to share whatever information Drew was referring to, but still, the thought that they might have information that could help someone and choose to not use it didn't sit well on her shoulders.

"If you don't want to—"

"Of course I'll do it, Drew. I was just thinking that I'm glad I'm not the one who has to make these decisions. I'm glad I'm not the one who has to weigh the value of sharing information against the lives it might help or harm." She took another sip of her drink and set it down with a small smile. "I'd totally suck at it," she added.

Drew smiled back—a real smile. "That's because you have a heart and you're human."

Kit rolled her eyes. She was a softy; she'd freely admit to that. But Drew wasn't giving himself any credit. He had a tough job, and she knew how much he cared about just about everything. Maybe too much.

"So then," she continued. "Now that we've settled that, what are the particulars?"

Drew slid two business cards across the table to her. Both were printed with her name and generic contact information. One had a small, Celtic design in the upper right corner, a design taken from her first book, *Celtic Shelter*, and the other had a similar design, only it was in the upper left corner. The cards looked normal and bore nothing unusual that would draw attention to them.

"This one," Drew said, his finger tapping the card with the mark on the right side, "is for Ambrose."

Fabio Ambrose was a diplomatic liaison located in Rome. She'd met him on numerous occasions and had already been planning to see him, at Drew's request, on her upcoming trip to Rome. Ambrose was her official assignment.

"And this one," Drew said, sliding the other card over, the card with the design on the left, "is for Parker."

"And how will I meet Parker?" she asked, taking the cards and tucking them into her purse. She wasn't sure what information was on them or how the intended recipients would retrieve it, but she assumed that it was some sort of old-school dot technology where information was encoded in tiny pixels that made up the print.

"That's easy," Drew said, leaning back in his chair, looking a little bit more relaxed than he had just a few moments before. "His sister is a journalist who covers financial news."

Kit laughed. "And, let me guess, financial crimes as well?"

"The two do tend to go together," Drew answered with a grin.

"How fortuitous then, that the book I'm currently working on revolves around the impact such a crime has on a small community."

Drew's grin widened into a smile. "I thought so too. Isabelle Parker would make an excellent interview subject. She's older than Parker by several years and has been on the beat forever. A request from you to meet wouldn't be unusual."

Kit shook her head and smiled. "I'll do some research on her and have my publicist contact her tomorrow. Provided she'll be in town, I can fly through London and spend a few days there before heading to Rome for Marco Baresi's party."

Marco was a fellow writer and her mentor. He was also, at one point years ago, something more. Marco had recently received a very prestigious European book award, and his publisher was throwing him a huge party to celebrate. Of course she would be there. And when Drew had found out, he'd asked her to contact Ambrose while in town. It would seem she was adding Isabelle Parker to her list now as well.

She looked down at her purse and contemplated the two business cards inside. One was Drew doing his job. But the other, well, thinking of it gave her pause. She wasn't about to back out, but that didn't mean she wasn't concerned.

"Drew? Are you sure?" she asked, bringing her gaze up to his.

She knew he saw the seriousness of her question and her concern for him. His expression softened even as a world-weary look stole across his face.

He nodded. "Yes, I'm certain. He's a good agent and I've known him for years. When I heard what was happening, I knew it wasn't him. And when I found the information that could prove it, well, that just made it all that much more clear in my mind. But," he said, taking a deep breath and then letting it out, "as much as I hate to admit it, I can see why we don't want to share what we have with our counterparts in England. I even agree with the decision."

"But?"

"But Parker will know what to do with it. I trust him not to share it, but to use it to clear his name."

"That's a lot of trust to put in someone, Drew," she pointed out.

He gave her a wry smile. "Ironic, isn't it? Spies aren't supposed to trust anyone with anything, yet I'm entrusting him with information that could not only pose a threat to the US but also get me fired and likely imprisoned too."

Kit studied him for a moment and saw the resolve in his eyes. "Well, if it makes you feel any better, I'm not sure of the wisdom of your decision either, but I *do* trust you." She took the last sip of her beer and looked around the room. It was sometimes surreal meeting with Drew, knowing the shady world he operated in, then looking around and seeing couples laughing, families dining together, and the world going on.

"Is there anything else I should know?" she asked, bringing her attention back to her companion.

Drew finished his drink and set the glass back down on the table. He didn't look up as he answered, but kept his focus on his fingers as they caught the moisture gathered on his glass. "I'm not going to lie and say this meeting with Parker is like all the others, because it isn't. I haven't heard anything that would indicate that there could be problems, but just be safe, Kit. Be aware of what's going on around you. You have good instincts; use them. If something doesn't feel right, trust that feeling."

Kit frowned. Drew had given her this same speech any number of times when she'd first started shuttling information for him. But he hadn't given it in years. That he felt the need to now came as a surprise.

It made her want to ask, yet again, if he was sure he wanted to go forward with his plan. But remembering the look of certainty in his eyes the first time she'd asked, she knew she already had her answer. And so she nodded in response to his warning.

"Always," she said.

His eyes watched hers for a moment, then traveled down to her empty beer glass. "Shall we?" he asked, nodding toward the door, ending the meeting.

"You go on ahead," she said, suddenly feeling that she wanted a little time alone with a glass of whiskey. Drew frowned. She smiled. "Really, Drew, please. I know you have to drive back to New York City tonight, so go on ahead. I'm just going to have another drink, enjoy this view," she said with a gesture toward the picture window, "and then head home."

"You sure?" he asked, concern still lacing his tone.

"Yes, I'm sure. Go. Drive safe. The roads are cleared from the snow last night, but they still get icy."

"Yeah, yeah, yeah," Drew said, rising with a smile of his own and donning his black cashmere scarf and coat. "I know, the Taconic Parkway is winding, ice builds up, and people don't drive safely." He mimicked what she told him nearly every time he visited during the winter months.

"Just call me 'Mom,'" she said with a laugh as he pulled on his leather gloves.

Drew rolled his eyes, then bent down and kissed her cheek. "You're almost a decade younger than I am, but you do give my mom a run for her money in the worry department."

"Just be safe," Kit said, grabbing his scarf and stopping him from straightening away. He might joke, but she meant every word and wanted to make sure he knew it. His face was a few inches away from hers, and it occurred to her that the position was an intimate one. Though it had never been like that between the two of them, she knew that if anyone she knew saw them, gossip would ensue—the joys of a small town.

"Be safe," Kit repeated, quietly.

Drew's eyes held hers for a moment, then he gave a tiny nod. "You too," he said, then dipped his head and gave her one more kiss on the cheek. Reluctantly, she released him and watched him walk out the door.

Through the window, she saw him climb into his silver Mercedes SUV and back out of the plowed parking lot. She glanced down at her purse again, hoped like hell Drew knew what he was doing, then ordered a shot of whiskey.

• • •

It was just after ten when Kit finally made her way to her car. Consisting of a post office, a general store, and Anderson's, the restaurant she'd just come from, Old Windsor, was never a very happening spot. It was even quieter on this cold, Sunday evening.

Her boots crunched the snow as she crossed the street toward her car. Kit loved winter, but in temperatures hovering around zero this time of night, she was glad for her gloves, hat, and scarf, not to mention her long down coat that nearly reached the top of her boots. A small gust of wind blew, and the frigid air snaked under her scarf and down her neck. She hunched her shoulders in protection as she reached into her pocket for her keys.

Concentrating on where she was putting her feet, Kit was startled to hear the sound of a car door opening. Her head shot up and her step faltered. Parked next to her own vehicle was a black Range Rover. She knew a lot of people who drove Range Rovers, especially this time of year, but only one who would show up like this. Despite the cold, she paused about ten feet from her destination and watched as a jacketed figure unfolded itself from the ominous-looking car.

"Kit," her brother said.

"Caleb," she responded. She hadn't seen or spoken to her brother in five months, almost enough time to believe he wasn't a part of her life. Almost enough time to accept, again, that she was fine on her own; that she was fine with having no family.

"We need to talk," he said. Kit didn't respond for a moment. She and her brother didn't *talk*. They never *talked*. Not anymore. There had been a time in their lives when that hadn't been the case. There had been a time when she'd idolized her older brother, when he'd looked out for her, when they'd gone fishing together, and when she had believed that he had an answer for everything.

But that time had long ago passed, and they hadn't been in each other's presence for more than a few days a year for over a decade. Kit started to speak but stopped short when a second figure emerged from the passenger side of Caleb's car.

She was glad her face was hidden in the shadows of her hat and scarf as Garret Cantona, her brother's right-hand man, straightened to his full height. Kit was tall, easily five foot eleven, but Garret's six-foot-three form dwarfed hers. Like Caleb, he wore jeans and work boots, but rather than a jacket, Garret sported a black sweater and a gray beanie. She knew the hat covered light-brown hair that, if it got too long, curled in ways that bothered him. And she felt, more than saw, his light-blue eyes—eyes rimmed with thick, black lashes—studying her.

"And I see you brought your Mini-Me," she added, forcing

her gaze from Garret back to her brother in time to see a look of irritation flicker across Caleb's face.

"Kit," Caleb warned.

She let out a little breath of annoyance. It was too cold to be having this conversation now. "I'm going home. If you'd like to follow me, feel free. You know I have enough room for you. If you don't want to stay with me, there are dozens of bed and breakfasts around. I don't care either way, but I'm too cold to be standing out here right now." She almost added that they could feel free to camp on her property too, since that was exactly what Garret had been doing when she'd first met him. Her brother had been in town helping a friend of hers and had brought Garret along. She'd discovered Garret camping on the back edge of her eighty acres— close enough to a road to be easily accessible, but far enough away from everything else to be seen. Why her brother hadn't had him stay in the house with them was a mystery to her.

"Cantona will go with you," Caleb all but ordered.

Kit laughed. "I don't think so, Caleb. You can meet me there." Both cars had been backed into their spots, and Kit had to pass Garret as she made her way to her driver's side door. Keeping an eye mostly on the icy path, she glanced up at her brother's companion as she drew alongside him. His eyes were trained on hers, but she could read nothing in his expression. She wished it were the same for him—that he would find her expression as neutral as she found his—but she wasn't as good at this game as either of the two men who stood with her. Still, he stepped back and let her pass.

After unlocking her door, she slid onto the leather seat and shivered as her cold jeans pressed against the backs of her legs. She reached for the door but Garret was already there, closing it. And for a moment, for a very brief second, she thought she saw a question in his eyes. Then the door shut.

"Go with her," Kit heard Caleb say as she fumbled with her key in her gloved hands.

"No," Garret responded. "It's not as though she's going to

run, Forrester. You just dropped in on her after five months of no contact. Give her space," he added.

Kit heard Caleb start to reply, but whatever he said was lost to her as her engine roared to life. She pulled out onto the road and turned west, toward home. Through her rearview mirror, she saw both men climb back into Caleb's Range Rover. She wasn't sure what to feel when his headlights appeared through her back window.

Not wanting to think about the sudden appearance of both Caleb and Garret, Kit turned her mind to her meeting with Drew. She wasn't going to back out, but the more she thought about it, the more anxious she became—for Drew, not herself. She didn't know the half of what he did in his job, but she knew he was committed to it, almost too much so. She also knew he wasn't married, and from what she could tell—from her conversations with him and with their mutual friend, Dani Williamson, now Dani Fuller—he'd never even had a relationship that had lasted more than a month or so.

If the MI6 agent, Parker, was playing him, Drew could lose everything—everything he had worked so hard for would disappear. The thought made her stomach turn. Drew was one of the good guys, and he deserved some happiness in his life—in whatever form that came.

Kit made a promise to herself to do what she could to help Drew and she was already mentally planning the adjustments she would need to make to her schedule to accommodate his request as she pulled onto her long driveway. In the distance, she could see the top of her home. That sight, and the drive from the road to her abode, always brought her a sense of calm.

That sense of peace was why she lived in the Hudson Valley. She was young, almost thirty-two, with a career that kept her in the public eye to a certain extent and, over the years, more than one person had asked her why she chose to live alone in such a small, rural town. Ironically, even though she was a writer, it was a question she couldn't adequately answer with words—it was just this *thing* she felt each time she came home that drew and kept her here.

Her house came into view as she rounded a gentle curve. Unlike most houses in the area, hers was modern in design. From the driveway, it resembled the side of a staircase, with three levels climbing the hill. The lower level held a guest room, laundry room, and all those other rooms that only occasionally got used, like her TV room and gym. On the middle level was the main living area and kitchen, and the upper level had two more guest rooms and her massive master bedroom suite with an attached office. Every side of the house that wasn't tucked against the hill was lined with floor-to-ceiling windows.

It was bigger than she needed just for herself. But when working with the architect, she'd been adamant that the home be designed in such a way that it would be easy to sell if she ever wanted to—which meant standard things like more bedrooms, a big, easy living area, and nothing too crazily custom. At least that's what she'd told the architect. Although it was something she thought about less and less with each passing year, in rare moments she wondered if she'd really been hoping to fill the house with her own family. It wasn't that she thought she was getting too old; age had nothing to do with it, since she knew she was still young. But after having lived on her own since she was seventeen, she often wondered if she might be too set in her ways to ever be able to live with someone else, let alone raise a family.

Taking a deep breath and forcing those thoughts from her head, Kit pulled around to the parking area carved into the hill at the back of the house. After parking in her garage, she didn't bother to wait for her brother and was already in her kitchen pulling off her hat and gloves when Caleb and Garret came in, each carrying a duffel bag.

Her eyebrow went up. "So, I guess you're staying."

"We need to talk," Caleb repeated as he dropped his bag in the entryway and stepped into the kitchen.

"I wasn't planning on seeing you tonight and, believe it or not,

I don't actually have time to talk with you right now," she said as she removed her coat.

Garret had placed his bag on the floor and was leaning against the wall, arms crossed, watching her.

"Kit." Again, Caleb's voice held a hint of warning.

"Look, Caleb, as Garret pointed out, you just dropped in on me. I do have a life and, in fact, I'm not even going to be here very long. I'm heading to Europe the day after tomorrow to attend a party for a dear friend of mine. Between now and then, I have a number of things I have to do, some of which I need to do tonight." Like reschedule her flight through Heathrow so she could meet up with Isabelle Parker.

Her brother opened his mouth to say something, but she cut him off. "The downstairs guest room you use whenever you decide to show up is made up. You," she said, turning to Garret, "can either sleep on the sofa down where Caleb sleeps or there are two more guest rooms upstairs. Both are made up and both have attached baths."

"You can sleep on the sofa," Caleb interjected. Kit let out a sardonic laugh at the order issued from her brother. At one point in their lives, hearing the protective tone in Caleb's voice would have felt normal, would have made her feel cared for. Now it was just ridiculous. Not only were they all adults, but Caleb had long ago given up the right to be protective of her in any way.

Garret chuckled. "I don't think so, Forrester. Between a bed and a couch," he shook his head, "it's a bed for me." And to prevent any further discussion, Garret grabbed his bag and headed up the stairs. Neither she nor Caleb said anything as he left. And when they heard the door to one of the guest rooms click shut, the silence between Kit and her brother suddenly felt heavy.

"He won't bother you," Caleb finally said. "We've worked together for years," he added. *He wouldn't dare* was left unsaid.

"I know," Kit said. "Ian told me about Garret when he was here with you last fall helping Jesse with that mess." She didn't mention that she had actually met Garret; it seemed easier not to.

Saying she'd heard of him from Ian MacAllister, the county sheriff and a mutual friend of hers and her brother's, seemed reasonable.

Caleb and Garret had come to offer their help, and considerable expertise, to Ian when one of Kit's good friends, Jesse, had gotten caught in the crosshairs of a woman who had stalked and nearly killed her on more than one occasion. While Kit was grateful for the help Caleb and Garret had provided, the fact that both had up and disappeared from Windsor before she'd even had the chance to thank them served to remind her of just why Caleb was no longer a significant part of her life. Not even when he was standing five feet in front of her in her own kitchen.

They stood for another silent moment, and with every passing second, the gulf between them seemed to open wider and wider.

"I have some things I need to do," she said abruptly, breaking the building tension.

"We do need to talk, Kit," Caleb said as she started to walk away.

She paused at the bottom of the stairs, tempted to just keep walking. But she didn't. Instead, she turned to face him. He was watching her, still standing where he'd stopped when he walked in. She and her brother didn't have much of a relationship, but he was still her brother, and he *had* come to help her friend Jesse when he'd been asked.

"I have some things I need to do tomorrow, but I should be free by the afternoon," she said. She saw another look of irritation flash across his face, but it was gone almost as fast as it had come. He gave a small, curt nod. She waited for him to pick up his bag and head downstairs, but when he didn't, she said her good night and climbed the stairs to her own sanctuary.

• • •

Two hours later, Kit was still awake. She'd changed her ticket, adding a layover in England rather than flying straight to Italy as she'd originally planned. She had also researched Isabelle Parker, the journalist, and e-mailed her own publicist to see about setting up a meeting with Ms. Parker while she was in London.

The change to her schedule had been easy, but given that she was expected at a party in Rome on Friday and had anticipated arriving Wednesday, she needed to move her departure up a day to give herself enough time in London. That meant she'd be flying out the next day rather than the day after. Caleb wouldn't like that, but it wasn't as if he'd given her any warning that he was coming, so she shoved aside what little guilt she felt for not sticking around.

After finishing things up in her office, she'd taken a shower in an effort to quiet her mind and body. But it hadn't worked. And now, at just after midnight, she stood alone in her room, in her pajamas, staring out at the winter night through her floor-to-ceiling windows.

And it came as no surprise when, behind her, she heard her bedroom door click open and shut. Even without the soft sound, she would have known when Garret walked into the room. For good or for bad, it was just like that between them. Looking over her shoulder at him, she watched as he paused a few feet into the room and met her gaze.

"Mini-Me?" he said, his lips quirking into a shadow of a grin.

"If the shoe fits," Kit responded into the quiet of the night. He had showered too; his hair still looked damp. He was in jeans again, with a white t-shirt and bare feet.

"I'm three inches taller than your brother," he said, coming toward her.

She turned her attention back to the window. "Being a Mini-Me is more a state of mind than a physical state."

He chuckled as he came to stand beside her, but she didn't feel much like laughing. Running a finger down the side of her face, he brushed her hair away from her profile. "I've missed you," he said.

She couldn't deny the little hitch in her heart at hearing those words, but she didn't want to go there with him. It would be so easy to turn into his arms and finish what they'd started all those months ago. But all the months apart had made her realize something—while her body might want Garret, the life he could offer her, that he could offer *them*, wasn't one she wanted. So she changed the subject.

"It was for nights like this that I had all these windows put in," she said, placing her palm on the glass pane. It was cool to the touch, and the heat and moisture from her hand created a small ring of fog. She paused and watched as it disappeared. "There are maybe four or five nights a year when we have both snow and a full moon, and even fewer that are clear nights with new fallen snow," she said.

Kit kept her gaze on her little valley, letting the raw beauty of it seep into her soul. A fox trotted across the driveway several yards away from her house, then disappeared into the woods. The full moon hung in the dark sky, its light reflecting off the snow and casting the night into an encompassing kind of blue. Trees created shadows that fell in muted patterns onto a ground that looked blanketed with diamonds.

"The beauty of it is almost enough to make me believe in magic," she said quietly as she let her hand drop.

"Kit," Garret said. He made a move that would bring him closer to her but stopped when she shrank away. The peace that had flirted with her as she'd looked out at the night vanished.

"You're upset," he said.

The funny thing was, she *wasn't* upset. She had every right to be, but she wasn't. She was something much worse; she was disappointed. Sad.

She shook her head. "I'm not going to deny that we have chemistry, Garret."

"Just chemistry?" His voice was flat as he cut her off.

"Yes, chemistry," she repeated, then finally turned to look at him again. In the light of the moon, she could see his blue eyes locked on hers. The physical pull she felt when she held his gaze seemed to mock the idea that what they shared could be "just" anything.

"Chemistry," she said one more time. As if saying it would make it so.

He didn't blink. He didn't so much as move a muscle. Then he seemed to take an internal deep breath and relax. His shoulders dropped an inch and a small smile played on his lips.

"I read an interesting article on my flight here," he said.

His non sequitur caught her by surprise and she frowned in response.

"It was about love at first sight. Do you know how many women believe in it?" he asked.

Too many, she thought to herself, but she said nothing and shook her head.

"34 percent," he answered. "Do you know how many *men* believe in love at first sight?" he continued.

"A lot less," she guessed, feeling cynical.

"73 percent," he stated.

She simply stared at him for a long moment. He couldn't possibly be telling her he was in love with her. They did have some something—something she had never experienced with anyone else—but they had only spent less than three days together.

She cleared her throat and looked away. "Well, it's not the love at first sight that's most important, it's the love at the one-hundredth or one-thousandth or ten-thousandth sight that really matters."

For a moment, Garret said nothing. Then he sighed. "I'm sorry I didn't call. I could have," he admitted. "But I wasn't sure what I would say. Or if you would even have wanted me to."

That last sentence was said more as a question. Would she have wanted him to call? The girly girl in her said yes, of course he should have called, but the woman in her, the woman who had her life figured out and knew what she wanted out of it—including what she did and didn't want out of a partner, was a little bit glad he hadn't.

"I don't know." She answered what he hadn't really asked. And Kit knew her honest response hurt him. She felt his energy change.

She hadn't intended to upset him, but she wasn't going to lie—not to him, not to herself.

Gathering her strength, she turned to face him. Kit could feel the heat coming off his body and was once again struck by how easy it would be to slide her arms around his waist and bury herself in him. But she wouldn't.

"There is *something* between us, Garret. I've already conceded that. But what I want for my life isn't what you can give, and I'm not interested in asking you to change."

"Then don't," he said.

She shook her head. "I'm not, Garret. The man you are is someone I admire and like and, yes, am attracted to. But don't ask me to change, either. Sometimes love or lust or chemistry or whatever you want to call it isn't enough. A wise woman I know who has been married for over fifty years once told me that it's often not the big things that ruin a relationship but all the little things. And though I don't doubt your sincerity and I believe your feelings for me are real, I've had enough people in my life like you—people that can't or don't talk about their work and who come and go as the job dictates—to know that it's not what I want for *my* life."

She saw his jaw tick at that. But she needed for him to hear this. It wasn't him she was rejecting, it was the kind of life he led, and she wasn't about to try and change him. She'd been honest with him about that, too.

"It doesn't have to be that way," he said.

"It doesn't?" she challenged. She couldn't see any other way it *could* be. Garret led a life of secrets. A life that required him to be places within a moment's notice. A life that didn't allow him to share when he'd be going, where he'd be going, or why he was going, let alone when he might come back.

"It doesn't," he insisted.

"Fine, then," she said. "What are you doing here?" she asked.

Garret shrugged. "I don't actually know. Caleb said he needed to talk to you, and I came along for the ride because I wanted to see you."

"Where did you fly from?" she pressed.

He gave her a hard look as he realized what she was doing.

"How long will you be here?" She hated throwing these questions at him, but he *had* to see her point.

"I don't know, Kit." He didn't like that she was pushing, but she needed him to understand.

"And where will you go when you leave?"

"I don't know," he bit out.

"And how long will you be gone?"

"I couldn't say," he managed as his jaw ticked again from the tension.

Kit paused as exhaustion suddenly overwhelmed her. Letting out a small sigh, she spoke. "I know, Garret," she said, her voice quiet in the darkness. "I know you can't say or don't know. And I know you're okay with living like that, but I'm not. So, as easy as it would be to lead you to my bed right now, I'm trying to be a grown up about this and put some value on what I want—what I really want for the long term rather than just what I want right now."

She felt the tension radiating from his body and knew this was as hard for him as it was for her, because she did believe he was sincere in whatever feelings he had for her. Which made it all that much more important to be honest about where she stood and what she was feeling.

"And I think you know as well as I do that if we end up finishing tonight what we started five months ago, it's going to be more than a one-night stand," she said. "We can't cross that bridge and expect to be anything other than completely involved."

Even as she said the words, a sense of sadness swept through her. She'd half expected the emotion, but it still didn't feel good. And though she knew in her heart she was doing the right thing—she knew in her heart that now was not the time or place for her and Garret—she still felt the sting of loss.

Maybe Garret felt it too, but his expression shifted from one of frustration to something infinitely more kind and intimate. He didn't take a step toward her, but he did raise his hand and slip his fingers under her hair at the nape of her neck. His thumb brushed across her jaw and she stood still under his touch. After what seemed like forever, he bent forward and softly, gently, brushed his lips against hers. For a heartbeat, she allowed herself to close her eyes and just feel him.

Her eyes opened when he pulled back a few inches. He held her gaze. "I understand what you're saying, Kit, I do. I even respect it. But this isn't the last conversation we're going to have on the issue."

She wasn't sure what to say to that, but even if she'd had a response, Garret wasn't going to wait around to hear it. He dropped his hand, turned, and walked away.

For a long time after the door had closed behind him, Kit just stood and stared at the place where he had been.

CHAPTER 2

LYING IN HIS BED UPSTAIRS, Garret could hear Caleb rummaging around in the kitchen. Caleb wasn't much of a rummager, and when he moved around a room, he was naturally quiet as a mouse. That Garret could hear him up a flight of stairs, down a hall, and through a closed door said more about his friend's state of mind than Caleb would ever actually say himself.

A bird flying by the massive window caught Garret's attention. He had the same kind of floor-to-ceiling windows in his room that Kit had in hers, and he turned his head and took in the snowy scene.

Sort of.

He did let his eyes take in the sweeping landscape—he and Caleb had spent the majority of the past few months moving in and out of South America's jungles and crowded cities, so he had to adjust to the expansive views—but mostly, as his eyes adjusted, his mind was on Kit.

She was right, of course. Not about not being together. In that, he knew she was very wrong, and he could work on that. What she had been right about was his love at first sight comment—it was true that the "at first sight" was the easy part; it wasn't as though either of them had had to work at or even think about the instant attraction they had felt. But sticking with it over years and decades—through the good and bad times—took a lot more effort and said a lot more about a couple and their love for each other than what they had felt in the first seconds after they'd met.

But even knowing that it was only with time that they would

ever really discover if they were good together, he was hard pressed to forget the day, the instant, he'd met Kit. Caleb hadn't wanted him to stay at her house five months ago when they'd come to help a friend of hers, so he had camped on her property instead. But somehow she'd found him—or his camp, rather, while he was in town picking up supplies. And the moment he'd come upon her, sitting on a log near his tent as if she had been waiting for him, was indelibly seared into his memory.

He remembered coming to an abrupt stop, gripping his backpack of supplies, and simply staring. It hadn't been so much the surprise of finding someone at his camp as the shock he had felt reverberate through his body when she'd looked up at him with her golden eyes. For a moment, he'd actually contemplated going down on his knees to thank god, or whomever, for sending her.

He hadn't, of course. Instead he'd walked slowly toward her. Her eyes had been wary but curious, following his movement. He'd told her his name and held out his hand; she had taken it in her own and offered him a tentative smile—as if to seal a deal neither of them had yet understood.

Down in the kitchen, a drawer slammed and Caleb cursed, bringing Garret back to the present. He smiled. Kit's brother rarely swore out loud; it just wasn't his thing. It seemed that being in the presence of Kit had affected them both.

Then Kit's question from the night before echoed through his mind: *What are you doing here?* His smile turned to a frown. What *were* they doing there? And did it have anything to do with how Caleb was acting?

Jackknifing off the bed, he rested his feet on the cold floor as he dug in his bag for a pair of socks. He was already dressed, and had been since he'd heard Kit leave earlier that morning, but he hated socks. That said, even though the house was well heated, coming from the South American summertime to a North American winter required some adjustment, even for him.

Tugging a sock onto one foot, he let his eyes trail back to the windows. Again, Kit's voice echoed in his ears: *It's almost enough to make me believe in magic.* He could almost see that too. The morning light was just barely starting to make its appearance and, from Kit's southwestern views, the shadows were shortening and the snow was starting to glisten and sparkle. It reminded him of a Christmas years ago, when some relative or another had tried to expose him to a little bit of culture by dragging him, aged eight, and his four-year-old sister, to The Nutcracker.

He didn't have many memories of the dancers, but he did remember the set—a snowy forest. As an adult, he'd seen his fair share of snow, but back then—back when he was eight and living in the bayous of southern Louisiana outside Baton Rouge—snow was about as foreign to him as ballet. He'd been captivated.

Now, looking out Kit's window, a tiny bit of that awe crept back into his soul, because it was stunning. Pristine and clean. And quiet. Too quiet, at the moment.

After pulling on his other sock, he ventured down to the kitchen, unsure of what he would find. What he did find when he walked into the room was Caleb sitting at the kitchen island, glaring at the cabinetry, resting his chin in his palm.

"There a problem?" Garret asked, not bothering to stop the grin that tugged at his mouth.

Caleb turned his glare on Garret for a full ten seconds, then finally threw his hands up.

"I can't find the fucking coffee," he growled.

Garret studied his friend for a long moment before turning to the freezer, opening it, and pulling out a bag of ground beans. After holding it up on display for a moment, just to needle Caleb, he went to the coffee maker on the counter and started making a pot. A big one.

"How the hell did you know that?" Caleb finally demanded once the water had started to perk in the machine.

Garret kept his back to Caleb as he shrugged. "It was just a guess." Only it wasn't, not really. Caleb knew nothing about Garret's meeting with Kit last fall, and Garret had no desire to enlighten him. Thinking back on those three days he'd spent with her, during which they'd mostly just talked, he didn't remember her drinking any coffee—though she'd had quite a few cups of tea. But even if Kit herself preferred tea, she was too conscientious not to have coffee available for visitors or friends, so in his mind, it made sense that she would have some coffee stored somewhere, and the freezer seemed to be the most common spot.

When the coffeemaker beeped, Garret poured two cups, handed one to Caleb, then leaned back against the counter and studied his partner over the island. They'd been working together for nearly seven years and he had never seen Caleb so clearly agitated and tense.

"What's going on, Forrester?" Garret asked.

Caleb took a sip of his coffee, then another, before he spoke. "I can't find Kit."

Garret's stomach dropped a bit. "What do you mean, you can't find Kit?"

"I've called her four times and every time it goes straight to voicemail," he said, gesturing to his cell phone in disgust—as if it were the phone's fault. "And I have no idea what time she left."

That settled Garret somewhat. He remembered she had mentioned errands, so it wasn't as though her being away from the house was completely unexpected. "She left around six-thirty," Garret supplied. "I heard her get up around six and get ready and then leave about thirty minutes later," he added.

"And you didn't stop her?" Caleb demanded.

Again, Garret studied his friend before speaking. "Why would I have stopped her, Forrester? What's going on and why, exactly, are we here?"

Caleb opened his mouth, shut it, and after a beat, responded. "I didn't exactly invite you," he pointed out.

Garret's curiosity increased tenfold at that comment. "You're right. You didn't. But you also didn't tell me not to come. And since the only times we've ever *not* been together during the past six plus years was when we'd specifically scheduled R & R, and because this most definitely isn't R & R, even though we're at your sister's, I'm thinking it's a good thing I'm here, so why don't you just tell me what's going on?"

He crossed an arm over his chest and took a sip of the hot, strong coffee. He should have paid more attention and asked more questions when Caleb had said he was coming to visit Kit, but the thought of seeing her again had pretty much overwhelmed what little sense he'd had.

"Forrester." Garret added. His demand for information was implied, and thankfully, it worked. Caleb shot him a glare, but he didn't leave the room.

"You're a nosy bastard this morning," Caleb commented.

"I'm always a nosy bastard, but I can usually read your mind or at least see the logic in what we're doing, but this is different. Not that I mind coming here," he said, gesturing to the luxurious surroundings with his coffee cup.

Caleb took another sip of his coffee, then drummed his fingers on the island's granite. Twice, he took a breath as if preparing to speak, but said nothing. When he finally looked up, Garret saw something in his friend's eyes he'd never seen there before: worry.

"That last deal we worked on, not Heinlach in Argentina," he said, referring to the job that had so abruptly pulled them away from Windsor five months ago, "but the arms transfer we documented in Venezuela."

Garret nodded, remembering the last-minute favor they'd done for a friend, running surveillance on a transfer of illegal arms. It had been a quick and easy job because documentation was all their friend had needed—images, details on the cargo, transfer times, and those sorts of things.

"Well, two of the people on the tarmac that day were faces I knew," Caleb continued, ignoring Garret's raised eyebrow. Caleb hadn't said a thing as the transfer was going down, and that didn't give Garret the warm fuzzies now.

"One is a guy I had my eye on years ago. He showed up in an investigation I was running on the trafficking and transfer of arms and humans. Circumstances," Caleb paused, and for a moment, his gaze seemed to take him back in time—a look of regret flashed across his face. Then he cleared his throat and continued. "Circumstances changed and I never had a chance to follow up on him, but from what I had gathered, he wasn't a good guy."

This wasn't surprising to Garret. They didn't meet a lot of good guys in their business. "And the second guy?" he pressed.

Again, Caleb looked away, and by the tensing of his jaw, Garret could tell it was this man whose presence really bothered Caleb.

"He's someone I knew growing up. Someone Kit knew. His name is Henry Michaels," was all Caleb said.

Garret took another sip of his coffee as he mulled over what Caleb had said, and what he hadn't. In their line of work, it wasn't unusual to see the same people crop up in different places at different times—it wasn't like they were targeting dime-a-dozen petty thieves. No, in Garret's experience, once a person had crossed the line far enough to come onto his and Caleb's radar, they were already the kind of person who would pretty much do anything for anyone for the right price.

And so it was the second person, the new guy, Michaels, who also caught Garret's attention.

"Tell me about Michaels," Garret said.

But Caleb shook his head. "I'm not going to get into it until I talk to Kit. Which is why I'm so pissed off that I can't find her. I need answers."

Garret blinked and then very carefully picked his words. "Just what do you think Kit might be able to tell you? What kind of 'answers' do you think she'll have?"

Caleb's eyes shot to his, no doubt responding to the measured, careful tone in his question. For a split second, Garret saw a question flash across his friend's face. And then it went neutral.

"I'm not sure," Caleb said after a beat. "I just don't like that two men from my past, one of whom Kit knows, showed up like they did—in the same place, at the same time, participating in the same thing."

"And you think Kit might be able to enlighten you as to

why? Surely you don't think she is involved in anything that even remotely touches our world?" Garret pressed.

Caleb didn't immediately agree, and Garret felt his blood pressure rise.

"You've got to be kidding me," Garret said. "No way Kit is involved in anything, let alone arms dealing." And as if to prove how ridiculous the notion was, he rose, turned his back on his friend, and began to wash out his coffee cup.

"I don't know," Caleb finally answered.

Garret had an urge to tell Caleb he *did* know, and there was no way Kit was involved in anything Caleb seemed to be questioning. But such certainty was bound to raise Caleb's curiosity, so Garret carefully placed the mug in the drying rack and turned back around.

"What do you know?" he asked.

Caleb ran a hand over his face and shook his head, then seemed to think better of whatever he was about to say. "The first guy I mentioned? Well, I came across him years ago while I was tracking the movements of one of his colleagues. That colleague is now dead but Michaels also had ties to that same guy—ties I had always assumed were just social," Caleb paused then shook his head. "But seeing those two together all these years later did not make me feel all warm and tingly inside," he added.

"So, someone you knew growing up has ties to the trafficking business, and you're just now learning that he might have been involved in the business all along? Is that what's bothering you?" Garret clarified.

Caleb hesitated for a moment, then nodded.

"And what do you think Kit will be able to tell you about him?" he asked, still unclear where she came into play.

Caleb ran his hand over his face, then rose from his seat. "Honestly? I don't know what, if anything, Kit will be able to tell me, but I do have some questions about him, and at the very least, I'm hoping she might be able to give me some insight. She knew him much better than I did."

Garret didn't like the sound of that and frowned in response. "In what way? There were five guys on the tarmac that day. Which guy was it?"

But Caleb shook his head and started toward the stairs that led down to the lower level. "I'm going to try calling her again. Why don't you try? Maybe if she doesn't recognize your number, she'll pick up. I'll text you her number," he added, unaware that Garret already had it.

Garret watched Caleb's form disappear down the stairwell, then stared at nothing in particular for a long moment. His number would show up on Kit's phone, he'd programmed it in there five months ago. But whether or not she'd take his call was anyone's guess. The good news was he knew he could get under her skin in a way that Caleb, as her brother, couldn't. So with a smile, he pulled out his phone and dialed her number as he headed back to his room.

It rang twice as he walked through the door, then it went straight to voicemail. He hung up and smiled. If her phone had been turned off, it would have gone straight to voicemail—no, she was just ignoring him. Or trying to. It was kind of cute.

He laid down on the bed and typed out a quick text message. "I'm in bed thinking of you." Then he hit send. As expected, nothing came back. So he sent another, and another, and yet another. All along the same lines. Finally, he got a response.

"Busy, go away," she finally messaged.

He laughed. "Where are you?" he typed.

"Busy, go away."

"Busy where? Your brother is worried about you."

"My brother doesn't worry." She responded, and he could all but see her roll her eyes.

"You're right. He's pissed he didn't get to talk to you this morning. Where are you?"

"Too bad. I'll be back in a couple of hours."

"WHERE ARE YOU? BTW, I can keep bugging you all day."

There was a long pause before she responded. "I don't doubt

that. I'm at breakfast with some friends in Riverside. I'll be home in a few hours."

He liked that he could hear her voice in his head as he read her messages, even if her tone was clearly one of annoyance.

"See you then," he typed and set his phone down. He knew Caleb hadn't told him everything that was on his mind, and for a moment, Garret debated letting Caleb stew about Kit's whereabouts just to get back at him for not telling him what they were really doing there. But then he realized he didn't care all that much about what had brought them here, only that they were here now. Garret sent Caleb a quick text letting him know where Kit was and when she would be back—he could have gotten up and walked down to the lower level of the house, but Kit had excellent taste in beds, and he was rather enjoying the king-sized luxury. And he hadn't really been kidding when he'd said he was thinking of her.

CHAPTER 3

"**Who was that?**" Kit's friend Vivienne DeMarco asked as she tucked a blanket around her five-month-old son, Jeffery. Kit looked at the baby lying comfortably in his baby seat; with his father's green eyes and his mother's dark hair, he was obviously going to be a heartbreaker when he got older. And as if agreeing with her thoughts, he flashed a big, toothless smile at her and waved his hands. She smiled back at the little flirt.

"Who was who?" Kit asked as she reached over to tickle Jeffery's belly. He let out a squeal and kicked his feet and, because she couldn't help herself, she reach over, unclipped him, and lifted him onto her lap. With a delighted gurgle, he started playing with her hair.

"Nice try, Kit. Who were all those texts from?" Jesse pressed. Jesse Baker was another one of her close friends gathered around the table for an early breakfast.

"Where's Emma this morning?" Kit asked, ignoring Jesse and Vivi's questions. For a moment, it worked.

"She and David are shoveling snow," Jesse answered with a smile. Emma was Jesse and David's soon-to-be-adopted daughter. At nearly two years old, Emma had dropped into their lives at a point in time when neither Jesse nor David had had any plans to raise more kids. Having both been young parents—David with a grown daughter and Jesse with two grown boys—they were just starting to enjoy having lives of their own for the first time. But life threw curveballs whenever it felt so inclined, and less than a year after meeting each other, Jesse and David were married and raising Emma.

"But we knew that already," Matty Kent, the third friend in their group, interjected with a pointed look. "Jesse said so when she sat down. Now, stop avoiding the question, because you know doing that just piques our curiosity even more. Who were those texts from?" Matty repeated as she grabbed Jesse's cup of coffee and took a sip.

"You know," Kit said, watching Matty take a second sip of Jesse's coffee before setting the cup down and sliding it back in front of their friend. "If you drink all of Jesse's coffee, it's kind of the same as having your own cup." She glanced at Matty's growing belly. At five-and-a-half-months pregnant, Matty looked fabulous—very pregnant, but fabulous.

Matty shrugged. "I know, but this way when Dash," she said, referring to her husband, "asks how much coffee I ordered, I can just say one cup and it will be the truth. Now, who were the texts from?"

"He's just looking out for you," Kit pointed out. "And for good reason. How many cups *have* you had today?" she demanded as Jesse reached over and pulled Jeffery into her own lap. The baby's attention immediately switched from Kit's hair to Jesse's necklace.

"That was my last, I promise," Matty said, eying Jesse and Vivi's cups longingly. Kit studied her friend and knew that while she was probably drinking more coffee than many pregnant women, Matty would never do anything to jeopardize the twins she was carrying. So, with a smile and a shake of her head, Kit reached for her own cup—of tea, not coffee—and began to futz with it.

"Uh oh, she's futzing," Matty said. Kit looked up to see three sets of eyes, well, four if she counted Jeffery, staring at her, waiting for an answer.

"My brother came into town last night and Garret, his partner, is with him. They were just texting to find out where I am since I left this morning without saying where I was going," she answered.

Predictably, Jesse's eyes lit up. She and Caleb had formed a unique kind of friendship when he'd helped her out of a sticky situation last fall. Her brother wasn't the most social of creatures, and hadn't endeared himself to David when he'd all but accused David of being involved in the several attacks on Jesse, but something between Caleb and Jesse had just clicked. Not in a sexual way, of course—not in the same way things had clicked between Kit and Garret.

"How is he? Will he be staying for long? He needs to come by and meet Emma," Jesse said.

"Caleb never stays around for long," Vivi pointed out.

"Or comes for no reason," Matty added. "So what's going on? Is everything okay?"

Before Caleb had come to town last fall, Kit hadn't talked too much about him to her friends. She and her brother had been more or less estranged for years, so she'd had very little *to* say. But after he'd come and met her friends, and helped Jesse, they'd asked questions—not so much about him, per se, but about her relationship with him and why they weren't close. Kit had done her best not to reveal too much about that piece of her past and had, instead, provided basic facts. Like the fact that Caleb rarely came around and that, when he did, she never knew when, why, or how long he would stay.

Kit shrugged, "I don't actually know why he's here. He just showed up last night and said we needed to talk. I haven't seen him since that day—that day," she paused and looked at Jesse.

That day when Jesse's deceased husband's former mistress had kidnapped her son and then tried to blow them all up. With Caleb and Garret's help, they'd each made it out alive and mostly in one piece. Marcus Brown, one of the police officers involved, had been severely burned and injured, and it had been touch and go for a while, but he was now well on the way to recovery—not a full recovery, but a good one, given all his injuries. So while the story had the best kind of ending it could, considering what had happened, it still wasn't something any of them looked back on fondly.

Kit was brought back to the conversation at hand when Jesse

reached over to give her hand a squeeze, then asked, "Where did he go?"

"And who is his partner?" Matty joined in. "Call me crazy, but my guess is that the blush that crept up your neck a while back wasn't from a message your brother texted you."

Kit tried to glare at her friend, but Matty was unrepentant and just grinned back.

"I remember Ian saying something about Caleb having a partner, but well, Jeffery came along so unexpectedly that I never bothered to ask after that," Vivi added. Ian, Vivi's husband and the county sheriff, had been there that day too. But when Marcus had been injured, he and Vivi had followed him down to the burn unit in New York City. Who knows if it was the stress of that day or just Jeffery being impatient, but while they were waiting for word on Marcus, Vivi had gone into labor four weeks early. Thankfully, Jeffery was more than ready to come out and hadn't even had to spend a night in the NICU.

"So who is this masked man?" Matty pressed, again with a grin.

Kit rolled her eyes. "What are you, fifteen?" she teased.

Matty waggled her eyebrows as Kit scooted her chair in to let two men from the next table over pass by.

"Good god, you're a menace," Kit muttered.

Matty grinned "And by the way, those guys that just left were talking about you," she added with a nod toward the two men who had made their way past her chair and were now exiting the restaurant.

Kit frowned. "How do you know?" she asked.

"And were they saying anything interesting?" Jesse added, her eyes sparkling.

"They were speaking Spanish and saying they wouldn't mind being in London with you but thought Rome would be too distracting for their taste," Matty supplied.

Kit frowned; it felt disconcerting to know those men had been eavesdropping on her conversation with her friends when she'd been discussing her travel plans. Of course, people eavesdropped all the time, and if they were sitting less than five feet away, like those two men had been, it was probably not even intentional. But still, it surprised Kit that they'd spoken about her in such a way. Having traveled as much as she had, she always assumed that at least someone around her would speak English and be able to understand what she was saying—the good, the bad, and the inappropriate. Apparently, not everyone made the same assumption.

"I don't even know what that means," Vivi said. "How can Rome be too distracting?"

"You, my friend, have no imagination. London is gray and drab this time of year, Rome is not," Matty offered.

"And?" Vivi prompted.

Matty turned to Jesse, "Is this what I can expect after these babies are born? That any kind of sexual adventurousness just up and disappears?"

Jesse laughed. "No, on the contrary, actually. I just think that maybe you and Vivi have different ideas about what that might mean."

Vivi arched an eyebrow at Matty, who laughed. "When it's gray and drab outside, what better to do than hole up in a hotel *all day*, if you get what I mean," Matty elaborated.

Vivi huffed a laugh. "Yes, I do actually *get* that," she said. "I'm just not sure why Rome would be different."

"Because it's not as gray as London and it's a great walking city," Kit jumped in. "That's not to say London isn't, but Rome is seductive; it makes you want to be out and about, seeing, tasting, and touching it." Rome was and would always be one of her favorite cities.

"You make it sound like Rome itself would compete with any lover," Vivi said with a smile.

Kit thought back to all the times she'd been to the city. She'd never really thought of it that way, but what Vivi had said actually had a bit of truth in it. Kit inclined her head in agreement, but then added, "Of course, any lover worth his salt would know how to use the city as part of his own seduction, rather than compete with it."

"So, speaking of lovers?" Matty pushed with a not-so-subtle smile, bringing the topic back to Garret.

Kit shook her head, laughed, then let out a deep breath. "Garret Cantona is my brother's partner. He was here last fall. We met then," she finally supplied, knowing her friends would never drop the subject unless she complied with their demands.

"You *met* or you *met met?*" Vivi asked, an eyebrow arched.

"We *met met*, but we didn't, uh," she paused for a moment, "we didn't *meet meet*, if you know what I mean."

"Meaning you made out with him but didn't have sex," Matty clarified. "Or at least not hot monkey sex. Judging by the blush creeping up your neck again, I'd wager there was some sex involved."

Kit tried to glare at her friend again, but Vivi and Jesse jumped in.

"You didn't tell me anything," Jesse said.

"You didn't tell any of us," Vivi added.

Kit held up her hand to ward off further comments. After a moment, her friends seemed to comply. When they were all quiet, she spoke. "Look, I didn't tell anyone because I never heard from him again after he was here for those few days. My brother has no idea—I suspect if he did, he wouldn't have brought Garret back into my house. And as for not telling you guys, well, there was a lot going on back then, if you recall," she gave them each a pointed look. "Jeffery had arrived," she said, looking at Vivi. "And you and David got married and were in the middle of starting the adoption process," she said, looking at Jesse. "And you," she directed her gaze at Matty, "you were newly pregnant and barfing your guts up about every fifteen minutes."

Matty turned a little green at the reminder of just how sick she'd been that first trimester. "It just didn't seem like a big deal considering everything else that was going on," Kit continued. "Especially since I didn't hear from him." But saying those words out loud made it clear to her just how big of a deal it had been.

Because she remembered how much she had *missed* him after he'd left so suddenly. She hadn't known him long, but during those first few days and weeks after he'd gone, she'd craved his company and wanted it like nothing else. But then the weeks had turned into months and her memories had turned into reminders—reminders of just why someone like Garret didn't fit into her carefully constructed life.

"But he was manically texting you just now," Jesse pointed out.

Kit forced air into her lungs, fighting against the weight of her memories—she didn't want her friends to catch a glimpse of how much Garret affected her. If they saw it, she might have to face it herself.

So she slowly exhaled and gave what she hoped would come across as a lighthearted shrug. "Like I said, he and my brother are just looking out for me," she said. "I have no idea what Caleb wants to talk to me about, but I should probably get home and have it out with him. I told him we could talk tonight, but then I had to rearrange my trip to Europe and I now leave tonight. He's not going to like that."

"Your brother doesn't like anything that doesn't go according to his plans," Jesse pointed out in support. Kit smiled because what Jesse had said was true, but also because her friends were letting her change the subject.

Vivi laughed, "Yeah, I know a thing or two about men who are addicted to plans," she added. Ian was notorious for making plans. "But the good news is planners can generally re-plan so don't feel too bad about upsetting him."

"And besides, it's not as though he called and made plans with *you*. I mean really, he can hardly expect you to put your life on hold for him," Matty offered, making Kit smile again. Actually, all her friends made her smile.

Gathering her hat, gloves, and jacket, she rose from her seat. "I love you guys. I'll be in touch when I get back from Europe."

"I want pictures of the event, including some of you in all your finery," Matty, a fellow writer, said as Kit donned her gear.

"And then when you get back, I want to hear just how you *met met*, but didn't *meet meet*, Garret Cantona," Vivi added with a glint in her eye.

"I think we all want to hear that," Jesse said.

"Prurient, all of you," Kit responded with a laugh. "Love you all, and I'll see you next week."

Holding the warmth of her friendships close, she stepped out into the cold and went to face her day.

Before heading home, however, she had one more stop to make. Pulling onto Main Street back in Windsor, Kit scouted for a parking spot as close to the police station as possible. She liked the winter, but walking on frozen sidewalks wasn't her favorite thing. And though there weren't a lot of cars out this early in the morning, since most of the stores didn't open until ten, the snow banks left by the plows seemed to take up half the street, leaving scant room for parking.

Half a block from the station, she found a spot and pulled in. Three minutes later, she was entering the building, stomping her boots more out of habit than to rid them of any accumulated snow.

"Hi, Sharon," she said to the receptionist. "I'm here to see—"

"Me, I take it," Carly Drummond said, walking out of her office into the main room.

Kit smiled at her friend. "I am." Taking off her jacket, she followed Carly into her office and shut the door behind her.

"How are you?" Kit asked as they both took seats.

Five months ago, Carly had become the acting deputy chief of police. At twenty-nine, she was the youngest person—and the only woman—ever to hold the position. Kit had always sensed that Carly had some misgivings about her choice of careers—even when she'd been just an officer. But then Carly'd had the deputy chief position thrust upon her when Marcus Brown, the previous deputy chief, had been injured and, well, the additional responsibility seemed to exacerbate the somewhat edgy, dissatisfied energy Carly emanated at times. She was good at her job, Kit knew this from talking to Vivi and Ian, both of whom worked in law enforcement, but she never seemed very comfortable with it.

Carly shrugged. "I'm fine. You know, Vic is being Vic," she answered, referring to the current chief of police. "And I saw Marcus last night," she added.

"How is he? Still in Albany?" Kit asked. Marcus was still technically the deputy chief, and Carly's role, though five months and running, was temporary while he was on a leave of absence as he recovered.

Carly nodded. "He is. The Albany Police Department has given him some administrative tasks, and he's actually been spending some time at the state lab with Vivi and Dr. Buckley, the director. He's edgy though; he wants to get back to work."

It was interesting to Kit that Carly had used the same words to describe Marcus's desire to get back to work that Kit would use to describe Carly's potential desire to get out of it.

"But he's still focusing on his physical therapy?" Kit asked. While Marcus had survived the explosion, he had still needed a knee replacement and skin grafts as well as time to heal a broken hip and collarbone and a dislocated shoulder.

Carly nodded in response to Kit's question. "He is. He's diligent about that, which I find somewhat surprising because he also complains about it every time I see him. But he goes," she said again. "And then spends a few hours a day doing administrative work or helping at the lab."

"That's good, I'm glad to hear it. When I'm back from Europe, I'll head up and see if he can meet for lunch one of these days."

Carly laughed, "He'd like that. He'll jump on any chance to get out of his routine. Besides, you don't coddle him like Vivi does."

Kit smiled, "Yeah, I'm not really the coddling type."

Carly snorted. "So, your trip?" she asked.

"Yes," Kit said, sitting forward and sliding a spare key across Carly's desk. "I had to move my trip up a day so I'm leaving tonight, and I wanted to let you know." Carly lived in a small apartment over an appliance repair shop in town and often housesat for Kit when she traveled. "The thing is," Kit continued, "my brother arrived last night with a friend of his, and I'm not sure if they will be staying and if so, for how long."

"So, do you think I should stop by?" Carly asked, adding the key to her keychain.

Kit wagged her head. "I'll see if I can get any more information from him this afternoon, and I'll text you if I hear anything. He says he came to talk to me about something—what that 'something' is, I don't know. But whatever it is, if I'm not here, he won't be able to talk to me about it, so I suspect he'll take off too."

"I can stop by tonight and check in, if you want," Carly offered.

Kit wagged her head again. "If he leaves, it will probably be tomorrow, so why don't you plan to come by tomorrow after you get off your shift. But if anything changes, I'll let you know. Sound good?"

Carly nodded and they both rose. "Are you looking forward to the trip?" Carly asked as Kit donned her jacket again.

Kit let out a little laugh. "I am. I really am. It's been about a year since I've seen Marco, and it's always fun to get dressed up."

"I bet," Carly said as they exited her office. "I put on a dress for the Fallen Policeman's benefit last month, and though I wouldn't want to wear one every day to work, I have to admit, it was fun."

"We should plan a girls' weekend in New York when I get back," Kit said. The suggestion had come on a whim, but the idea grew on her immediately. It would be fun to get dressed up, take in a good dinner, maybe a show, and then hit a club. With three best friends all with young kids or pregnant, it had been a while since she'd had a good girls' night out.

"We definitely should. I could use a little girl time," Carly responded just as Vic's door flew open. Both women jumped at the sudden noise, and much to Kit's surprise, Lucas Rancuso, a good friend of Vivi's from Boston, walked out.

"Lucas?" Kit said, not bothering to hide her surprise.

He stopped, shot a glance in her direction, then quickly

looked away. At well over six feet tall—really, closer to six and a half—Lucas was an imposing man. But the somewhat furtive expression on his face made him appear almost boyish.

"Kit, Carly," he said, nodding to the women. "How are you?"

"Fine," they replied in unison as Vic came out of his office behind Lucas. The chief was a bit of an enigma to Kit—he was pleasant to her and she knew he'd been good to Carly, but he'd been a complete asshole to Ian, Vivi's husband, during Ian's short tenure with the department. And it didn't look as though he'd been any nicer to Lucas.

She suspected that maybe his volatile nature had turned away more than one interested party—personally and professionally. Professionally, the department had been understaffed by more than one officer for over a year. And personally, well, Vic Ballard was a good-looking guy—tall and slim, with brown hair that was graying slightly at his temples. He looked fit, and Kit had seen him out with women, having drinks at Anderson's or The Tavern a time or two. But she knew he'd never married.

"Kit," Vic said, with a nod in her direction. "It's good to see you."

She held back a frown at the tension in the room. "You too, Chief. I hope you're doing well?"

He nodded.

"Good, well, I—well, I guess I'll be heading out now," Kit said. With a last look at Carly, who gave a small shrug, Kit headed toward the door.

"I'll join you," Lucas said, striding after her, not bothering to say good-bye to either of the police officers.

"You okay?" Kit asked when they hit the sidewalk outside.

"Fine," Lucas managed to say.

"Are you up visiting Vivi and Jeffery?" she asked. Lucas had been life partners with Jeffery DeMarco, Vivi's brother and her son's namesake, before Jeffery had been killed in action a little over two years before. As close to Vivi as her real brother, Lucas now stood in for one, showering baby Jeffery with lots of love and way too many toys.

"I am," he answered as they reached her car. "I know you had breakfast with her this morning. She mentioned she was meeting you."

"They look great, don't they?" Kit responded as she placed her hand on the car door handle.

Her remark elicited a smile from Lucas. "Yeah, they do."

Meghan, the young woman who ran the ice cream store in town, pulled into the lot across the street and waved when she saw Kit. Kit waved back and smiled—it was the dead of winter, but Meghan had started to sell her ice cream to local stores, so lately she was in her shop making and packaging her product more days than not.

"So, what were you doing in the police station? Is everything okay?" Kit asked, bringing her attention back to Lucas, even though she knew she probably didn't have the right to pry.

Lucas just gave a little shake of his head, then let out a long breath that fogged around him. "Everything is fine. Vic attended a seminar I taught a few weeks ago, and we disagreed on a process and procedure issue. I figured since I was in town, I'd come by and see if we could have a rational conversation about it."

Lucas was a homicide detective in Boston, and what he said seemed more than plausible, but something about the expression on his face when he'd come out of Vic's office made Kit think the conversation had been more heated than one about processes would warrant. But still, it wasn't really her business.

"Well," she said, opening her car door. "I hope you worked it out."

Lucas gave a short but harsh laugh. "Not hardly. But I hear you're headed to Europe soon?"

"Tonight."

"Well, have a safe trip and all that," he said. He was too polite to leave until she'd gotten into her car. She had the feeling she should ask him something else, something more, but for the life of her, she didn't know what. So rather than make him stand around in the cold, she nodded, thanked him, and got in her car.

She flipped the heater all the way on, flexed her gloved fingers to ward off the cold, and girded herself to face her brother.

CHAPTER 4

THROUGH THE KITCHEN WINDOW, GARRET watched Kit's car make its way up her long drive. He was both curious and a bit concerned about what might happen next; as he heard her garage door open, he braced himself to watch the convoluted dynamics between the siblings.

"Where have you been?" Caleb demanded as soon as Kit stepped into the entryway.

Garret was now leaning against the counter with his back to the window, and Kit's eyes came up to meet his—she seemed to be asking him if he'd told her brother what she'd texted him. Garret nodded and she went back to toeing off her boots and removing her winter gear.

"Well?" Caleb stated.

"As I'm sure Garret told you, I was having breakfast with my friends down in Riverside. By the way, Jesse says 'hi' and that she'd like to have you to tea if you're going to stick around long enough."

Judging by the tone in Kit's voice, Garret doubted that Jesse had issued such an invitation. He rather suspected Kit had thrown it out as a not-so-subtle way of pointing out her brother's lack of social graces, such as letting people know when he was coming to visit or making the time to catch up with friends.

Garret didn't think the comment had the intended effect, but even so, Caleb did seem to rein in his frustration a bit. Garret watched as his partner ran a hand through his spiky blond hair, then rested both hands on the back of a stool at the kitchen island.

"I was just surprised to see you out of the house so early," Caleb said in lieu of an apology.

Kit inclined her head and made her way to the stove to put the kettle on. "Jesse had to be at work by nine, so we met early. Vivi and Matty were there too," she added. The temper had gone out of her voice, and though Garret knew the antagonism between the two wasn't all together gone, they were both trying to get hold of it. He frowned as he watched her put a tea bag in a mug and return to wait by the stove. Caleb had rarely talked about his sister, and Garret had always assumed it was to protect her from touching any part of the sometimes-ugly life they led. But watching the two of them together, it was clear that something else bubbled underneath the surface of their relationship.

"So, what do you want to talk about?" Kit asked, turning toward them after she'd poured hot water into her cup.

"Have a seat," Caleb gestured.

"I'd rather stand, thank you. I have a lot I have to do today," she added.

Caleb's eyes narrowed, and he looked about to argue but then seemed to change his mind. "What do you know about Henry Michaels?" he asked abruptly.

Kit stilled, then blinked. "The father or the son?" she asked, her voice barely audible in the quiet kitchen. Garret shifted his gaze to Caleb, who had gone so still he looked unmovable, like a statue. Garret's eyes went back to Kit, who looked like a deer in headlights.

"The father—either, really," Caleb answered.

And damned if Kit didn't go pale. She swallowed and shook her head. "I haven't seen either of them since about a month after our father's funeral."

"You haven't talked to either of them? Wasn't the younger one close to your age? He never tried to get in touch with you?"

If anything, Kit seemed to go a little green as she gave a rapid but small shake of her head. "No, I haven't seen or spoken to either of them in years. Now, if you'll excuse me, I've had a change of plans, and I'm now leaving for Europe tonight. I need to get packing." And she was gone.

Garret stayed where he was, letting the scene sink into his mind and memory. After several minutes had passed, he turned to look at Caleb, who also hadn't moved, other than to meet Garret's gaze.

"She changed her plans," Caleb repeated.

Garret shrugged. "I guess so."

To get away from them or for some other reason, was the question. Caleb looked to be pondering the same thing.

"She knows something," Caleb finally said, acknowledging what Garret knew he didn't want to. But while it was obvious Caleb thought he knew what Kit's reaction to the name Henry Michaels meant, to Garret—to someone not entangled in the sibling relationship—her reaction could have meant any number of things.

"The name did have an impact," was all Garret was willing to concede.

Caleb drummed his fingers on the back of the chair, then after a moment, he looked up. "How do you feel about a trip to Europe?"

The request didn't come as a surprise. Garret inclined his head. "I'll make the reservations."

CHAPTER 5

GARRET DID NOT LIKE WHAT he'd been seeing. Or the fact that his mind couldn't seem to untangle the events of the past few hours. He could blame it on jet lag, but he had extensive traveling experience, and jet lag had never been an issue for him in the past. Still, he might invoke it if he couldn't figure out just what the hell was going on and fast.

"Fabio Ambrose?" Caleb repeated on the other end of the cell connection.

"Yep," Garret responded, keeping his eye on Kit, who was seated in a café across the street, apparently waiting for someone. It was close to four in the afternoon, and it was already getting dark in London. He and Caleb had made their way into London just over seven hours ago, about an hour before Kit's flight from New York had landed at Heathrow. They'd managed to get the name of her hotel out of her before she'd left Windsor and were checked in and waiting for her before she'd even arrived. Of course, she didn't know any of this. Not yet, anyway.

"Why would she have met someone like Ambrose?" Caleb demanded.

While Garret was keeping an eye on Kit, Caleb was going through her hotel room. Garret didn't much care to think about that, or the fact that it felt like he was betraying her, but if for some reason Kit was mixed up with Henry Michaels, or people like him, it was up to Garret and Caleb to keep her safe.

"I think there is a lot you might not know about your sister,"

Garret managed to say as his attention was drawn to an older woman joining Kit.

"Ambrose works for Vatican intelligence, how the hell would she know him?"

Over the phone, Garret heard a door close and figured Caleb was done with his search.

"Find anything?" he asked. Caleb answered in the negative, which was probably a good thing. Maybe this wasn't as bad as it looked.

"Well?" Caleb asked again. What little patience Caleb possessed was clearly running out.

Garret shrugged even though he knew Caleb couldn't see him do it. "I don't know how she knows him. They talked about publishing, and it sounded like they had some newspaper people in common," Garret said, reciting what he'd gathered from Kit's meeting earlier that afternoon—a meeting he'd been able to eavesdrop on from a behind a newspaper a few tables away.

"Publishing?" Caleb repeated.

"Yeah, you do remember that your sister is a world-renowned writer, right? And she was featured in the Times last weekend for winning that big award?" Garret didn't think Caleb gave his sister enough credit and tried to drive the point home with sarcasm. The only indication that Caleb had been listening was a grunt that came over the phone line.

"And that's all they talked about?" Caleb pressed.

Garret nodded out of habit, then spoke. "Yes, she told him she had expected to see him in Rome. He said he'd had a change of plans and needed to be in London, so he was glad they could meet here instead. They had lunch together and talked about the news in Europe, then he asked if she would be willing to chat with a friend of his who is with one of the papers in Italy, so she gave him her card to pass along." Garret summarized the ninety-minute lunch in a ten-second wrap-up.

Caleb grunted again, and Garret was just about to hang up when something caught his eye. He watched as a man, somewhere in his mid-fifties, joined Kit and the other woman. The man stooped to place a kiss on the other woman's cheek, then shook hands with Kit before sitting down.

"Cantona?" Caleb demanded across the line, likely sensing the tension that had just shot through Garret's body.

Garret watched for a moment, not believing what he was seeing. "No fucking way," he heard himself mutter.

"Cantona," Caleb warned.

"You're never going to guess who just sat down with your sister."

"I swear to god, I'm going to kill you if you don't just tell me," Caleb answered.

"Jonathon Parker," Garret mumbled as he focused on the table across the street. The three of them were chatting and laughing about something.

"Tell me you don't mean *the* Jonathon Parker? From MI6? The one being investigated for the leak and the deaths of all those assets?"

Garret heard Caleb's question, but his mind was too wrapped up in trying to figure out how to get closer so he could hear what they were saying.

"Cantona? Where are you?"

Garret rattled off his location as he jogged across the street to see if there was another way he could get into the café without being obvious. Without being seen.

"Stay put, I'll be right there."

And with that, Caleb hung up. Garret slid his phone into his pocket and surveyed his options. Unlike the restaurant where she'd met Ambrose for lunch, the café where she currently sat didn't offer much in the way of anonymity. It was too open, too small, and there was nowhere that would get him close enough to Kit to hear her conversation but keep him hidden enough so that she wouldn't see him. He cursed the fact that he was tailing someone who would recognize him, someone who knew him well enough to recognize even his frame or way of moving. Hiding from people he didn't know was a hell of a lot easier than hiding from someone who knew him intimately.

Not happy with his options, he jogged back across the street and stepped into a shadowy doorway.

Knowing Caleb was on his way, Garret pulled his collar tighter around his neck, leaned against the cold wall, and watched. Twenty minutes later, his partner pulled to a stop in front of him, driving yet another black Range Rover. Garret was never sure where the cars came from, but he knew that if given a choice, Caleb would always pick the same style.

Climbing into the vehicle without a word, Garret kept an eye on traffic as Caleb circled around until he found an alley they could park in that would give them a view of the threesome. Over the years, Garret had developed a slight ability to read lips—he wasn't great, but he could make out most things. And in the shadow of the car, Garret pulled out his binoculars to see if he could pick up anything they were saying.

"Well?" Caleb asked. His own binoculars were trained on the window where Kit and her two guests were visible.

"More publishing. Actually, I think Kit is asking the woman about some financial scandal that she—oh wait." Garret stopped talking and focused. After a few minutes passed, he thought he had a little better understanding of the specific situation happening on the other side of the street, even if he felt like he was looking at the trees rather than the forest.

"The woman is Isabelle Parker, Jonathon Parker's sister. They're talking about that international oil scandal where the company was charged with facilitating the raping of women and the pillaging of villages along the pipeline. Kit seems to be asking her all sorts of questions about how the multi-national company worked, who hired who, and that sort of thing."

"And Jonathon?" Caleb asked.

"Just weighing in with his opinion. If he's giving her some sort of coded message, it would be a very subtle one since the opinions he's expressing, as far as I can tell, aren't all that different than general public opinion."

In silence, they sat and watched for another forty-five minutes, Garret occasionally passed a comment or two to Caleb, though nothing the three at the table talked about seemed to relate to anything Jonathon Parker might do, or had done, professionally. Still, the fact that Kit had met with not one, but two foreign intelligence officers within hours of each other was something that boggled Garret's mind. And if the moody tension coming from the driver's seat was anything to go by, it was bothering Caleb too.

Finally, after what seemed like an eternity, the three diners rose from their seats and began donning their winter-wear. Kit and the Parkers exchanged cards, and Isabelle and Kit gave each other a hug as they prepared to part ways.

"What are your thoughts?" Caleb asked as Kit and company exited the café.

Garret knew that one or the other of them would need to trail her, and since Caleb was driving, the task would, thankfully, fall to him. He was about to exit the car, but Caleb held out a hand to stop him so he turned back to the scene. Kit and Jonathon were still talking as Isabelle made her way toward the Tube station on the corner. After a bit, Kit and her male companion started walking in the opposite direction. They weren't far from the hotel, maybe a thirty-minute walk, but the most direct route wasn't a path he and Caleb could drive because of various one-way and blocked streets.

"Now follow her," Caleb ordered.

Garret was more than happy to slip out of the car and make his way down the street in her direction. From his following distance, about a block behind and on the opposite side of the street, they looked to be doing nothing more than walking and talking. On occasion, Jonathon would point to something or other, but they continued on toward the hotel.

They reached a large roundabout and at this peak traffic time, Garret was beginning to get annoyed at the number of times he'd lost sight of Kit due to some bus, or five, blocking his view. He had just reached the edge of the circle himself when he jogged around the back of a bus, expecting to see Kit and Jonathon ahead of him on the street leading back to the hotel.

Only he didn't see them. His heart skipped a beat as he craned his head around, searching for them everywhere. He scanned the buses and cars in the area. Chances were, she couldn't be taken from the street, not in this traffic, but there were any number of things a man like Jonathon Parker would know what to do with a person—willing or not.

The panic started to settle in his stomach and he darted between the cars, ignoring the blaring horns, and made his way toward where he had last seen them. Again, he scanned the area, looking for Kit's hat in the crowd. The darkening night and dim streetlights didn't do much to help, and he was just about to reach for his phone when he saw her rise from the sidewalk.

A wave of relief swept through him, followed closely by one of confusion. It appeared that Jonathon Parker had fallen down; Kit and another woman, presumably someone who had stopped, were helping him rise.

When Jonathon was standing upright again, Garret watched as he and Kit said something to the woman—something that looked like thank you—and then the woman walked away. Kit turned to Jonathon and seemed to be speaking to him; Garret couldn't see what she was saying, she was too far away and her back was him, but she had a hand resting on Jonathon's sleeve in a gesture of concern. Jonathon shook his head and said something in return. Kit didn't seem to like this answer, shaking her head as she pointed something out to him on his other arm.

Whatever else occurred in their exchange was lost to Garret as yet another bus passed in front of him as it exited the roundabout. When it finally moved out of his line of sight, all he could see of Kit was the back of her coat as she entered a nearby pharmacy.

• • •

Kit all but dragged Jonathon into the pharmacy two doors down from where he'd fallen. He hadn't wanted to come, but she'd threatened to make a scene if he hadn't. She wasn't sure if she would have followed through on it, but thankfully, he hadn't pressed the issue.

She glanced over at her companion who was standing meekly at her side, cradling his injured arm. For the moment, he looked okay, even if his eyes were looking everywhere but at her.

She hadn't a clue what had happened. One moment her hat was blowing off in a sudden gust of wind created by a passing bus, and the next Jonathon was on the ground, bleeding from his upper arm. He tried to tell her he'd simply fallen. She wished she could believe that, but even though she saw no indication of anything else, the way he tried to rush away made her think something else was going on.

As she reached for some antiseptic and bandages, she noticed her hands were shaking. She knew she'd hold it together, but she didn't like where her mind wanted to go. Jonathon was a spy. A spy who was being investigated for something—she didn't know for what exactly, but chances were that if Drew had gotten involved, it couldn't be good. And now he was injured. From a "fall."

Fall, her ass. He had no more fallen than she had.

"I'm fine. If you'll just let me go, I'll take care of it," he said with a gesture of his head toward her shaking hand.

"You'll do no such thing," she snapped. The fear of the unknown was putting her at less than her best. He sighed as she reached for some first aid tape, the last item she needed before cleaning him up. If she'd had a first aid kit in her hotel room, she would have just insisted they walk the short distance remaining, but as it was, she had nothing that could do the job.

"Fine, Florence Nightingale. You go pay for those things, then meet me at the loo in the back of the store. I have a few calls to make," he said.

She turned and met his gaze. He was a man that her mother would have called classically handsome, even in his mid-fifties. His hair was still a rich brown color, but it was streaked with enough gray to make him look even more distinguished than his strong cheek bones, above-average height, and trim figure did. She knew his brown eyes, eyes that appeared soft and warm, saw more than they let on. And though his manners had so far been faultless, she was beginning to hear a bit of an edge creep into his voice.

"You're not going to run away, are you?" she demanded, trying to get a better look at his arm as he twisted away in an attempt to prevent the same thing.

"I assure you, Kit, that I do not run away." His British accent held that trace of sarcastic condescension that Brits were so good at. She glared at him. He sighed again. "I promise you, Kit, that I will be in the loo, and I will let you have a look and bandage me up." His voice had become much gentler, more sincere. It crossed her mind that he was a spy and probably more adept at lying than she.

"Promise?" she asked again. Although she wasn't sure what a promise from a man like Jonathon might mean.

But he nodded and turned, heading toward the back of the store. She watched his figure retreat behind a half door and then enter the bathroom the cashier had pointed out when they'd first entered the store.

Kit took a deep breath and tried to calm her nerves. She grabbed one more item, then managed to make her purchase and explain to the cashier that her friend had been hurt in a fall so she was going to help him clean up his wound. The young man with the four eyebrow rings seemed singularly disinterested so without another word, Kit made her way back to where her charge was waiting.

When she entered the room, she turned and locked the door. Jonathon slid his phone into his jacket pocket and made a gesture indicating that he was at her mercy.

"Sit," she said, pointing to the closed toilet lid. "And take off your jacket."

He sat and after a minimal amount of male wincing, his jacket was off and lying across his lap. Gingerly, she fingered the rip in his shirt. It was a straight rip about three inches long. Under the torn material was a gash in his bicep almost as long as the rip—a gash that was still oozing blood. Following the line of his shirtsleeve, she could see the trail it had made as it tracked its way down his arm. When her eyes landed on his hand, she noted there was much more blood than she had anticipated, and though mostly dry, it was caked around his knuckles, fingers, and nail beds.

"Your shirt needs to come off too," she sighed.

He sighed too. "If only that were said under different circumstances, luv."

She laughed a bit at that. "If circumstances were different, *luv*, I wouldn't be so polite."

"No, she wouldn't," came a voice from behind her.

Stifling a scream, Kit spun, even as Jonathon rose to push her behind him. For a split second, they froze in that tableau, until her mind processed what she was seeing.

"Garret? What are you doing here?" she demanded. He nodded to her and relocked the door he had somehow managed to get open.

"Kit?" Jonathon asked, still keeping her behind him.

"He's, uh," she paused and gave herself a mental shake. Even though she could no more explain what Garret was doing there than what had happened to Jonathon, she knew she needed to get the introductions done quickly so both men would stand down.

"He's a friend of my brother's," she said. "They uh, they work in, well, I don't really know what they do, but it's a lot of stuff for the government that neither of them can tell me about," she managed to say.

"And what is he doing *here*?" She heard the suspicion in Jonathon's voice and mild panic set in. She didn't want to put Drew's friend in danger, nor did she want to find herself in a position where Drew was wrong about his friend and she, or Garret, ended up paying the price. The thought really hadn't crossed her mind until now. Until now, their conversations had been about politics and the weather and the royal family. But with these two men in the same room, the dynamics had changed. A lot.

"I'm watching over her," Garret said.

"Why?" Jonathon said.

And at the same time, she asked, "You are?"

"Because obviously, she needs it," Garret shot back at Jonathon, ignoring her question. "If that is what I think it is, you've been shot, my friend," he added with a nod toward Jonathon's bleeding arm.

Shot? *That* thought hadn't occurred to Kit and she moved in to get a closer look. She'd never seen a gunshot wound before, but as soon as Garret mentioned it, she realized that it looked exactly how she would have expected it to look—how she would have expected a graze from a bullet would look. She felt a little ill.

"Kit, you need to sit down," Garret ordered. Once the tone of his voice had sunk in, she looked up and glared at him.

"You, I will talk to later," she said, pointing to Garret with the hand carrying antiseptic. "You," she said, pointing to Jonathon, "sit."

She saw Jonathon look to Garret, more in question this time than in assessment—asking whether or not he should listen to her or if Garret wanted to deal with the situation. She spun around.

"Garret Cantona," she said with a very pointed look at him, "if you even consider trying to whisk me off somewhere because of some lame male caveman thing, I will make sure you regret it every day for the rest of your life. He's been shot, I just want to clean it up and make sure I don't need to force him to go to the hospital."

She saw a hint of hint of something, maybe promise, play in Garret's eyes, then he lifted a shoulder and grinned.

"You heard the lady, Parker. Sit."

She turned back to Jonathon and would not have been at all surprised to hear him say "We are not amused" as his eyes bounced between them. But like a good spy, he sat and began to remove his shirt.

Ten silent minutes later, Kit taped the last piece of gauze around Jonathon's bicep. She'd cleaned it up, made him wash his arm and hands in warm water to the best of his ability, and used the antiseptic before closing the wound with butterfly bandages. Then she covered the whole thing with gauze.

She pulled a clean, white t-shirt from the bag of stuff she'd bought and handed it to him. "It's not as nice the one that's ruined, but at least it's clean."

Jonathon said nothing as he stood, handed her his jacket, then pulled the t-shirt over his head, sliding his injured arm gingerly through the sleeve. Once it was on, he held his hand out and she handed the jacket back, frowning at the tear in the sleeve. "Are you sure you're all right, Jonathon?" she asked.

She watched him wince as he slid his arm into the sleeve of his jacket; then he straightened his collar and looked her in the eye. "I will be fine, I promise you. I've made a few calls and though I hate to say this, I would like for you to have some company, at least until you leave for Rome."

"Company?" Kit asked, arching an eyebrow at him. "Is that your way of saying you'd like me to have protection?" The thought was both ridiculous and sickening.

Jonathon's eyes went to Garret then came back to hers. "Yes, I would. And while under different circumstances, I would volunteer for the job—"

"Not happening, Parker. Not for a whole list of reasons I'm not even going to go into," Garret interrupted.

"No," Jonathon replied, his eyes never leaving Kit, "Perhaps that isn't the best of ideas. But I think you shall be in good hands with this one," he added with a nod toward Garret. "Now, if you would both excuse me."

Kit stood silently as Jonathon leaned down and gave her a kiss on the cheek. He then nodded to Garret, unlocked the door, and walked out. Kit was fairly certain she would never see him again. But truth be told, that didn't bother her all that much. She'd liked him—he'd been interesting to talk with, but there were any number of people she'd met over the years of working for Drew that she'd never seen again. And she tended to trust that it was for the best.

"Kit?"

Garret's voice brought her mind back to where she was. She

turned her head and met his gaze. She couldn't begin to understand what he was doing in London and why he'd been keeping an eye on her. She didn't think it had anything to do with Drew; neither her brother—and there was no doubt in her mind that her brother was behind this somehow—nor Garret had ever met Drew, as far as she knew, at least. And, come to think of it, she hadn't done any CIA work since meeting Garret five months ago.

But the alternative was something she didn't want to think about. Because the alternative reason for her brother and Garret following her was likely something she'd been avoiding for over a decade. She swallowed and pushed aside the memory of Caleb asking her about Henry Michaels.

"Kit? Let me get you back to your hotel. We can talk there."

Numbly, she nodded. She didn't want to spend any time with Garret, and remembering Henry Michaels made her want to hide from everyone. But she knew she needed to get back to her hotel. And since the chances of him not accompanying her were slim to none, she decided not to fight it.

Out on the sidewalk again, she took a deep breath of the cold, night air and burrowed deeper into her jacket. Garret walked between her and the street, and for the most part, she was able to ignore him and try to figure out what she needed to do next.

About halfway back to the hotel, her phone rang. Garret glanced at her for a moment before returning his vigil to the streets. She reached for the device and recognizing the number, she answered.

"I heard what happened," Drew said. "Are you okay?"

"Yeah, I'm fine," she mumbled, not sure how much Drew wanted her to talk in front of Garret.

"And Garret Cantona is with you now?"

That surprised her, though she supposed it shouldn't have. "Yes."

"Good. I assume your brother is also there, so don't be surprised if you see him too."

Garret shot her a look when a sardonic laugh escaped her.

"Yeah, Click and Clack, those two. I haven't seen him but assume he's here somewhere," she answered, referring to Caleb.

"Good," Drew said again. "Don't head back to your room yet. Make an excuse, go for a drink or something, just give me another hour and I'll have someone else in place to stick with you."

She slid a look at Garret who was, despite looking like he was out for an evening stroll, radiating tension. "Uh, I don't think that's going to be very easy."

"Yeah, I'm sure it's not. But I have faith in you. You're a younger sibling, surely you have some devious tricks up your sleeve."

Kit gave this a moment's thought. "Yeah, I suppose I might."

"Good, then use them. I don't need long and I'm actually going to give you permission to tell your brother and his partner everything about what you've been doing, but I need you to give me until tomorrow morning before you do. Can you do that?"

"Everything?" she asked. The unspoken question was, even about Parker?

"Yes, everything. I've looked into your brother and Cantona, and I'm comfortable with you telling them whatever you feel comfortable telling them. I just need you to wait until tomorrow morning," he repeated.

Well, this was new. But Kit didn't need to think too much about it. "Of course."

"Thank you. And like I said, I'm sending someone to look after you for tonight, so don't be too surprised."

And before she could ask who, he'd hung up.

"Who was that?" Garret asked as they approached the hotel. The doorman held the door for them and she walked in ahead of her companion.

"A friend," she answered. "I think I need a drink before I go up to my room," she added. With that implicit command hanging in the air, Kit walked straight into the bar, confident that Garret would follow.

• • •

An hour and a half and two martinis later, Kit was making her way to her room flanked by her brother and Garret.

In the hotel bar, Caleb had peppered her with questions, most of which she'd ignored by keeping her nose buried in a *Times of London* someone else had left behind. Garret had said next to nothing, though toward the end, when it had become clear that Kit wasn't going to talk, he had told Caleb to back off. It was then that she'd allowed herself to look at him for the first time since they'd sat down. And for a moment, she'd had the strongest urge to crawl into his lap and let him hold her. The look he'd given her in return seemed to say that he'd welcome such a move on her part. But she hadn't been brave enough. Not with her brother there. Not when she didn't know why they were both in London. Not when she didn't know what she really wanted from Garret.

And now that she'd spent the last ninety minutes establishing how she was going to address what had happened with Jonathon Parker—in that she was *not* going to address it at all—what came next would be an interesting test and she knew it. She needed to get rid of both of them before she entered her room.

She'd been mulling it over since she'd taken the first sip of her dirty gin cocktail and was pretty sure she had a good plan. Getting rid of Garret, who seemed a bit more respectful of her wishes, would be easier; it was her brother she was most concerned about. So she opted to tackle him first.

"Your key," her brother demanded as they neared her room.

"I have it, thanks," she replied as she pulled out the unremarkable card.

Caleb let out a breath. "You were shot at today, Kit. You aren't going to stay alone tonight."

"I wasn't shot at. Someone I happened to be with was shot at. And I *am* staying alone tonight," she retorted. "Because, dear brother, I'm still beyond pissed that you're here following me and haven't even told me why."

It wasn't exactly a lie. She *was* curious why he was there, but since she suspected it had something to do with Henry Michaels, a man she wanted to say nothing about, she didn't actually want to press the issue. But Caleb didn't know that, and she'd noticed that despite his eagerness to ask her about the man before she'd left for Europe, Caleb hadn't brought him up since. Of all the questions he'd asked her in the bar, not a single one was about either of the Michaels men. So she hoped that his reticence to talk to her about that and about what he was doing in London would hold him back.

"I would think it's obvious why I'm here—I mean, really Kit, how many times have you been shot at?" He crossed his arms and stood beside her door. She didn't dare slide the key in the lock because she knew he would slip right into the room. She also didn't bother to point out that he'd followed her to London long before the events of a few hours ago.

"I told you, *I* wasn't shot at. But I *am* jet lagged and I *am* annoyed at you. So if you really don't want me to be alone, leave Garret."

Predictably, Caleb snorted, though behind him and out of his sight, a single one of Garret's eyebrows went up.

"Well then, that solves that," she pronounced, gesturing for her brother to step aside. "I don't want you anywhere near me until tomorrow and then only if you're willing to talk to me. So, since you won't let Garret stay with me, I guess I'll be on my own, thank you very much."

Caleb eyed her for a moment, then stepped aside. Easily. Almost too easily. She eyed him right back and motioned with her head for him to step even further away from the door. He rolled his eyes but took three more steps away.

"I'm not going to rush tackle you, Kit," he said sarcastically.

"Forgive me if I don't trust you when for years you've come and gone from my life without so much as a 'how are you' and now you want to stayed glued to my side." She shook her head. "You were following me before Jonathon was shot, which means you're here for some reason other than to protect me. Sorry, Caleb, I'm sure even you can see how I must feel that you're here only because you want something from me. And at this point, that's not a feeling I care to continue to inflict upon myself. So, if you'll excuse me," she let her voice trail off, surprised by the sting in her own tone. And judging by Caleb's reaction, she'd hit a nerve. She hadn't meant to and honestly hadn't known that was how she felt until the words had come out. But now that they were out, she could scarcely deny them. There was no other explanation for Caleb sticking so close to her when he'd all but ignored her for years.

The realization hit her as hard as it seemed to hit him; in an instant, all the fight went out of her and a wave of loss and sadness swept into her soul. Maybe Garret recognized it, or maybe not, but when Caleb made to move toward her as she slid her key in the lock, he put a hand on Caleb's shoulder, halting him. And Caleb didn't fight him. She was pretty sure that was a good thing.

She stepped into her dark room and let the door click shut behind her. Turning to flip the lock and hit the light switch, she let out a deep breath. When she felt more collected she turned. And for the second time that day, barely stifled a scream.

"Kit?!" Garret's response was immediate from the other side of the door. She heard him try the handle, then let out a curse. She frowned, it was in Spanish, if she wasn't mistaken, a language she'd never heard him use before. But his pounding didn't let her mind absorb the information, and she frantically looked around her room.

At the two people lounging there.

One leggy blonde lay on the bed flipping through a magazine, and a dark-haired man sipping a glass of amber liquor relaxed in one of the side chairs. When Garret's knocking got a bit more insistent, the blonde gestured to the corner of the table, then nodded toward the door. Kit got what she was trying to say.

"I'm fine, Garret," she said, turning her head toward the door so her voice would carry. "I just walked into the corner of a table and it hurt like a son-of-a-bitch."

"Then let me in to see you," he demanded. Caleb echoed the sentiment.

Kit sighed and opened the door but left the top lock on. "See, I'm fine. I'll probably have a bruise tomorrow, but I'm fine."

Both men eyed her suspiciously, but Garret finally stepped back. And then it occurred to her why Caleb had given in so easily a few moments before—because he wasn't planning on going anywhere anyway. Oh, to be sure, the hotel would kick him out of the hallway eventually, but she didn't doubt he would be watching the hotel, watching out for her.

"I'm fine," she insisted. "And now I'm going to go to bed, so good night gentlemen," she said, then closed the door with a finality that she felt in her bones.

Turning back to her guests, she gave them a questioning look. The woman shook her head as she rose silently from the bed and gestured toward the bathroom. Kit got the message and glanced at the man who nodded to both women and waved them into the relative privacy of the attached room.

When they were both inside, with the door shut, Kit flipped on the water, because that was what she saw people do in spy movies, and faced her visitor. A huge smile broke across her face, the first real one all day.

"Dani Williamson Fuller," Kit said. "What the hell are you doing here?"

CHAPTER 6

KIT LET DANI ENGULF HER in a huge, warm hug. It felt good to be in the presence of her long-time friend—a woman she both trusted and admired. But it was completely unexpected. The last time they had talked, Dani and her husband, Ty, had just been settling in for a long winter in their hometown of Portland, Maine. TJ, their two year-old son, was just learning to sleep in his big boy bed. And now Dani was here. For her.

Dani let out a quiet laugh. "Drew did not send us over here just to meet you, so you can stop worrying that you've interrupted my life. Not that any visit with you would ever be considered an interruption," she added.

Kit studied her friend and saw the honesty in her eyes, which was even more confusing. "Then why are you here? Not that I'm not glad to see you."

"Ty and I never really had a honeymoon," Dani said as she propped herself against the counter. "So we decided to take a couple of weeks away. We spent a week in Greece and just landed in London a few days ago. When Drew called and told me what had happened, he asked if we wouldn't mind helping out for a few hours. And since I rarely get to see you in person, it was, of course, no question."

Kit wasn't sure what to think of the coincidence, but there was no doubt she was happy to see her friend, so she just smiled.

"How are you?" Dani asked. "I can't imagine you've ever been shot at before?"

Kit rolled her eyes. "I was not shot at. Someone I was *with* was shot at." She repeated what she'd said to Caleb just a few minutes ago, but Dani waved her off.

"Whatever. Being anywhere near a live shot can be scary as hell, so how are you?" she pressed.

Kit slid her coat off, and in the process, caught a glimpse of herself in the mirror. "Geez, I look like hell," she said, eyeing the dark circles under her eyes.

"Jet lag, lack of sleep, and stress can do that. Did Drew get you involved in something he shouldn't have?"

Kit shook her head as she reached for an elastic band to tie her hair back. Adjusting the temperature of the running water, she avoided Dani's knowing gaze.

"He did, didn't he?" Dani pushed as Kit bent to wash the travel and city grime off her face.

She didn't talk as she splashed water on her face, but when she'd finished and Dani had handed her a towel, Kit knew she had to say something. Dani and Drew were like brother and sister, she didn't want to get Drew in trouble with Dani, but she also didn't want to hide anything from her friend.

"Not intentionally, I don't think," Kit answered as she patted her face dry.

"Meaning?" Dani asked as she handed Kit a small bottle of face lotion.

"Meaning he asked me for a favor, a *personal* favor. He's never done that before, and considering everything he's done for me," Kit raised her hand to stave off the objection Dani's lips were already forming and continued. "After everything he's done for me, I wanted to help him. It's as simple as that. I knew what he was asking and why. He didn't hide anything from me," Kit insisted.

"But he almost got you shot," Dani pointed out.

Kit gave her friend a pointed look. "Gun violence in England is so rare, he never could have suspected this might happen. And before we rat hole on this, let's just agree to let it go. It happened, it's over, now what do I do? I assume Drew has some sort of plan for dealing with this?"

Dani's big brown eyes studied her for a long moment, and Kit knew her friend was searching for any sign of doubt or fear. Fear she'd find—it was true, it wasn't every day she was with someone who'd been shot—but she wouldn't find any doubt. If there was one thing Kit knew how to do, it was move on.

Finally, Dani nodded in acquiescence. "Once your brother and his colleague stop loitering in the hallway, we'll get you out of here and somewhere safe."

That got Kit's attention. She flipped the lid of the toilet closed and sat down. "Do you really think I'm in actual danger?" It sounded like a dumb question, considering the events of the day, but there was something about Dani's tone that made it seem more *real* than it had felt up until this point.

Coming to sit on the edge of the tub beside her, Dani gave Kit's arm a gentle squeeze, just like she had all those years ago when they'd first met and Kit had been a scared little six-year-old shipped off by her dad to some rich-kid summer camp for four weeks. Kit managed a smile at the memory.

"Who would have thought," Kit said. "All those years ago when you agreed to be my big sister at camp and shepherd me through my first time away from home, that we would end up like this."

Dani rubbed Kit's arm again, then dropped her hand. "We haven't 'ended up' anywhere, Kit. This isn't the end to anything. Like so many other events in our lives, it's a bump. And considering what *has* gone on in our lives, it's a relatively minor bump, at that."

Kit had to give her that. Between the two of them, they'd make one hell of a made-for-TV movie. She shook her head. "You're right. It's the jet lag and the stress. When I think about what happened today, it *was* scary, but I don't feel unsafe now. Right now, I just want to get to bed."

On cue, Ty poked his head into the bathroom. "Ready?" he asked, directing his question to his wife. "And by the way, Kit, hello to you. You look great. Sorry you got shot at today," he added.

Kit thought about pointing out for the umpteenth time that she hadn't been shot at, but then saw the spark in Ty's eyes and just shook her head and laughed. "It's good to see you too, Ty. Dani sent me some pictures of TJ; he's the spitting image of you."

Ty's mouth split into a grin at the reminder of his son. "I know, right?" He cast a look at Dani, then laughed. "It makes Dani grumpy. She thinks that since she did all the work, he should look at least a little bit like her."

"I did carry him for nine months, then breast fed him for a year," Dani pointed out.

"Maybe you'll get lucky next time," Ty teased, coming over to kiss his wife on the top of her head.

"You aren't—" Kit didn't even get to finish the question before Dani started shaking her head.

"No, I'm not pregnant."

"Not that we know of," Ty added. Dani elbowed him in the hip then turned back to Kit.

"We're thinking we might try for another," she said. "It was part of the reason we wanted to take this trip now. We figured if we ever wanted to spend some time alone, we should do it before we start trying for another and life becomes engulfed by two kids."

Kit smiled. "Whether TJ gets a sibling or not, you guys are great parents."

Dani and Ty both smiled. "Thanks," Dani said. "It isn't always easy, but between our families we have great support."

And that they both knew how fragile life could be was something they didn't say. They didn't need to, not to Kit, who knew all about both their pasts. At the age of thirteen, Dani had witnessed her parents' murders and then, years later, she'd almost lost Ty when he'd gone after the man who had killed them. Ty had been caught in the cross fire during the mission and had been presumed dead. He'd missed nearly all of Dani's pregnancy while recovering in the jungles of Africa before finally making it back to the States just before their son was born.

Knowing they were putting their much-deserved vacation

together on hold for her, Kit took a deep breath. "So tell me then, what's the plan?"

• • •

Stretched out on a bed three floors above Kit's room, Garret gazed up at the ceiling. He and Caleb had left the hallway outside Kit's room when it had become clear that one guest or another was going to report them. He'd then taken a shift keeping an eye on the most common exits, first sitting in the bar with a view of the elevator and stairwell, then moving to the street with a view of the main door as the night wore on and the bar closed. Caleb had gone off to only god knew where, but had returned at about three in the morning to relieve him.

It was close to five and he still hadn't slept a wink. Garret didn't like leaving Kit one bit. And he didn't like their makeshift surveillance of her either. There were a hundred and one ways someone could slip into her room outside of their surveillance. Actually, by his count, there were one hundred and twenty-seven ways.

But he hadn't seen her leave, nor had he seen anyone who raised the hair on the back of his neck while in the bar. And once he'd moved to the street, he'd actually caught a glimpse of her silhouette as she'd moved toward the bathroom and flicked on a light. It wasn't much, but that small sighting had soothed some of his nerves.

Rubbing a hand over his face, he tried to will himself to sleep. But the events and the conversations of the day before were still bouncing around his head like a coked-up jackrabbit. He didn't believe for a second that she was involved in what Caleb was concerned that she might be involved in. But then again, she'd been seen with two spooks and been shot at. And she seemed to have taken it all in stride. Of course, Kit wasn't really the type to wallow in hysterics. She'd been frightened after the shooting, he'd seen that, but she'd pushed it aside and bandaged Jonathon up. When he'd sat with her at the bar afterward, he'd noticed that her hands shook as she'd raised her drink. But her voice had been strong—soft, but strong.

So if she wasn't involved in whatever it was Caleb thought she might be involved in, why had she reacted to the name from her past in the way she had, and why was she so comfortable around spies?

He had no idea what was going on in her head or her life because five months ago he hadn't stuck around to find out. A rueful bark of laughter escaped his lungs as he thought about that and the pain he'd heard in her voice when she'd accused Caleb of following her and only sticking around because he needed something from her. He couldn't help but wonder just how many people there were out there using Kit for their own purposes. Caleb was one, to be sure—he thought she had information he might need. And Garret would wager that whatever circumstances had brought Kit to cross paths with Jonathon Parker involved someone using her for their own reasons as well.

And then there was her job. Her agent used her and made money off her. He knew from his conversations with Kit five months ago that she wouldn't characterize her relationship with her agent that way, but the long and short of it was that whether the woman was a true friend to Kit or not, she only made money when Kit did.

And then there was him. Was he just one of many who looked at Kit as a means to an end? He tried to look at things objectively but not surprisingly, he came up short. He could see how Kit might see it that way. He could see how she might resent his waltzing back into her life and looking to pick up where they left off.

Only that wasn't how he saw it at all. He wanted her to be happy and he knew, bone deep, that she'd be happy with him. He just had to convince her of that. Of course, it wasn't entirely about her. What he felt for her, the almost physical punch to the gut he'd felt when he first saw her in his campsite, was something he would never forget. He didn't *need* her. He didn't need anyone.

But he sure as hell wanted her—mentally, emotionally, and most definitely physically.

That last little thought brought a smile to his lips. The memory of his brief time with Kit, especially the physical parts, had kept him going throughout the last five months. He couldn't wait to touch her again, to feel her hands on his skin.

Finally, as his mind focused on Kit, the other thoughts and worries slowly slipped from his mind and he drifted off to sleep.

* * *

Five hours and one cryptic phone call from Kit later, Garret stood on the bank of a tree-lined, narrow canal in South London and stared at his phone.

"Cantona? Are you there?" He could hear Caleb's voice despite not having the device anywhere near his ear. He looked at the houseboat he'd been studying again. Looked at the woman standing on the deck and shook his head.

"Garret!"

Finally, Garret put the phone back to his ear. "Yeah?"

"What the hell?" Caleb demanded.

"I just," he paused and looked at the woman again. She raised a mug in his direction, silently inviting him aboard.

"You just what?" snipped his partner.

Garret felt the last of the cobwebs shake free of his brain and he narrowed his eyes. "I think you need to get down here," he said.

"I think you need to get back to the hotel," Caleb countered, his measured tone revealing just how irritated he was. "It's ten o'clock and I haven't seen hide nor hair of my sister. It's time she woke up."

"She's up," Garret said, taking a step toward to the boat.

"How would you know that?"

"Because I'm looking at her. In fact, she just offered me a cup of coffee," Garret said. He still had no idea what was going on, but as he got closer, he was relieved to see Kit looking fit and well rested.

"Like hell. You saw her in her room last night and she hasn't left."

"Well, she didn't leave by the lobby or the front door, but I assure you she left because she's here."

He heard Caleb grumble something under his breath before speaking again. "You're sure?"

Garret stepped onto the deck of the houseboat and handed Kit the phone. She wore a thick, wool sweater that fell to her mid-thigh and a hat and gloves to ward off the February chill. Her auburn hair fell free down her back and her golden eyes looked more alert and less ringed with fatigue than they had the night before. Whatever she'd been up to since he'd last seen her, she'd gotten a good night's sleep.

"Good morning, Caleb," she said, then grinned at Garret as she listened to her brother's response on the phone.

"Well, I have a few tricks up my sleeve," she said into the phone as she motioned Garret inside the quaint and warm cabin. She listened to her brother as she pulled off her hat and gloves, laid them on the small table, then walked to the tiny kitchen. Grabbing a mug, she poured him some coffee.

"You know, Caleb," she said, handing Garret the steaming beverage. "You do realize that whatever you say isn't going to change the fact that I am, in fact, on a boat and not in my hotel room."

She met Garret's gaze and rolled her eyes at something her brother was currently saying. He removed his leather jacket and slung it over one of the chairs.

"Be that as it may, if you would like to know what *is* going on, you are more than welcome to join us. Garret and I were just getting ready to sit down and have a cup of coffee. Well, I'm having tea, but you know what I mean."

With that, she handed the phone back to Garret, and he provided Caleb with their location then ended the call.

"You really shouldn't take such glee in one-upping your

brother, you know," he said as he sat down at the small table, not meaning it at all. As far as he was concerned, it was about time someone one-upped Caleb Forrester. Garret had the utmost respect for his partner, and actually liked him as a person, but that didn't mean eating a slice of humble pie every now and then wouldn't be a good thing for Caleb.

"Of course I should," she shot back, taking a seat beside him. "He's too arrogant and too controlling for his own good. I don't often get the chance to talk to him, let alone needle him, the way a sibling should." She grinned again and took a sip of her tea.

Sitting back, he took a sip of his coffee. The hot liquid tasted good and felt even better sliding down his throat. Logically, he knew it wasn't as cold in London as it had been in Windsor, but there was something about being in a city in the winter that made him feel like he'd like entered an ice palace, like he'd never be warm again.

They sat in companionable silence for a few minutes. He wanted to know what was going on, but figured it would be better to wait for Caleb to arrive so that Kit wouldn't need to repeat herself.

"You look good, well rested," he said, studying her face as she sipped her tea.

She offered him a smile. "Thanks, I am. This boat is surprisingly comfortable. I don't know what I was expecting when I came here last night, but the bed is a real one and there's always something nice about being on the water."

She liked the water—a little something he'd file away. "What time did you get here?"

She wagged her head. "I don't know, I guess at around ten last night."

He coughed and set his mug down. "I saw you through the window of your hotel much later than that." He'd assumed that she'd snuck out at some point this morning, maybe when Caleb had stepped away to grab some coffee.

Kit laughed. "I'm not sure whether to be offended that you

were all but stalking me or offended that you couldn't differentiate my form from someone else's. Especially, considering . . ." She let her voice trail off.

Yeah, considering he'd spent a good deal of time remembering her form, it seemed surprising that he would have mistaken hers through the window.

Kit laid a hand on his arm and gave him an indulgent smile. "I'll let it slide this time, since it's been five months and Dani and I are built a lot alike."

He looked at her hand on his arm and a sudden surge of frustration swept through him. How did they come to this? Kit shouldn't be in a position where she was sneaking around, hiding out, and hanging out with spies and people that got shot. She should be hanging out with him, maybe on a beach somewhere, laughing and driving him crazy with her golden eyes.

"Garret?"

He raised his eyes and saw a frown of concern touching her lips.

"I'm fine, I was just wondering how we ended up here," he managed to say.

"I was wondering the same thing," Caleb said, as he opened the door and stepped into the lounge area. Garret hadn't heard him approach, and the boat hadn't rocked at all when he'd boarded.

Kit let out a little yelp of surprise and her hand went to her heart. "Jesus, you startled me," she said.

Caleb gave her a hard look. "Good," was all he said. He stood there for a moment and just looked at her. She didn't bat an eye at his scrutiny, but Garret suspected Caleb's study was more to assure himself that his sister was okay than to intimidate her, which seemed to be the way she was reading it too.

"Coffee?" Caleb finally asked. Kit waved to the pot on the counter behind him. After pouring a mug, he joined them at the table.

Kit's eyes went from her brother, to Garret, then back again.

"Well?" Caleb demanded. "What the hell is going on, Kit?"

Her eyes dropped to her hands wrapped around her mug, then she looked up and met Caleb's gaze.

"Several years ago, I met a few people who work for the CIA. We became friends and since then, as my travel and schedule permits, I occasionally carry and deliver information for them."

Garret blinked. That sure wasn't what he'd expected to hear. He glanced at Caleb, who wasn't bothering to hide his expression.

"Try again, Kit."

Garret swiveled his gaze to Kit in time to see her eyes drop and a look tinged with disappointment and resignation wash over her face at her brother's reaction.

While Garret hadn't initially believed her either, that look changed his mind. When she turned to look at him, he met her gaze. "For how long?" he asked and was gratified to see her shoulders release some tension at his belief in her.

"You don't believe her, do you?" Caleb asked.

"Actually, I do," Garret responded, holding her gaze. "Honestly, it's the only thing that makes sense. Why else would she be hanging out with spooks and have people to step in for her to make it look like she was somewhere she wasn't," he added, referring the figure he'd seen in the window. "I don't know how or why, but I do believe her."

Her eyes softened and her lips tipped up into a small, fleeting smile. "Thank you, Garret."

"Why don't you tell us about it," he prompted.

Caleb, who for some reason was being more of an ass than usual, sat back and crossed his arms over his chest, not saying a word.

"There's not much to tell," Kit began after she'd taken another sip of her tea. "I was introduced to Drew Carmichael by a friend right around the time our father died. I knew they both worked for the CIA, so when my travel schedule picked up and I started attending some of the events I attend, Drew and I just started talking one night about ways I could help."

"Ways you could help?" Garret repeated, not sure he'd heard

right. "In what ways would a CIA operative ever need to drag in a civilian?" He actually knew a few, but he was starting to feel a little pissy that this Carmichael guy had dragged *Kit* in.

"Don't get so moody, Garret," Kit shot back. "It was my idea, actually. I was at an embassy party in Cairo several years ago and happened to overhear something. When I got back to the states, I called Drew and told him what I'd heard. That started the whole thing and I've been doing it ever since."

"You're a CIA asset?" Caleb clarified, disbelief still ringing clear in his voice.

Kit shook her head. "No, I'm not an asset, more like a mule. I just carry information around. I don't do anything else, and I only do it if I happen to be going to a particular place. And just to clarify, I don't think Drew is an operative—he used to be out in the field a lot when he was younger, but now he does a lot of work out of Langley."

Garret shook his own head. In his mind, once CIA, always CIA. Whether Drew was active in the field or not, he shouldn't have dragged Kit into his game.

"When he was younger? How old is he?" Garret asked, suddenly realizing what else she'd said. It would just be so much worse if the guy behind all this was some old-school spook.

Kit lifted a shoulder. "He's not old by any means, late thirties, maybe forty, but he's always saying field work is a young man's game."

"He may not be old in years, but I tell you he's an old man at heart," a woman said, stepping into the lounge much the same way Caleb had. In an instant, both he and Caleb were on their feet, blocking Kit. He had a gun, so did his partner, but neither wanted to pull it unless necessary.

A tall, blonde woman stepped farther into the cabin and a dark-haired man came in behind her. Her big brown eyes bounced between them and she let out a little laugh. "Stand down, gentlemen. I'm a friend."

Neither of them did, but then, judging by the way she seemed perfectly at ease with their vigilance, Garret would guess she hadn't expected them to.

"You okay?" the woman asked, her eyes landing on Kit, who was still sitting.

Kit nodded. "I'm fine, well rested. Thank you."

"My husband didn't keep you up with his snoring?" the blonde teased.

The man snorted. "You're the snorer in the family, babe," he shot back.

"Am not," she retorted with a smile that led Garret to think this was a long-standing faux argument between the two.

"Yeah, you are," Kit interjected. "Caleb, Garret, meet Dani and Ty Fuller," she added making the introductions.

Dani gestured with her hands in mock exasperation. "So much for girl power, Kit. Did you tell them?"

Again, Kit nodded. "Yes, but my brother doesn't believe me."

Dani's sharp brown eyes flitted to Caleb. "I can hardly blame him for that, Kit. You're too good to be a part of this world in any way."

Garret found himself liking this woman, whoever she was.

"You're CIA," Caleb said, meeting her eyes.

For a moment, she didn't answer, then she glanced at the man beside her and spoke. "Former CIA," she clarified. "And my husband is former vice and a former SEAL. We both work with a private security-consulting firm now. But," she paused and let her eyes fall to Kit again. "What's relevant for this conversation is that I'm a friend of Kit's. We've known each other a very long time."

"So you're the one who brought her into this?"

"Don't be a jerk, Caleb. Dani didn't do anything I didn't initiate," Kit cut her brother off. "And it's none of your business how it all started or even whether I'll keep doing it, but it *is* the reason I was seen with the two gentlemen you saw me with yesterday. So, now that you know my deep, dark secret, you can go back to whatever it was you were doing before you followed me here," she snapped.

"Are you ready?" Dani asked.

"Ready? Ready for what?" Caleb demanded.

Garret could see Caleb's tone was quickly wearing on Kit's temper. He could see her startlingly colored eyes debate whether or not to even answer her brother. Finally, she sighed as she rose.

"If you recall, I'm expected at a gathering in Rome. Dani and Ty are going to escort me."

"Like hell. I want to know what you were talking to Jonathon Parker about. You must know—" Caleb cut himself off, and for the first time in probably ever, Garret saw Caleb act unsure. He could tell that his partner of so many years didn't know how much to say. He wanted answers, but didn't want to drag his sister in any deeper.

"I must know that Jonathon Parker is being investigated by MI6?" Kit supplied, surprising everyone there.

Caleb blinked. "Yes."

"Yes, I do know. Drew told me everything when he asked if I would meet with Jonathon to begin with. That meeting was different than others, obviously. But Drew and I have been good friends for a number of years and he asked me to do him a personal favor. He didn't hide anything."

Garret saw Caleb's jaw working furiously. He wasn't ever sure what Caleb thought of Kit, but Garret was pretty sure her brother had never suspected she did anything other than write. Finding out she was hooked up with the CIA and had been for years was a lot for someone like Caleb to stomach. It was a lot for Garret to stomach too—and he wasn't doing it very well either. He ran a hand over his face and through his hair.

"Kit, why don't I take you to the airport?" he said. And get on a plane with you, was what he wanted to say. He didn't doubt her, not for a moment. And that was what made it all worse. Now that he knew what she did, even if she didn't think much of it, he was pretty sure he was going to have an ulcer every time she traveled out of the country.

"*I'll* take her," Caleb interjected.

But Kit shook her head. "Neither of you will take me. Dani and Ty will. Caleb," she said, turning to her brother. "I don't know why you came to Windsor a few days ago or why you followed me here. This," she said with an encompassing gesture, "was obviously news to you, so not the reason. I know there's something you want from me."

Caleb opened his mouth to say something, but she cut him off. "Whatever it is, it can wait. I have friends I want to celebrate with in Rome, friends who mean a lot to me. Please, just leave it be for now and we can talk when I get back. I can't imagine what you think I might know, but all you ever had to do was ask."

Something in the vicinity of Garret's chest ached at the sorrow he heard in her voice. One day, he'd figure out what had happened between the siblings. If he couldn't make Caleb be a better brother, maybe he could at least help Kit feel less sad.

"Ready, honey?" Dani asked her friend, her voice quiet.

Kit moved her gaze from her brother to Garret, and they shared a brief moment in which he told her much more than he could say in words. She dipped her head in a small acknowledgement.

"Yes, Dani, I'm ready."

CHAPTER 7

GARRET STOOD AGAINST THE WALL and watched Kit dance in the arms of another man. Another man who, if the way his hand was spread across her lower back was any indication, felt completely at ease with Kit's body pressed against his.

Marco Baresi. The celebrated writer. The good friend. The author Garret used to enjoy reading.

He watched them turn slowly, engaged in conversation as they flowed across the floor with a familiarity that would be hard to mistake. Kit, clad in a dark red silk dress that draped across her shoulders and down her body to mid-thigh, leaned back and smiled at something Baresi said. Her auburn hair, held back with a clip above her ear on one side, swayed as they danced.

A few people walked by and eyed Garret, no doubt trying to figure who he was and whether or not he was important. The party was invitation only, so no one doubted he belonged there, even if they couldn't place him.

Garret waved to one of the servers, who immediately brought him a glass of champagne. He sipped it as the music played, waiting for the dance to end. He tried to turn his eyes from the couple to take in other parts of this opulent party he'd managed to snag an invitation to through an old contact who'd owed him a favor. But he didn't try very hard; after only a few seconds, his eyes drifted back.

The tightness in his chest didn't let up as Kit and Marco turned and glided to the other end of the dance floor. It took everything he had to fight his primal urge to intervene. It wasn't that he thought

Kit was going to jump into the other man's bed, but Garret was jealous, ridiculously so, of the time they were spending together and of the ease they seemed to share. And he couldn't help wondering if Kit would ever feel that comfortable in his arms.

Finally, the song ended. Baresi continued to hold Kit in his embrace as he finished saying something to her, but the couple stopped moving. Unable to stay away any longer, Garret took the last sip of his champagne and set the glass down on a nearby table.

"May I have the next dance?" he asked, having moved across the floor.

With a surprised gasp, Kit spun. Baresi released one of her hands when she turned, but kept his arm wrapped around her waist as she stayed tucked against him.

"Garret?" she said, sounding as confused as her expression looked. "What are you doing here?" Her perfectly framed eyebrows came together. Then came together even more, and not in surprise.

"Let me guess, my brother sent you?" she asked, all but turning away from him. Dismissing him.

"Actually, Kit, your brother is back in New York. I came because I wanted to be here."

For a moment, she was speechless and just stood there staring at him—while she was still in another man's arms. He was going to have to change that. Soon.

"Darling, why don't you introduce me to your friend?" Marco Baresi said, nudging Kit out of her silence. She gave herself a little shake and eyed Garret warily, but dutifully turned to Baresi and spoke.

"Marco, this is a, well, this is Garret Cantona. Garret, this Marco Baresi, my good friend and the reason for this party."

Garret didn't miss the lack of a qualifier attached to his name, but ignoring that for the moment, he turned to the author. Garret acknowledged that the man—though bald, just a hair taller than Kit in her heels, and more than a few years older—might hold a certain appeal to women. He was unquestionably okay looking, but he also had the kind of confidence and easy sensuality, judging by the way his hand remained on Kit, that women might find attractive.

"I hear congratulations are in order, Mr. Baresi. I've been a fan for many years." *But not so much anymore*, he appended in his head.

His statement not only surprised the author, but Kit too. She drew her head back and looked at him as if she was trying to figure out if he was poking fun. But he wasn't. And to prove it, he continued.

"I've heard rumors that you had a muse for *10,000 Yearnings*, and from what I gather, most people have assumed it was Kit," he said putting two and two—and two—together, from everything he'd read about Baresi. "But," Garret continued, "I think that if you've ever based a character on Kit, it would have to have been Marta in *Comings Away*."

For a beat, no one said anything. Then Marco Baresi threw his head back and laughed. Garret glanced at Kit—who was frowning at him, or maybe at Marco—and took a moment to study her. He was relieved to see she still looked well rested, though if it was possible, he'd wager she'd lost a pound or two in the past two days.

When he finally stopped laughing, Baresi smiled at Garret. "You know her well, then," the author said in his thick Italian accent.

"Well enough for now," Garret answered.

Baresi gave him a speculative look that he soon turned on Kit.

She met her old friend's gaze for moment then Baresi turned back to him. "No one has ever suggested Marta was based on Kit. Most of them assume it was the lovely, lithe, and seductive Genevieve from *10,000 Yearnings*. But you are, of course, right, my friend," he added. "I'm curious, if you will, what made you see that?"

Garret could tell from the look on Kit's face that she was anything but curious. In fact, she looked like she wanted to be anywhere in the world but in the middle of this conversation. Too bad.

"There is no denying the appeal of the young Genevieve," Garret started. "Her sensuality, her seductiveness, is rather," he paused searching for the word. "It is rather irresistible. And easy for one to attribute to Kit without reserve."

Kit shifted and looked away. Still looking for an escape she wasn't going to find.

"But Marta," Garret continued, keeping his gaze on Kit, who finally, with obvious reluctance, met it. "She possesses a spirit, a will to not just survive but to make her life better. To live better, to love better, to be better. A strength that goes beyond the sexual realm—one that is more subtle but stronger than any aspect of Genevieve's character. And that," he said, his eyes locked on hers, "is Kit."

He felt more than saw Baresi's eyes bounce between the two of them. But in his mind, in this place, there was no one in the room but him and Kit. Her golden eyes watched him as he noted the flush of her skin and the rhythm of her pulse beating in her neck.

"I suppose then, *mi amore*, that tonight, I shall be lonely."

Garret heard the words, but it seemed to take more than a few seconds for them to register with him—and with Kit. But after a moment, she gave a little shake of her head and turned toward her old friend.

"Marco, don't pretend you'll be lonely tonight," she chided. "We would have stayed up drinking, smoking Cuban cigars, and rehashing old times. But you know Cara is always willing to accommodate any of your *other* companionship interests."

Marco gave a good-hearted tsk-tsk and shook his head. Saying something in Italian, he leaned forward and brushed a kiss across Kit's cheek before facing Garret.

"She is my muse in more ways than one, my friend," he said. "And she is perfectly capable of taking care of herself, as I well know. But do not assume that because she is competent, she needs no one."

"Marco!" Kit protested, but he silenced her by raising her hand to his lips and pressing a kiss there, like a gentleman from days gone by.

"Be good, be kind, and if she comes back to me," he said,

placing Kit's fingers in Garret's hand, "rest assured, I *do* know how to heal her and will not hesitate to do so again." With that, he turned and walked away, leaving the two of them standing on the dance floor as the orchestra struck up another song.

Garret hesitated for a split second before he pulled her into his arms and began moving to the music. Judging by Kit's silence, they were both contemplating what Marco had said, and what he hadn't. Then again, she could just be plotting his demise for crashing the party and disrupting her evening.

"Kit?" he asked, pulling back a bit to see her face. Her eyes were fixed over his shoulder for several strains, then finally met his gaze.

"I don't want to talk about it tonight, Garret. I don't want to talk about why you're here or what Marco said. I just want to dance and visit with my friends and then go back to my room, *alone*," she added. "And get a good night's sleep before I fly home tomorrow. Can you just let me do that?"

He studied her, not just her eyes, but the feel of her body against his, the way her feet moved with his, the tilt of her head, and the feel of her fingers brushing his neck. What she was asking wasn't what he wanted—good god, it wasn't what he wanted. But if it was what she needed, then yes, he could do that.

CHAPTER 8

KIT WALKED INTO HER KITCHEN and smelled coffee. And maybe something cooking. She paused. Since Carly was usually gone by the time Kit returned, she wasn't used to entering her home after a trip to find someone there.

"Caleb," Garret said from behind her. She glanced over her shoulder at him and not for the first time in the past twenty-four hours did she wish things could be different between them. He'd stood by what he'd promised her the night before, and they'd spent most of the evening mingling with her friends, talking, and even doing a little more dancing. A few times, he had brushed her hair or her hand with a light kiss, but at the end of the night, he'd seen her to her room and left her. She hadn't seen him again until he'd shown up to take her to the airport. And she was mostly sure that his leaving her alone was a good thing.

But after her time with him in Rome, then their time cooped up together on the flight from Rome to New York, and then again in the car for a few hours on the way to Windsor, Kit found herself beginning to wonder—to wonder if maybe Garret could be good for her. He was definitely good *to* her, of that there was no doubt. But he was also good company and an easy traveling companion. They'd talked when the mood struck, laughed a time or two, and enjoyed some companionable silences. She'd learned that when he wasn't working, he liked to explore cities and often spent hours roaming the streets of various metropolises. And she had told him her favorite places to travel and why. All in all, over the past fourteen hours, she had been more comfortable in his company than she'd ever imagined, especially considering that she still wasn't sure what had motivated him—or her brother—to come back after all these months.

But even though the wall she'd built to keep him out was starting to show signs of fracture, she couldn't forget that what he could offer, what his lifestyle offered, just wasn't what she wanted to sign up for. And though it was hard, she kept reminding herself that what she *did* want, a partner that stuck with her, wasn't actually all that much to ask for. And she'd compromised enough in her life with the men closest to her, and learned enough of a lesson from it, that she didn't want to let go of this one fundamental thing she wanted from a relationship.

Taking off her coat and boots, she stepped into the kitchen as Garret went to deposit both of their bags upstairs.

"There's coffee," Caleb said, appearing at the top of the stairs that led down to where he slept. "No more lunch," he said gesturing to the dishes in the sink, "but there's coffee," he repeated.

She murmured a thank you, poured herself a cup, then joined Caleb at the kitchen island. She didn't normally drink coffee, but sliding onto a stool, she wrapped her hands around the liquid energy—energy she knew she'd need for whatever was coming next—and looked at her brother. Really looked at him.

His eyes were the same unusual color as hers and their skin was a similar tone as well, though her hair was auburn while his was closer to blond. But where Caleb had inherited their father's bone structure, she'd taken after their mother. Despite her height, which she had inherited from her father, her features were fine, almost delicate.

"How was your flight?" he asked.

For a moment, she thought about answering, about engaging in small talk. But she was tired, both physically from the jet lag and mentally from everything that had happened in the past week.

"What do you want, Caleb?" she asked instead.

His eyes didn't leave hers as he drummed his fingers on the countertop. Garret pulled up a seat beside her.

"You came here for a reason, so just tell me what it is and then we can both go on our merry way," she added when his silence extended.

Finally, he let out a breath. "What do you know about Henry Michaels? The dad and the son."

She'd been expecting to hear the name, but even so, she felt her fingers constrict against her cup and a tightness spread across her chest. Again, she thought about just answering the question. But if she was going to go through hell, she damn well wanted to know why.

"Why do you want to know?" she asked.

Predictably, Caleb's eyes narrowed on her. Next to her, Garret made some sort of noise she assumed was meant to warn Caleb from doing or saying anything stupid, but she kept her focus on her brother. Caleb's eyes moved to Garret, then came back to her. His hand fisted on the table as he studied her.

She sighed. "Look, Caleb," she said. "You haven't been around for the past fifteen years or so, so let me assure you that I'm a big girl. You know who some of my friends are, you know some of what I do, and though my life may not be what you thought it was, I'm an adult. So I'll ask again. Why are you interested in the Michaels men?"

He was silent for a moment. Then he sat back, ran a hand through his hair and over his face, and spoke. "You don't like me very much, do you?" he asked.

Kit blinked in surprise. It wasn't what she'd been expecting to hear, but she could see the honest, though reluctant, curiosity in Caleb's expression.

And so she thought about it, really thought about it.

She knew deep down she loved Caleb as her brother. But as for liking him? There had been a time when the sun rose and set on him. Five years older, he'd watched out for her, played with her, indulged her to the extreme—especially after their mother had died when she was ten.

But then he'd left. Without a word. Without any explanation, without leaving any contact information, and without telling her where he was going. He hadn't called or written. He'd just vanished. Leaving her to the hell that was their home.

She'd been fifteen and confused as hell when it happened. She'd felt hurt, then angry. But looking at him now, sitting across from her, with the expanse of time between those events years ago and now, she realized she was no longer angry. Just hurt. Deeply hurt. Because everything she had gone through after he left, she'd had to do on her own.

She looked down at her coffee cup and blinked back tears. When she was sure she had herself under control, she looked up again.

"Honestly, Caleb, I don't know you enough to know if I like you. I love you as my brother. But any more than that?" she shrugged, letting her voice trail off.

"But you're angry with me," he pressed.

She tilted her head in acknowledgement. "Yes, but more hurt by what you did."

"By what I did?" he asked, looking confused.

Kit blinked at him. His confusion seemed genuine. How could he not know how much his leaving had affected her?

"You left, Caleb. You left without a word to me. Without letting me know how I could reach you or where you were going or when—or if—you'd be back."

For a moment he stared at her. Then he ran his hands over his face again. "I can't. I don't want to get into that right now, Kit," he said with a look at Garret.

Of course he didn't. The strength of the anger that Kit had thought she'd mostly gotten over came roaring back. It took a moment to rein it in, but she'd be damned if she was going to let Caleb control this conversation.

"Fine," she said, her voice cool. "Then tell me why you want to know about the Michaels men."

"Kit," Caleb responded, his voice holding a hint of what

might have passed for pleading if it had come from anyone other than her brother.

"Tell me," she demanded. She set her cup down with a sharp thunk to make her point.

Again, Caleb's eyes went to Garret, lingered there for moment, then swung back to her. "I don't want to tell you why, I just want to know if you kept in touch with them or know what either of them is up to now."

"I don't care what you *want* to tell me, Caleb. If you want me to answer the question, you don't have a choice."

"So you do know something," he responded, his eyes narrowing on her.

She took a sip of coffee but said nothing.

"Kit?" he pushed.

"Why do you want to know?" she asked again, aware that Garret, still at her side had said nothing, hadn't even moved, throughout the exchange.

Caleb pushed himself off his stool and spun away from her. Several seconds passed before he turned back. "Why can't you just answer the fucking question?"

That got Garret to move. Not that she needed him to, but he too came off his stool and positioned himself even closer to her side. Presumably in a show of support.

"Back down, Forrester," Garret said.

"This is none of your business," Caleb shot back.

"Like hell, it's not."

Kit turned and looked at Garret, then swung her head back to Caleb. Both men looked ready to do some damage if needed.

"Tell me," she said. "And you have five minutes to decide because after that, I'm going to bed. And after that, you'll be leaving."

Doubt flickered across Caleb's face. He didn't believe her. Fine. She rose from her seat and headed toward the sink.

"You don't want to know, Kit," Caleb said.

She turned back and didn't bother to bite back the harsh laugh that escaped her. "I don't *want* to know? How could you possibly know what I want or don't want, Caleb? Do you have any idea what my life was like after you left? Do you have any idea what I know and what I've seen? Oh, I know you think you have the corner on life's horrors, Caleb, but you need to get over that. Now, either tell me why you want to know or get out and leave me alone."

She saw doubt flicker across his face and mentally she started counting down from ten. If he didn't speak by the time she reached zero, she was done.

"It's about Dad," he said. Finally.

If he had expected to shock her, he fell far short. She let out another not-so-nice laugh. "Dad?" she said.

He gave a hesitant nod.

"Just what is it you think you can't tell me about our father, Caleb?"

She paused and spared a glance at Garret who was standing, arms crossed, watching them.

"Do you honestly think anything you have to tell me about our father is going to shock me?" She was incredulous at the thought. And even more so when she saw the expression on Caleb's face that told her he had assumed she knew nothing about their father's activities.

"You *left* me in that house, Caleb. What did you think was going to happen? Oh, we both know how it looked from the outside, all perfect and beautiful and grand. A house worthy of Southern gentry, filled with the prodigal son and beautiful daughter and doting father.

"But it was all a lark, wasn't it, Caleb? And you left me to figure that out on my own." Kit was breathing hard and not done yet. Fifteen plus years of pain, frustration, shame, and anger continued to pour out of her.

"You want to know about the Michaels men and why I reacted when I heard their name? Fine." She paused to take a breath and prepare herself to speak about something she hadn't spoken about for over a decade.

"I reacted to the name because our *father* sold me to them— lost me in a game of poker, actually. Yes, you heard that right. It wasn't just people from foreign countries and illegal weapons he traded in," she continued. In front of her, Caleb had gone sheet white and she was dimly aware that Garret had moved a step closer to her. She held out a hand to stave him off and finished.

"He sold me off, Caleb. Or rather, my virginity. Henry Michaels senior thought it would be fun to win that for his son. And then again, a second time for himself once I was broken in," she added. "I was seventeen when I found out. Too late to take it back from junior, but at least I caught on before the father had his chance. I thought I was in love. I thought Henry was in love. He played it well. Then again, it's probably not hard for a twenty-two-year-old man to play a seventeen-year-old girl."

"How," Caleb's voice broke. "How did you find out?"

"What he did to me or about everything else?" she bit out, not interested in, or probably not even capable of, taking any pity on her brother, though clearly he'd had no idea.

"Both," he managed to say.

"Men talk," she waved a hand absently in the air. "You know how our father was—have the guys over, drink some whiskey, play some pool. I happened to come home early from the lake one day and overheard him talking to Henry Michaels senior over another game of poker. It seems the only thing our sweet father was concerned with when he gambled me off the second time was that I not be physically bruised in the process. You know, because the social season was starting and he didn't want to see any marks on me in my dresses."

Caleb went from white to an interesting shade of green. And still, she continued.

"And as for the rest? As for his activities trafficking women and children and illegal arms? Well, he always was a bit of a technophobe, so he kept those stupid journals all the time. After I realized what he'd done to me, I wasn't about to lie down and take it. I'd done that already, hadn't I? So I broke into his office, photocopied the information, and contacted Dani.

"I knew she was working at the CIA by then, and she and Drew took it from there. I know for a fact that they ruined several of his enterprises. I had the pleasure of watching his life fall apart for a few months even though he tried to keep it from me." She paused again and suddenly, all the fight went out of her. She took a deep breath and let it out.

"So there it is, Caleb. Yes, I know both of the Michaels men but no, I haven't seen them since I moved out of the house after our father died. Nor do I ever wish to do so." She paused, then shook her head. "I changed my mind. I don't want to know why you want to know about them. All I know is that I don't want to talk about it anymore. You know what you came here to find out, so now you can go."

Never in her life had she seen Caleb at a loss, but he seemed to be now. She knew he had a right to feel bowled over, but her concern was fleeting.

She turned toward her room, toward her sanctuary, needing to get away.

"I didn't know," Caleb said, his voice hoarse. "About you, Kit. I mean, I knew about the rest, that's why," he paused and took a deep breath. "I knew about the rest and that's why I left. I left to see what I could do to stop him," he explained.

Kit turned back to see a myriad of emotions raging on her brother's face.

"Please, Kit, believe me," he said, taking a step toward her, though he was blocked by the kitchen island. "If I had known, I never would have left. Or I would have taken you with me."

"You were twenty when you left, Caleb. How could you have *not* known what he was like? Especially now that I know you knew about everything else, how could you not have known what he was capable of?" It was the question that had haunted her since the moment she'd found out just the kind of man her father was. How could her brother have left her when he had known?

"I mean, look," she said, feeling sick and dirty just talking about it. "Look at what he named us for Christ's sake! Caleb: a fearless leader, faithful and bold. And me, Kitten. Who in their right mind names their daughter Kitten?" Kit felt like she was going to be sick. She turned and pushed past Garret, who was smart enough to let her go.

Her foot was on the third step when Caleb spoke again.

"I swear to god, Kit, if I'd have known, I would have taken you and killed him."

She turned and studied him. He met her gaze and she had no doubt he was telling the truth. It was a small salve to her soul. But just a small one.

She offered him a sad smile. So much had already been said, but there was one more secret to tell. One more dark part of her to share with her brother.

"But you didn't have to, Caleb, because I did."

CHAPTER 9

IT WASN'T SO MUCH WHAT Kit had said but how she said it that froze Garret's blood. Her words were tinged with sadness, but what really echoed in his head was how matter of fact she'd sounded. Dimly, he recognized that he'd been standing in the same place for a long time, frozen in the onslaught of information.

And then all that information, everything she'd shared, slowly filtered into his mind and formed a story. Only it wasn't fiction. And at the thought of Kit being used, yet again, fury ripped through him.

"What the hell, Forrester?" he said, turning on his partner.

Caleb was sheet white and backing away from him. The island stood between them, but Caleb was smart enough to know that if Garret wanted to go for him, the granite centerpiece wouldn't stand in the way.

"I didn't, I . . ." His voice trailed off and he held up his hands in a defensive gesture. "I swear to god, I didn't know. Any of it," Caleb clarified.

Garret felt the tension in his own body coiling through his arms and squeezing his chest. But he forced himself to look at Caleb, take a deep breath, and try to figure out what the hell had just happened. And though he wasn't inclined to admit it, the way Caleb looked—pale and maybe even a little bit scared, slowed the pounding anger into a steady thud.

"You knew something," Garret pointed out. Caleb shot him a wild look, then spun away from him, though he didn't move to leave the room. Finally, after a long moment, Caleb ran his hands over his face, laced his fingers behind his neck and let his head fall back.

"I think I'm gonna be sick, Cantona," he said.

Garret studied the line of his friend's back. "No," he said after a moment. "No, you're not. You'll figure this shit out and when you've made things right with Kit, *if* you can make them right, then you can get sick. But right now, your sister is more important than anything you're feeling."

And Garret believed that too. He was even pretty sure Caleb believed it, but he had to admit that the magnitude of what had been said in this room was probably beyond anything Caleb had ever experienced. The guilt alone might do him in.

"Why did you ask her about Henry Michaels?" Garret asked.

It was so long before Caleb finally turned around that Garret had been just about ready to repeat himself.

"Michaels?" Caleb repeated as he shook his head, possibly trying to shake it all off. "Remember? I recognized him on the tarmac of that deal we watched just before we came here."

"And?"

"And the other guy, one of the other guys," Caleb clarified, "was someone who had cropped up when I went off to investigate what my dad was into. So when I saw the two of them together, I just," again, his voice trailed off.

"You just wondered how someone who was involved with your dad all those years ago and one of his old friends ended up on a South American tarmac with illegal weapons some fifteen years later," Garret supplied.

Caleb gave a sharp nod.

"Any chance that guy, not Michaels but the other guy, showed up a few months before your dad died?"

Again, Caleb nodded.

"So he was probably the spook Dani and Drew sent in once Kit handed over her father's, your father's, papers."

Caleb gripped the back of a stool. "Probably," he conceded, not sounding at all happy about it. Not because he was unhappy that the intelligence communities already seemed on top of whatever it was Michaels was into, but more likely because, had he known they were already involved, he never would have confronted Kit. Never would he have forced her to relive that part of her life.

But even in the few short minutes that had passed, Garret was beginning to think that maybe it hadn't been such a bad thing to get everything out in the open. Obviously he wished the events themselves hadn't happened—he felt like he could take something, or someone, apart if he let his mind actually begin to contemplate everything Kit had gone through. But they had. And nothing was going to change that. What might change was Caleb and Kit's relationship and maybe, just maybe, her relationship with Garret. It was hard to hide behind a wall after shining the light on everything.

"But what about now?" Caleb asked, the question sounding more habitual than out of any real curiosity.

Garret gave this a moment of thought, but it didn't take too long for him to land on a decent theory. "My guess is that Drew keeps an eye on things your father was involved with. He and Kit seem close, and we know now that they've known each other since she was seventeen. I bet Drew got wind of Henry Michaels trying to enter the game and sent in the same guy they used the first time to figure out what was going on. Based on his friendship with Kit, I wouldn't be surprised if Drew does this as a matter of course. She might not even know, probably doesn't even know," he amended, "that Drew does that sort of thing."

Caleb seemed to contemplate his statement, but as he did so, Garret began to feel edgy. He'd let Kit walk away because it had felt as though they all needed some time to process what had just been said. And in Caleb's case, what it all meant.

And though Garret hadn't necessarily sorted through everything yet, he had done enough that Kit, who was never far from his thoughts, was moving back into them, front and center. And he needed to be with her. More than he had needed anything else in his entire life.

Without a second thought, he moved toward the stairs leading to her room.

"Where the hell are you going?" Caleb barked.

Garret didn't bother to turn around or even answer. What would he say, anyway? So he kept walking until he reached her door. Leaning against it, he heard the sound of her shower running. After stopping off quickly in his own room, where he kicked off his shoes and removed his sweater, he returned to Kit's door and quietly entered room.

The shower was still running, but the bathroom door was open so he approached and leaned against the doorframe, waiting. After a few moments, Kit turned the water off and stepped into view at the entry to her walk-in shower.

As she reached for her towel, she caught sight of him. Her hand froze. She stood like that for a moment, then grabbed the towel. He wanted so much to go to her, to wrap his arms around her and tell her everything would be okay. But even from where he stood, he could feel her pushing him away, so he remained at the door.

"I always feel so dirty when I talk or think about that time in my life," she said, running the towel over her wet hair. She didn't bother to try to hide the rest of her body and so, with the exception of parts occasionally hidden by the towel, Garret was gifted with the sight of her.

"None of it is your fault," he said, "but that doesn't mean you're not entitled to feel how you feel."

Her eyes caught his for a moment, then bounced away. He could feel her defensiveness relaxing just a bit when he didn't push, but still, he didn't trust himself to go to her now—she might not resist as much as she would have just a few seconds ago, but with the strength of what he was feeling for her at this moment, he feared he would overwhelm her.

"That's what Baresi meant, wasn't it?" Garret asked instead of reaching for her. "You went to him after you left your father's house. After he died," he clarified.

Kit stepped out of the shower and wrapping the towel around herself, walked toward him. Stopping a few feet away, she looked at him and spoke.

"I met Marco in a bar in Rome one night. After the funeral, as soon as I had access, I'd taken some of the trust money my mother had left me. A few months later, I found myself in Italy. We talked, we became friends, and then yes, we became more." She took another step toward him; he could smell the musky scent of her shampoo and feel the heat from her water-warmed body.

"He was good to you?" he managed to ask.

"Yes," her answer was instant. "He was," she added softly. He watched her as her mind seemed to travel back to that time. When she spoke again, her voice was filled with the weight of her memories—only this time they weren't all bad. "He taught me about trust and respect and, yes, even love," she said. "But I think the most important thing he taught me was that sex, and maybe even love, didn't have to be tainted. It didn't have to be soiled by greed or pride or arrogance. He taught me to give as freely as I chose to give and to take what I needed from a partner. He taught me that being physical with someone didn't have to be a war that someone won and someone lost, but that it could be a dance, something shared. He taught me all of that when I most needed to learn it," she added, her voice soft. "And in learning that, I also learned so many other things about myself—what I wanted and who I was. He said he healed me once before and he wasn't lying, Garret. I was broken when we met, and he helped me put the pieces back together into something that was better than what I had started with."

Garret reached up and brushed a lock of wet hair from her face; it was all he would allow himself. "For that, I am in his debt," he said.

For a moment, she just looked at him, then she stepped forward, closing the space between them. She placed one of her hands on his chest and slipped the other behind his neck, pulling him forward until he dipped his head and his lips met hers.

All sorts of logic and reason screamed in his head, telling him that this wasn't the time or the place. But it all took a back seat as her body leaned into him and she brought her other hand up, linking her fingers at the back of his neck. Instinctively, his arms wrapped around her waist.

"Kit," he said, pulling away. He was unsure of where she wanted things to go. If she needed him to stop, he would. It would cost him dearly, but he would. "Tell me what you need," he added before dropping his forehead to hers and looking her in the eye. He could feel the blood racing through his system and, try as he might, he couldn't get it to quiet.

Her golden eyes stared up at him and for a moment, she said nothing. Then she spoke. "I need you to heal me, Garret. Remind me that everything that happened all those years ago wasn't what it was supposed to be like. Remind me of how good something can be. Take me away from that place and that time, Garret. Help me make it better."

"Kit," he said on a breath. Did she even know what she was asking? He would give everything he could, but would it be enough?

"I know," she said, touching his lips with a single finger. "I know it's a lot, Garret. But I know, from the bottom of my soul, that you can do this with me. I *need* you to do this with me, Garret."

And though it wasn't how he had imagined things would go between them, it wasn't the wine and roses and white tablecloth service he'd always imagined when he thought of being with Kit, he took one last look in her eyes and knew, beyond a doubt, that she wasn't the only one who needed this.

• • •

Garret lay beside Kit, gently stroking her hair, her cheek on his chest. Everything they'd done in the last few hours was more than the sum of the individual acts. That much he knew. But he also hoped, lying there, feeling her body against his, that the honesty they had shown each other—that they had demanded of each other—was enough. Not enough to make her forget, he doubted Kit would ever forget what her father had done, but enough to help her remember, remember how good and true it could be between two people.

"Do you think my brother will be surprised?" she asked, referring to the fact that there was now no way they would be able to hide anything from Caleb. Garret let out a slow laugh.

"I think he's probably already planning exactly how he will kick my ass," he answered. Her head popped up.

She frowned. "Caleb long ago stopped looking out for me," she said. When he said nothing in return, she gave him a little poke. "What?"

Garret lifted a shoulder against the cool sheets. "I just think that maybe there was more going on than you know about."

She watched him for a long moment, then abruptly rolled away. "Undoubtedly," she said. "There's always more going on with him than I know about, which is part of the problem."

"Kit," he said, sitting up as she rose from the bed and walked to the bathroom. "I'm not defending him for leaving you there. God, no. I wanted to kill him myself not two hours ago. But your brother isn't as complex as you think he is."

She stopped by the bathroom door and, as if she suddenly felt very exposed, grabbed a towel and wrapped it around her. Turning to face him, she leaned against the doorframe and arched a single brow. "In my experience, most men aren't."

He sat up more fully now and shot her a look. "Resorting to clichés is so beneath you, Kit." He raised a hand to stop her next retort. "Caleb didn't talk about you or your dad often, but when he did, it was usually a comment about how happy you were at home and how close you were with your dad, and how your dad doted on you. Like I said, Caleb never said much, but when he did, it was obvious he cared about you."

"So much so that he left me with a man who was a criminal," Kit shot back. He heard and even understood the bitterness in her voice, but still believed there was more to it. "I wasn't there, Kit, so take what I'm saying for what it's worth. But I do know your brother cares about you. A lot. I do know he thought you were happy at home."

"And?" she pressed, crossing her arms over her chest.

"And I wouldn't put it past him to have left because he knew what your father was but wanted to keep you out of it as much as possible. Wanted you to continue to have the life he thought you had."

He was surprised when Kit didn't immediately reject his suggestion; instead, she stood there, a far-off look on her face. He got out of bed, pulled on his boxers, and went to her.

"Kit?"

Her eyes came back to him and in them he saw her own questions, her own doubts. Finally, she gave a small shake of her head. "I don't know, Garret. What you say actually does sound like Caleb, like the Caleb I knew all those years ago. If he actually thought he was protecting me by leaving, by keeping me away from whatever it was he was looking into about our dad, I *can* see that. But . . ." Her voice trailed off.

"But so much has happened since then it's kind of hard to see the forest for the trees?" he offered.

She nodded. "I just don't know anymore, Garret. Protecting me while I was young does sound like him. But then to stay away for so long?"

He heard the hurt and pain in her voice and wished he could explain it, but there was only one person who could do that.

"Why don't you get dressed and go talk to him?" he suggested. A look of panic crossed her features. He cupped her face and tilted her eyes up to his. "You already laid everything out, Kit. If you and Caleb have any chance of repairing your relationship, of getting back what you had as kids, you need to let him tell his side of the story."

She swallowed and after a few beats, nodded. "I'll get dressed and be down in a minute. Can you go down and make some tea?

Between the jet lag and the time of day and what we need to talk about, it could be a long night."

He nodded, then kissed her forehead. "You're an amazing woman, Kit," he said.

She gave a small, sardonic laugh. "If only that were the case, but I'm glad you think so."

And he did. He watched her move into the bathroom and start brushing the tangles from her hair before he dressed himself and prepared to meet her brother. He had no doubt that Caleb was going to go to extreme measures to make things right with his sister. That was just the kind of guy he was. But Garret was pretty sure Caleb wouldn't be extending the same understanding to him.

And it didn't take more than ten steps out of Kit's bedroom for Caleb to confirm that for him. When he was halfway down the hall, Caleb came bounding up the stairs and sucker punched him with a mean left hook. Garret crashed against the wall, but didn't otherwise defend himself. He could have, but he figured he'd let his friend get it out of his system.

He was just straightening up when Kit flung her door open and quickly took in the scene. He noticed she'd pulled on a pair of yoga pants and dark green sweater, but her hair still looked a little wild.

"Jesus, Caleb. What did you do?" she demanded, coming to Garret's side.

Neither he nor Caleb answered. She raised her hand and gingerly touched what he thought was probably a pretty decent sized red mark on his cheekbone.

"Are you okay?" she asked him.

"He's fine," Caleb grumbled.

She turned and shot her brother glare. Garret thought Caleb looked suitably guilty.

"Come on, let's get some ice on that," she said, taking Garret's hand and leading him to the kitchen. Caleb followed and soon enough, Garret was propped on a stool with Kit tending to him. He thought it might have been worth the hit just to have her nursing him, standing there looking concerned, holding a bag of ice against his cheek.

"He's fine," Caleb repeated.

Again, Kit glared at him. And in turn Caleb glared at Garret, who smiled.

"Jesus, he wasn't such a baby when his arm all but got blown off a few years ago," Caleb muttered.

"That's because she's a better caregiver than you are. Prettier. She smells better too," Garret shot back.

Kit made a face. "I smell like sex," she said quietly.

Caleb all but growled and Garret's smile got wider.

"You," she said with a pointed look at Garret, "don't have to look like you're enjoying this so much."

"But I am," he answered.

She gave them both one of *those* looks. "Well, I'm not. Caleb, why on earth would you do something like that?"

"Because he's sleeping with you," came his matter-of-fact reply. As if that alone explained everything. And it kind of did, to Garret. But Kit did not look so appeased.

"Right," she said with a roll of her eyes. "As if you've never had sex before. Geez, Caleb, grow up."

He grumbled something.

"And let's get one thing clear, dear brother," she continued, fixing him with a look. "Short of you needing to protect someone's life, if you ever, and I repeat *ever* hit someone in my house again, or even on my property," she amended, "you will *not* be welcome in my home."

Caleb just stared back at her.

"Do you understand?" she demanded.

Finally, after a long pause, her brother gave a single nod.

"Good, now that that is out of the way, I think—" But she never got to finish her sentence. The bell indicating that someone was turning into her driveway rang.

With a frown, she handed Garret the ice bag and moved toward the security monitor she had in the kitchen. Garret watched as her head cocked to the side. He couldn't see her face but judging by her body language, he'd wager she wasn't sure about something.

"Kit?" Caleb seemed to sense the same thing.

She shook her head and turned around. "It's nothing. Or rather, I think it's nothing, but Drew is coming up the drive. He just," she said with another glance at the monitor, "he just doesn't usually visit without calling first. But I guess we'll know why soon enough," she added as they heard the car pull onto the parking pad.

Garret watched Kit, who looked more curious than concerned. Which was exactly what he was *not* feeling. Anxiety crept up his back and into his shoulders as the seconds ticked by. He didn't like the idea of the agent coming to visit Kit unannounced. As far as he was concerned, it was a little like getting that middle-of-the-night phone call.

By unspoken agreement, he and Caleb stayed in the kitchen when Kit went to answer the door. One look at Caleb told Garret that his long-time partner was thinking the same thing—nothing good was going to come of this.

He heard Drew and Kit greet each other and then the sound of a kiss being given, a jacket being removed, and gloves coming off. A few seconds later they both walked into the kitchen.

Garret didn't know what he had been expecting when he'd first heard about Drew, but it wasn't this. The man looked like he'd just stepped out of some yuppie catalog or off some yacht. He was tall and lean. His blond hair was the right length to fall over his forehead just so and his blue eyes tracked Kit. Garret hadn't been inclined to like him before meeting him. He liked him even less now.

Kit made the introductions, but none of the men offered to shake hands. Then, after a few seconds of awkward silence, Drew turned back to Kit.

"Kit, is there somewhere we can talk?" *Privately* was left unspoken.

Kit glanced at Garret, then at Caleb. Garret could tell from the look in her eyes that she was getting a bad feeling about this too. He was about to step in when she nodded to Drew.

"Yes, my office."

Drew inclined his head and she gestured for him to follow.

"Kit?" Garret said, rising from his seat, not wanting her to go anywhere with a man who no doubt knew more than he should about the way the world worked. He didn't want her exposed to that any more than she already had been.

"It's fine, Garret. I'll be right back," she said before disappearing up the stairs with Drew following behind her.

He tracked their footsteps down the hall, through her room, and into her office, then heard the office door slide shut. He looked at Caleb.

"What the hell?" Caleb said. And again, Garret was struck by just how much this situation was stressing Caleb out. He'd heard him swear more times in the past two weeks than in the previous five years.

"Any idea what it's about?" Garret asked.

Caleb drew back and made a face. "How the hell would I know? I just found out she *has* friends in the agency."

"You can't tell me you didn't look into it while I was in Rome," Garret pointed out.

Caleb shrugged. "Yeah, I did. No one seems to know much, but those who did know something didn't seem to think," he paused, presumably looking for the right word, "didn't seem to think she was involved in anything more than what she told us. No reason for her to be in danger."

"She carries information for the CIA. There's always the possibility of danger," Garret pointed out.

"Yeah, well, their view of danger is relative, and in their estimation, she isn't in any."

Garret considered this as they fell into an expectant silence. He didn't like the direction his mind was taking, but until Kit came out and actually told them what was happening, he wouldn't be able to keep his thoughts from going to all sorts of dark places.

Finally, he heard the office door slide open, but it wasn't Kit who came down the stairs. Drew's boots made an appearance and the man himself soon came into view. Taking a look at the two of them, he leaned casually against the wall and crossed his arms.

"Where's Kit?" Caleb asked.

Drew's eyes flicked to Caleb's, held them for a moment, then landed on Garret's face.

"She'll be down in a minute. That's some hit you took there," he commented with a nod toward Garret's eye.

Garret tipped his head.

"You hit him left-handed," Drew added, directing his comment, if not his attention to Caleb.

"I'm left-handed," Caleb countered.

"No you're not," Drew answered. "You're mostly ambidextrous but your right hand is your lead." On the surface it was an innocuous statement, but no one in the room was fooled. Drew had very subtly thrown down the gauntlet, letting them both know just how much he knew and what kind of detailed information he was privy to.

"But it's not as though I haven't been there before," Drew added with a smile and a nod toward Garret's bruised face, "Dani, who you met in London, and her sister Sam are like sisters to me. We grew up together." His eyes danced to Caleb, then seemed to grow thoughtful. "Of course, with Dani there was a time or two when it was *her* I wanted to throttle," he added.

"Ready?" Kit said, jogging down the stairs. Carrying an overnight bag.

Both Garret and Caleb shot out of their seats.

"Like hell," Garret said. "You aren't going anywhere," he added, making a move to stop her. She ignored him and focused on pulling on her boots.

"Kit," Caleb warned.

"Oh, stop," she said, straightening and reaching for the coat Drew had retrieved for her. "You come and go all the time. And I mention that not to sound spiteful but to remind you that what is good for the goose is good for the gander."

"What the hell does that mean?" Garret demanded. Then, rounding on Drew, he added, "Where the hell are you going because she sure as shit isn't going without one of us."

Drew tugged his gloves on with infuriating nonchalance. "I'm afraid she is. We've had a little chat and she's agreed to come with me for a few days."

"On company business?" Caleb demanded.

"Kit," Garret said, trying to stop her.

"Ready?" Drew asked, ignoring Caleb's question. Kit nodded.

"Jesus, Kit. You can't just leave," Garret erupted.

The look she gave him seared into his brain. She could and she would. But then her eyes seemed to soften and she stepped back into the kitchen. She walked up to her brother and gave him a kiss on the cheek. Caleb stood stalk still and Garret had no doubt his friend had no idea what to do—let her go or steal her away. He recognized the look because he could sympathize.

Then she approached Garret. Gently she brushed the hair beside his growing bruise. "Take care of that," she said. He reached for her hand and she let him take it, if only for a moment. "I'll be back soon," she said. Then she leaned into him and brushed her lips against his.

He wasn't sure how it happened, but the next thing he knew, the door was closing behind her and once again, he and Caleb were left in a hollow, empty silence.

The sound of Drew's car faded into the distance and he brought his eyes around to Caleb's. The gaze that met his wasn't that of his friend. It was that of his partner of the last seven years, his colleague, his brother in arms. Without a word, they formulated a plan. They both knew what they had to do.

"I'll make the calls," Caleb said.

"I'll make sure the plane is ready."

CHAPTER 10

BY SEVEN THE NEXT MORNING, Garret and Caleb were making their way through security at CIA headquarters in Langley, Virginia. They'd learned a little bit about what was going on through the various phone calls they'd made during the night, but they didn't know too much more than they had when Kit walked out the door.

What they did know was who was running the show and calling the shots, and that was who they were dropping in on this morning. The plan was to be read in and given the details of where Kit was—and why—and then go find her. Garret had an additional plan, but at the moment, he was keeping it to himself.

Given their level of clearance, they made it through security quickly and were assigned a young soldier to escort them to their destination.

Five minutes later, over the objections of his assistant, they walked into Drew's office without knocking. Sitting behind his desk looking immaculately put together, he glanced up at them from over the lenses of a pair of reading glasses, then waved off his worried assistant. The door shut behind them.

"Have a seat," Drew said, returning his focus to his computer.

"You don't seem surprised to see us," Caleb commented.

Drew looked back up at them and as his eyes travelled to Garret he let out a little laugh. "No, I'm not surprised to see you."

"We're here to see Rina," Garret said.

"I know, but she's finishing a meeting. Like I said, have a seat. She'll be here as soon as she's done." Neither Caleb nor Garret sat; after a moment, Drew shrugged and went back to his computer.

Garret gave Caleb a look.

In response, Caleb pulled out his phone and dialed. "Rina?" he said.

"Jesus," Garret heard her muffled reply, then realized as the door swung open behind them that he hadn't been hearing her voice through Caleb's phone. "I told Drew to keep you entertained while I finished my meeting, but you always were an impatient bastard, Forrester," she said through the now open doorway.

Rina Ahmed strode into the room, took everyone in, then narrowed her eyes. At five foot nothing, the older woman had grown plump with age and her black hair was streaked with gray. Wearing a dark blue dress and blazer, pearls, and sturdy heels, she looked a little like the stereotype of a librarian from the fifties—bun and all. But Garret knew enough about her to know that the phrase "don't judge a book by its cover" had probably been created with her in mind.

Rina was one of a handful of people who ran the show at the agency. Not the public parts—no, that was a more politically savvy appointee who was not much more than a figurehead—but the parts that actually got things done, that worked with operatives, analyzed intelligence, and planned operations. That was all her. At least when it came to their foreign operations. Having been one of the best operatives of her time, she was well respected—by those who worked for and with her—and she was also one of the most blunt.

"Sit down, Forrester, Cantona. Drew, do you have anything new coming in?" she asked, closing the door and moving toward the small, round table at one end of Drew's office.

"Yes, they're just departing from the military base near Stanwick now. We should have more information in a few hours."

"Then join us," she commanded. Picking up a few files from his desk, he did so, and in short order, the four of them were sitting around a table that was way too small. Garret looked at Rina.

"As you know, Jonathon Parker is an MI6 agent who was recently put on leave pending an investigation into the release of certain information that compromised several key MI6 assets," she began. "No one likes a leak, especially one with those kinds of consequences, and it was even less fortunate that a few of those assets worked with us on occasion as well." As she spoke, she slid a file in front of each of them.

"We were doing our own investigation, of course, and have known for about ten days that Jonathon wasn't the problem. But until we knew the extent of the problem within MI6, we decided to hold the information close to our vests."

"With the exception of what Drew had Kit give him," Garret interjected, not hiding the bitterness he felt.

Rina carried on without missing a beat. "And I'm glad Drew did so because we concluded our investigation last night, and based on our findings, three people at various levels in MI6 are involved. Jonathon was an easy one to frame, given his travel schedule and contacts, so when someone at MI6 finally started to suspect a leak and they began putting the intel together, including the fact that assets were being killed in a subtle but systematic way, one of those three men involved in the leak, someone higher up on the food chain, had everything lined up to point to Jonathon."

"So they're clearing him," Caleb said.

"And why do we care about this?" Garret interjected. He was getting impatient to get to the parts relevant to Kit.

"Because," Rina continued with an irritating lack of response to his tone, "two more assets that Jonathon worked with were killed yesterday." She gestured to the folders with her head. Garret flipped his open and saw the face of a young mother with a toddler in one photo and in the other, a man, also on the young side, hanging off a boat, grinning. He felt sick.

"We know Jonathon isn't the leak, but when these two were killed yesterday in separate incidents, we didn't want to take any chances with Kit. She's not an asset and has never been an asset, but given that she was with him when he was shot at in London, her identity isn't exactly a secret."

"And so you've taken her into protective custody," Garret

finished. He'd expected as much, had even figured it had to do with Jonathon Parker, but to hear it out loud settled like a rock in his stomach.

"Yes," Rina confirmed. "We have."

"Where is she? Stanwick?" Caleb asked, repeating what he'd heard Drew say when Rina had walked in.

Drew shook his head. "No, that's the team going after one of the three men involved. They are flying out of Stanwick as we speak."

"So, how many do they have in custody?" And by "custody" he meant dead or alive.

"One for certain, one they are on their way to handling, but the third man is in the wind," Drew answered.

"Fuck," Garret said. "So until all three are accounted for one way or another, Kit's in custody."

Drew inclined his head. "We don't think she's a target, but we'd rather be safe than sorry. And she agreed."

Garret took in all the information. For as bad as things could get, this wasn't the worst. Kit was somewhere safe and as soon as MI6 cleaned up their mess, she'd be even safer.

He took a deep breath and let it out. "Fine, where is she? We'll be taking over protective duties."

Rina and Drew shared a look.

"What?" Caleb demanded.

"She said you'd come to me for this reason," Drew responded.

"Yeah, so?" Garret pressed.

"And she made me promise not to tell you anything about where she is," Rina answered. "You may think it's best for you to stand guard. But she feels otherwise."

At that, Caleb shot out of his seat and paced away a few steps. "She has no idea what she's talking about," he snapped, turning back to the group.

Rina's eyebrow arched. "On the contrary, I think she knows exactly what she's talking about," she countered. "In fact, I think her exact words were 'They got what they came for, now they can go back to doing whatever it is they do.'"

Caleb paled, looking like someone had just delivered a blow to his solar plexus.

Garret, on the other hand, felt the impact a bit higher in his chest; for a moment, it was hard for him to breathe. Then he cleared his throat, "Rina, is there somewhere we can talk?" he asked. "Privately," he added when she cast a pointed look at the closed door.

She eyed him for a moment, then let out a sigh as she stood. Without a word, he followed her out the door. He had expected to be taken to her office, but was surprised when she stepped into a coffee room. He was not surprised, however, when the single other occupant took one look at Rina and discreetly exited.

"So talk," she said, reaching for a coffee mug.

"Look," he started, not sure exactly where to start. "Kit, well, she has every right to think and feel the way she does. I'm not sure how much you know about her father, but he traveled a lot, never bothered to tell her anything about where he was going or why, and then when she was seventeen, she found out all sorts of things about his 'business' and just what he was doing on those trips—"

"I'm well aware of the 'work' Edward Forrester did before he died," she cut him off.

Garret crossed his arms and leaned against the counter as Rina took a sip of coffee. "And then there's her brother," he continued. "Caleb took off when she was fifteen without any reason, left her in a, well, to call it a terrible situation would be an understatement. And though I think he regrets it now, he hasn't spent much time with her at all. He's come and gone as he's pleased."

"And you? What have you done to her?" she asked.

Garret flinched, then forced himself to meet her eyes. "I left her too. The first time I met her we spent three days just talking." And maybe a little more, but not much. "No one knew. It was like we were living in a world of our own."

"And then?"

"And then I left. With Caleb. She was comforting a friend of hers who had just come through a sticky situation when Caleb and I got a call about a man we'd been trying to track for years."

"And so you left."

He nodded.

"Without a word."

Again, he nodded.

For a long moment, Rina held his gaze. Finally, she let out a sigh and moved to the other side of the room. "From what I've heard, Kit knows her mind very well and has every reason not to want you and her brother involved," she said.

"I'm not going to argue with that. But she doesn't have all the information right now," he said.

Rina turned around and arched a single brow at him.

He took a deep breath. "She's had a lot of people come and go from her life. But, well, here," he said, handing Rina a letter.

She eyed it for a moment, then set her coffee down, took it from his hand, and read. A minute later, she looked up at him.

"You're terminating your arrangement with the Agency?" she asked. Under normal circumstances, Garret would have been pleased to have managed to surprise Rina. But as it was, he simply nodded.

"And what about your other engagements?" she asked.

"Between last night and now, I've contacted everyone," he responded. It was drastic and a little scary, but he knew it was what he wanted to do.

"What are you going to do?" she asked, folding the letter back up.

"A former colleague of mine runs the organization that handles all the security for, among many entities, the United Nations. The role of Director of Security Operations for the UN has opened up and he's offered it to me. It's based out of the city, but would let me work from anywhere as long as I'm close enough to come in for meetings."

Rina blinked. "So you're quitting your job to be with Kit?"

He nodded.

"And because of that, you want me to go against my word to her and let you and your brother handle her security?"

"You know how good we are. And we'll be free," he added in an attempt to bring some levity to the conversation. It didn't work.

"Kit is a woman I have a great deal of respect for, Cantona," Rina said.

"You and me both," he responded.

Rina pursed her lips and Garret stayed silent. He didn't even bat an eye, worried that any move he made might sway her in the direction he didn't want her to go. He knew Rina had the power to say no and mean it. He was just hoping she didn't.

Finally, she let out another long breath. And nodded.

Garret felt the tension leave his body.

"I'll let you go. But I want to get one thing straight, Cantona," she said, walking up to him. He looked down and met her piercing eyes. "If you mess this up, if you so much as even *think* about bailing on Kit before this thing is long over, it will become my personal mission to make sure that you regret every moment of every day for the rest of your life."

He blinked at her vehemence. Not that it surprised him, the loyalty Kit inspired in others, but well, it actually did kind of surprise him.

"Do you understand?"

"Yes."

"And do you understand that this new job you mentioned goes away if you mess this up?"

He nodded.

"And those contracts you just terminated? None of them would be open to you again."

"I get the point, Rina."

She fixed him with a long stare. Then a hint of a smile appeared on her lips. "I'll give you the location and details when we get back to Drew's office."

"Thank you, Rina." They started making their way back.

"She's on Cape Cod. If you fly yourselves up, you can be there by this afternoon."

He said nothing as he opened the door and Rina preceded him inside.

"And I really wish I could be a fly on the wall when you tell Kit you quit your job for her," she added under her breath with a small laugh.

CHAPTER 11

KIT LET THE HOT WATER from the shower cascade over her head and flow down her back. The steam warming her bones. There wasn't much to do holed up in a house somewhere between Hyannis and Hyannis Port on Cape Cod, so taking a long, hot shower seemed a reasonable option. She'd already spent several hours writing, figuring her exile could be put to good use, but other than that, she was already bored and it hadn't even been twenty-four hours.

The below-zero temperatures would take her mind off things if she were allowed outside. But she wasn't. She wasn't allowed to do much of anything. Staying in, essentially alone, shouldn't be a problem. After all, she lived alone and had for years. But really, if she cared to admit it to herself, what was making this isolation harder than it normally would have been was having left Garret and her brother in Windsor.

She didn't harbor any illusions that they wouldn't try to come after her; she knew they would. But after telling Rina her concerns—about her history with her brother and Garret coming and going as they pleased—the older woman had given her word that she wouldn't tell the two about the house on the Cape.

And besides, the truth of the matter was that they *did* both have jobs that she assumed they would eventually need to get back to. She could even twist things around to make herself believe that she was doing them a favor. But even though there was some truth to it, she couldn't bring herself to lie to herself that much. And it *was* a lie. Because she didn't have to dig very deep to realize that

Garret and Caleb would have taken over her protective detail in a heartbeat *and* stayed as long as needed, if she had asked them to. In the last few days, everything had changed between them—between her and Caleb and between her and Garret—and there was no denying that this time, this visit, had been different.

So, yes, while everything she'd told Rina had been true, it hadn't been the whole truth. The whole truth left her feeling like a bit of a coward. If she were honest with herself, she would admit that there was a tiny piece of her that wanted to use this enforced exile as a way to avoid the possibility of Caleb and Garret leaving her *again*. Because the next time it would be so much worse. It would hurt so much more. At least it had been *her* decision to leave this time; she wouldn't wake up one morning to find that *they* had left *her*.

With a sigh, she turned the water off and reached for her towel. Pushing thoughts of her own cowardice aside, she let her mind wander back to the conversation with her brother in the kitchen. It hadn't been her finest hour, that was certain. But all the hurt and pain of what had felt like Caleb's abandonment had come flooding back. And he'd been standing there, demanding that she relive the worst few months of her life. Demanding it like a father talking to an errant teenager.

And she'd snapped.

Kit finished drying off and wrapped her hair in the towel as she stepped out of the shower. She hated feeling like an ostrich with her head in the ground, so she forced herself to consider the very real possibility that Caleb hadn't known what their father would do to her. It was true that up until the summer after she'd turned seventeen, her father had doted on her, given her everything she'd ever wanted, treated her like a princess. As a kid, she had thought it was normal, but looking back on it now, it had reeked of nothing but condescension and patronization.

Standing in front of the mirror, Kit smoothed lotion on her face and body. Glancing out the small bathroom window, she unwound the towel and grabbed her hair dryer. She could see nothing but the snow-covered beach and beyond that, the ocean. It was beautiful in a bleak sort of way and with the not-very-charitable assessment she was forming of herself, she realized it suited her current temperament.

Switching the blow dryer on, she turned over the events in her mind. She still remembered the gut wrenching confusion—and grief—that had engulfed her in the few weeks after Caleb had left. Garret had suggested that Caleb had been trying to protect her, and truth be told, that *did* sound like something Caleb would have done for her back then.

Could she give her brother the benefit of the doubt when it came to him thinking their father would never hurt her? As she let the hot air stream through her hair, she realized that yes, she could. But even so, she thought, as she pulled on a pair of yoga pants and a thick sweater, they'd been so close and then he was just gone. And then he'd stayed gone. For so long.

With another sigh, she stepped from the bathroom, vowing not to wallow completely in the past. Yes, she needed to sort out how she felt about Caleb and Garret, but she couldn't do it twenty-four hours a day, and she could also use this imposed break for good. She was halfway to her makeshift computer desk when a movement to her left caught her eye.

Backlit against the light from the hall, a man loomed in the doorway. Her heart lurched and panic shot through her body.

"Kit, it's just me," came a familiar voice. A too familiar voice.

The hand that had shot to her chest at the sight of the intruder dropped, but the residue of the panic took a little longer to subside.

"Garret?"

"In the flesh," he said, moving into the room and closing the door behind him.

"Don't ever . . .don't do that . . .don't . . ." Her voice faltered as her surprise faded; surprise that was quickly being replaced by frustration. "What are you doing here?" she demanded. "I told Rina I didn't want you here." Her guilt over the real reasons she didn't want Garret and her brother there was making her sound angrier than she was.

"I know," his voice was soft as he took a few more steps into the room. The light from the bathroom fell across his face and he looked like he'd seen better days.

"But you don't have all the facts, Kit," he said and for the first time, she detected the weariness in his voice. And maybe a hint of wariness too.

Her eyes narrowed on him. "What 'facts' would those be, Garret?"

For a long moment, he said nothing but just stood there taking her in, as if assuring himself she was indeed there and was in fact safe.

"Garret?" she pushed.

His eyes came up to meet hers. "I quit my job and took one that has me working mostly from wherever I want, although I do need to be close enough to New York to make it into the city for meetings on occasion. But I won't be starting the new job until this thing," he said with a gesture to her and the room in general, "until this thing that involves you is wrapped up."

She heard him, she really did. But her mind refused to accept what he was saying. He couldn't just quit his job. Could he? Wasn't there some weird mercenary or spy thing that actually prevented him from quitting and moving into another job? But before her mind went too far down that track, it bounced onto another. Why? Why would he quit? As far as she knew, he'd been at it for years and when they'd first met, he hadn't spoken about—couldn't speak about it—but he'd seemed to genuinely *like* it. What would make him quit?

She searched his face in silence, but there was nothing to give away what he was thinking. Or was there?

She focused in on his eyes and there, there it was.

Taking a step back, she shook her head and held out a hand as if to ward him off. "No," she said.

"I'm afraid so," he answered, calm as could be as he took a step forward.

She blinked again, the weight of the situation hitting her like a ton of bricks. Then, rather than move away from him, she flew at him.

"How dare you?" she demanded, trying to shove him back toward the door. "How dare you quit your job to do this," she gestured wildly about her. "You can't just up and quit your job," she argued, even as he grabbed her hands in his and wrapped his arms around her.

She struggled against him, against the gravity of what he'd done and why he'd done it. And he let her. Holding her loose enough to squirm but not loose enough to get away.

"Garret, please. Please tell me you didn't quit your job to be with me," she demanded. She thought she felt the fight draining out of her, but with so many other emotions whirling inside her, it was hard to tell.

"I can't do that, because I did," was all he said.

She looked up and met his gaze. His body was hard, firm against hers, but his blue eyes were soft. And sure.

"Why?" she said. Her voice was quiet but she didn't bother trying to hide the desperation she was beginning to feel.

He took a deep breath and released her hands, but his arms stayed wrapped around her. She raised her palms to his chest and felt the steady thud of his heart under her touch. For a moment, she absorbed it. Then she raised her eyes back to his, silently demanding an answer.

"That night, last week, when we got back to your house and you peppered me with questions about my job. Questions you knew I couldn't answer, but that you asked anyway to make a point. Do you remember that?" he asked.

She nodded.

He took another deep breath. "I heard you that night, Kit, really I did. I heard what you were saying and maybe even understood why you were saying it. But I didn't really *get* it. I didn't really, fully understand what you were saying—what you were saying about how hard it would be for you to live with someone who just came and went as needed with no warnings and no explanations. I've been in this job so long that it's hard for me to look at it objectively.

"There's the logistical part to be sure, juggling a life like mine with a family. Honestly, I've never actually even seen it done. But that wasn't what you were talking about, was it?"

She shook her head; her heart beat rapidly in her chest. She stilled for a moment when she felt a small shudder run through Garret's body; his arms tightened around her.

"When you left with Drew yesterday, when you left without saying why you were going or where you were going or when you'd come back. It," he paused and she felt his heart rate kick up under her palm. "It almost brought me to my knees, Kit," he said on an exhale as his eyes closed.

"I was terrified," he continued, opening his eyes and locking his gaze back on hers. "My mind went all sorts of places—bad places—and it's a feeling I never want to experience again. In those hours when I didn't know . . ." He let his voice trail off for a moment, then he took another deep breath and straightened just a bit. "I understand now what you were saying that first night, Kit. What I felt yesterday is what you would feel every time you woke up and found me gone or got a call saying I had to leave. And it would be worse for you. At least I have the contacts and skills to track you down. You don't. You," he paused and brought a hand to her cheek. Laying his palm against her face, he continued, "You'd be alone with no one to answer your questions. And yes, I do believe in love—or something—at first sight, and yes, I do think we should be together. But more to the point, I don't ever want you to feel even a fraction of what I felt yesterday when you walked out that door."

Kit stared at him. She pushed aside the idea of him quitting his job and her mind zeroed in on one salient thought—Garret *got* it. He really did. Her father had always come and gone and she hadn't really given it much thought until she'd learned of his activities. In the years following his death, wondering whose lives her father had ruined each time he'd walked out the door—each time he'd walked out the door and left her to her pampered, spoiled existence—had nearly crippled her with guilt. And then, with Caleb up and disappearing too, then coming and going as he pleased with no explanations later on, the thought of living with someone who held, for good or for bad, so many secrets was something she knew she couldn't handle. At least not with any grace or constancy. That gut-wrenching feeling of being left to wonder was something she hadn't wanted to sign up for, and it had taken a turn of the tables for Garret to understand.

But she hadn't wanted to change him. She respected him, knew he did good work, or believed he did, and she was sure that he loved his job. Him leaving it all for her was something that sat like a pound of day-old bread in her stomach. Because never in a million years would she have asked him to quit.

"I don't want you to quit your job for me, Garret," she said.

"Too late," he responded.

Her eyes narrowed at his flip tone. "It's not funny, Garret. My issues and my thoughts and my feelings are my own—*my own* to deal with. I don't want you to change who you are so that you can give me what I want." She noticed that she'd used the word "want" instead of "need."

Garret sighed. "Kit, everyone changes, all the time. If I'm going to make a change, why shouldn't it be for something we both want?"

For several seconds, she said nothing, just thought about what he'd said.

"You still don't look happy about my decision," he said, brushing a piece of hair from her face. A face that must have revealed her unease.

She took a moment to answer, knowing that this was important. What she said and how she said it was important to him, to them.

"I won't lie," she started. "I won't lie and say that the idea of you being near me and knowing that you're safe and close isn't appealing. But," she paused again for a moment before continuing. "But it's a lot of pressure, Garret. On me. On us. What if we don't work out?" she asked, gesturing with her hand to the two of them. "What if we do this, but in five months you realize you hate your job and can't do it another day? You'd be torn between me and the job you love and that's not a place I want to be. That's not a place I want *you* to be."

"That's not going to happen." He sounded so sure, so confident.

"What if *I* decide it's not working, but here you've given up your job for me. Do you know how much stress that will cause to both me *and* the relationship?"

He sighed and combed his fingers through her hair, forcing her to look at him. "Listen to me, Kit. I will say this now and I will repeat it as many times as you need to hear it. You are not responsible for my decision. Yes, if it weren't for you I wouldn't have made it, but it was *my* decision. Not yours, not your brother's, not Rina's. And as it was my decision, it is my responsibility to live with the consequences. What those consequences may be, we have no idea, but I want to find out, Kit. I want to know if they are good or bad or possibly better than anything we could have imagined.

"If you want me to walk away after all this stuff with the CIA and MI6 is over, I will. But I needed to make this decision for myself because I never could have lived with myself if I didn't try to make this work between us."

He held her head tilted up to his, but she dropped her eyes to his throat and watched the steady pulse there. She swallowed. "What if you decide I'm not what you want?"

On the one hand, she knew it would be easier if things between them didn't work out and if he was the one to decide they weren't good together. That way, he could go back to his job and feel like he'd given it the old college try. It wouldn't be her responsibility.

But on the other hand, just the thought made her feel like throwing up.

He sighed, then dropped a kiss on her forehead and pulled her close. "I don't think that's going to happen, but I also don't think this is something we're going to resolve right now. You've been through a lot, both recently and with other men in your life, and I'm starting something new, leaving the work I've done for years. Maybe we should just focus on where we are now, and once things quiet down, you and I can talk about what we want to do."

That sounded reasonable, so she nodded. "And no pressure?" she asked.

"No pressure," he answered. "Provided of course, you trust Caleb and me to do our thing."

"So, that's the deal? I let you and Caleb stick around until all those people are caught and Drew thinks I'm in the clear, and in return we table the conversation about your new job and about us?"

"We table it for the moment," he clarified.

It wouldn't be easy, but it also wouldn't be the hardest thing she'd ever done. And just because they didn't talk about it didn't mean she couldn't think about it and figure out how she felt.

She nodded and he let out a long breath.

"Good," he said before sealing the deal with a deep kiss. She didn't even try to resist him. It felt good. He felt good.

When he pulled away, he studied her face for a long moment, then dropped his hands and stepped away. In an instant, the heat from his body flooded away from her, leaving her chilled.

"Where's Caleb?" she asked, wrapping her arms around herself.

"He's making the rounds but he should be back in a few minutes. Drew pulled two people from his team off the detail so there are still four of us," he answered. He reached back up and traced a line down her jaw. "How are you? Really?"

She smiled. It was small, but it would have to do. "I've been better. I'm bored, but there's not much I can do about that, so I'm trying to make the best of it."

"Getting some writing done?" he asked with a nod to her laptop open on the small desk in the room.

She bobbed her head. "An outline of the story I'm just starting to work on."

"When we have more time, you'll have to tell me all about it."

She studied his face and thought about what he was saying and what he wasn't. When everything was sorted with the MI6 leaks, she and Garret had a lot to talk about; a lot to get to know about each other.

"I'd like that," she said softly.

A brief smile touched his expression, then he leaned forward and gave her another quick kiss. "I need to get downstairs and debrief with your brother and the rest of the team. I'll come up to check on you later, but if you need anything, someone will always be downstairs."

She nodded and he paused for a moment to look at her before leaving. He was at the door when she called him back.

"Yeah?" he said, turning to look at her over his shoulder.

"Thank you," she said.

This time his smile lasted longer. "Anytime."

• • •

Garret jogged down the stairs of the small, efficient house. It looked like most of the other houses on the Cape with its white clapboard siding, beach-facing porch, and paned windows. He had no idea when it had been built, but it looked to be in the style of the houses built when this part of the Cape was more heavily settled in the 1800s. Other than its location, there was nothing special about it, which made it a perfect safe house.

But right now he was thinking the house was the *only* thing that was perfect. His talk with Kit hadn't exactly gone as planned. Or as he'd expected. In all honesty, he'd thought she would be beside herself with his decision to quit his job. Or at the very least, marginally happy or excited.

He scowled as he grabbed a mug from a kitchen cabinet and dumped hot coffee into it. If she'd come to him and told him she was rearranging her life to be with him, he would have grabbed her and taken her straight to bed to celebrate.

Wouldn't he?

He took a sip of the scalding brew and gazed out the window toward the waves barely visible over the small dunes. The gray of the ocean, with its churning white foam, blended with the snow-covered ground to give new meaning to the word bleak.

Pushing aside what a blow to his ego Kit's reaction had been—which was harder to set aside than he thought it should be, considering he wasn't an ego-driven person—he took another sip of coffee and conceded at least one of her points. The fact that he'd changed his livelihood for the sole purpose of being with her *did* sound like a lot of pressure. He could understand, in a theoretical sense, why she would be concerned. If they didn't work out, would he blame her or would she blame herself? If they didn't work out, how long would it take for him to resent her or for her to become preemptively defensive? While he stood in the small kitchen, he kind of got her point and understood her concerns. From a theoretical perspective, anyway.

Because in his mind, it was all theory. Because in every cell of his body, he knew that whatever life brought him and Kit, they would face it together. Maybe he would hate his new job, but he had no intention of letting that change the way he felt about her. He probably couldn't change the way he felt about her if he tried. No, whatever life brought them, he knew that what he felt for Kit would be his anchor, would be *their* anchor. As far as he was concerned, the rest of the world—their jobs, families, friends—could swirl around them creating chaos, or not, but he and Kit would stay the course.

"I'd say a penny for your thoughts, but they're probably about my sister, so then I'd probably have to kill you," Caleb said from behind him.

Garret turned to see his partner standing in the doorway that led from the kitchen to the small sitting room at the front of the house. He thought about making a joke about how much Kit had already been through and that by killing him, Caleb would only make things worse. But then the light caught the shadows in Caleb's eyes and the dark circles under them. Caleb hadn't recovered from learning what had happened to his sister after he'd left home. And Garret knew he was being eaten alive by guilt.

Instead of joking, Garret shrugged, pulled another mug out, and poured Caleb some coffee. Handing it to him, he asked, "Everything all right?"

Caleb took the mug and nodded. "We've got two people in the house that's visible just up the road. It sits higher and they have a good view of this place. This time of year, no one will be coming in by the water, so we're pretty well tucked in here. You can stay here full time, but I may alternate with one of the other guys between here and the other house."

The plan sounded fine to Garret and he said so. "How'd they get access to two houses on Cape Cod?" he asked, realizing for the first time what a costly piece of real estate the government owned.

Caleb shrugged. "They own this house; the house behind us, the bigger one, is owned by Drew Carmichael. His family owns stuff all up and down the Eastern seaboard."

Garret shot a questioning look at his friend, but he wasn't sure he wanted to know more, considering how close Carmichael and Kit were.

"The family is über wealthy. They run one of the last major private conglomerates left in the US. Of course, they have international holdings as well. It's still mostly run by Drew's father, but Drew's younger brother, Jason, and his wife, Samantha, who is, by the way, Dani Fuller's twin sister, are involved in the operations as well. Drew's involved too and becoming more so as he's getting older and wanting out of the game, I imagine," he added.

The information was neither here nor there to Garret, but still, he let it sift through and sink into his brain. He had no problem picturing Drew, with his urbane presence and yuppie looks, gallivanting around the world conducting business. But one fact floated into his mind and stuck.

"Holy hell, that woman has a twin?" he said, referring to Dani. Caleb chuckled.

No wonder Drew had made the comment about knowing what it was like to have sisters after he'd seen the damage Caleb's fist had done to Garret's face. He reached up now and rubbed the spot—there wasn't a bruise, but it was still sore. He imagined having two "sisters" who looked the way Dani Fuller looked—even in her late thirties—with her attitude to boot. Must have been hell on the guy.

With a shake of his head, Garret turned back to the coffee pot and topped off his mug. "So, now we're in the waiting game?" he asked, knowing the answer full well.

Caleb pulled a chair up to the small table, sat down, mug in hand, and nodded. "Now we wait."

Garret grabbed a deck of cards he'd seen sitting on the window ledge and sank into a seat of his own. "At least this time we have cards. Poker?"

And by unspoken agreement they fell silent on the topic of Kit, opting not to talk, for the moment, about what was bringing them all together under this one roof.

• • •

"Where's Garret?" Kit asked as she walked into the kitchen.

When Caleb looked up from the table where he sat playing a game of solitaire with actual cards, she didn't miss the fleeting look of discomfort that flashed across his face. They'd been living in the same tiny house for two days, and she still hadn't spent any time alone with him. She didn't love the thought of another trip down memory lane, but seeing the somberness in his eyes when he looked at her now, she recognized just how tormented he'd been feeling about the whole thing.

And while she wasn't exactly "over it"—after all, what had happened wasn't something someone "got over"—she was starting to feel the need to address the elephant in the room. It wasn't going to be easy. There were still moments when a wave of nausea would wash over her, leaving her feeling almost unable to stand up or even to breathe. It was the same feeling that had hit her like a tsunami when she'd first heard—and understood—what her father and the Michaels men had agreed upon. And occasionally she'd feel a burst of panic, and maybe even fear, when she remembered what she'd done to her father. It was that part she tried not to think about too much. She didn't condone her behavior. Being both judge and jury of her father and sentencing him to death was something that, if she let herself think about it much, would probably give her panic attacks.

And if it had been just about what he'd done to her, she never would have gone through with it. She would have waited a few months for her eighteenth birthday when the trust fund her mother left her came into her possession, then simply taken off.

But it wasn't just about her. There had been so many people killed by the weapons her father had dealt. She knew it for a fact because she had heard him talking to one of his buyers one day after she'd started to snoop around. Her father was *laughing*, telling whoever it was on the other side of the line that he never had any doubt the launchers would do their job.

Kit hadn't known what he'd meant when she had first heard him, but she'd looked into it and realized that whoever had bought what her father had been selling had attacked a refugee camp in Africa. Two hundred people had been killed. Mostly women and children.

And then there were the women. The women and children her father's network trafficked and sold. Yes, she'd read all about them too. Along with his assessment of each broker he worked with, based on her father's personal experience "testing" the goods the broker provided.

The more she had learned about her father, the more she had realized that while what he'd done to *her* was deplorable, what he was doing to hundreds and maybe even thousands of *others* had to stop.

And so she'd stopped it.

"You okay?" Caleb asked, bringing her back to the present.

She gave a little shake of her head and moved to put the teakettle on. "Fine, where's Garret?" she repeated.

"Walking the perimeter; checking things outside," he answered. She didn't look at him but could feel his eyes on her as she pulled out a mug and rummaged for tea bags. She heard him gather up the cards and shuffle, but he didn't re-deal them. He just shuffled and reshuffled while she waited for the water to boil.

The kettle finally whistled and she poured the water into her mug, then turned and joined her brother. Judging by the look on his face, he wasn't sure if this was a good thing or not.

They sat in silence for a long moment before Kit decided she couldn't take it anymore. Someone had to be the first to bring it up and it didn't look like her brother was willing to be the one to do it. Because he was scared or because he was worried about her, she couldn't tell.

"Why did you want to know about Henry Michaels and his son?" she finally asked. The question had been bothering her since he'd first asked and now that everything was out—well, almost everything—she wanted to understand what had happened to bring it all about.

Caleb looked away for moment, then with what looked like great reluctance, brought his gaze back to hers. "I saw him, the son, on the tarmac of a small airport in Venezuela participating in a transfer of weapons."

He didn't have to specify that it was an illegal transfer. In fact, Kit didn't need much more information than that to figure out why Caleb had come to her after seeing what he'd seen.

"And you wondered if I was still friendly with them after Dad died and if I'd given them any of his journals," she stated. Whether he thought she might have known what was in them and willingly handed them over or not, she didn't want to know.

"When I left the house, I photocopied some of the same journals you probably did," Caleb started to explain. "I didn't know my ass from a teakettle, but I was determined to do something to stop him. I used some of the money Mom left me in the same kind of trust I know she left you and I armed and trained myself."

Kit thought she was beyond being surprised but found herself speechless at his words. Who in his right mind trained himself to go after a brutal trafficker single-handedly? But there, in the question, was the answer. Caleb hadn't been in his right mind. Just as she hadn't been when she'd realized what a farce their home life had been.

"I can't imagine what that must have been like, Caleb," she managed to say.

He waved her off and kept talking. "There was a guy who came onto the scene about two years after I started tracking our father's activities. I didn't know who he was, and I couldn't buy any intel on him. But he seemed to suddenly show up a lot in our father's transactions."

"Not one of the Michaels men?" Kit clarified.

Caleb shook his head. "No, I would have recognized either one of them."

"Who was it?"

Caleb lifted a shoulder. "I don't know for certain, but based on what you told me—us," he corrected, "in Windsor about what you went through and what you did with Dani and Drew, I'm thinking he might have been someone Drew sent in after you handed over the information."

The timing of what had happened back then made sense. But she didn't know why he was important, so she asked.

"I saw him again with Henry Michaels on that tarmac," Caleb answered. "Not knowing what I know now, it was too big a coincidence to see someone I *knew* had worked with our father show up with someone from our father's social circle. It was obvious Michaels was, or rather *is* trying to get into the business, and I had to wonder how he knew who to make contact with."

"And you thought I might have known and told him."

Kit's heart sunk a little at the realization that her brother could have thought so little of her. Not to mention that it seemed to conflict with Garret's suggestion as to why Caleb might have left. If Caleb had in fact left to protect her, it would have been because he'd thought her *worth* protecting. But here he was now, thinking she was the kind of person who would help their father's friends enter the playing field—the kind of person she knew he would never in his life protect. So if he thought of her as that kind of person, then he hadn't been protecting her when he left. To him, she must have been the kind of person worth leaving in that hell-hole, not someone worth saving.

"I see," she added softly, willing her eyes to stop welling.

"No, you don't, Kit," Caleb said. His voice was strong enough that her eyes came up to meet his.

"I don't?"

Caleb shook his head. He hesitated, then continued. "There was one brief moment when I wondered if maybe you had taken up where our father had left off. But it didn't take me long to realize that the thought was based on everything ugly I had seen in the world. It wasn't based on who I knew you to be. I know," he said, staving off her objection. "I know I don't really know you as an adult—neither of us really knows each other. But what I knew of you as a kid and even as a teenager? There was no way you'd be carrying on our father's legacy. You were constantly trying to save things—animals, people, even spiders for god's sake. You weren't about to start selling children or arming terrorist groups."

Okay, that made her feel marginally better. "So what *did* you think?"

He took a deep breath and let it out. "I knew about the journals too. I already told you I photocopied them, just like you did. After I realized you weren't the head of some new crime syndicate, I wondered how Henry Michaels got into the business and if the journals had had anything to do with it. I thought maybe you'd given them to him after our father died. After all, if you hadn't known what they contained, you wouldn't have known to ask why Michaels would have wanted them. It was much easier for me to imagine you trying to make our father's friends feel better by giving them some of his things than it was for me to think of you taking his place."

"Then why did it feel like you were accusing me of something?"

She saw regret flash in his eyes, but to his credit, he didn't look away. "Because I was angry. I didn't know how Michaels got involved, I still don't really know who that other guy was, and I was angry at myself because I thought maybe I missed something all those years ago. And if I missed something, then how many people have suffered since?"

Kit had to bite her lip at the self-recrimination she heard in Caleb's voice. She had a feeling that if he could, he would probably blame all the world's problems on himself.

Finally, Kit shook her head. "I don't know how Henry, father or son, would have gotten hold of our father's journals, but I do know that they were both around a lot after he died. They more or less had free rein of the house for several weeks and helped in sorting out the estate. I would bet that one or the other of them either knew about the business beforehand and offered to help in order to find the details of our father's business, or they didn't know and just came across the information when they were going through his things."

After a long pause, Caleb inclined his head, seemingly in agreement.

So, now she knew why Caleb had asked about Henry Michaels. Even with her soothing tea, her stomach roiled at what she was about to say. But after everything Caleb had just told her, he deserved to know.

"He got good and drunk at the club one night." She started telling her brother the story of what had happened the night their father died. "It wasn't anything new, but for some reason I noted it. Maybe because I was more sensitive to everything he did by that time." She paused, remembering. "I don't know why it seemed more pronounced to me that night, but it did. I had my own car, thankfully, and left a few minutes before him, I didn't want to be on the road at the same time he was. Anyway, about two miles from home, right at that sharp curve up the hill to the right," she said, knowing Caleb would know the spot she was talking about, "my tire blew. It wasn't a big blowout, but just around that curve is a small pullout. I parked there, thinking I would call for some help. But then I heard him coming." Again, she paused, thinking back on that night. She remembered exactly what she'd done. But now, as she let herself really think about all the details for the first time since it happened, she realized that even though she'd known exactly what she'd been doing, she didn't remember anything about what she'd been feeling or even thinking. It was almost as if she'd been an automaton, programmed to do what she'd done.

With a shake of her head, she continued. "His car had such a distinct sound, you could hear it coming from a mile away. Especially up in the hills between the club and our house. Anyway," she paused again to take a sip of her tea, vaguely noting how pale her brother had become. "Anyway," she started again, taking a deep breath, "I was parked and when I heard his car, I simply got out and walked out into the road. I knew he would be driving too fast and I knew he was drunk. So I stood and waited."

And Kit saw the moment Caleb realized exactly what she had done. A look of horror flashed across his face as his head drew back and his eyes went wide. She saw him swallow.

"Jesus, Kit. He could have killed you," he all but choked out. "What if he hadn't swerved? What if he hadn't even seen you? What if he'd been on his phone and hadn't noticed?"

For a moment, she said nothing. Playing with her tea bag, she knew her brother would figure out the rest. And when he let out a strangled sound, she looked up. He knew.

"Why, Kit? Why did you do it?"

And she knew he wasn't asking why she'd killed their father.

"I did it because I didn't care anymore, Caleb. I didn't care if I lived or died. My life, in so many ways, had been turned inside out and eviscerated. You were gone, the father I'd thought I had was gone. I couldn't trust any of my 'friends' anymore because I had no idea who was involved with him and who wasn't. I figured that, if I died, who would really care? It hardly mattered to me. And if I took him with me, or even just hurt him a little bit, then so be it."

And that was the truth of it. That time in her life had been the darkest time she had ever experienced. Her father was a murderer, a rapist, and a man capable of selling his own daughter. She was seventeen and had no one to go to, no one to rely on, no one to trust. And so yes, looking back on it, what she had done was the act of a desperate and scared teenager. She remembered the constant, searing hurt she had lived with since she'd had her world turned upside down, so she'd done—or tried to do—the only thing she knew could stop all the pain.

"But Drew and Dani, they were helping you," Caleb pointed out, his voice quiet with desperation.

Slowly, Kit nodded. "They were. I had made copies of the journals, given them the pages, and they were working on it. But they didn't know everything. They didn't know what he'd done to me. I was too ashamed to talk about it."

"Kit, that wasn't your fault," Caleb interrupted.

She gave a bitter laugh. "I know, but that's the thing about shame: it often overwhelms logic. I couldn't talk about it; I still don't talk about it much. To this day, there are only three people I have ever told." She paused for a moment and let that sink in. For the longest time, Marco was the only person she'd ever told—now two more knew. With a sigh, she shook her head and continued.

"But it wasn't just about me and about what he'd done to me, Caleb. Dani and Drew knew about the arms and trafficking. But what they didn't know was how personally involved he was. They didn't know that he raped some of the young girls he smuggled into various countries. They'd never heard him laugh as he was told about the death and destruction the weapons he sold had caused," she finished, her voice quiet in the confines of the kitchen.

In the silence, she waited for Caleb's censure. Waited for him to condemn her decisions, her actions. Waited for him to point out that their father would have been brought to justice in a court of law had she not intervened.

Her heart was thudding heavily in her chest and each breath she took felt labored. Her tea was cooling in its mug and she was still playing with the tea bag, avoiding looking at her brother. Staring at the dark brew, she flinched when Caleb's hand came into her line of vision. Gently, he tugged her fingers off the tea bag string and wrapped his hand around hers, resting them both on the table.

She looked up.

"I'm so sorry, Kit. More than you will ever know. I'm so sorry."

She blinked back the tears gathering in her eyes, not aware until now of just how much it meant to be relieved of her brother's judgment hanging over her head.

"I shouldn't have left you there. I shouldn't have left you in a position to ever have to make the decisions you made. I know you made the best ones you could, and while to my dying day I will regret that you had to make them at all, I can't find any fault with what you decided to do."

A single tear tracked down her cheek. She cleared her throat and looked away. "Even though I'm not sorry he died? I may not have meant to kill him, but I'm still not sorry he died."

"I know that most people would believe that he should have seen justice through a court of law, but I've been around long enough to know that most people like our father—those rich enough to hire the best lawyers or emigrate to a country with no extradition laws—get away with what they do far more often than the average man. Our father wasn't dumb. Arrogant and maybe careless toward the end, but not dumb. He already had bank accounts the courts couldn't touch and houses in countries that would have let him not only live out his days but probably continue what he was doing."

He stopped talking for a moment and held her hand in his, their roughness and heat reassuring her like they had when they were kids.

"I'm not going to judge you, Kit, especially not after some

of the things I've seen and done and allowed to happen. But god, am I sorry you had to live through any of that." His voice cracked toward the end and Kit looked up from their hands to a pair of eyes that mirrored hers. A pair of eyes that not only saw her and what she'd done, but that reflected regret and held not only his pain but hers as well.

She squeezed his hand and a flicker of hope flashed across his face. She knew that someday they'd talk about everything. They'd talk about everything she had heard, everything she had done to get information to Drew and Dani, everything she had felt during that time. But now was not that day. And that was okay. Because she had hope now. Hope that maybe she would get her brother back. Hope that maybe she'd let herself want him back.

• • •

Later that afternoon, Garret stood at her window staring out at the snowstorm. From Kit's position at her makeshift desk, she had a perfect view of his profile. It had been two days since he had told her about leaving his job. She still wasn't sure what to make of it all. She hadn't been joking or overreacting when she'd told him it was too much pressure. She didn't want to be the cause of any regrets in his life.

But the more time they spent together, and granted it had only been two days holed up in a CIA safe house, the more she started to wonder if he'd been right. If *not* giving themselves the opportunity to even try would be what they'd both end up regretting.

It was so tempting to let her thoughts fixate on where her relationship with Garret was going since there really wasn't much else for her to think about while stuck on Cape Cod, especially after unburdening herself to her brother. But her good sense stopped her every time her mind went down that path—the path of happily-ever-after or, alternately, the path of what-the-hell-have-we-done. Being in protective custody with the potential for someone to come after her because of her random association with someone from MI6 wasn't really the time to be thinking about whether or not she and Garret made a good couple.

"It's too bad we're not alone on vacation. This could be so much more entertaining, so much more fun," Garret said, turning to give a pointed look at the bed, her bed, a bed she'd been sleeping in *mostly* alone, "if that were the case."

Her lips twitched. Here she'd been thinking all sorts of deep relationship thoughts and Garret had been thinking about sex. Well, now that he'd brought it up, she had to admit he wasn't the only one who'd been thinking along those lines. Both nights she'd gone to bed early, and at some point he'd come in and slid between the blankets next to her. But all he had done was wrap an arm around her and fall asleep. And when she'd awoken in the morning, he'd been gone. When this was all over, it might actually be nice to lounge around in bed with him for a few days. Or weeks.

"Any news from Drew?" she asked.

He'd turned back to the window but she saw him shake his head. "Nothing of any consequence."

She sat up straighter. "What does that mean?"

He turned to face her, his hands shoved into the pockets of his jeans. "Of the two men they were still looking for, they found one but the other is still in the wind, which means we do nothing different."

Kit thought about this for a second. It made sense that they do nothing since the potential threat was still out there. But still.

"Did he have anything to say? The guy they caught?" she asked.

If she hadn't been watching Garret closely, she wouldn't have noticed his nearly imperceptible hesitation. But she had been and she did.

"Garret?" she prompted.

After a moment, he lifted his shoulders. "The guy didn't say much of anything. He wasn't interested in being tried for treason."

Kit blinked. And frowned. This was so not her world. "Are you saying he killed himself?" she asked, her eyes narrowing.

Garret nodded in response.

She let out a huff of air and sat back in her chair. "So, what about the guy MI6 *does* have in custody, and how close are they to finding the third guy? Do we know if they know anything about me? Has the man in custody said anything about seeing me with Jonathon that day he was shot?"

Garret took his time answering, which didn't sit well with Kit. She thought his hesitation came either from some mistaken belief that she didn't need to know the details, or because he himself wasn't sure what to think. Neither option made her feel very comfortable, so she let him take his time.

Finally, he answered. "The one they have in custody hasn't said anything about hiring out a contract on Jonathon Parker. In fact, he denies it."

"But he would, wouldn't he? I mean, in the spy world, isn't it worse to kill one of your own agents than a civilian, someone not officially in service?"

Garret wagged his head then moved to the side of the bed and took a seat. "In the US, it's definitely worse to kill someone on active duty—police, soldier, anyone—than another civilian. But in the world of the CIA and MI6? Well, it's a little different. There's this weird code that, once you've entered the game, you're fair game. And since the premise of organizations like these are to protect the people from what they don't know, killing a civilian is often frowned upon way more than killing another agent."

In her experience, civilians were far less innocent than anyone wanted to admit, but she took a deep breath and let it out. Life in the world of international intelligence was way more complex than she cared to know about. All she really wanted to know, as cowardly as it sounded, was that she was safe enough to go home. Safe enough to spend some time with Garret when he didn't feel the need to carry a gun. Safe enough to go on with her life. She wanted justice too. Justice for the assets who'd been killed and for Jonathon, who'd been framed. But that was beyond her control. In fact, it was all beyond her control.

THE FRAILTY OF THINGS

"I hate this," she said.

Garret's head swiveled toward her and he smiled at her. "I know. But you're doing great."

She rolled her eyes. "Yeah, it's really hard to sit on my ass all day and do nothing."

"It's a very fine ass, though," he said after a beat.

Her eyes lifted back to his, but this time with less frustration. "I'm just saying that it will be nice to be home," she said, rising from her chair. Garret's eyes tracked her as she moved toward him. He leaned back as she stopped in front of him and then lowered herself onto his lap, her knees straddling his thighs.

"It will be nice to just relax," she said, draping her arms over his shoulders, brushing the nape of his neck with her fingers. His hands came to her waist and he leaned forward just a touch. She didn't need more of an invitation than that; her lips met his eagerly.

She felt his hands tighten on her body and her own arms pulled him closer. Tugging her against him, her body came flush with his as he tilted his head and encouraged her to take their connection deeper. Happy to oblige, she met his demand as his fingers inched up under the sides of her sweater, caressing her skin.

She wanted him. In every possible way. Just like she had the very first time she'd seen him. She wanted him heart, body, and soul. And she knew he wanted the same from her.

And she also knew that, like so many things lately, now was not the time.

They eased away from the kiss at the same time and when she finally broke free, she let out a breath and laid her head on his shoulder. He ran a hand up her back and simply held her. She could feel his heart beating in his chest and realized that she didn't think she would ever forget it, how his heartbeat felt against her, an indelible tattoo on her own body.

She was enjoying the quiet moment when Garret suddenly stiffened beneath her. Drawing back, she looked at him. His eyes were fixed out the window.

"We have company," he said. And then she heard it too, the

sound of a car making its way toward the house. Sliding from his lap, she said nothing as he rose, gave her a quick kiss, then headed downstairs with a warning for her to stay put until he or Caleb came for her. It was a warning she didn't need, but nonetheless, she stood to the side of the window and craned her head, hoping to catch a glimpse of whoever was visiting.

She wasn't all that worried—anyone making as much noise as this visitor was wasn't trying to sneak up on them. But she was being cautious, as she suspected Caleb and Garret were too.

"It's Drew," Garret called up to her, just as she saw the Mercedes pull into sight. She debated for a moment whether to go down and join them or just let Caleb, Garret, and Drew talk. It was a short debate; she pulled on a pair of thick socks and jogged down the stairs.

By the time Drew entered the kitchen from the back porch, stomping the snow off his boots, Kit, Garret, and Caleb were all there waiting for him, hot drinks in hand, with expectant looks on their faces. After getting most of the snow off his boots, Drew looked up and a flicker of surprise crossed his face. Then he allowed himself a rare smile.

"Waiting for something?" he chided.

Caleb rolled his eyes. "Well?" he said.

"Do you want some coffee or tea?" Kit asked. She was just as anxious to hear what Drew had to say as her brother and Garret were, but she wasn't going to forgo her manners completely.

Drew shook his head. "We have the third man in custody," he said simply.

Kit hadn't realized how tense she'd been until she felt her body sag in relief. She smiled. "So I can get out of this joint, then?" she asked. Not that the house itself had been that bad. Actually, it would make a great writing retreat in the summer. It was just the enforced stay that had worn on her.

When Drew didn't immediately answer, she darted her gaze over to Caleb and then to Garret. And then back to Caleb, who stood with eyes narrowed in thought and his arms crossed over his body.

Her chest constricted. Again.

"What? What I am missing?" she demanded.

"I don't know," Caleb said. "What are we missing?" He repeated the question but directed it to Drew.

Kit swung her eyes back to her old friend. He was watching her with a guarded, curious look. She didn't understand either. "What?" she asked again, or more implored this time.

Drew let out a deep breath. "Neither of the two men captured alive have copped to hiring the hit on Jonathon Parker."

Kit blinked at him, trying to sort out the significance of this statement. Because it was significant. That much she could tell from the way both Garret and Caleb's eyes focused in on her.

She frowned. "I don't get it. That doesn't seem like that big of a deal. Criminals don't confess to things all the time. I don't find it all that surprising that they didn't confess to hiring an assassin to kill one of their own agents on the streets of London. In fact, I'd be surprised if they *did* confess."

Once again, she got the feeling she was missing something when all three men shared looks with each other.

"What?" She was beginning to sound like a broken record and it was starting to piss her off.

After a beat, Caleb answered. "They didn't go through a regular interrogation, Kit. Not like what you see on TV."

Kit's eyes narrowed on her brother. She hadn't given it much thought, but she supposed he was right. After all, the men they had caught were going to be tried for treason. Her mind flitted to Guantanamo Bay and she wondered if the British had anything similar. But even she knew that confessions gained through torture weren't the most reliable. Then again, maybe that was the point. They *hadn't* confessed. At least not to what had happened to Jonathon.

"Did they confess to anything?" she asked, not sure she wanted to hear the answer.

Drew gave a short nod. He met her gaze, not shying away, but she could see the crease of worry around his eyes.

She took a deep breath and let it out. "Okay, so if they confessed to some things, but not to what happened in London, what do you think it means?"

For a long moment, Drew just looked at her. Studied her, even. But what he was looking for, she hadn't a clue. A wild thought entered her mind that he knew about her father and what she'd done and maybe it was somehow tied to what had happened in London. She felt a surge of panic that she tried to tamp down as she turned a questioning look at Caleb. He seemed to read her mind and he gave a small shake of his head—something she would have missed if she hadn't been staring right at him.

"Has anything strange happened to you recently?" Caleb asked. She didn't miss the subtle emphasis on the word "recently."

She forced herself to breathe and held his gaze. His eyes, identical to hers, held a kind of comfort she hadn't experienced in a long time. And in a rush, childhood memories came flooding back. Memories of Caleb helping her up and dusting her off when she was learning to ride a bike. Caleb meeting her at the schoolyard and walking her home when she was being picked on by the other girls for her gangly height and "weird" eyes. Caleb making her an ice cream sundae in their kitchen at midnight the night of the first school dance she never went to.

A sense of calm washed over her. She didn't need him to take care of her anymore, but knowing that he could, that he would, gave her a new strength.

"Other than what happened in London? No," she answered. "Why? What do you think is going on?"

"We're not sure," Drew answered and everyone looked back to him. "It's possible, they just didn't confess. It's possible that the man who wasn't captured alive ordered the hit . . ." His voice trailed off.

"Or?" Garret prompted, as he took a step closer to Kit.

"Or maybe the shot was meant for you, Kit," Drew said, meeting her eyes again.

Her stomach protested at the thought. More importantly, so did her logic.

She shook her head. "I can see why you might think that, but I have no idea why someone would be interested in killing me."

"Not just shooting her," Garret interjected, "but that shot was not a shot taken by amateur. I'd stake my life that it was a professional with a silencer who pulled that off."

"Someone who's hired to do that kind of job," Caleb added, seemingly in agreement with Garret.

That statement was so far out of left field that it almost made her feel better. It was ludicrous to think she'd done something worthy of even becoming a target in the first place, but add to that the suggestion that a hit man had been brought in to do the job? Well, that just made the whole idea even easier to dismiss.

But having Garret and Caleb contemplate it so matter-of-factly made it difficult to *completely* deny the idea.

"Has there been anything?" Drew pressed. When Garret frowned, Drew gave him a dismissive wave. "We have to think about it, Cantona. Even if it's unlikely. Even if we don't like it."

Kit was about to shake her head, but she forced herself to slow down and actually give it some thought. *Then* she shook her head. "Really, Drew, I can't think of anything. I've been in Windsor most of the time in the last year or so. And mostly just writing and spending time with my friends."

"Where else have you been in the past year?" he asked.

She frowned as she recalled her schedule. "I went to Europe last July—Barcelona," she added, knowing Drew would want specifics. "I was in Boston for one night with Vivi, Matty, and Jesse when Jesse dropped Matt at college last August. I went to San Francisco for a week in the end of October, right around the time the Giants won the World Series, and then I was in New York City for a few days in January when *The Times* did an interview and photo shoot after I won that award." She paused for a moment to run through the last year in her mind and make sure she hadn't forgotten anything. And when she knew she hadn't, she shrugged. "That's it. Other than those trips, I've been in Windsor."

Drew kept his gaze on her but she got the sense he was looking into the empty space between them as he gave her recital some thought.

"And did anything strange or unusual happen on any of these trips?" he asked.

A smile teased at her lips. "Jesse actually got drunk in Boston. That was a first. Not falling-on-her-butt or puking-her-guts-out drunk but enough that she wasn't looking her best the next day." She knew, even as she said it, that this kind of information wasn't what Drew, or judging by the intent looks they were giving her, Garret or Caleb were looking for, but honestly, it was all she could come up with.

She shrugged in frustration and a bit of tea spilled onto her hand. It had cooled enough not to burn, but she wiped her hand on her pants to dry it as she walked to the sink to dump the rest out.

"Sorry," she said over her shoulder. "I know that's not exactly what you were asking, but that's it. Really." She watched the nutty-brown liquid slip down the drain. "I was in Barcelona for five days at a conference and it was just like every other writers' conference. I spoke on a few panels, had a few dinners, lots of drinks, and that was about it. San Francisco was a four-day trip that I didn't plan well since the city was flooded with people celebrating the games when all I wanted to do was some basic research at the historical society. And as for New York, I did the interview and photo shoot, met with my agent and publisher, and spent most of the rest of the week in my apartment."

When she'd finished talking, she turned to find three sets of eyes staring at her. She leaned back against the counter, crossed her arms, and sighed. "I'm sorry," she said again with a shake of her head, "I don't know what to tell you. I haven't done anything that I know of that would make anyone want to hurt me, let alone kill me." She paused for a moment; a strange sense of vertigo washed over her as she said those words, words no normal person should ever need to say. "I haven't done, or seen, or heard anything strange," she repeated.

Drew regarded her, and for a moment it looked as if he was about to say something, but then he seemed to change his mind, switching his gaze to Garret. Some sort of silent conversation took place—it wasn't difficult to guess it was about her—then Drew turned back to her.

"I had to ask," he said simply. "It just didn't make sense that they wouldn't say something about the hit considering some of the other things they *did* talk about."

"At least as far as MI6 told you," Caleb interjected, noting that it was possible that MI6 hadn't shared everything with the CIA.

Drew inclined his head, not so much in agreement but in acknowledgement. "Regardless," he continued. "Given what you've told us, it's probably likely the man who died ordered the hit and you're not involved at all, Kit. But not being able to confirm that bullet was meant for Jonathon, not for you, is a loose thread I don't like."

"What does that mean?" she asked. She had to admit she was on the same page as Drew on this one. She would much rather have confirmation that whoever had shot at them on the streets of London had intended to hit someone other than her. As callous as that sounded.

Drew shook his head and shrugged. "We have no reason to keep you here," he said with a gesture to their surroundings. "But I would ask you to be careful and maybe keep thinking about whether or not there is *anything* you might know, no matter how insignificant, that might lead someone to want to prevent you from sharing it."

That sounded like such a nice way to say someone may want to kill her. And she might have laughed if Drew and the other two men hadn't looked so serious. It was such a preposterous idea, but for their sakes, she nodded.

"Of course," she said.

Drew seemed to believe her and with one last look at Caleb and Garret, he walked over to her and dropped a kiss on her cheek. "You're free to go on with your life now," he said. And she didn't miss the way his eyes lifted just a tiny bit in the direction of Garret. "But please be careful, and let me know if you think of anything. *Anything.* I would be greatly disturbed if something were to happen to you, Kit."

And she knew he would be. He was a good friend and had been for years. Yes, they worked together, but she knew their relationship was deeper than that of colleagues.

"You too, Drew. Stay safe and I'll let you know if I think of anything," she said.

He held her gaze for a moment, then looked up at Caleb and Garret. With a brief nod to each of them, he made his exit.

Kit let the gust of cold air that flooded the room as he left wash over her. She kept her eyes on the door for a long moment, not wanting to turn around and face Garret and her brother. She knew they'd both be staring at her, concerned. And she wasn't quite sure what to do with that. She understood what Drew had been saying to her and why he'd asked what he'd asked, and she wasn't being dumb or willfully ignorant, she just really couldn't think of any reason why anyone would want to kill her. Her life was in Windsor, with only a few side trips each year. And those trips, even her short stays in New York City, were made up mostly of visiting friends and conducting business.

"Kit?" Garret said from behind her.

She let out a breath and turned to face the two men. "Yes," she answered.

"What are you thinking about?" he asked.

She glanced at the clock and realized she'd been staring at the door for almost five minutes. She shook her head. "Nothing, really," she said. "Other than I don't think there's any reason to worry." She paused and looked at each man, then added, "I think I'm more worried about how you two took the news than about the news itself."

A ghost of a smile touched Garret's eyes. Predictably, Caleb's narrowed.

"I think we need to come up with a plan to figure this out," Caleb said.

Kit rolled her eyes and moved back to the stove to make another cup of tea. "There's nothing to figure out." She put the kettle on, rinsed her cup, and grabbed a new tea bag. She was staring at the kettle, thinking of nothing in particular when she realized her brother had been silent for too long. She looked up at him, but it was Garret who spoke.

"Why don't we go spend a few days in New York? I need to meet my new employer, get up to speed on the job—"

"Figure out where you're going to live," Caleb interjected, clearly not liking the thought of Garret moving in with Kit. Come to think of it, she wasn't sure what she thought of it either. She liked the idea of being able to see him, of having him around, of knowing where he was and what he was doing. But living together seemed a bit overwhelming.

She looked over and met Garret's gaze.

"Figure out the living situation," he added with a small nod meant for her only.

It didn't escape her notice that he'd said "the" living situation rather than just "his" living situation.

The kettle whistled and she turned her attention back to her tea. After adding honey to the green tea steaming in her cup, she sat down at the small kitchen table. The table wobbled under her forearms as she set her mug down, and a few drops sloshed over the side.

"New York might not be such a bad idea," she said. She could see the surprise in both men's expressions—closely followed by a look of hot anticipation from Garret and one of suspicion from Caleb. She let out a long sigh, wondering just what it was in her brother's life that made it impossible for him *not* to be suspicious when things went his way.

She flicked her gaze back to Garret. "I have some meetings I can schedule with my agent and she and the publisher have been trying to get me into town to celebrate the award. I haven't had a chance to make it because of obligations in Windsor and then my trip to Europe, but I do need to let them do their thing and market me."

And as she said it, she realized how much she actually liked the idea. She had never loved the publicity side of writing, but understood it was a part of her job. Having Garret to go to dinners with her, and maybe even to a party or two, would make it easier. Or at least more interesting. And it would give him time to sort out his new job in the city. She still couldn't quite wrap her mind around him taking what was essentially a desk job, but only time would tell if it would have staying power or not.

And aside from all the business they could accomplish, being in New York had the added benefit of allowing her some time alone with Garret in her small apartment on the Upper West Side. Staying a week or two in her apartment would have more of a temporary feel to it, rather than having him come home to Windsor with her—kind of like a living-together trial.

"I have a place," she continued. "We can stay there. You can do your thing and I can do mine and we can see how things go." Judging by the way Garret looked at her, he knew she meant more than just how things went with their work.

And judging by the pig-like grunting noise her brother was making, he knew it too.

"Seriously, Caleb," Kit turned on him.

He blinked at her tone then his eyes narrowed. "Seriously, what?" he said.

She sighed. "I get that you don't like the idea of your younger sister being in a sexual relationship with someone, but this is getting a little old."

He made another grunting noise that she supposed indicated his disagreement.

"How long have you worked with Garret?" she asked.

After moment's hesitation, he answered, "Nearly seven years."

"And is he good at what he does?" she pressed.

He snorted, "I wouldn't work with him otherwise."

"Which also means you must trust him."

Caleb's eyes narrowed to slits as he recognized the trap he'd just stepped into.

"Well?" she pressed, wanting to make her point. "Do you trust him?"

"Yes," Caleb ground out.

"And has he ever, to your knowledge, treated any woman he was with poorly?"

"No," her brother managed to say, though the fact that the word made it through his clenched jaw was somewhat amazing.

"Does he sleep around? Does he lie to or cheat on women? Does he drink too much? Does he waste his money?"

Caleb didn't bother answering, but he did manage a single shake of his head.

"Then I think it's about time you just got over it. I mean really, what kind of man do you *want* to see me with if you don't want me with someone you know—probably better than you know me—someone you trust, and someone you know treats women well?"

She let the question hang, not expecting an answer. At this point, she knew her brother well enough to know she just needed to walk away and let what she'd said sink in. Taking the last sip of her tea, she rose from her seat and placed the mug in the sink.

"I'll go pack. I'll be ready to leave in twenty minutes. I need to go home to Windsor for a day or so to get some clothes, but I can head to New York after that."

"*We* can head to New York," Garret corrected. She gave a small nod and made her way up the stairs, leaving the two men behind.

CHAPTER 12

GARRET STOOD ON THE SIDEWALK, leaning against the wall beside the door to Kit's apartment building, and waited in the evening shadows. The past two weeks had been unlike anything he'd ever experienced. Mostly good, but it still took some getting used to. He'd never had a desk job, and though this desk job was about as minimally "desky" as a job could get, it took a different kind of focus than his usual gigs. Over the last several days, he'd familiarized himself with the UN building, met the heads of security for most of the ambassadors to the organization, and had begun to get to know the city, including traffic patterns and all the ways into and out of the borough of Manhattan. It was a jungle of a different sort.

He shoved his gloved hands deeper into the pockets of his leather winter jacket as the line of rush hour traffic moved slowly up the street. Even on Kit's residential Upper West Side road, the cars were moving at less than ten miles an hour. Of course, the recent ice storm hadn't helped. For the most part, the streets were clear, but drivers still seemed more cautious than usual. Which wasn't a bad thing.

His phone vibrated in his pocket and he pulled it out. He smiled at the message Kit had sent, letting him know she was right around the corner. He pulled off his glove and keyed in a quick response to tell her he was waiting.

They had plans to walk across the street for dinner before retiring for the evening—far and away his favorite part of the day. And he could have waited in the apartment, the cozy little two-bedroom place she owned five stories above where he stood, or at the restaurant. But waiting outside was just as easy as waiting inside, and at least this way, if she'd put on heels when she'd left that morning, he'd be able to make sure she didn't slide all over the place while crossing the street.

He ignored the cold air seeping in between his jacket and his scarf as his mind flitted back over the past two weeks. Things with Kit were going well. Better than he'd even expected. They'd gone to a few receptions held in her honor, a couple of dinners, and even to a play with a friend of hers. But his favorite nights were the ones when they stayed in, or maybe grabbed a bite to eat out but then came home and just spent time being together. Sometimes they'd play cards, sometimes he'd work or she would, but the familiarity of it felt good. It might not be the most exciting life, but he'd had enough of that—enough dodging bullets and chasing bad guys— that quiet nights at home suited him just fine. Which also told him just how ready he'd been for a change. He hadn't realized how ready until he'd actually quit. His fast adjustment to staying put, staying in, and doing all the things normal people do, said more than any shrink could ever say on the topic.

But what really brought it all home for him was the fact that he now *liked* it when he woke up in the middle of the night to find Kit gone. The first time it had happened, he had gone into full alert, upright with his gun in his hand before he knew it. Then he'd heard the typing of the keys on her computer in the extra bedroom she used as an office. It had taken a moment for his adrenaline to drop, but by the time he'd climbed out of bed and padded silently to the office doorway, a smile had played upon his lips. Hovering in the shadows, he had watched her reflection in a mirror hanging on the wall. Head down, an intent expression on her face, and a pencil held between her teeth, Kit had plied her trade.

There'd been more than a few nights now that he'd found her that way. And always after watching her, after reveling in the intimacy he felt as she poured her soul into whatever she was working on, he left her alone to do her work. And in the morning, when she was back in bed, he slipped out quietly, leaving her a pot of fresh coffee to wake up to when he left for work.

He didn't know why watching her work, or knowing that she was doing it so close to where he slept, had such an effect on him, but it did. For some reason, whether right or wrong, he took it as a sign of trust. She trusted him to let her do her thing, to let her focus shift completely to another world, another world he wasn't a part of. And he had no intention of violating that trust. Especially because he knew that when she felt it was time to leave her fictional world, she would come back to him.

He smiled at the thought of Kit living in so many worlds—her city world, her Windsor world, her fictional world, their world, and the world that was solely and completely hers. The small, silent laugh he let out created a cloud of fog in front of him; as it dissipated, he saw a taxi making its way to the curb.

Straightening away from the wall, he stomped his nearly frozen feet and visually plotted a course toward where he suspected the taxi would stop. Satisfied that the ice wasn't going to do him or Kit in, he watched the taxi as it rolled the last twenty feet toward him. From where he stood he could see Kit's silhouette in the back seat and could tell from the movement of her head that she was digging in her purse for her credit card.

Out of habit, he glanced around, taking in the crowded post-work streets. Seeing so many people all the time, for more than a few days at a stretch, was something he was still getting used to. Figures moved in the shadowed darkness. The fog and steam created by humanity glowed in the dull light cast by the streetlamps. At this time of the evening, more often than not, it was difficult to make out a person's features until they were less than ten feet away. But still, he could tell by the way they walked and what they carried that most were professionals of some sort returning home after a long day.

He frowned as a man caught his attention. He looked like many of the other office workers making their way west of Central Park. Only he wasn't carrying a bag of any sort. His head was covered by a black knit hat and he wore a long, wool jacket over a pair of khaki pants. His boots were sure on the ice, his hands were shoved in his pockets, and his eyes were focused down as his shoulders hunched against the freezing temperatures.

If he had been carrying a bag or briefcase of any kind, Garret would have overlooked this particular man. But as he was not, Garret's curiosity was piqued as the man paced up the street, about twenty feet behind Kit's taxi, which had just come to a stop at the curb in front of Garret.

Hearing the door to the car open, Garret's attention swung back to Kit, who was listening to something the taxi driver was saying and laughing as she gathered her purse and made to exit the cab. When he took a step toward the car, her gaze came up and met his. Her brilliant smile turned into another laugh when Garret was abruptly pushed back against their building as a sea of people moved between them on the sidewalk. Waiting impatiently for the group to pass, he watched as the taxi pulled back into traffic, leaving Kit alone at the curb.

Glancing left to see when the crowd would ease and he'd be able to cross and greet her, his eyes caught again on the man in the knit hat. He was less than five feet from Kit, and when he looked up and exposed his profile, Garret felt the hairs on the back of his neck stand on end.

Without apology, he made to move across the wide sidewalk, no longer willing to be patient and wait for an opening. Ignoring the muttered curses of the people he bumped into, Garret looked up to catch a glimpse of Kit's head suddenly dipping below his line of sight as if she'd fallen.

His heart rate kicked up, but once he was about five strides away from her, her head came back into view. The crowds thinned the closer he got, and he kept his eyes on Kit and the man in the knit cap who seemed to be holding her arms.

Garret's heart leapt into his throat. But then Kit laughed. His eyes focused on her and then it became obvious that, judging by everything he could see, the man was simply apologizing for having bumped into Kit, steadying her as any decent person would before continuing on. It was just an accident; completely understandable, given the slippery sidewalks.

But something was making his skin prickle in a way he couldn't ignore.

"Are you all right?" he asked, reaching Kit's side.

"Of course," she said, smiling and leaning in for a kiss.

He obliged, but his eyes and mind where still tracking the man in the hat, who was now walking away.

"Garret? Is something wrong?"

He heard her voice, he heard the question and the concern. But his mind was taking stock and memorizing everything he could about the form quickly disappearing down the road.

Even as he was cataloging the details—height, race, gender, movement characteristics—another part of his brain was already telling him to let it go, that he was overreacting. And despite his instincts and all his training, he was two seconds away from listening to that part of his brain. Then the man turned around. Garret's eyes looked directly into those of a man he had both hoped to meet again and hoped to never again see walking the face of the earth.

Garret's blood turned to ice and he gave a moment's thought to running after the man. He even lifted a foot in that direction. But the grip of Kit's hand on his sleeve stopped him.

"Garret?"

Her voice already sounded weaker than it had even seconds ago. Torn between running down the road to catch the man who had "bumped" into Kit and turning back to her, he could barely choke back a growl of frustration.

And then Kit's hand tightened again and his eyes shot to hers. She was frowning and swaying a bit.

"I actually—actually, I don't feel so well," she said, sounding more confused than concerned. Her gold eyes met his with such a look of trust—as if she believed he could make everything better— that he realized there was no decision to make.

"I'm sure you don't feel so great, honey. But I know how to

make it better," he said as he swept her into his arms, even as he was dialing Caleb's number. Because no matter how much he loved her or how much he knew exactly what was happening to her, he knew that what was coming next was nothing he could handle on his own.

CHAPTER 13

KIT WOKE WITH THE MOTHER of all headaches. And backaches. And aches *everywhere*. But even though she recognized that she was awake, her mind and body seemed to float in and out of consciousness as if not quite sure. The thought of opening her eyes drifted through her mind, hovering on the edges, but even the mere idea of it caused a bout of dizziness that rivaled even the worst case of the spins. And as the sounds around her shifted from muted hums to distinct noises—the honking of horns, the hushed voices talking somewhere nearby—the feeling of being disassociated from herself intensified, sending fresh waves of nausea that washed over her as if her corporeal self and her mental self were locked in a battle that left her reeling.

Instinct kicked in and she took a deep breath, fending off the worst of the nausea. The air seemed to do her some good; seemed to clear a bit of the fog away, and as it cleared, she mentally searched for something to which she could tether her mind and spinning thoughts.

The voices.

Recognizing the hushed sounds, if not the words, gave her something to focus on other than her aching body. And slowly, ever so slowly, she came to full wakefulness.

Forcing her eyes open, Kit was surprised to find herself in her own room, in her own bed. Not quite willing to get up yet, she managed to cock her head, frowning as she tried to discern the speakers of the voices coming from what she now knew was her dining room.

She heard the timbre of Garret's voice and then an answering one, one she had a vague recollection of, but couldn't quite place. Then a third voice, again, too indistinct for her to recognize.

More confused than ever, she started to sit up and was hit with a brick wall to the head. Or at least that was how it felt. Her entire body screamed in protest, the pain so intense that for a brief moment, she thought she might actually vomit.

Taking another deep breath to prepare, Kit braced herself and managed to roll onto her side and slide her feet to the ground. Another few minutes passed as she battled to retain the contents of her stomach—even what little there might be. When she felt confident that everything was under some sort of control, she pushed herself up to a seated position.

Her head spun and pain shot up her neck and down her back. What the hell had she done? Sitting there, eyes closed, head hung, feet resting on the ground, Kit thought back, trying desperately to figure out just how she had ended up like this. Trying desperately to figure just what *this* was.

With another deep breath, she remembered being in the taxi on her way home. She remembered the cab driver telling her stories about teaching his son to drive. She remembered texting Garret; they were supposed to go to dinner. He was going to meet her.

She frowned. She didn't remember much after that. An image of standing on the street with Garret flashed in her mind. Of his concerned expression. And there was something else too, but what it was, she couldn't remember.

Any more than that was lost. She remembered nothing. Not how she got upstairs and back into her apartment and certainly not how she'd ended up feeling like she'd been on the losing end of a fight with semi-truck. Or how, or why, she now had an IV needle in her hand.

She stared at the needle she'd just noticed taped to the back of her right hand. It wasn't currently attached to anything, but when she managed to bring her head up and look around, she saw a bag of fluid hanging from an IV stand.

For the first time since she'd roused herself into consciousness, fear took hold as her strongest emotion. Her heart started beating faster and she could feel her palms getting clammy. The adrenaline must have sharpened her hearing because she could now hear not just Garret, but Caleb and Drew talking too—each voice as distinct as the man himself.

With a firm grip on the headboard, Kit pulled herself up to a standing position. And after the initial nausea from the movement passed, she felt, if not steady on her feet, at least capable of walking into the dining room.

After a few shaky steps, she seemed to find some sort of equilibrium, and she managed to make it to the door without being heard. There she paused, listening, getting more confused by the moment.

"There's no way she would have ever come across him," Garret was insisting.

"Is there any way he was associated with your father?" Drew asked.

"I never came across him when I was tracking my dad's activities, but I can't rule it out altogether," Caleb answered.

"At this point, I don't give a shit how she came onto his radar, I just want her off of it. Permanently," Garret interjected.

All three of the men seemed to agree on this point as they shuffled papers around on the dining table. Taking a closer look, Kit realized that each one of them seemed as though they'd seen better days. Garret and Caleb both had stubble growing on their chins; Drew was actually in jeans and a t-shirt. She didn't think she'd ever seen him in jeans and a t-shirt.

Pain lanced up her neck and she must have made a sound alerting the three to her presence. In an instant, Garret was at her side, holding her arm and helping her to the chair Caleb had jumped up to pull out for her.

She slid into the seat, the wood of the chair cool against the backs of her thighs. Glancing down, she realized she was wearing a t-shirt and a pair of boxers that belonged to Garret. Knowing she hadn't put them on herself, she figured he must have picked them because they were loose enough to slide on without much hassle. It seemed practical, but now that she was up and about, sort of, a chill swept across her body and goose bumps broke out on every surface of her skin.

"Here," Garret said, reaching for her hands and tugging them gently through the sleeves of a sweatshirt which he then pulled over her head. Drew appeared at her side to hand Garret a blanket that he swiftly wrapped around her legs. It all happened so fast, or what felt like fast, that she was surprised, once she was settled, to see Caleb standing before her with a cup of tea in his hand.

She opened her mouth to say thank you and immediately felt like shards of glass were being forced down her throat. Tears sprang to her eyes and though the pain was intense, she didn't miss the look of grim concern etched on her brother's face.

Without a word, he handed over the cup and urged her to take a sip. "It will help," he said, reassuring her. She couldn't fathom getting liquid down her throat, but something in her brother's surety gave her confidence to try. She raised the cup to her lips and took a tentative sip. The tea was warm, not hot, and sure enough, she could almost feel it acting like a balm sliding down her throat.

She had a million and one questions to ask, but judging by the looks of the three men staring at her, she would be better off finishing her cup of tea and *then* trying to talk. As if sensing her decision, Drew and Garret sat down, Garret beside her and Drew across the table. Caleb hovered, waiting for her to finish, and as soon as she was, he took the cup from her and stepped into the kitchen to fill the mug again. Once he was done, he brought it back to her and then took a seat beside Drew.

"How do you feel?" Garret asked, taking her free hand in his.

She swallowed, and given that the pain seemed to have dulled a bit, she decided to try and answer. "Sore," she managed to croak. "Tired," she added.

No one seemed to have anything to say to that, so she took a few more minutes to finish the second cup of tea. Setting the cup down, she looked at each of the men sitting with her.

She swallowed again. "My throat," she said.

Caleb's lips thinned. "I know. It feels like a cat crawled in and tried to claw its way out, doesn't it?"

She blinked. Because actually, that was exactly how it felt. And then it occurred to her. "You *know*?" she managed to scratch out. Caleb's eyes jumped to Garret for a fleeting moment before landing back on hers. "What happened to me?" she asked.

Garret must have given Caleb some signal because her brother was the one to answer. "You were poisoned. It was a weapons-grade form of bacterial meningitis, transferred to you subcutaneously." As Caleb spoke, Garret reached over, pushed up the sleeve of her sweatshirt, then gently raised her arm up onto the table. She caught sight of a small dot surrounded by red, irritated flesh about midway up the inside of her forearm. It looked a little like an infected mosquito bite.

She blinked again and wondered if her brain was ever going to feel sharp again because what he'd said made no sense. "Weapons-grade bacterial meningitis?"

Drew took a deep breath and when her eyes shifted to him, he answered. "It's a biological weapon that, like all biological weapons, is banned by international treaty. That said, there are a number of countries that haven't signed the treaty, or began development of it before signing and still hold the technology. It's not a common form of biological weapon, but we have seen instances of it over the past several decades."

So maybe her brain wasn't in such a fog. Maybe what she was hearing actually *was* crazy. "Biological weapon? Who would use that? And who would use that on *me*?" she asked. And when none of her companions immediately answered, she turned her eyes to her brother. His eyes, so like hers, looked back at her with concern. "And how did you know how I felt? Have you been infected too?"

He hesitated, then nodded. "I was in Kosovo when I had the

pleasure. Luckily, Cantona found me and figured out what had happened. Otherwise, I would have died within twenty-four hours."

Her gaze swung to Garret. His blue eyes were watching her, filled with concern. And something else—anger, or maybe frustration.

"Is that why you were able to figure out what happened to me so quickly?" she asked. But that didn't seem right. How could he immediately know what had happened to her? And Drew had said it was transmitted subcutaneously; Garret wouldn't have been able to see the mark on her arm through her coat, so how would he have known? She was obviously sick, and even the possibility that she had meningitis, knowing what meningitis did, made sense to her with her body aches, painful throat, and frequent chills. But *weapons-grade* meningitis? She'd never heard of it, and it didn't make any sense that it was the first conclusion Garret had jumped to when she'd started to feel unwell. So she asked.

Garret gave the other two men an uneasy look before meeting her gaze again. He dropped her hand, reached across the table for a piece of paper, and slid it toward her—no, not a piece of paper, a photo. She looked down at the image of an older man. His blue eyes were deep set, his nose a bit hawk-like, and his chin quite narrow. He was looking away, as if unaware that he was being photographed.

"Do you recognize him?" Garret asked.

She looked again; the face stirred no memories for her. But feeling the intensity directed at her by everyone else at the table, she forced herself to take a closer look and catalog what she saw. Not just the man at the center but everything around him, hoping that maybe, with some context, she might be able to place him.

But to no avail. Even after looking at the background for clues, she came up with nothing. Judging by the architecture, the picture was taken in Europe, or maybe some colonial city, but other than that, she truly had nothing.

She shook her head. "No, I don't. Should I?" she asked, her eyes traveling to each of the men.

Drew let out a long sigh. "No, you shouldn't know him. But just in case, do any of these look familiar?" he asked as he slid four more pictures in front of her. They were all obviously of the same man, but two of the four showed him looking much younger, with his hair dark instead of gray and his skin still youthful.

Again, she shook her head. "Who is he?"

When she turned an expectant look on him, Garret took her hand again and answered. "His name is Alexi Kašović. He was a general in the Serbian army during the Balkan War." Garret paused and looked at the photo again. "He was responsible for the deaths of a lot of innocent people."

It was more how his words came out than the words themselves that caused Kit to pause. She had been in Europe after the war and had met her fair share of survivors. She had no illusions about just what kind of brutality Garret was referring to.

She let her gaze follow Garret's and her eyes landed, once again, on the image of the now old man. Her mind couldn't, wouldn't, process just what he might have been responsible for, but she could ask one question.

"What does he have to do with me?"

She saw Garret's lips thin, and for a moment, she thought frustration might get the better of him. But he seemed to rein it in as he lifted his eyes to hers. "We don't know," he said.

She frowned. Not exactly the answer she was hoping for—although just what answer might have satisfied her alluded her. After all, it wasn't every day she was being connected to a war criminal—and though no one at the table had called him that, she had no doubt that was precisely what Kašović was.

"Okay," she said slowly, "what *do* you know?"

"That he's the one who poisoned you," Garret answered.

Kit looked at Garret. "But how . . .why . . .I didn't . . .what's going on?" she managed to stammer.

"As to how it happened, that we know," he said, picking up her arm. "He bumped into you on the street, and he injected you with the meningitis."

Kit looked at her arm, the information slowly sinking in. "And you saw this?" she asked Garret.

Garret shook his head. "No, I saw you get bumped into, but it wasn't until he turned around and looked back at you that I got a clear view of his face."

"And you recognized him," Kit finished his statement. "Okay," she said after Garret nodded. "That's *how* it happened. What about the *why?*"

Garret looked at Drew and Kit followed his lead. After a moment's hesitation, Drew pulled out a folder and opened it before them on the table. "There's a bit of background information here, so bear with me," he said. "Alexi Kašović is wanted by the international criminal court for committing Crimes Against Humanity. Unfortunately, within a year of the war's end in 1995, he disappeared without a trace," he began.

"How's that possible?" she asked.

Drew lifted a shoulder. "The same way it was possible for Nazi war criminals to escape—new names, new papers, old friends. And granted, we're a lot more connected these days than we were in the 1940s, but given the kind of people he did business with, arranging for a boat ride to South America probably wasn't that difficult."

She started to clear her throat and winced. Caleb reached for her mug and rose to pour her yet another cup of tea.

"You just said South America like you knew that was where he was though," she pressed.

"We do know that's where he fled to, but the international community hasn't been able to do anything about it due to the current political landscape. Does this woman look familiar?" Drew asked, sliding another photo in front of her.

This time, the image was of a woman who looked to be somewhere in her mid-to-late forties. She was dressed in a suit and her round face was surrounded by a mane of dark hair. She was pretty, but there was something hard in her eyes and she looked like a woman Kit would not want to mess with.

She shook her head. "She looks like a professional woman I

could know. Like someone I'd meet at a book signing, or a reception, or something like that, but I don't remember ever meeting her specifically."

Drew let out a little huff. She knew she wasn't being too helpful, but she really didn't know anything.

"What about him?" Caleb asked, pushing yet another photo in front of her. In this image, the woman from the previous photo was standing beside a man Kit assumed was her husband, based on the way his arm was wrapped around her and she was leaning into him. They were waving at something or someone and they struck her as a political couple—like they were standing there waving to their constituency.

"Is one of them in government?" she asked, handing the picture back to Caleb. He nodded.

"This is Maria Santana Costello. The Honorable Maria Santana Costello," he amended, pointing to the woman. "She's a judge in Colombia, the equivalent of a federal appeals court judge. Not quite the supreme court, but well on her way."

Kit eyed the photo from her seat and frowned. Neither the name nor the woman were familiar to her. "And why do you ask if I know her?"

"Because this man," Caleb said, sliding a picture of Kašović to the center of the table, "and this woman," he said, placing the picture of Costello beside it, "were recently seen leaving the same building within a few minutes of each other."

Kit paused. She was missing something. Or maybe they weren't telling her everything. She looked out the window to try and sort it out. She realized dusk was falling. "What day is it?" she asked.

Beside her, Garret spoke. "It's Wednesday."

That revelation, more than anything else they'd talked about, managed to take her breath away. She felt Garret's hand squeeze hers and Caleb shoved her tea at her, encouraging her to drink.

"Wednesday?" she repeated. Garret nodded. "I've been passed out for *two days*?" She could hardly believe them and even as she asked, she was searching for proof. As if sensing her panic, Garret placed his phone in front of her and hit the button to bring it to life. Sure enough, the date stared back at her, confirming what she'd just been told.

She swallowed. "Okay, I think it's time you tell me just exactly what you think is going on. And start from the beginning."

CHAPTER 14

DREW LOOKED AT THE OTHER two men, but Kit kept her eyes fixed on him. If anyone was going to tell her everything, it was him. And sure enough, after a long pause, he sat back in his chair and made himself comfortable.

"Alexi Kašović has been hunted for years, decades even, ever since the end of the Balkan War. There have been sightings of him here and there, but by the time anyone could be mobilized to do anything, he was in the wind. We've had a couple of confirmed reports indicating that, on occasion, he will hire out his services. We're not sure what motivates him—"

"Money, most likely," Caleb interjected.

Drew gave a single nod then continued. "Most likely, yes, but since we don't have a bead on his finances or even where he's living, it's not something we can confirm."

Kit digested this bit of information as she took a sip of her tea. So far it meant little to her, and she said so.

"And it shouldn't mean anything to you," Garret interjected before Drew picked up his narrative again.

"But it will," Drew said. "We're not sure why, but given what we know about Maria Costello's recent movements, as well as some interesting financial transactions we've tracked, we think she's hired him to kill you."

His bald statement washed over Kit for a long moment before it receded into her brain and actually registered. She blinked. "You think she," Kit said, pointing to the woman in the picture, "wants to kill *me*?"

Drew gave another nod.

"But why would she want to kill me, and how would you even know that?" Kit pressed.

Drew frowned and dropped his gaze to the pictures. After a moment, he spoke again, "I'm not actually sure *why* she seems to want you dead, but as to how we know, well, we have enough information to consider it an option. All credible, of course," he added.

Kit cast them all a skeptical glance. "What exactly is it that is 'credible'—the information you have or the theory of her wanting to kill me?"

"The latter," Drew answered immediately. "The information we have about Maria Costello's recent activities is sound. And it's what those activities have been—meeting with Kašović, transferring funds, holing up in her house for the last several days—that lead us to believe that Costello hiring Kašović to kill you is a credible theory."

Kit frowned. "There's more, though, isn't there?"

Drew nodded. "Maria Costello is someone the government tends to keep on eye on. She is considered an ally to the US based on her political persuasions, and she has a remarkably strong track record of advocating for the poor and disenfranchised, which makes her popular with the people."

"But?" Kit prompted, taking another sip of her tea. Drinking the warm concoction seemed to be the only way to tame the searing pain in her throat enough to have this conversation.

"But she's the illegitimate daughter of Emmanuel Salazar and niece of Esteban Salazar. Esteban Salazar is the head of a mid-sized but very ruthless drug cartel. They aren't wide-spread, but in the market in which they operate, they operate deep," Caleb added.

Kit's eyes narrowed. "But if she's a judge who's considered an ally of the US, how can she also be tied to what sounds like a pretty well-known drug cartel?"

Drew let out a deep breath. "Maria has managed her career better than any other politician I know. She recuses herself from cases that directly involve drugs, thus keeping an air of partiality, but she's an active advocate for human rights and has been up front about her relationship with her father's family."

"Which is?" Kit asked.

"Distant," Garret answered. "Neither side claims the other side, though it is common knowledge who Maria Costello's parents were. But to date, she has not so much as spoken to or been in the same neighborhood as anyone from Salazar's cartel."

"How is that possible? What about her father?" Kit asked.

"Emmanuel Salazar died almost twenty years ago," Garret supplied.

"And Maria Costello's mother, Olivia, died when she was four, and she was raised by her maternal grandparents," Drew interjected, "For all intents and purposes, until now Maria and her extended family haven't spoken or had any contact at all."

"But you think things have changed?"

Drew nodded.

"Why?" she asked.

"Because the last assassination that Kašović is believed to have carried out was on behalf of the Salazar cartel," Drew said. His flat tone brought her eyes up from the picture and she studied him. Then, without moving her head, she shifted her gaze first to Garret, then to Caleb. Each one of them looked tense enough to spring out of their skins at any given moment.

"But if she doesn't have any contact with her family . . ." Kit's voiced trailed off as she put two and two together. If Maria Costello had hired Kašović, what Drew was hinting at made sense—she'd likely done so through her family connections, connections she'd built her career on declaiming. But if it were true, whatever had brought her to that decision must have been momentous; it must have been something that was bigger than her career; bigger than her own life. And for the life of Kit, she still couldn't figure out what she had to do with any of it.

She thumbed through the photos again, thinking. The three men surrounding her remained quiet. Her life was staid and quite boring, so how could she possibly be the cause of Costello casting off everything she'd built her life on? Had Kit seen something or heard something somewhere? If so, she hadn't a clue. She wasn't the kind of woman who was linked to war criminals and drug cartels—at least not now that her father was dead. She paused at that thought, then raised her eyes to Caleb.

"You were talking about whether or not this could be about our father. Do you think that might have something to do with it?" she asked.

For a long moment, Caleb was silent. Then he shook his head. "Carmichael thinks it's worth exploring, but I don't think that's it. It's been years since he died. Why now? Why you? It just doesn't make a lot of sense," he finished.

She mulled his answer over before answering herself. "But you said yourself that the Michaels men were trying to step into our father's shoes, or at least use some of his old methods. Maybe that has something to do with it?" she suggested.

Caleb lifted a shoulder and she felt Garret's fingers tighten on her hand that he still held. "I suppose it's possible," Caleb said. "But I have a hard time imagining it, knowing what I now know about the Michaels."

She swung a questioning gaze to Drew, whose expression was flat as he began speaking. "We're exploring it as a potential lead, but I have to agree with your brother. It doesn't seem likely. Our man on the ground says Henry Michaels is incredibly incompetent and isn't likely to survive more than a year in the business. We're hoping that's the case and we don't have to do anything about it, but it certainly doesn't inspire confidence that he could be behind hiring Kašović to kill you. The biggest impediment being that Kašović himself doesn't suffer fools lightly."

Kit heard them, but her mind still lingered on the possibility. She hadn't been close to any kind of violence since her father's death, and it only made sense that he was a part of what she was going through now. Even after being nearly fifteen years in the grave.

Or was he?

Her heart caught in her throat as she pulled another photo closer. She blinked and stilled. And then in a rush, the blood seemed to pour through her veins, pounding through her heart.

"Kit?" Garret said from beside her. She felt him lean toward her and heard the concern in his voice. But her eyes were focused on one thing.

A face.

The face of a young man. Waving at someone. Handsome and smiling. Like he didn't have a care in the world.

And it was a far cry from the way he'd looked when she'd last seen him.

"I know him," she managed to say, pointing to the man. She set her mug down and focused on the image, she asked, "Who is he?"

Drew leaned over the table to get a better look. She flipped the photo around to face him. "This man here," she said, pointing him out. "Who is he?" she repeated.

"That's Louis Ramon," Drew said. "Maria Costello's son."

CHAPTER 15

"HER SON," KIT REPEATED AS she dragged her eyes away from the image. Drew nodded. She looked to Garret and Caleb, who both confirmed Drew's statement with their own nods.

"I saw him in San Francisco when I was there in October," Kit said.

"Impossible," Drew cut her off. "He hasn't been allowed entry into the US for years. Not even when his parents are traveling here for business. His ties to his mother's family aren't as severed as hers are," Drew continued. "That fact, and a minor drug bust he was involved in when he was partying on South Padre Island at age sixteen, have landed him on the list of those not welcome in the US."

Kit looked at Drew and frowned. "I have no reason to doubt you, but I can assure you, I saw him in San Francisco last October."

Drew met her gaze and she held it, certain in her bones she'd seen that young man in the US less than six months ago. Something in her expression must have caused a shadow of doubt to creep into Drew's frame of reference.

"Tell me what you saw," he all but commanded.

She took a breath as deep as her aching body would allow and spoke. "I was in the city for business, doing some research, like I already told you. It happened to be right when the San Francisco Giants swept the World Series. People were dancing in the streets, partying everywhere." She paused to both catch her breath and to remember the scene as precisely as she could.

"I was down on the Embarcadero early in the morning the day after they'd won. I'd gone for a run along the bay and ended up down near the park where the Giants play. Of course they weren't there, since they'd won the series on an away game, but people were celebrating everywhere. I stopped to watch for a bit." She paused as another cup of tea was placed in front of her. She hadn't even noticed Caleb get up.

"Anyway, I was standing next to a young woman and we got to talking. Turns out she was from Israel but studying with the San Francisco Ballet. We didn't exchange names or anything, just talked the way strangers talk in crowds sometimes. We chatted for, oh, I don't know," she paused to remember, "maybe five minutes, maybe ten? But no more than that. And then she spotted her boy-friend, or someone she said was her boyfriend."

"You didn't believe her?" Garret interjected.

Kit pursed her lips and thought back. After a moment, she answered. "It wasn't that I didn't believe her, but she just didn't seem happy about it. I remember thinking at the time that if the guy was really her boyfriend, he probably wouldn't be for long. She just didn't seem happy to see him, or even to have him nearby."

She drummed her fingers on the tabletop for a moment, then took a sip of tea. "But I don't know," she said. "Maybe I was wrong, because she left with him. With *him*," she said, pointing to the photo of Louis.

For a long moment, everyone was silent. Then Drew leaned forward and fingered the picture she was pointing at. "Are you absolutely certain it was this man you saw in San Francisco?"

"Yes," she answered without hesitation. "And if you want proof, I have a video."

"A video?" Drew repeated.

She nodded. "I was filming the antics of the partiers with my phone, and I know I caught the two of them on video—Louis and the young woman I was talking to."

"You have a video of Louis Ramon in San Francisco?" Caleb repeated.

Kit spared a glance at him, just barely containing an eye roll. What was so hard to believe about what she was telling them?

"Yes, I do. And I can show it to you too, if you give me a minute," she added.

"And your phone," Garret said, holding out her cell phone to her. She glanced at it, then really did roll her eyes.

"I lose phones like every two months. I think that is my second replacement since October," she said, still scanning the room for what she needed.

"So then you *don't* have the video?" Caleb asked with equal parts irritation and disappointment.

"Of course I do. Like I said, I lose phones all the time, so after the first two times, I learned a valuable lesson. I always buy insurance, and I always set my phone to wirelessly back itself up to a cloud storage account every four hours."

"Are you telling me you have a video of Louis on your cloud storage account?" Garret asked. He dropped her hand to rummage in his bag for a laptop.

She didn't deign to answer and as soon as he was logged in, he pushed the computer over to her. She typed in her account information and pulled up the videos. "It's here," she said, sliding the computer back to its owner. "They're date stamped. You'll find it in the October folder. I'd find it for you . . ." Her voice trailed off as Garret began opening files.

"Have I told you lately that I love you?" The excitement in Garret's voice made him sound younger than he ever had before. But still, that didn't excuse him.

"No, you haven't *ever* told me you love me, and if you think that counts as the first time, I would strongly urge you to reconsider." She meant to tease him, and really she was, but she hadn't done a very good job of keeping the fatigue she felt crawling through her body from affecting her voice.

He glanced up sharply and took one look at her face. Less than ten seconds later, the computer sat in front of Drew as Garret helped her out of her chair.

"You need to get back to bed," he said, guiding her back to their room. "We're fine here for now. You've given us a massive tip, something that will take us a while to dig into. You rest and we'll fill you in when you wake up."

He was babbling. A bit. But he was doing it to make her feel better, to make her feel that she wasn't quitting on them. And though she saw through it, she appreciated the effort. And slowly, as he held her, she sank back onto her bed and back into a dreamless oblivion.

CHAPTER 16

ONCE AGAIN, KIT PULLED HERSELF from a deep, dizzying sleep to hear voices in the other room. Only this time, she knew what they were talking about, if not exactly what they were saying. She glanced at the IV bag beside her and noted that it was empty. She frowned and looked down at her hand. The needle was still there. Garret must have hooked her up at some point while she was asleep.

And he would have had plenty of time too. A look at the clock told her that six hours had gone by since she'd slipped back under the sheets. It was long dark by now, more than forty-eight hours had passed since she'd first fallen ill. At least now she was starting to feel, if not better, a little less like she'd been stuck in a vise and squeezed from every which way.

She lay still for a moment longer, letting the conversation she'd had earlier with Drew, Garret, and her brother filter through her mind. It was still somewhat unbelievable that a hit man had been hired to kill her—and a war criminal assassin at that. But she had to trust what she'd been told—whether or not she found it believable would have no impact on whether it turned out to be the truth.

Kašović wasn't a name she'd heard before, or that she remembered having heard during her time in Europe. Then again, that wasn't exactly surprising. The Balkan War was more complex than the media portrayed it to be, as most wars were. They wrote of Milošević, Karadžić, and Mladić often, but Kit knew enough about life and had met enough people who were survivors of various wars to know that while there were often a few names and faces that grabbed the attention of the international community, there were usually hundreds, if not thousands more that perpetrated similar crimes without ever coming into the glare of the media spotlight.

She took a deep breath and let it out slowly as this truth sank in. She wished they could find a way to capture Kašović. The people he'd hurt, those whose lives he'd ruined, deserved to see him brought to justice. But how? Kit knew that the most obvious way would be to use herself as bait. And the idea, as soon as she let it form, felt as right as it felt terrifying. She didn't like it one bit, but what was her fear when measured against the lives of so many who deserved justice?

But to put such a plan into place, she'd need Drew, Garret, and her brother to buy into it. The thought of relying on them wasn't as scary or improbable as it had been a few weeks ago. She'd been living on her own for so long, however, that even though Garret and her brother were proving to be steady and reliable, the thought of her life being in their hands still didn't come easy. And it would be in their hands, of that she had no doubt. If she—they—had any hope of capturing Kašović, it was something she couldn't do alone. It was something she wouldn't just *want* help with, but something she would *need* help with. And Kit hadn't needed help with anything since she'd taken a stand against her father and realized just what she was capable of.

Then again, if she was willing to risk her life to capture Kašović, would it be so hard to let Drew, Garret, and Caleb run the show? With a rueful laugh at her arrogance, Kit shook her head at herself. Of course it wouldn't be hard to turn over the planning of something like what she was contemplating to the three men in her living room. Because ultimately, capturing Kašović wasn't about her. It wasn't about her damaged relationship with her brother or her fledgling relationship with Garret. It wasn't about the life she'd built for herself or the years she'd lived on her own. It was about something much more than any of those things—something far greater than her own fears.

Of course, that meant she was going to have to convince them to go along with her idea. Which she didn't suspect was going to be even the slightest bit easy.

Silently, she slid from the bed. She was still wearing the sweatshirt Garret had given her, but when the cool air hit her bare legs, which were still clad in boxers, chills broke out along her body. Giving herself a moment to adjust, she stood still and listened.

"There are very few people I'd like to bring in more than Kašović," Garret said.

"Have you ever worked with Ivo Delic? Or his son Zoran?" Caleb asked, presumably to Drew since Caleb and Garret always seemed to work together.

"His entire family, with the exception of Zoran, was wiped out because of Kašović's army. His wife, daughter, and two other sons, just gone, along with most of the inhabitants of the town," Caleb continued.

"The only reason Ivo and Zoran survived was because they happened to be visiting Ivo's parents in a neighboring town when Kašović and his men moved in," Garret added.

Kit heard Drew let out a disgusted grunt. "That isn't the only story like that I've heard about Kašović. He wasn't interested in waging a war, his driving force was always power and preferably power gained through torture and killing. He's a sadistic son of a bitch. And I say that having seen some of the worst sadists out there," Drew added.

Both Caleb and Garret mumbled an assent.

"Jesus, I wish we could find him," Caleb said.

"Then why don't we?" Kit said stepping into the room. She couldn't have asked for better timing to propose the idea she'd just come to. But even so, the carefully blank expressions on the faces of all three men did not bode well.

"If he's coming after me, use me to get to him," she continued as she walked toward the table they were once again gathered around. Only this time they were standing, moving a step here or rocking back onto their heels there, as if they were each trying to leash the urge to *act*, to do something.

"No!" Garret said.

"Not a chance," Caleb echoed.

She'd expected that reaction from them, so when she came to a stop at the chair she'd vacated earlier, she kept her gaze locked on Drew. His eyes, by their lack of expression, told her what she wanted to know. He was considering it.

Caleb and Garret must have sensed it too, as they both started objecting.

"Stop," she said, raising a hand. When they were finally silent, she asked, "Drew?"

Standing behind the chair opposite her, his hands resting on the back, he studied her. "It's possible," he said after a long pause.

She let out a deep breath and sat down even as Caleb and Garret did their best—or not—to curb the malice they were feeling toward the idea.

"You said 'possible.' What factors would come into play if we were to use me to lure him out?" she asked.

"Don't," Garret growled, taking a seat beside her. She waved him off and kept her eyes on Drew.

"His risk tolerance," Drew answered. She raised her brows in question and he continued. "He's already made two attempts on your life. With each attempt, it gets riskier. There's a greater chance he'll be caught or that he won't be able to complete the job, and if he can't complete it, why risk starting?" Drew elaborated.

"And do we know for certain it was Kašović?" Kit asked.

Drew nodded. "Once we realized who we were dealing with, we went to the various agencies and asked for assistance running facial recognition software. Our first hit was Kašović leaving Rome to fly to London. We think he must have been waiting for you there. How he found out about your London trip, we're not sure, but the day before you arrived, he flew into Gatwick Airport."

Kit frowned at that, then something niggled at the back of her mind.

"Kit?"

She dredged through her memories, then caught the thread. "This is going to sound strange, but would it have been possible for someone from the Salazar family to have been in Windsor? Or Riverside, more precisely?"

How Garret could get his face to look so emotionless, she had no idea.

"Why do you ask?" Garret asked.

She lifted a shoulder, giving a slow shrug, then told them about the two men who'd been seated beside her, Matty, Jesse, and Vivi that morning at breakfast. That morning when she'd told them all about her plans to stop in London before flying on to Rome.

Drew asked her to repeat what the men had said twice, then crossed his arms over his chest and fell silent.

"It would make sense that Kašović would prefer London over Rome," Caleb managed to say as he finally sank into a chair and joined Kit and Garret at the table. Garret glared at him, though she didn't know why. The situation was what it was; talking about it wasn't going to make it any worse.

"I was busy in Rome and barely left the hotel. Given that and the fact that, because the prime minister attended the event, security was incredibly intense, I agree with Caleb—London was a much better opportunity."

She glanced at the photos still lying on the table and noted that a picture of the young woman she'd met in San Francisco with Louis Ramon had now joined the others. Obviously printed from the video she'd captured, Louis had his hand gripped around the girl's arm, and the girl looked to be in pain. Louis himself was looking up at the camera, his face in full view.

"How do you think it all came about?" she asked, moving the photo around with the tip of her finger, still trying to soak it all in, to believe it all. "And while I have no reason to doubt you, it just seems so unbelievable that his mother would go to such extremes to hide the fact that her son was in the US," she said.

For a moment, no one said anything; then Caleb spoke.

"There's more to it than that. We think that Louis saw you taking the video and knew you could prove not only that he'd been in the US, but also, more importantly, that he'd been with her," he said, with a nod to the girl in the image.

"Why would he want to hide the fact that he'd been with her?" she asked.

"That's Yael David," Drew said, sitting down as he took up the narrative. "Her father is the public face of Mossad."

"The Israeli intelligence agency?" she asked.

Drew nodded then continued. "Yael was found dead in San Francisco the evening after you took that video."

Kit drew back in surprise. "Dead? Was she murdered?" she asked, the pieces starting to fall into place.

Again, Drew nodded. "Yes, she was. Strangled with a cord, her face beaten, and her body left for dead in an alley."

Unbidden, tears formed in Kit's eyes. She hadn't known the girl at all, hadn't even known her name. But that brief conversation they'd had, a conversation between strangers, had made Kit smile. The girl—Yael—had been sweet and happy and thrilled to be living and dancing in San Francisco. And now she was gone.

"The death was reported but her identity, or rather that of her parents, was played down because neither country was certain if it had been a random act of violence, something that had to do with Yael's new life, or something to do with her father. Everyone agreed to keep it mostly quiet until there were some leads."

"And did you have any? Before today, I mean."

Drew lifted a shoulder. "We have the print of the side of a fist, but nothing usable from a fingerprint perspective. And some DNA. But it didn't show up in any systems of offenders, so it was useless until we found a sample to match it against."

"Was useless?" she asked.

"We don't have Louis's DNA, but we do have a sample taken from his mother from when she toured some classified locations. We analyzed the two and there are maternal markers in the sample found with Yael," Drew said.

"So he killed her," Kit said softly, looking at the picture sadly.

"Yes, we think he did. And because you could identify him, we think his parents, or at least his mother, used her connections with her family to protect her son—her only child—by getting rid of you."

Kit let that information swirl around in her brain. The situation made more sense now that she knew about Yael, but she didn't understand that kind of allegiance to someone—not when what her son had done was undeniable. Hell, look what Kit had done to her own father—as far as she'd been concerned, locking him up in jail hadn't even been good enough. How could anyone, let alone someone sworn to uphold the law, do what Maria Costello was trying to do?

"Kit," Caleb said quietly, maybe sensing the direction of her thoughts. She looked up and met his eyes. "I don't understand it either," he continued. "We've seen a lot doing the work we do, and it seems like maybe we should be able to make some kind of sense of it sometimes, but I'm glad when we can't." *It's what makes us feel more human*, was what she heard, even though he didn't voice it.

Garret reached over and took her hand. For a long moment, they all simply sat there.

When she finally spoke, it was to ask an obvious question, but one to which she couldn't find an answer.

"So, if Louis recognized me, or knew I'd seen him, why did it take so long for him, or his family, to come after me? I mean, these events," she said, gesturing to the picture of Yael and Louis, "happened in October—five months ago. Does it take that long to find a hit man? With her family's connections, I wouldn't think so."

Caleb reached for a folder lying on the table and pulled out a piece of paper—a printout of the front cover of a *Times* book review from early February. A cover with her picture on the front in tribute to the award she'd won.

"We think he had no idea who you were, only that he knew you'd seen him," Garret said.

"And then, when that came out," she said with a nod to the

image in front of her, "he suddenly knew who I was. And where I would be," she added, remembering that she'd mentioned going to Rome in the interview.

"Yes," Drew said. "That's what we think."

She studied her own image for a beat. "And they say no publicity is bad publicity," she muttered.

No one answered, but Garret squeezed her hand.

She took a deep breath and let it out. "Okay, so where do we go from here? Are you going after Maria Costello? What about trying to get Kašović?"

"Let me handle Costello," Garret said, surprising not just her, but judging by the look on Drew and Caleb's faces, all of them.

"No." Drew's response was swift and certain.

Garret's eyes darted to her and then to Caleb before landing back on Drew. "I have connections that could be useful."

"I know exactly what kind of *connections* you have, Cantona—" Drew drawled.

"That's not what I meant," Garret interrupted.

Drew shot him a disbelieving look. "Whatever connections you think you have, do not, I repeat, *do not* use them. The US government has a vested interest in how this is all going to play out, and I do not want you to be the one responsible for screwing it up."

"You mean the US has an interest in using this little situation to turn Maria Costello into an asset," Garret snapped, not bothering to hide his disgust.

Drew gave him a withering look, but to Kit it looked more like he was disappointed that Garret didn't seem to place as much value on having Maria Costello dancing to the strings of the US government as he should.

"Whatever your thoughts on the situation, we have people on Maria Costello." Drew hesitated, then continued. "But we're holding off. For the moment."

Kit didn't need the oaths coming from Garret and Caleb to figure out just what Drew and his people had been waiting on. They'd been waiting on her.

"You don't want to alert Maria and risk her calling off Kašović, do you?" she asked Drew.

She saw the flicker of unease in his eyes. He was torn, that much she knew. And knowing Drew as she did, she'd wager that he'd argued with his own team against the idea of using her as bait, but had been overruled. Like her, she knew he saw the sense in it, at least in trying to get Kašović, though she appreciated the fact that he didn't appear eager to employ the tactic—using Maria as an asset was one thing, staking a friend out for a professional hit man was quite another.

"It's your call, Kit. If you say no, no one will think less of you," he said with dead certainty. A certainty she didn't feel sitting in a room with three men who regularly risked their lives, in one way or another, for king and country, so to speak.

She took a moment to mull over what she'd heard and what she hadn't. She had enough friends and acquaintances who had survived the Balkan War, and other wars, that she knew what it meant to the victims to bring war criminals to justice. But she needed to better understand this world she was stepping into— if she was going to go in, she was going to do it with her eyes wide open.

"You said he would likely weigh the risk of a third attempt once he learns this one was unsuccessful. What does that mean?"

"Kit, don't," Garret said from beside her.

She looked at him but didn't say anything. She knew she had to and so did he. He just didn't like it, which she could understand. She didn't either, but rarely in life was doing the right thing the same as doing the easy thing.

"Well?" she prompted, turning back to Drew.

"There are likely two things that motivate someone like Kašović. One is ego and the other is money. When he fled Serbia and was indicted as a war criminal, his assets were frozen. He probably had a chance to move some of them out before they were frozen, assuming he saw the writing on the wall, but we know he didn't move them all."

"So he probably had enough to live on for a while, but not forever?" she asked.

Drew inclined his head. "We're pretty sure that's why he took that first hit for the Salazar family. And probably why he took this one."

"So his risk analysis is going to weigh the risk of getting caught against the potential payout if he succeeds," she said more than asked.

Again, Drew inclined his head.

"And his ego?" she said.

"That's a little trickier," Drew responded. "By all accounts, his ego won't allow for an untrained woman to get the better of him."

"But?" she pressed.

"At his core, he's an egoist," Garret answered for Drew. "And in the end, the most important thing to an egoist is himself. So if he thinks he'll get caught, he's unlikely to proceed."

"But isn't it true that it's really not until the last minute that the egoist will admit defeat and try to preserve himself?" Kit asked. "Don't they, until that last moment, always think they'll succeed?"

She could tell by the silence at the table that she was right, although no one wanted to confirm it and send her further down the path of staking herself out as bait.

"How much money is at stake?" she asked.

Drew shrugged. "We don't know. We do know that several years ago, one of our undercover operatives was approached to handle a highly visible target, and the going rate was two-hundred grand."

"And I'm not highly visible. Not really," she added with a skeptical look at the newspaper copy.

"But given what's at stake . . ." Caleb said.

Because what was at stake wasn't the testimony or word of someone the Salazar family could easily impeach. She wasn't a drug dealer; she'd never touched that world. And not only was she who she was, she had irrefutable proof of what Maria Costello, and by extension her family, didn't want to come to light—that Louis Ramon had been in the US with Yael David.

If she made it onto the witness stand, she knew she'd be a prosecutor's dream witness. She wondered idly if what she'd seen would matter now that they had the DNA evidence; scientists could link Louis to the scene. They didn't need her. She assumed this would mean that maybe the Salazar family would take less of an interest in her since she was no longer the lynch pin.

But then again, maybe not. If anything she'd ever heard about the bigger cartels was true, her guess was that how much interest the Salazar family invested in the situation would depend on whether Louis himself held any significance for them or if having Costello indebted to them was important. If either of those factors held value to the Salazar family, they would be more likely to expand their circle of targets to include additional people—the scientists, the lawyers, and folks of that realm—rather than diminish it and cut their losses.

But that line of thinking was jumping the gun. As it was, since there had been no move made against Louis by law enforcement, the Salazar family probably thought she was still the only one who could identify him, the only one who could place him with the victim. So, until the family heard otherwise, it was likely that they still intended for Kašović to complete his task.

"He's tried shooting me and poisoning me. If he doesn't cut his losses, what do you think he'll go for next?" she asked, her question intended for no one in particular. But judging by the looks the three men exchanged, it was something they'd all considered, if not discussed.

Finally, after a long pause, Garret spoke. "It's hard to make a definitive guess, but if it were any of us, it would be something up close and personal." It was more the soft tone of his voice than the words themselves that sent chills down Kit's back.

"To make sure I'm dead," she said more than asked. "And it makes sense he would want to do that, wouldn't it? I mean, if he's an egoist and he's committed to the job of killing one naïve woman writer, he'd want to make sure I'm actually dead, right? Or it would be a blow to his ego."

"And his reputation," Drew added, earning him dark looks from Caleb and Garret.

She took in a deep breath and let it out. "Okay, so up close and personal, it is. But I guess that's a good thing, right? It means that if one of you is close to me all the time, then we're likely to catch him, right? It would be a lot harder if he set up another sniper shot from some building far away like he did in London. Or will he recognize you?" she asked Garret. "If he saw you with me on the street when he poisoned me and made the connection between you and my brother," she let her voice trail off.

Garret shook his head. "No, he won't recognize me. It was someone he used to work with that went after Caleb and even then, I wasn't there when it happened. I came along a few minutes later. I know Kašović's face, but he shouldn't know mine."

She could tell it had cost Garret to tell the truth. It would have been so much easier to lie and stop what they seemed to be putting in motion.

"So, what's the plan?" she asked.

There was some shuffling around the table as the men seemed to give it some thought. She supposed she should be giving it some thought too, but her mind was beginning to fog with fatigue.

"I have a cabin in Vermont," Drew offered. Everyone looked at him, and after a moment, he elaborated. "It's not very big, but it is isolated. I bought it years ago when I needed somewhere I could just, well, go and be alone."

Kit frowned. She knew Drew's job was tough, probably harder than anything she could imagine, but she had a difficult time believing that what he needed was more time alone. He was already one of the most "alone" people she knew. Even when he was standing within a crowd of people. There were some people who *did* need to be alone to heal, and she had no doubt Drew needed to heal after doing some of the things he'd done and seeing some of the things he'd seen, but she didn't think he was someone who should be doing it alone—like he did everything else.

Still, she held her tongue as he continued.

"I don't think anyone knows about it, I know my family doesn't. It's set out on about forty acres. The house is in a clearing of about four acres, but it's surrounded by woods."

"So, easy to see if someone is approaching, but also an easy escape route through the woods, if needed," Caleb said with an instantaneous level of understanding that Kit found disturbing.

"That's all well and good, but if we isolate her, how will he know where to find her?" Garret asked.

Kit blinked and realized she could actually contribute to this conversation. "I'm scheduled to go on *The Nation's Morning Show* on Monday," she said. It was the flashiest appearance her publisher had scheduled for her during the few weeks she and Garret had decided to stay in the city. The show was broadcast across the country, and the fact that they'd been interested in her had come as a surprise. Yes, she'd just won a very prestigious award, but the show tended to cater to celebrities, self-help gurus, and the kind of chefs who could cook a four-course meal in ten minutes with two ingredients. But still, they'd been interested and her publicist was not one to let the opportunity slip through her fingers.

"You're not well enough to make an appearance," Garret said, rubbing his thumb over the back of her hand.

"I am too. Or I will be by Monday," she countered. "And I could let slip during the interview that I'm headed to an isolated cabin in Vermont to work on my next book."

No one said anything for a long time, then Drew cocked his head. "It has promise," he said.

"I hate it," Garret grumbled.

"I'm not a big fan, either," Caleb muttered. And with that, she knew they had the start of a plan.

CHAPTER 17

"Thanks for having me, Lara," Kit smiled as she spoke to the petite host of *The Nation's Morning Show*. Kit and Lara Downey had known each other for a few years. They'd never worked together, but had been to receptions and dinners in the same company, so the smiles between the two came easily.

"I know we don't have too much time, since you're still recovering from some mystery illness?" Lara asked.

Kit let out a little laugh and prepared to lie. It was all part of the plan, but she still felt her heart rate kick up a bit. "I am. It's the strangest thing," she said, imbuing her voice with as much good-natured confusion as she could muster. "About a week ago, I fell ill very suddenly, but luckily a good friend was with me and had the smarts to get me to a doctor right away. I've been doing some traveling lately and I think my body just shut down, you know?" she finished her story, laying the groundwork should Kašović be watching. The story she'd just told was one she and Drew had agreed on—Caleb and Garret remaining quiet—to put it out there that she had no idea what had made her sick in the hopes that Kašović would believe it and not think she'd been tipped off to what was really going on.

"I can certainly understand that," Lara responded. "But I have to ask—you attended that fabulous party for Marco Baresi in Rome, didn't you? The one the Italian prime minister and all those celebrities attended? In fact, haven't you known Marco for some time?"

And so the conversation went for another five minutes or

so—they discussed Marco's award and career; they chatted about the glamorous party whose guests had taken up the entirety of one of Rome's most exclusive hotels, and they even touched on Marco's dashing reputation. When the topic of Marco had run its course, they moved on to other authors Kit knew, appearances she'd been making in the past few weeks, and Kit even managed to squeeze in a few mentions of her own book. Lara was the perfect host, a true professional. Kit knew that what Lara was really doing was putting a human face to a very literary book, and for that she was grateful.

"So, what are your plans now?" Lara asked as they approached the end of their time together. "Are you working on something new?"

Kit smiled. "I am, actually. But it's always slow going for me in the beginning. A friend has a cabin in Vermont, outside of Burlington, that I'm going to 'borrow' for the winter. It's pretty quiet where I live, but it's still easy for me to get distracted by my friends and all their cute babies, so I've decided to hie off to the tundra, so to speak."

Lara's eyes went big. "So you're planning on staying up there all winter? I assume there's hot water and heat and all that? It sounds isolated."

They both laughed. "Not quite *so* isolated, Lara. But it is quiet and it should be a good place to spend a few months focusing on this story that's been floating around in my head for nearly a year now."

"Well, that actually sounds perfect. After all, who wouldn't enjoy the chance to really get away from it all for a bit, right?" Lara responded.

And with that, they wrapped up the interview. When they cut to commercial, Lara and Kit turned their mics off and stood.

"Are you really doing okay?" Lara asked. "You still look a little pale."

Kit wagged her head. "I'm still pretty tired," she said, handing the audio equipment to an assistant. "But feeling much better, thanks. I do think some time away will be good for me," she added, wishing it were true. Well, it was true that time away would be good, she just wished she were actually going to be able to have down time rather than using the next month or so trying to lure a war criminal into custody with help from two mercenaries and the CIA.

"And I wager you aren't going to be totally alone?" Lara asked with a not-so-subtle nod in Garret's direction. He was leaning against a post, ankles and arms crossed, watching them both.

Kit let out a little laugh.

"I like the sound of that," Lara said as they made their way toward him. "What's the story there?" she asked with a smile and small gesture of her head in Garret's direction. When he noticed their approach, he straightened up.

"He does some security work for the UN; we met through my brother," was all Kit said. Then decided to add that yes, he was coming to Vermont with her. To which Lara muttered something that sounded like "lucky girl" under her breath as they stopped in front of him.

"Garret, this is Lara Downey; Lara, this is Garret Cantona." Kit made the introductions even as Garret held her coat out for her.

"Nice interview," Garret said to Lara as Kit slid into her coat.

"She's an easy guest—gorgeous, smart, and funny—my favorite kind," Lara responded.

"You'll get no argument from me," Garret answered as he slipped his hand into Kit's.

"So, are you headed up to Vermont soon?" Lara asked, walking them toward the studio door.

"Right now, actually," Garret said. "My car is packed and waiting for us."

Lara laughed, no doubt because she mistook the anxiety she heard threaded in Garret's response for an anxiousness to get Kit away and have her all to himself. Garret smiled noncommittally and let Lara think what she would.

A few moments later, after Kit had hugged her friend goodbye and promised to stay in touch, she was seated in the passenger seat of Garret's Range Rover heading north out of Manhattan.

She stared out the windows as they moved through the borough, Garret expertly navigating the morning traffic. The life and energy of the city seemed to juxtapose itself against the stark reality of what was to come for them—the isolation of the cabin they were headed to, but also the secrecy of the actual plan they had just begun to execute. Kit let her head fall back and rest against the back of the seat as she thought about what they were doing. She wasn't foolhardy enough not to be filled with anxiety, but she didn't for a minute doubt herself or her decision. There were too many people who deserved to see Kašović tried and jailed for the crimes he'd committed during the Balkan War, what he'd done to so many men, women, and children. It was surreal that she was the one who was—hopefully—going to help bring about some sort of justice and possibly even closure. But if there was one lesson life had taught her, it was that opportunities to make a real difference in the world didn't come along all that often and that, when they did, she needed to seize them.

"You okay?" Garret asked, reaching over and taking her hand. She rolled the back of her head along the headrest to look at him. And smiled.

"Yeah, I'm fine," she said. Then, as if to prove her point, she closed her eyes and drifted off to sleep.

• • •

Kit pulled on her slippers, leaving her shoes behind in the entryway as she went into her house. They were stopping in Windsor on their way up to Vermont so she could pick up a few things she hadn't needed in the city, like her heavy winter snow boots and her favorite big down coat that covered her nearly to her ankles. She also wanted to grab a few more items of clothing since, dishearteningly, she had no idea how long they would be up north.

She had barely pulled out a bag from her closet when the quiet alarm went off to notify her that someone was coming up her drive. Curious, she padded back to the kitchen to find both Garret and

Caleb, who'd come up the day before, hovering over the monitor. Nudging them aside, she recognized Matty's truck and caught a glimpse of both Jesse and Vivi in the double cab with her.

She wasn't sure how they had found out she was home—she'd only been there for less than fifteen minutes—but Vivi quickly answered that question when the three women, and little Jeffery, came bundling in.

"Ian saw you guys pass him on the Taconic," Vivi explained. "Since you've been gone for a while and none of us had set eyes on you recently, we decided to pay you a visit." Welcome or not, was left unsaid. Kit gazed at the women standing before her—three of her closest friends—then shook her head and laughed.

"I'm fine," she said. "There have been some unexpected issues that have cropped up, and I'm going away again, but I'm fine," she answered. "Aren't you supposed to be at work?' she asked, looking at Jesse. Vivi and Matty had flexible schedules, but as the hospital administrator in Riverside, Jesse was usually at the office this time of day.

Jesse waved her question off, "I had the day off. Unexpected issues?" she pressed from her position next to Caleb. Kit's tiny friend and Caleb made an odd pair, but for some reason, since the previous summer, the two had been close. As soon as she'd entered the house, Jesse had gone over to give him a hug.

"Ahem," Matty cleared her throat and gave a not very subtle nod in the direction of Garret, even as she tugged her sweater further down over her growing belly.

"Matty, Jesse, Vivi, this is Garret," Kit said by way of introduction. To his credit, he took their scrutiny well, nodding to each and not looking the least bit disturbed.

"Garret, what brings you here?" Matty asked as she sidled up the kitchen island and sat on one of the stools. "I hear you're a friend of Caleb's, who we all met last year. But if I recall, Kit's the only one who met you," she added. Her eyes twinkled at her reference to the conversation all the women had had before Kit left for Europe—their conversation about just how much "meeting" Kit and Garret had done in those few short days.

Garret inclined his head. "I was a little preoccupied last fall, but it's nice to meet you now."

Matty grinned, then opened her mouth to say something that was cut off by the more discreet Vivi. "What kind of unexpected things?" she asked Kit.

Kit shot a glance at her brother and Garret whose expressions seemed to say it was up to her how much she wanted to say. She looked at Jesse and thought about everything Jesse had been through recently, then to Matty, her stomach growing each week with her twins, and then to Vivi, totting her almost-six-month-old on her hip.

"Don't even think about protecting us," Vivi spoke up as the other two voiced their consensus with that statement. "After everything we've been through and seen together, you should know better than to try to do that," she added as the alarm from the driveway went off again.

"That will be Ian," Vivi said. When everyone looked at the monitor then her, she shrugged. "You know how he is. He worries," she added by way of a simple explanation.

A few minutes later, Ian had toed off his boots in the entryway and made his way to Vivi's side. Giving his wife a quick kiss, he reached out for their son. Vivi handed Jeffery over to his father, to the delight of the baby, who cooed and smiled before tucking his head into his dad's neck.

"So, what's going on, Kit?" Ian asked without preamble. "Where have you been and why do you look like you've seen better days?"

"Ian!" Vivi said, nudging her husband with her hip. He shot Vivi a look before returning his steady, all-too-knowing gaze back to Kit.

"Well, she does," he pointed out. "And you all know exactly what I'm talking about, you're just not mentioning it because you don't want to hurt her feelings. But it's obvious that whatever has run her down *isn't* a beauty issue. Something else is going on. Isn't it, Kit?" he asked.

She took a deep breath and let it out. With the exception of her brother, she may not have known everyone in the room for very long, but with everything they'd all been through over the past few years, they were all very close to her. And they deserved to know.

"Yes, something else is going on, and no, you aren't going to like it. There's more to it, which I'll let Garret and Caleb fill *you* in on," she said with a pointed look at Ian. She held up her hand to stave off the complaints from her girlfriends and continued. "I'll fill the three of you in as I pack. Garret and I are leaving for Vermont in a little bit, and we want to get up there before it gets dark. But as for why I look like shit, which Ian was kind enough to point out," she added, the humor in her voice taking the sting out of the words, "it's because I was poisoned."

"Poisoned!"

Kit wasn't sure who had spoken, or more precisely, who hadn't, when the word filled the kitchen. Again, she held up her hand. "First, I want to say it's not contagious. *I'm* not contagious," she said, nodding to both Jeffery and Matty as the two most delicate humans in the room. "But it was a weapons-grade meningitis that was administered to me through a tiny prick in my skin when a man who has been paid to kill me bumped into me on the street in the city a week ago."

Silence. Complete and utter silence filled the kitchen at the end of her pronouncement. Ian, still holding Jeffery, fixed her with an expressionless look while her girlfriends all gaped at her. She let a rueful smile touch her lips; for the first time ever, she'd rendered all three of them speechless.

But of course, it was only a moment before they started hurling questions at her. She staved them off and directed the women to follow her; if she didn't get to packing soon, she and Garret would never reach Vermont before dark. So, leaving Ian to interrogate Caleb and Garret, she led her friends up the stairs, down the hall, and into her room. All three of them plopped down on the bed and started firing questions at her as she packed.

She'd pretty much answered them all by the time she was done. And feeling tired herself, she decided to join her friends on the bed for a few minutes. Lying crossways by the pillows, she took a moment to register the fatigue thrumming through her body. She had no doubt that Garret would be facing another long, quiet drive on the way to Vermont; she knew she'd drift off to sleep as soon as they hit the expressway.

"You're still not feeling well, are you?" Jesse asked sympathetically.

"I'm tired, mostly," Kit answered. "I was really sore for a while. But now that's just an occasional twinge."

"I'm sure someone in the kitchen would be more than happy to give you a massage," Matty said with a grin.

Vivi arched an eyebrow, but then looked at Kit expectantly. For a moment, Kit said nothing. Then a smile crept across her face, one she couldn't have stopped even if she'd wanted to.

Vivi laughed first, followed by the others. "So, am I to take it that your relationship with Garret has gone beyond wherever it was last fall?" Vivi asked.

"Waaayyy beyond," Kit replied.

"And I assume that's a good thing," Jesse interjected.

Kit nodded. Unfortunately, her friends didn't miss her slight hesitation. Nor did they miss the opportunity to jump on it, all demanding to know what the issue was.

"It's just, well, it's hard to say," Kit started. She frowned and thought for a moment before trying to voice some of the emotions that would hit her, seemingly out of the blue, every now and then when she thought about Garret. "Well, you all know he used to work with my brother."

"Used to?" Vivi asked.

Kit nodded. "Yes, used to. He quit his job so that he wouldn't have to travel—so he could be closer to me."

With that statement, she'd managed to stun her friends for the second time that day.

"Um, wow," Jesse said. "Not that you're not worth it, of course," she hastened to add. "It's just that, well . . ." Her voice trailed off.

"It's just that that is a tremendous amount of pressure to put on you." Matty finished Jesse's thought.

"No kidding," Kit agreed.

"But is it going okay?" Vivi asked. "I mean, if you don't think about all that and what it might mean, do you enjoy spending time with him?"

Again, Kit nodded. "I do. Very much. But that leads to the second issue. How can I know what's real and what's lasting when I'm trying to start a relationship with someone who has just quit his job and started a new one, is spending all his time with me, and is protecting me from a war criminal who's trying to kill me? I mean, I have a lot of adrenaline around this, so it's hard to tell what's real and what's not."

"But until a few days ago, you didn't even know about Kašović," Jesse pointed out.

"That's true," Vivi agreed. "So before then, how did you feel about Garret? How were the few weeks you spent together in the city?"

Kit let her head fall back and gazed at the ceiling. "They were good," she admitted. "Really good."

"Then maybe you should just focus on the 'good' part," Vivi suggested.

"And as for the rest, look at us, Kit," Jesse said.

Kit raised her head and looked, but she wasn't sure what she was supposed to be looking for.

Jesse continued. "Vivi met Ian when they were tracking a serial killer. Matty met Dash when her half brother went missing. And I met David when my dead husband's mistress decided to try to kill me. I'm not saying everything is always easy for us, but none of us are the flighty or flippant type. If you *feel* that there's something real between you and Garret, chances are there *is* something real between you. Something that will withstand this admittedly scary bump in the road."

Kit took a moment to ponder Jesse's words and realized her friend had a very valid point. Kit had never been one to get caught up in much of anything. She was the youngest of the four women, but given her past—given her father and what he'd exposed her to—she was much wiser than her years. And what she felt for Garret was something she'd recognized as true long before her own life had been put in danger. In fact, she could still recall with absolute clarity the way her heart had skittered and her stomach had dropped the first time she and Garret had locked eyes.

Jesse was right; she was overthinking everything. All she really needed to be thinking about right now was getting through the next phase of their plan and, hopefully—god willing—bringing Kašović to justice. The rest was something she and Garret would figure out.

She smiled, "Did you just refer to a crazy, genocidal war criminal trying to kill me as a *bump in the road*?" she teased.

Jesse smiled and shook her head as she swung her legs off the bed. "I did, and unfortunately it just means you can now also officially join the Crazy-Things-Happen-To-Me Club—our membership is now four," she said, making a gesture that encompassed all of them.

"Four what?" Garret asked, walking into the room.

Kit pushed herself up off the bed; Vivi, Jesse, and Matty joined her. "You don't want to know," Kit said, as they all made their way down to the kitchen.

Garret made a noncommittal noise behind her but followed them back to where Caleb and Ian stood waiting. Judging by the look on Ian's face, Caleb and Garret had filled him in.

"You okay?" Ian asked softly. Kit gave him an answering smile, appreciating the man her friend had married.

"I'll be okay. It will be nice when this is all over, but I'll be okay," she answered. It was the understatement of the year and everyone knew it.

• • •

Rather than take the interstate north to Vermont, Garret opted to drive the more scenic, albeit slower route through the Green Mountains. He had been to nearly every state in the nation, and many nations in the world, but there were very few routes he liked more than the drive through the Green Mountains.

The two-lane highway snaked through a picturesque valley, never more than four or five miles wide, that was dotted with farms and large, open fields. It was spectacular in every season, but in the deep of winter, when old buildings peeked out from under thick blankets of snow that covered everything but the road and smoke rose from chimneys that jutted up from pitched roofs, he felt a little like he was traveling back in time—like a horse and buggy might come around the bend at any moment.

Glancing up at the mountains that seemed to shoot up from the valley floor, he couldn't stop his brain from recognizing that these hills, this valley, would be a good tactical spot from which to ambush someone. Logically, he knew that wasn't going to happen, not today. But with the height provided by the granite mountains and the thick cover of snow on the trees, hiding in them-thar-hills would be easy.

"What are you thinking?" Kit asked from beside him. He looked over at her, her eyes still hazy from the nap she'd just woken from, and smiled.

"Do you ever feel like part of a Norman Rockwell painting when you drive around here?" he asked in answer.

The flat look she gave him in return let him know that she wasn't fooled, that she knew he hadn't been thinking about the famous painter. But she sighed, turned her head toward the window, and went with it.

"Actually, he had a house not far from Windsor, in Stockbridge.

He lived there for a number of years. There's a museum there now. And," she paused. "If I remember correctly, before he moved to Stockbridge, he actually lived here in Vermont," she added.

He smiled. "Well, then, it would make sense that this drive reminded me of him, then," Garret answered.

"Hmm." She was silent for several long moments before she spoke again. "What were you really thinking, Garret?" she asked. "Was it about what's going on?"

He took in a deep breath and let it out, debating how to answer. "In a way, yes, but mostly no," he finally said.

She rolled her head toward him. "What does that mean?"

He lifted a shoulder and felt somewhat uncomfortable, though he didn't really know why.

"Talk to me, Garret," Kit said, placing her hand on his thigh as he continued to drive.

He shrugged again, but this time he spoke. "It's hard to explain. I did the kind of work I did for a long time. Certain habits were ingrained into me as a matter of survival."

"Such as?" she pressed.

He hesitated, then answered—if she was in it with him for the long haul, she needed to understand how his mind worked. At least, to the best of his ability to explain or describe it.

"These mountains would make a perfect spot to ambush someone," he said. "With a long range sniper rifle, it would be really easy to hit a driver or someone in a car."

Kit sat up and her eyes shot to the mountains. "You don't think Kašović is there, do you?" she demanded.

He reached down and wrapped his hand around hers as he shook his head. "That's the thing. I no more think he's up there than Santa Claus, but that's the way my head works. I see things and I assess the risk and options. I do it all the time, constantly. It's a part of who I am at this point."

"And you wonder if that will affect your ability to live a so-called normal life, don't you?" she asked, putting his worry to voice. To be honest, it wasn't that he doubted he could *live* a normal life, but he did wonder if he would ever be able to just simply *enjoy* it.

"I don't know, Kit. And I don't even know if it's worth thinking about all that much since, right now, it's serving us well, and I'm not sure I can change it anyway," he said.

She said nothing for a long moment but he could feel her eyes studying him. "I'm—"

"Don't, Kit," he cut her off. "Don't apologize for any of this." Because he had no doubt that was what she had intended to say, to do—to apologize for bringing him into this mess. "There is no other place I would want to be right now, and to be honest, at the risk of sounding a little love sick, I'm not sure there is anywhere else I *could* be right now, Kit."

"You know you can't always protect me from everything, don't you?" she pointed out.

He slid her a rueful look, "And that's *exactly* what keeps me up at night," he responded.

He felt her gaze on him for another moment before she turned her eyes back to the countryside. Several more miles of snow and turns passed as they started climbing up again, nearing one of the local ski resorts.

"How long do you think this will go on?" she asked.

Garret weighed his answer. "I'm not sure," he said. "My guess is not long. If he's going to come after you, he'll want to do it sooner rather than later."

"Because?" she prompted.

"Because the longer he stays here in the US, the harder it is for him to stay under the radar. He'll need money and places to stay, and I would guess the places he'll be staying are not quite the standard he's used to at home. Like anyone who travels a lot, getting home is probably a priority."

"And he can't go home unless he finishes the job," she muttered.

"Not if he wants to get paid," Garret added. "Or if he doesn't want to piss off some really bad dudes who know where he lives."

Kit inclined her head, "I guess we have that going for us," she said with a wry laugh. "And your job?" she asked. For about the tenth time.

"My job is fine," Garret responded, giving her the same answer he'd been giving her since she'd first expressed concern that their open-ended visit to Vermont might affect his new job. "They have what and who they need in place already. I was ramping up and not contributing too much yet anyway. The cabin has Wi-Fi, and I'll be able to stay in touch. Besides, being sequestered away will give me a lot of time to study the city's roads and transportation systems. It's stuff I need to know for incident management, but probably wouldn't have been able to spend much time on if we were still in the city."

She gave another short laugh. "Always looking on the bright side, aren't you?"

He lifted a shoulder, "It's practical, Kit. You know better than most that life doesn't always go the way you expect it to, and that when it doesn't, you have two choices: you can let it get to you or you can figure out how to deal with it and move on. You're a master at moving on; I'm not bad at it myself."

"But does it ever get to you?" she asked. And he knew she wasn't asking about *this* situation.

The car downshifted as they headed up another grade. He let the feel of the motor vibrating beneath them wash over his body, as if it were shaking up bits of his past.

When they reached the top, he let out a long breath and answered. "Yeah, it does sometimes."

"And what do you do when it does?" she asked.

He had to smile a little at that. A lot of people were more interested in *what* he did for a living rather than what his living did to him. He shrugged again, feeling a little uncomfortable. It's not that he thought Kit was going to judge him, he was just, well, out of practice was the best way he could put it. He was out of practice when it came to talking about himself, about things he cared about, about what he did to stay sane, or even how hard it *was* to stay sane sometimes. But he wasn't reluctant to try.

"There are a few places I go when we have down time, when I need down time."

"Such as?" she pressed.

"I have a place on the beach in a remote part of Mexico. I go there when I," he paused, not so much debating what to say, but surprised at the truth that was coming out of his own mouth. "I go there when I need to regroup, when I need to find my own humanity. There are other places I go too. There are a few orphanages where I like to spend time—in Afghanistan and Rwanda and Guatemala. I go and play with the kids. We kick the soccer ball around, I help the staff a bit."

"But the place on the beach?"

He took in another deep breath before answering. "The place on the beach is where I go when I can't be around other people. I'll go there sometimes, for even a few days, before going to spend time with the kids." He paused again, struggling to find the right words to describe what his life was like at times, to describe who he was.

"Sometimes," he started, "the things we do, Caleb and I—the things we see, the people we have to deal with—can strip me of my own humanity. Or they try anyway. I know this sounds crazy, but there are times when I don't feel alive at all, like some of the things I've done or seen have killed something inside me."

He felt her hand curl into his, but he kept talking. "And that's when I go to the beach. Because I *know* I'm dead inside. I have a healthy sense of self preservation and no interest in dying, literally or figuratively."

"And so you go to the beach," she said softly.

He nodded. "And so I go to the beach and sit on my porch and watch the tide come in, day in and day out. Sometimes there are whales and sometimes there are dolphins. But there is always an immense horizon and the ocean stretching as far as I can see."

"And that helps?"

"It helps to remind me of how small I am in this world. And although I don't belittle what I do or what Caleb does for a living, the truth is, we're not here all that long. And while we're here, we have choices."

"To let it get to us or to figure out how to deal with it and move on," she said, echoing what he'd said earlier.

Again, he nodded. "And once that knowledge resettles itself in my body, I usually pick up and go spend time with the kids."

A companionable silence filled the car for several long moments. Then Kit gave his hand another squeeze. "You're amazing, you know that?" she said.

He let out a little laugh. "I'm not. But I'm happy to let you think I am," he answered, echoing her words from what now felt like eons ago.

She smiled and leaned over to brush his cheek with a kiss. "Thanks, Garret. For doing this, for doing what you do, for being who you are."

"You're going to make me uncomfortable," he said, his skin itching from the compliments.

"Too bad, because I *am* grateful. But if it will make you feel better, I can give you something else to think about."

He turned and raised his eyebrows at her question.

She grinned. "If it will make it easier for you to accept the compliment, when we get to the cabin, I'll be happy to *show* you how grateful I am."

He chuckled. "Yeah, that might make it a *little* easier."

• • •

Having been lulled back to sleep by the miles of road, Kit came awake as they pulled up a long, gravel driveway that had been recently plowed. Snow banks were piled several feet high on either side, making the drive's one lane feel even tighter. But just as a twinge of claustrophobia washed over her, they rounded a gentle bend and the cabin came into view.

Drew must have told his groundskeeper that someone was coming as a few lights were on, lighting the covered parking area, walkway, and porch. The walkway between the parking area and the front door had also been cleared of snow.

With the stop in Windsor on the way up, the drive had been long; night was already falling. As Kit stepped from the car and inhaled a sharp breath of frigid air, she looked up to see a crystal clear sky full of stars.

Tugging her hat down and pulling her coat tighter across her body, she took a minute to absorb the beauty around her. Her eyes drifted to the full moon. It was hard to believe that only four weeks ago, she'd stood in her own bedroom looking at the same moon, Garret newly returned.

The footsteps of the man on her mind sounded in the snow-dampened silence as he came up behind her.

"You should go inside," he said, slipping his arms around her.

She leaned back into him. "I know. It's just so beautiful up here, isn't it? I mean it's not all that different than Windsor, but it just *feels* a little different. A little wilder, a little tougher."

He chuckled behind her. "It is Vermont, you know—the 'Live Free or Die' state."

She laughed back. "That's New Hampshire; Vermont is something about freedom," she responded as she turned toward him.

"I think I like the thing about freedom more than the thing about death," he murmured, nuzzling her ear the best he could given that it was mostly covered by a hat. When his attempt proved fruitless, he sighed, moving his arms from around her waist to her hips and giving her a little nudge. "Inside," he ordered, "we can look at the stars through the windows."

The cold was seeping through her pants and her thighs were starting to go numb so, obligingly, she turned and headed inside. Walking through the door, she stepped right into the eat-in-kitchen area. The cabinets, counters, and floor were all made of a thick-grained, unfinished wood and a sturdy table for four was pushed against the wall opposite from where she stood. Next to it was a staircase leading upstairs. The right wall of the kitchen was a half wall that was shared with a living room and into it was built a wood-burning stove that opened to both rooms.

She moved into the cozy living room to allow Garret to pass by her as he carried the bags upstairs. Though still a bit chilly, the whole place was inviting and, well, relaxed. Which is what really struck her, since "relaxed" and "Drew" didn't really go together in her mind. But still, the large sofa and chair looked well worn and welcoming, and the bookshelves overflowed.

Unable to resist, Kit walked directly to the shelves along the back wall of the living room; she was someone who firmly believed that everything you ever needed to know about a person could be discovered by browsing his or her bookshelves. Perusing the titles before her, she was both surprised and not. Drew had quite a few history titles and even all of Kit's books, but what surprised her was a cluster of what she would call self-help books. They weren't really self-help—well, at least not the old-school you-can-be-anything-you-want-to-be kind of self-help books—but a number of them dealt with issues ranging from PTSD to depression and all sorts of other mental health topics that survivors of trauma, in all its forms, might experience. Thumbing the spine of another book, she frowned. She knew if she asked Drew about it, he'd likely say that they were to help him understand the people he worked with. But seeing how dog-eared some of them looked, she wondered.

"Everything okay?" Garret asked, coming to a stop at the bottom of the stairs.

Not wanting to call attention to anything that might be so deeply personal to Drew, she turned and smiled. "There's a bedroom down here, along with a bathroom and an office. It's not exactly what I expected from Drew, but now that I'm here, it's kind of funny how perfect it seems for him." She'd peeked through a door between the bookshelves and discovered the three rooms off the main part of the house. They could be closed off with a door, but the extra space would be perfect for them to use as offices.

Garret inclined his head then knelt behind the half wall to build a fire in the stove. "There's a bedroom and bathroom upstairs for us," he said as he stacked the wood and lit a match. She watched him study the fire as it flickered then caught. Garret stayed kneeling before the stove a few minutes longer, making sure the fire would grow, then closed the door and rose.

She loved the look in his eyes when he looked at her. Sometimes it was tender, sometimes it was hungry, and though it hadn't happened yet, she had no doubt that sometimes it would be angry. But whatever tone it took, the underlying intimacy of what she saw reflected in his eyes, what she felt when her gaze caught and held his, was something she'd never experienced before.

Garret came around the half wall and walked toward her. She couldn't help the smile that touched her lips as she watched him.

"We can each take one of the rooms down here for our offices," he said, wrapping his arms around her.

That gave her pause. "I know I said in the interview that I was going to hole up in Vermont for the rest of the winter, but how long do you really think we'll be here?" she asked again. It was March and the "rest of the winter" wasn't actually that long, but it was still longer than she hoped to be there.

Garret shook his head, then took her hand and led her back to the kitchen. After ushering her into a seat by the fire, he started rummaging in the cabinets. Drew's groundskeeper had also apparently left them, if not well-stocked, stocked enough for a day or two.

"Like I said, I don't know, but I don't think it will be that long," he answered, pulling a pot out of a drawer and placing it on the stove. In silence, she watched as he found milk in the refrigerator, added it to the pot, and then added some cocoa and sugar to the mix.

"How did you know he'd have stuff to make hot chocolate?" Kit asked, her thoughts momentarily off of the more serious question at hand.

"A guess," Garret answered with his own smile as he stirred the pot.

"A guess?" Kit queried, realizing that in some ways Garret

and Drew were probably more alike than she would have thought. And that this place in Vermont was probably Drew's equivalent of Garret's place in Mexico—the place he went to find his humanity again.

"Do you all have places like this?" Kit asked.

Garret didn't pretend not to know what she was talking about, but he didn't raise his eyes either. "I don't know. Probably not," he answered.

"Why? Is it money?"

Garret shrugged, still watching the milk. "Honestly, I doubt it. I mean look at us—me, Caleb, Drew." He let his voice fade and was silent for a moment before continuing. "I mean, I know Drew has a lot of personal wealth so that's not an issue for him, but even for someone like me who had nothing when I started in this business," he paused again, then lifted his eyes to meet hers.

"People like me who have no one. We don't have family to spend money on, we aren't around long enough to want to buy a nice house somewhere, we're on the road three hundred and fifty days a year. No family, no expenses, and no way to spend the money we do make. So, while I'll never be rich, I can tell you that for people like me, if we *don't* have a stockpile of all our wages in some bank somewhere, there's probably something wrong."

Kit let that sink in for a moment. She hadn't ever thought of it that way—the bleak way—Garret had just laid it all out. She knew how much her brother traveled, and had some insight into how often Drew traveled, and she could see the honesty in Garret's words about everything else. She didn't know what her brother did in his spare time, but she knew he didn't have anyone or anything else that needed whatever resources he had. On occasion, he'd send her little gifts, but certainly nothing that would drain a bank account.

"So, if not money, then what?"

Garret lifted the pot from the stove and poured the hot chocolate into two mugs. He placed one in front of her as he sat down across the table.

"I don't know, really," he said. But she thought he did.

"It has to do with who you are, doesn't it?" she pressed. "And I don't mean what you do. I mean who you are as a person and how you see your place in this world. An awareness that maybe not everyone has." She knew the moment she said the words, she was right. In the line of business Garret and Caleb and Drew were in, there would be those who would not only place a value on maintaining their humanity but would have the insight to know when they were losing it.

"You know, don't you?" Kit asked. "When you've reached a point where maybe there will be no returning if you keep going?"

Garret met her eyes and nodded.

"But not everyone is like that, are they?"

He shook his head. Then he seemed to hesitate about something before taking a sip of his hot chocolate.

"Tell me," Kit pressed again.

He was silent for so long that Kit wondered if he would answer her, but then she watched how his eyes focused on his mug and she could see thoughts—anxiety, stress, pain, and a myriad of other emotions—flashing in his eyes. She knew a thing or two about needing to sort through emotions before speaking, so she let him be.

A full five minutes later he spoke. "I've worked with guys who haven't been able to tell where that line is and it's, well, it's not easy. Don't get me wrong, almost nothing about what we do is easy, but when we're working together, we need to trust each other to a certain extent. Caleb and I trust each other implicitly, but the others we work with, when we work with them, have to earn our trust before we go into dangerous situations.

"And sometimes they fool us. When they do, it can get ugly. I mean, I don't think . . ." He paused. "I don't think they turn into sociopaths in the true sense of the word, but some of the people we work with, some of the people who do the work I've done, have seen so much and been a part of so many things, that in some ways, the lines start to get blurry."

"Like when undercover cops begin to sympathize with the people they're investigating?" Kit asked. Garret looked up in surprise. Kit gave him a soft smile. "My first book had a character who was a recovering undercover cop, remember?"

Garret nodded.

"Not many people know this, but I based him on a man I met when I was living in Italy. He was Italian but had been undercover investigating the Russian mafia for eight years—from the time he was twenty. It didn't end well for him. When I met him, he was homeless and living on the streets of Rome. I'd buy him coffee and some food, and we'd sit in a park and talk. Even after being out for ten years, his eight years undercover still confused him. He didn't understand how he'd gone from the boy of his youth to the man who'd done some of the things he'd done or allowed some of the things he'd allowed."

Garret was watching her as she spoke. She remembered the man she'd found by chance, a man who'd had such a profound impact on her writing, but also on how she viewed the actions of people who lived through situations she didn't understand. In some ways, talking to him had helped her to heal herself, had helped her to better understand what she thought of herself and her role, knowing or unknowing, in her father's life and business.

"Then you know," Garret said, reaching across the table to take her hand.

"I know what I experienced. Tell me more," she said with an answering squeeze of his hand.

"Not everyone is strong enough to stay grounded, to stay true to who they are, when they live in those kinds of worlds day in and day out for years. Some people fall to the wayside and leave, some people switch sides, and some people, the most dangerous of all, try to play all sides."

Garret paused again as he rubbed his thumb across her palm. "I saw a lot of good people struggle to make it in our line of business. And I saw the destruction and pain they left in their wake. I don't know what made me realize it or what made me stick to the promise I made to myself early on when I vowed to do everything in my power *not* to become a casualty of one of those secret wars. I think I figured that if I was going to self-destruct, there were easier ways to do it."

"And so you promised yourself you'd do everything you could to stay true to yourself. To stay human. And that's why you have the beach and the orphanages and probably some other things you haven't told me about yet," Kit finished for him.

Garret let out a long breath, looked up, and nodded. "And that's a very long answer to the question of how I knew Drew would have stuff to make hot chocolate," he said with a smile.

Kit let out a small laugh. "It's the comforts, right? That would be my guess. You have your creature comforts at your place in Mexico, and you assumed Drew would have his here?"

Garret nodded again.

Strangely enough, Kit followed this logic as she took her last sip of the rich brew. Then she frowned. "I will say, though, that had I tried to think of creature comforts for Drew, I'm not sure hot chocolate would have come to mind. Champagne maybe. Or caviar."

Garret chuckled and pulled her to her feet as he took her empty mug. Placing a kiss on her forehead, he deposited their mugs in the sink. "Drew may like all those things, but deep down he's a family man. The way he cares about the people he works with makes that clear. My guess is that he might have been raised with a silver spoon, but I bet that silver spoon was used to stir hot chocolate more often than it was used to eat pâté."

Kit had to laugh at that and as Garret stepped closer to her, she wrapped her arms around his neck and leaned in to kiss him. "You're an amazing man, you know," she murmured against his lips.

"I could argue with you," he said, backing her toward the stairs. "But I think that would be counterproductive. If I recall, you offered to show me just how amazing you think I am."

She smiled, then gave him the kind of kiss that brought out just the reaction in him she was hoping for. "So I did," she said.

A few hours later, they lay in the dark looking out the large bedroom window onto the clear night. The moon now hung high in the sky, casting so much light the stars were nearly invisible.

Kit smiled as she lay against Garret's bare chest.

"What are you smiling about?" he asked, gently stroking her hair.

"You know you don't eat pâté with a spoon, right?"

CHAPTER 18

To say they fell into a routine over the next several days would be a great misnomer. They had made one trip to the local grocer and they usually went for a couple of walks a day, but about the only thing that happened on a predictable schedule were the morning and evening trips Garret made to the small barn to get more firewood. That was okay by him. As he sat in his office, maps of New York City spread out in front of him, he wondered when in his life, if ever, he'd had such unstructured time. Of course, he wasn't diminishing the fact that Kašović was still out there, and in his heart of hearts, he knew that if there wasn't some sign of the man soon, they'd have to provoke him, but in the meantime, he was rather enjoying himself.

Which was just a little bit wrong.

"What are you thinking?" Kit asked from the doorway of the room he'd taken as his office.

Garret chuckled. "That I'm a little sick and maybe a touch twisted to be enjoying it here so much."

He was graced with a wide smile from the woman he'd known for a while was going to be his future, but was only now starting to understand what that meant. Every day that they were together, they learned more about each other—their likes and dislikes, their quirks. Again, he knew their environment was contrived, but he also knew that that fact stopped neither him nor Kit from being very real.

"How about enjoying some lunch?" she asked. "I made soup."

With a last look at the maps, he rose and joined her. It had snowed overnight, giving them an excuse not to go into town, so the soup was a bit of a kitchen-sink concoction, but one other thing Garret had learned was that Kit could cook. She didn't cook fussy food, but she had a knack for everything comfort. Or at least that's how it seemed to Garret.

They were halfway through their meal when the call that Garret had known would eventually come finally came. He excused himself and stepped away from the table.

When he returned, Kit gave him an expectant look. Resting his hands on the back of one of the dining chairs, Garret let out a deep breath. He didn't like what he'd just heard, what he'd just agreed to, but that didn't mean he hadn't expected it.

"That was Drew," he started.

Kit took a sip of her tea and nodded.

"He wants to schedule a book signing for you in Burlington and to make a big deal of it."

Again, Kit nodded.

"You know what this means, right?" he pressed.

Kit set her tea down but left her hands wrapped around the mug. She looked calm, contemplative, but he could tell from her grip that she was anything but. "Yes, I know what the signing means," she said. "It will, hopefully, draw Kašović out so we can end this thing." Her voice was calm and sure. Too calm, too sure.

Garret took a step back and crossed his arms over his chest. "This was your idea, wasn't it? You talked to Drew?" he asked, a pit gnawing its way through his stomach.

Slowly, she inclined her head.

He locked his jaw to keep from yelling in frustration. Yes, he was upset that she and Drew had worked up this scheme without him, but what caused him even more irritation was the fact that the reality of their situation had just come crashing back down on him and the whole thing, truth be told, terrified him.

He turned toward the wood stove and knelt to add some firewood, just to give himself something to do.

"You're angry," Kit said, her voice soft behind him. She hadn't moved, and for that he was grateful.

After a long moment of silence, during which he shoved a few logs into the burning stove, he let out a deep breath and answered. "At the situation, Kit," he said, watching the fire dance around the logs, their orange and blue flames licking the new wood as if testing its suitability.

"I am too, Garret. That's why I suggested the book signing to Drew. I want—no, I *need* this to end."

And then he heard it. He heard all the stress in her voice, all the fear and anxiety that he'd recognized and dismissed as they'd been holed up in their cozy little cabin for the past five days. He couldn't ignore it now, he couldn't dismiss it and turn their attention to more interesting and diverting pursuits the way he'd been doing. He couldn't try to make this better for her by forcing it under the rug.

He let out a rueful laugh.

"Garret?" she asked. He hated the tentativeness in her voice.

Rising, he walked toward her, then pulled her up and wrapped his arms around her. She gave him a wary look, but he just pulled her in tight and laid his cheek against her hair.

"I'm not going to lie and say it's fine, Kit, because we both know that nothing about this situation is fine. But you're right, we need it to be over."

"You don't sound happy about it," she said, pulling back enough to look into his eyes. As her golden ones searched his, a wave of love mixed with terror washed over him, leaving him nearly shaking with its power.

Leaning his forehead against hers, he spoke. "I want this to be over, Kit. I want us to be together in a way we want to, not in a way we have to. I want to see you laugh freely. I want to get to know your friends. I want to argue over the dishes and the trash, and maybe even get a dog we can take on long walks with us."

"But?"

He shook his head against hers. "But nothing. I laughed

because you're right. Here I am, the man who has done this kind of work for over a decade, and I'm happily shoving the danger under the rug because in the past few days, I've been living a life I never thought I would. And there you are . . ." His voice trailed off.

"And here I am?"

He nodded. "Strong, clear headed, and wanting to move forward. You did what I should have been doing. You're the tough one here, Kit. Tougher than me, I think. Don't ever forget that."

She smiled at that—a small, hinting smile. "I'm not that tough, Garret." Her smile faded. "I'm scared half to death, actually. But I want this over with for all the same reasons you do. Well, maybe not so we can argue over who takes the trash out because you'll be doing that, but so that we can go home. So that you can get to know my friends, so we can go into town for lunch or dinner, so we can maybe get a dog and take it for long walks whenever we want to."

She paused, then ran her fingers through his hair, forcing his head back enough so that they could get a better look at each other. "I'm not going to say I'm sorry you've never lived the kind of life we've had these past few days. Who you are now, the man I love now, is a mix of everything you've done, everything you've seen, and everything you've thought and felt in the past. Your past and how you've lived it, how you've understood it, has made you understand what you want for your future. And I know you want me and a life with me. And that is something I'm not ever going to regret or belittle or forget. And *that* life is something I want to start sooner rather than later."

For a long moment, he stood and simply looked at her—at this amazing woman he now had as the center of his life—and let her words sink in. She was right. They both knew too well how frail life could be and how sometimes fighting for it came at a cost—a cost that could not, or should not, be underestimated.

Their pasts, the good and the bad, helped make them who they were standing there in that kitchen. Their pasts, and what they wanted for their futures, made them stronger together. And he knew it would always be like this—he had found someone who didn't need him to be strong all the time. He had found someone who was as strong and tough and determined as he was. Someone he could trust to share that burden. Because being that way, tough and strong, *was* a burden sometimes; it was a burden for anyone to carry some of the time and almost impossible for someone to carry all of the time. And in each other, he knew that they would carry it together, that when he didn't have the strength for whatever was happening, Kit would bear the burden. And when she faltered, he'd be there too, carrying them through.

This was a new kind of trust and Garret was humbled by it. "You know I love you, right?" he said.

Her lips tilted up before she leaned in and brushed a gentle kiss across his lips. "Yes, I do. I not only know it, I'm counting on it."

• • •

Garret still wasn't happy about the plan a few days later when he and Kit drove into Burlington to meet with the owner of the bookstore that would be hosting her. He wasn't happy about being out in such a public area and he wasn't happy that every time he set foot into a new room or onto a new street, all he could think about was how easy it would be for Kašović to take Kit away.

On the other hand, he *did* like seeing Kit and Joseph, the host of the signing and owner of the bookstore, talking, planning, and gushing over their favorite books. He'd seen Kit smile a lot in their few days together, but this was different. This was her world, and judging by the time on the clock he was watching, she could live in it indefinitely.

His phone vibrated in his pocket; he briefly turned his attention from Kit to the device. Glancing at the number, he answered. "What's the plan?"

"Everything is in place," Caleb replied.

"And Drew agreed?" Garret asked.

"Drew didn't have much of a choice, but yes, he agreed."

"When?" On reflex, Garret took a casual look around him. Other than Joseph and Kit, there were two older women and five younger people who looked like students milling about.

"They'll be on their way tomorrow."

"Perfect." And with that, he hung up. He'd talked to Caleb after Kit had told him about this little excursion, and while she would play her part, he had a few ideas of his own. Including bringing in backup he could trust. He wasn't sure if it would be enough—no, scratch that, he knew it wouldn't be enough to cover her from the moment they left the house the day of the signing to the moment they returned. But without an army, there was no way he could keep Kit protected on all the open land they had to pass through to get into town or on all the streets they had to drive on to get to the store. At least they would be able to park at the back of the shop and walk straight in. It was a small thing, but he'd take it.

Still, he hadn't wanted to set Kit out as bait without more than just himself to watch over her. Thankfully, Caleb was on board—not that that was ever in doubt—and, apparently, in agreeing to his plan for backup, Drew too. There would be just four of them, but at least he wasn't alone.

"Ready?" Kit asked as she approached him wearing the most relaxed smile he'd seen on her face outside the bedroom in a long time.

"Did you get everything arranged?" he asked, pushing off the wall he'd been leaning against, his eyes going between Kit and Joseph. Joseph looked to be beside himself to have the opportunity to host Kit Forrester, which made Garret smile.

"Yes, it's all taken care of. I can't tell you how thrilled we are to host this event. She has a lot, and I mean *a lot* of fans around here," Joseph said.

Kit gave a self-deprecating laugh, "That's only because two of the professors use my second book in their lit classes."

"Because they have good taste," Garret said, pulling Kit close and brushing a gentle kiss on her temple.

Joseph nodded in enthusiastic agreement as they made their way toward the parking area behind the store. Passing through a door and into a storage room, Joseph continued to talk about the promotional plans that were already underway. Garret half listened as he scoped out the room through which they walked. He'd checked it out on their way in; it wasn't his favorite kind of space—filled with boxes piled in no particular order. He couldn't see around all of them, and he had already made a not-so-subtle request to Drew to have the room changed around a bit before they returned in three days for the big event.

At least the back door was locked, Garret noted as Joseph unlocked not one, but two hefty deadbolts before giving the door a shove and opening it onto the well-plowed alley behind the store. "Alley" wasn't quite the right word, it was more of a back byway, big enough for delivery trucks to use, but not used by the general public; only owners of the stores had permits to park back here. And selected guests.

Garret's feet crunched on the frozen snow. It had warmed up the day before, then dropped to well below freezing overnight and hadn't quite hit thirty-two degrees yet. As a result, a thin layer of ice coated almost everything, including the snow.

"So, we're all set then," Joseph said as they stopped at the car.

Kit nodded. "I think so. And please, don't hesitate to e-mail or call me between now and Saturday if something comes up and you need to make adjustments, or if you think of something you specifically want me to read or talk about."

"I can't imagine picking anything better than what you've suggested, but I will keep that in mind. And please, you do the same. If there's anything you think you'll need or want that we haven't talked about today, please call me and I'll make sure it's taken care of." Joseph spoke as he shook their gloved hands.

After a quick round of good-byes, Garret and Kit were seated in their car, the heat blasting and the seat warmers set to high.

But they didn't move.

Kit shot Garret a curious glance but didn't say anything. They'd talked for hours about just what this little planned baiting might mean and what it would require of the both of them. Rather than try to keep things from her, he'd made it his mission over the past few days to immerse her into his world. They'd gone over maps of the area, he'd coached her on what to look for when walking into a room, he'd trained her on evasive tactics in a crowd, and he'd impressed upon her just how important it was to have one person in the lead throughout the day. Yes, he wanted her aware, on her toes, and able to take care of the basics of watching out for herself, but after many hours of *discussion*, he'd finally convinced her that if they did this—if they willingly held her out as bait—she had to allow him to be the leader of their new two person team.

Truth be told, she hadn't argued his right to be the leader whatsoever. After all, she could hardly discount his experience, but she had argued about wanting to be more prepared. It shouldn't have come as a surprise, knowing Kit the way he knew her now, but it seemed that once he'd unleashed her into his world, she'd wanted to devour it whole. She'd wanted to know everything about everything. She had even wanted to go out into the woods and practice things like escaping without leaving a trail or sneaking up on him and catching him by surprise. He'd indulged her a bit, but the truth was, she wasn't going to learn everything that had taken him over a decade to learn in only a few days.

And so they'd argued. Their first real fight. He had wanted her to focus on perfecting what he had taught her, what he believed to be the few things that would be most helpful given the situation they were in. She'd wanted to learn more and more. And then, yesterday, he'd found her writing notebook when he was picking up the kitchen. It had been open to a page full of notes on everything he had been teaching her.

It might have seemed like a small thing, but to him, it wasn't. And he'd lost it. Not only did she want him to try to teach her more than she could possibly learn instead of focusing on what she most needed to know, it seemed to him that the the only reason she wanted to learn any of it in the first place was as research for one of her books. His stress level had been so high that when he'd found the notebook—and what he had believed to be proof that she was not taking anything about the situation seriously—well, the conversation hadn't been pretty.

Kit had denied peppering him with demands to know more, to learn more, for her research and had tried to convince him that she did take the situation seriously. But even then, even as she'd been fighting back in the peak of passion, he'd sensed a half-truth in her words. Knowing that they would both say things they'd regret if they'd kept arguing, he'd stepped out of the house for a while and gone for a walk in the snow—not far from the house, of course, but enough to clear his mind and let his jumbled thoughts, thoughts mixed up with emotions like fear and frustration, settle.

When he had walked back into the house, he'd found her sitting at the table, waiting for him. Without a word, he had sat down across from her and taken one of her hands in his. They had each taken a figurative deep breath and come back to the table to talk.

And talk they did. It had been a tough one, not so much because of what was said, but because navigating their shared desires to both listen and be heard was a new dance for each of them—the give and take of a relationship was something they were both learning.

But in the end, he'd come to realize and accept that she *was* taking everything he'd been teaching her seriously. The reality was that, even despite her experiences with her father, there was no way she could possibly understand their current situation in the same way he did. He had years of experience to fuel his fear, experiences that had seared into his brain exactly what it looked like when the shit hit the fan. She knew about it all in theory alone. And because she didn't *know* it the way he did, she'd defaulted to her usual response to the unknown: researching and attempting to under-stand everything there was to know about the topic. Because then maybe it wouldn't be so scary.

And that was what had been driving them both—fear. Fear of

losing each other, fear of dying, fear of the unknown. It had finally blown up between them but, not surprisingly, they'd come through it stronger.

Now, Kit sat silently beside him as they watched Joseph disappear back into the bookstore. Another minute passed, then he climbed out of the car and walked back toward the door. After squinting at the sliver of space between the door and the doorframe for a moment, he was satisfied.

"What were you looking at?" Kit asked once he'd buckled himself back in.

He picked up her hand and gave it a kiss before putting the car into gear and backing out of their spot. "He had the door locked when we arrived and unlocked it when we left, I wanted to see if he locked it again when he went back inside."

Kit inclined her head, "To get a sense if he's vigilant about keeping that door locked."

It wasn't so much a question, but he nodded. "I still couldn't say for certain if he is always vigilant, but based on his behavior today, and the way he went through the motions of locking and unlocking the door—like he'd done it a million times before—I'd wager that Joseph is on top of it."

They made their way through the streets of Burlington and within twenty minutes they were on the outskirts of town. They'd planned to stop at a diner closer to home for dinner, which gave them about forty minutes of driving time.

"You okay?" he asked when Kit was silent for several minutes.

In his peripheral view, he saw her nod, then shrug. "It's funny, I do all these high profile signings and New York City dinners and events, but really, what I most enjoy is meeting people like Joseph. People who love books—all kinds. People who understand that a good book can teach you and touch you and take you someplace you've never been before. And not just that, but people who are *excited* about discovering just what the next book will reveal to them."

"It's been a while since you've done a signing like this, hasn't it?"

Again, she nodded. "But I think after all this is over, maybe I should change that. Maybe I'll plan a few signings in smaller towns, maybe college towns. Or maybe I'll start a new trend of author chats where I can actually talk *with* readers rather than just *to* them."

She paused and he could tell her mind was working things out. A few minutes later, she let out a quiet laugh. "I guess that's one good thing to come of all this. I've been reminded of what it is that I really like about the literary world."

At that pronouncement, he let out his own bark of laughter. Leave it to Kit to find the silver lining when someone was trying to kill her.

• • •

Kit was nervous. She hadn't been nervous about a book signing since her first book had been featured on Oprah. But this was different. Yes, this event was more about being bait for Kašović than an actual signing—but it *was* an actual signing, and what was making her the most nervous was not the events that had gotten her here, but the man standing against the front wall of the store watching her while looking deceptively casual.

She'd had any number of friends attend her events before, but having Garret there, inviting him into this part of her life, felt big. After today, there would be no facet of her life that he wasn't a part of or hadn't yet had a glimpse into. And in some ways, this was the one that was most important to her. Yes, she wanted him to get along with her friends, maybe even grow to love them like she did and, yes, she wanted him to like living in Windsor, a town she felt rooted in even though she'd been there less than a decade. But this part of her was something that was deeply, deeply personal.

Her books were so much about her and how she viewed the world, or wished she viewed the world, or hoped she didn't view the world, that they had no free will—they were not, in her mind, distinguishable from herself. That's not to say she loved all the characters in her books or only wrote about that which she had lived or wished she had lived, but there was a sliver of truth in every one of her characters. Most of the time that sliver was something she liked or admired about someone, but sometimes it wasn't.

Sometimes, it was something she feared in herself.

And that was what made her nervous about inviting Garret into her world. Because he would know. While most of her readers would never guess or assume that the most unlikeable characters in her books were usually based on herself—she was too nice for that, too kind and pleasant—Garret would know. He would know that she'd dived into her soul, caught one of her fears by its tail, dragged it into the light, and dressed it up with someone else's name. And standing here in the bookstore in Burlington, Vermont, talking about one such character with her readers, he'd know what no one else, not even her mentor Marco Baresi, knew about her. He'd know one of the things she feared the most about herself. It was all laid bare for Garret, and it was a power she was handing to him uneasily, because never in her life had she been this honest about herself with another person.

She hadn't been intentional about it; it wasn't as if she'd sat down with him and told him all about her writing process, but she knew that by watching her talk, watching her move, watching her expressions, and hearing her voice, he would *know*.

It was both freeing and terrifying to have that kind of truth between them.

Kit spared a glance at him as she engaged in a conversation with a young woman who'd come to the signing. He was still leaning against the wall. He had a faint smile pulling up the corners of his mouth. Just as he knew her, she knew him, and she knew that smile on his face was one of pleasure, not one of courtesy.

She let her own pleasure at his reaction show in her eyes as she looked at him, and he answered by letting the smile that had been threatening his visage shine through.

Turning back to the young woman, Kit continued to chat for another minute or two before an older woman stepped up and placed her book on the table. As often as she could, Kit liked to have a meaningful, if short, conversation with each person who came to one of her signings.

So she spent the next few hours signing books and chatting with readers. When all the books were signed, Joseph brought her a cup of tea and she spent another hour lingering in the store, chatting informally with those who remained. All the while, Garret stayed within sight, only occasionally making a round through the store. And those rounds, she suspected, were more to get his body moving than to keep an eye on things.

When the last reader left and Joseph brought her and Garret's coats out from the back, reality slammed into her with the force of a truck. In less than a minute, she felt her energy level switch from the high that always came with meeting readers to something close to panic.

"You're fine," Garret whispered in her ear as he helped her with her coat.

She swallowed. She wasn't sure if she was fine. Kašović hadn't shown up—they hadn't expected him to, not here. But that meant if he *was* planning to come after her today, he was most likely going to do it sometime between the time she set foot outside the bookstore and when she arrived at the cabin.

Hand in hand, they let Joseph lead them through the store and out the back. He chatted the entire time, thanked her for coming, talked about how thrilled he was to host her, and invited her back anytime. She rather liked the young owner, and she really liked the fact that, even knowing that bookstores were going out of business left and right, at his young age he'd decided to make *this* store his business. That took guts.

They stood at the back door and she made a promise to come back, her mind even mulling over the idea of launching her next book there. She didn't want to mention it to Joseph since she'd have to run it by her publicist, but the more she thought about it, the more she liked the idea.

Finally, Joseph opened the door to the alley where they'd parked. The metaphor of doors opening onto opportunities crossed her mind, but this one felt more like one of the gates to Hades with the drive home being like judgment day. Maybe she'd get a reprieve, maybe not.

Garret stepped out first and gave her hand a gentle, reassuring tug. She turned and said one last good-bye to Joseph, then made her way, at Garret's side, to their car.

Snow flurries had started to come down about an hour earlier, but now it looked to be gearing up for an actual snow shower. Small flakes landed on her black coat as they walked the short distance to the car and as she glanced around, she noted a fine dusting covering everything around them.

Great, a killer *and* a snowstorm, she thought. A laugh almost, but not quite, managed to sneak out of her as Garret held the door open for her and she slid into her seat.

"What?" he asked once he'd climbed into the driver's seat.

Kit shook her head. "I think I might be getting a little punchy about this whole thing," she answered.

He cast her a sidelong glance before turning the car on and cranking up the heat. She felt a moment of panic burst through her as thoughts of car bombs exploded into her mind. She must have shown some sign of her state of mind, because Garret took her hand, kissed it, and spoke.

"I asked Drew to have someone watch the car while it was parked. We're fine in here."

She looked at him. He'd had someone watching the car. She let that sink in. Of course he'd had someone watching the car. After their big fight a few days ago, she should have known better than to think he wouldn't have thought about things like that. And with that realization came the guilt—she should know better than to underestimate him; she should trust that he knew what he was doing and that he was doing everything he could to stack the deck in their favor.

Blinking back frustration with herself for being so dense, she turned and looked out the window as Garret began driving out of the alley.

"Kit?" he said, his voice not so much a question but invocation.

And his intimate tone made her feel even worse. "I'm sorry, I didn't mean to panic. I should have trusted you. I mean I *do* trust you, it's just that . . ." She let her voice trail off as he picked her hand up again and brought it to his lips.

"Kit, it's fine. I didn't read anything into your panic about the car. One of the things about situations like this is to say that they are emotionally fraught would be just about the biggest under-statement of the century. And while things like panic and fear can be good some of the time, the constant swirl of what sometimes feels like competing emotions can be hard to deal with." He made a left turn onto the two-lane highway that would take them back to the cabin.

She took a deep breath beside him. "Is it always like this?" she asked, knowing he'd know what she was really asking was whether it was always like this for him. Whether he felt the same maelstrom of emotions that she did.

"Most of the time, yes. Not all the time, but most of the time."

She stared at him. Then blinked. "You mean every time you and my brother go out and do whatever you do, you subject your-self to the same chaos I'm feeling now?" That had to age a body, she thought. Or make you feel like you couldn't let yourself feel anything for fear of feeling everything.

And then everything he'd told her about his place in Mexico and the orphanages made even more sense. They were places where it was safe *to feel*.

"Oh, god, Garret," she said, not bothering to hide the sadness in her voice.

He lifted a shoulder and rueful smile touched his lips. "It's not that bad. After a few years, you don't so much as sift through the emotions, but you do get a sense of the pattern."

"Meaning?"

Again, he shrugged. "It's hard to explain. But after a while, you can recognize the pattern in the chaos. I could tell, depending on what we were doing, if it was going to be emotionally intense, and while I couldn't always anticipate what all those emotions would be, I did know that feeling them, that their existence, was something I would have to recognize and dismiss if I wanted to do my job."

"So, kind of like a process—like step one is planning, step two is prep, step three is panic, step four is moving through the panic, step five is implementing, step six is, well, whatever step six is—and so on?" she asked, trying to understand.

Garret inclined his head. "It sounds very clinical, but yeah, that's about right. You know it's coming and you know you have to move through it, so you recognize it and keep going."

"If you're going through hell . . ." she started.

"Just keep going," Garret finished the same quote she'd heard a time or two from Ian, who'd had it burned it into his mind from the days he was a Ranger.

"That sounds easier said than done," she said after several minutes of silence. The snow was really starting to come down now and Garret had adjusted his driving. They had a good car for the conditions and he was an excellent driver, but the weather would slow them down.

"Sometimes it is. But for you, it most definitely is, since you don't have the same experience I do." He paused, let out another sigh, then reached for her hand again. "This will pass, Kit. I promise you that. I can't give you a magic tip or skill for dealing with the myriad of emotions I know are battling inside you right now, but I can remind you of what we've been working on, of the skills and plans we've been making and practicing this past week. If you ground yourself in what you know, it can sometimes help quell the questions and doubts about what you don't. Do you want to go through it again?"

They'd been through it a million times. In the dead of night, he'd sometimes woken her up to ask where their safe place was if they were separated or what she needed to do if she was forced into the woods and was lost. Dutifully, she'd repeat what he'd taught her. It made her grumpy to be woken up, but she knew why he did it—because when she most needed to remember those things would likely be when she was most unprepared to remember them.

And thinking back on how second nature some of what he'd taught her had become, she realized he was right. Focusing on what she *knew* was a hell of lot better for her confidence than focusing on what she didn't know—or what might happen.

Straightening in her seat, she adjusted the heat, then turned to face him. "I'm ready," she said. "Fire away."

And so for the next forty minutes, he did just that. They went over how she could tell direction from the sun and wind, he drilled her on how best to cover her tracks in the snow, and they talked about the protocol for using the hiding spot he'd found their first day in Vermont—a place they would go to if they were ever separated in the woods.

While Garret's drilling came fast and furious, the drive itself was slow going, and getting slower by the minute as the snowstorm turned almost blizzard-like. Kit was grateful she wasn't driving and kept her eyes trained on Garret rather than the near whiteout conditions of the road in front of them. She had no idea how Garret managed to continue to test her, talk to her, and still stay so calm and focused as he drove. But she was grateful for it. His confidence in driving and in coaching her had the calming effect he no doubt intended.

A small smile played on her lips as he asked her yet another question about how best to maneuver around the lake in conditions such as those they were driving in. She was about to answer when she heard his phone vibrate in the console where it sat between them.

He cast a quick glance at her before reaching for it. She knew he shouldn't be driving and talking at the same time, but she said nothing. Her stomach had dropped at the sound of his phone going off, and coward that she was, she was pretty sure she didn't want to hear whatever message was being relayed to Garret. She didn't know for sure if it would be about her or Kašović, but if she didn't hear it, maybe she could deny the situation for just a little bit longer.

Or not.

Garret glanced at her one more time as he asked several one-word questions. "Where? When? How?" Those words were evidence enough that Kašović was finally making his play, but the final confirmation came when Garret eyed the clock on the dashboard, paused in thought for a few seconds, then replied to whoever was on the other line. "Plan B it is then," he said. "I'll be there in about thirty minutes." He paused again, listening to the unknown speaker. "Okay, let me know if things change," he responded, and then he hung up.

Kit watched him stare out the windshield onto the snowy road. He seemed to be gathering himself up for something. And in that short moment, Kit realized that while Garret was confident in his abilities, he still didn't like what was going on and he, like she, needed to prepare himself for what would come next.

"Garret?" she said, laying a hand on his shoulder. He shot her a quick smile, one that was more burdened than fun, before returning his eyes to the road.

"It's going to be fine," Kit continued, feeling the need to comfort him, reassure him.

He let out a small laugh at that, but he reached for her hand and gave it a squeeze. "Yeah, it will be fine, but we have to get through this part first."

"And what is this *part*?" she asked. "Kašović is here, isn't he?"

Garret nodded.

"Who called you?" she asked.

"Caleb," he answered, slowing the car as they rounded a turn.

When they were back on a straightaway, he continued. "Your brother's been here for a few days. Camping out in the woods," he added.

At that, Kit did have to let out a little laugh. "I don't know what it is with you two and camping, but whatever works for you—as long as you don't make me do it."

She saw the sides of Garret's mouth tip into a smile. "I was only camping on your property all those months ago because your brother thought it would be less complicated if he didn't have to introduce me to you or explain me to anyone."

"Fat lot of good that did," Kit interrupted. "Not, of course, that I'm complaining."

He did smile at that. "I liked coming back to my camp that day to find you sitting there, just waiting for me. It was a surprise, and I hadn't been surprised in a long time. I don't know what would have happened if Caleb had brought me into your home, but being out in the woods kind of gave us a neutral place to meet and talk for the first time. So, I'm not complaining either."

Kit brought his hand up to her lips and brushed a kiss across his knuckles before releasing it so he could have both hands on the wheel. "But I assume that's not the reason my brother is camping? And he must be beyond freezing."

Garret lifted a shoulder. "It's wet and snowy here, but we've been to a lot colder places, and no, you're right, he's not camping to make things less complicated. He's camping because we wanted someone watching the house while we're out, and even when we're not, but we needed someone who couldn't be seen around the house itself."

"You didn't want Kašović scared off," she interjected.

"Or tipped off," Garret added. "We've gone to all this trouble to lure him up here, we didn't want to take the chance that he'd think it was anything more than a writer's getaway once he got up here."

Kit accepted this with a nod. "Okay, so what did my brother say, and assuming he said Kašović has been spotted, what is plan B? And why not plan A?"

She knew Garret would answer, but he took a long pause before doing so. Finally, he let out a deep breath and spoke. "Plan A doesn't work because, while our backup team is on its way, they aren't quite in place yet. So plan B means I'm going to drop you about a half mile from our meeting spot. I want you to walk there and stay there. With the all-weather gear we have here in the car, and that you're going to put on, you shouldn't have any problems staying warm."

Their meeting spot was a cave on the northeast side of the lake that Garret had found on one of their first walks. It was about a mile from the cabin and it was a place she'd been to many times before—a place she could find blindfolded which, in the storm, she practically would be.

She didn't relish the thought of being there alone, but despite the ominous sound of calling it a "cave," it was actually a fairly large opening once you made your way past the narrow entry. Formed years ago by the quarrying in the area, the opening was well hidden by a copse of trees and together, they'd cleaned out the interior enough so that she didn't have to think about things like snakes and spiders—although in the winter, neither was a huge issue. But still—caves, spiders, and snakes just seemed to go together, if only in her mind.

"Okay," Kit nodded, knowing she could make the walk to the spot on her own. She gave more than a moment's thought to saying they should stick together when she remembered her own thoughts from earlier in the car ride. She needed to trust him. She didn't need to like it, but she needed to do it.

Garret slid her a look, his brows raised as if he was waiting for her to protest to being dropped off. She leaned over and kissed his cheek. "Whatever we do, I won't like, because it will put us, all of us, including my brother, in danger. But at this point, what I know I *can* do is trust you."

"And you do," he said. It wasn't a question and though he was still tense, she could see in his shoulders and hear in his voice how much of a relief it was that she did.

"I do," she repeated. "So what happens now and where do you go after you drop me?"

He took another breath, then spoke. "First, I'm going to pull into the lot at the little community store and we're going to get you changed into the gear I have for you so you'll be prepared for the walk. We've got everything in our kits in the back of the car, so you should be set. Once I see you on your way, I'll meet up with your brother and we'll take it from there."

"Do I want to know what 'take it from there' means?" she asked.

"It doesn't mean what you think it means, but even so, I can't tell you exactly what it does mean since however this turns out will depend in large part on what Kašović himself does. What I *can* tell you is that our intent is to capture him."

Not kill him, she noted to herself.

"Okay, so it'll just be you and my brother out there? What about this backup you mentioned?"

Garret lifted a shoulder. "Caleb is checking in with Drew on that. He's sending two men, and last Caleb heard, they were on their way, but we don't know how far out they are."

Kit frowned. That didn't sound like Drew. Drew was one of the most prepared people she'd ever met; it wasn't like him to send people who may or may not make it in time to help. And she said as much to Garret.

Garret inclined his head. "Caleb and I specifically requested the men Drew is arranging for our backup. Drew's been coordinating it and wanted to get them here sooner, but logistics got in the way. Our preference is to hold off on capturing Kašović until they get here, but even if they don't make it in time, your brother and I will be able to handle things."

How they would do that, she didn't know; how they were going to do that she didn't *need* to know—at least not right now, when he was preparing to do battle, so to speak. Even so, her mind and body felt like they were being torn apart by emotions; her anxiety about the situation was battling with the certainty she felt in Garret's ability to do what he said. But as he'd told her earlier, her only real option was to accept that nothing in the situation was going to feel "easy" and she'd just have to live with knowing that whatever was going to happen was going to happen and that, eventually, it would be over. So she swallowed her own panic and said nothing.

They rode the next ten minutes to the community store without another word. And in silence, Garret helped her into her all-weather gear. She changed her socks and shoes, added water-proof pants and a jacket, and checked her hat and gloves.

Once she had all her clothing in order, they methodically went through the backpack Garret had packed and put in the car almost as soon as they'd arrived at the cabin. He'd made one for each of them and she knew what was in it, everything she'd need to keep her warm and fed for over twenty-four hours. She didn't need to go through it again, but doing so gave her an extra few minutes with Garret, so she didn't complain.

When he was satisfied that she had everything she'd need and knew where to find it, he turned and shut the trunk of the car. The snow was still coming down, but he'd parked under the overhanging roof that extended from the store and only a few windswept flakes made their way to where they stood. One landed on her eyelash and before she could sweep it away, Garret slipped his hands into her hair to steady her as he brushed away the flake with his thumb.

When she looked into his eyes, she saw everything that he was leaving unsaid. Fear mixed with intimacy combined with regret and maybe even some guilt shadowed his gaze. Leaning forward, she rested her forehead against his. The mist from their breath mingled. She closed her eyes.

"I'll be fine, Garret," she whispered. His hands tightened in her hair. He said nothing, but drew her mouth up to his. It wasn't a scorching kiss or one meant to ignite her, but it was, without a doubt, the most intimate touch she'd ever experienced.

Feeling tears start to form under her lids, Kit pulled back. The last thing Garret needed was for her to show her own fears and panic. Opening her eyes, she cleared her throat. He was still watching her. Without taking her gaze from his, she slid her own hand over one of his and brought his palm to her lips. Placing a kiss there, she stepped back. His other hand fell away.

"We need to go," she said. His gaze lingered for a moment, but then he nodded. She gave his hand one last squeeze, then turned and made her way to the passenger side of the car. Garret was already in the driver's side when she reached for her seatbelt.

Pulling out of the small parking lot, Kit kept her gaze on the barely visible landscape. Every now and then she caught a glimpse of a house or smoke coming from a chimney, but it was hard to make out much more than that.

"So, is the plan what we already talked about? I'll just meet you at the cave?"

Garret nodded as a wave of melancholy swept through her at the thought of being alone—waiting. Garret had packed a satellite phone in the backpack for her, even though they'd checked the reception in the area and knew she'd be able to place calls from her cell. Both phones had all the necessary numbers programmed in and ready to go should she need them. She would never be truly alone. But still, all she really hoped was that Garret would return to her, in person, as soon as possible.

With everything confirmed and in order, there seemed nothing left to do or say. And so, for the short five-minute ride to where Garret would drop her, she said nothing more. When he pulled over onto the dirt road that led to the trail she would take to the cave, they said nothing. When he opened the door and she stepped onto the unplowed road, there was nothing but the sound of the car's running engine. And when he helped her on with her pack, she could swear she heard the sound of the snowflakes landing on the ground.

But when she turned and walked away, she heard him all but whisper, "I love you, Kit."

She didn't turn back to look at him when she replied, "I love you too."

CHAPTER 19

GARRET STAYED AND WATCHED KIT until her form was swallowed up by the snow and she was no longer visible. And then, for a moment, he stared into the empty whiteness in front of him. All his fears reared their heads in one fell swoop and he nearly dropped the plan and went after her. Nothing he had ever done—and he had done a lot—had ever been so difficult as watching her walk away.

Forcing his gaze and his body to move away from the road, Garret climbed into the car and dropped heavily into the driver's seat. For a moment, he sat waiting, hoping she'd come back. But as soon as he acknowledged the wish, he put the car in gear and pulled away. He didn't really want her to come back. Not if they wanted this thing with Kašović to be over. And if she did come back, he couldn't be there because he was pretty sure he wouldn't be able to watch her walk away a second time.

So he made his way down the snowy road to where he and Caleb had agreed to meet. Kašović was lying in wait near the house. The plan was to come at him from behind. Or at least *he* was planning on coming at Kašović from behind. Caleb would take the car straight to the house and circle back behind the building. From where Kašović had stationed himself, he was facing the southwest side of the house, more to the west. He would be able to watch the car make its way up the drive, but once it came around the last bend toward the parking area, it would leave his line of sight.

Both Caleb and Garret were counting on the reduced visibility and lighting to help ensure that Kašović wouldn't be able to see who was—or wasn't—in the car. There weren't many perks about working in these kinds of weather conditions, but it did make the element of surprise a little easier. Unfortunately, that worked both ways.

Forcing his mind to stay focused on the plan and not on Kit, Garret pulled to the side of the road. Rather than climb out of the car and into the snow, he crawled to the back and pulled out his own pack. He donned his own winter gear, checked his kit and then, once he was sure everything was in order, he checked the pistol he had strapped to his ankle. Confident it would stay dry and in place, he double-checked the weapon now strapped to his chest as well. Only then did he climb out of the car and around to the back.

Staying under the protection of the back door, he pulled out a locked box, keyed in the security code, and gently lifted the lid. His rifle lay there, cleaned and ready to go.

He examined it quickly, made sure it had ammunition loaded, locked it, and slung it over his back. He didn't think he'd need it, but just in case, he grabbed some extra ammo and shoved it in the pocket of his white jacket. Gently, he closed the trunk, took a deep breath, and began to make his way toward Caleb.

One of the other benefits of working in snow, Garret mused as he made his way to Caleb, half a mile into the woods, was that it didn't let you let your mind wander. There was no way he could spare any deep thoughts for Kit as he made his way through the conditions that were now rapidly changing from a snowstorm to an ice storm.

With a glance upward, he hoped the change would hold off long enough they wouldn't have to worry about any branches coming down under the weight of the ice. He was pretty sure they would have Kašović under control fairly quickly, but then they had to wait for Drew's team for the retrieval. Though he trusted Drew and knew he had everything covered, Garret wasn't sure how the weather would impact the arrival of the team.

Garret paused and checked his GPS. Caleb was less than forty feet away, and Garret couldn't even see him. For a moment, he wondered just how close his partner had had to get in order to see Kašović. But he pushed that thought aside and made his way a little farther into the woods. Two minutes later, he could make out Caleb's form against a tree.

Caleb stood, binoculars in hand, not moving from his position. But Garret didn't need a greeting to know that the other man knew he was there—not after all these years.

Garret came up beside his partner, who handed him the binoculars without a word. Putting them up to his face, Garret could see nothing but the heat signature of a man—or what he assumed was a man. Kašović.

One more benefit of the snow was that it certainly made heat signatures easier to spot.

Kašović was lying on one of the many big boulders that littered the area. From there, he would have a perfect view of the house and the path that led from the parking area to the front door, though not the parking area itself. Garret wished he knew what kind of rifle the man was holding, but while the binoculars were good for some things, they weren't good for that kind of detail, and Kašović was too far away to see anything else. Especially in this weather.

Lowering the binoculars, Garret unstrapped his rifle. "How did you even find him?" he asked, keeping his voice low.

Caleb shrugged and shoved himself off the tree. "I would have seen him anyway since he picked one of the five spots I've been keeping my eye on for his position. But he also happened to walk about twenty feet in front of me."

Garret shot his partner a look.

"Yeah, surprised the hell out of me too. Thankfully, lady luck was on my side and I'd been lying low on the ground with a thin layer of snow covering me. I don't know that he would have seen me even if he'd been looking, but he wasn't and I just blended in."

"You'll have to toast Mother Nature for that little bit of aid when this is all over," Garret answered as he handed Caleb the keys.

"Many times over," Caleb replied. "Hopefully, with some hot

whiskey. And maybe some hot women," he added with a grin. Leave it to Caleb to grin at a time like this.

"I'll join you in the whiskey and I already have a hot woman, so I'm good on that front," Garret said, bringing the binoculars back to his eyes. Kašović hadn't so much as twitched.

Caleb let out a little snort. "Yeah, that's my sister, so you'd better be good with just the one."

Garret smiled, but kept his eyes trained on Kašović. "What, no warnings, no threats to beat me up if I hurt her? Which I won't, by the way."

He heard the light rustle of Caleb's jacket and assumed he was shrugging. "I don't need to warn you or threaten you. You know perfectly well what I'm capable of, and it would just insult us both for me to spell it out."

Garret had to chuckle at that. It was true. Anything Caleb put into words wouldn't be half of what he was actually capable of doing. He was about to reply when his phone buzzed with a message. Handing Caleb the binoculars, he fished his phone out his pocket, tugged a glove off, and pulled up the message. A wave of relief washed over him; he keyed in a quick response to the sender and then another quick note to Kit before slipping the device back into his pocket.

"Our backup has arrived. They're getting their gear ready," Garret said, pulling on his glove and taking the binoculars back.

"Did you let Kit know to expect them?" Caleb asked.

Not taking his eyes from the binoculars, Garret nodded. "I told her our backup was here so she wouldn't worry. They know about the cave, of course, but the plan is for them to gear up at their vehicle and intercept us between here and there," he answered. "Kit should never even see them."

"Or any part of what we're all about to do." Caleb voiced Garret's thought.

It wasn't that what they were about to do would shock her, but if Garret had his way, Kit wouldn't see any of it and would only know when it was finished and Kašović was no longer a threat.

"You better get going or he's going to get suspicious about how long it's taking us to get back," Garret said. "I'm sure he knows what time the signing ended and the snow has bought us some leeway since it will be easy to assume it slowed us down . . ." His voice trailed off.

"I'm on my way," Caleb said without further ado.

But after he took two steps, Garret heard him pause so he swung around to look at his partner.

"Are you really okay?" Caleb asked.

Garret gave a tense nod.

"I know the mechanics of this operation are something you could do in your sleep, but this one, with Kit," even Caleb's quiet voice caught a little as he spoke her name. "Well, with Kit involved, it turns it all into a little bit of a nightmare."

Garret wasn't sure what to say about Caleb's concern, so he simply gave another short nod.

"But you're good with this plan? I could take your place," Caleb offered. "You could go be with Kit."

Garret bit back the "yes" he wanted to answer and shook his head. "You know it won't work that way. Not now that our backup is in place. We have to get Kašović walking toward the meeting spot and it has to be me who gets him there. I'm the only one he'll believe."

Caleb regarded him for a long moment then gave a sharp nod, not so much in agreement but in recognition of the truth of what Garret was saying.

"How long do you need?" Caleb asked.

Garret swung the glasses back to Kašović. He was about a quarter of a mile away, maybe a little more. "Fifteen minutes," he answered. He didn't need to see Caleb to know he'd heard; within seconds the sounds of Caleb moving toward the car were swallowed up by the dampening snow.

Ignoring the cold touching his cheeks and seeping through his gloves, Garret stood still and quiet as the mix of ice and snow fell around him.

With another look at Kašović, still flat out on the boulder, Garret pulled his eyes from the binoculars and glanced at his watch. Five minutes to go. Slinging the binoculars over his shoulder, he began to make his way toward the assassin. Moving quietly enough to seem as though he was trying to sneak up on his target but loud enough to alert Kašović, Garret approached the man from his left. A few times he paused, more for effect than for any other reason, but mostly he made his way steadily forward.

Garret heard Caleb intentionally rev the engine as he pulled the car into the parking area. By this time, Garret was close enough to see Kašović through the falling precipitation, which had now turned almost completely to ice. He paused for a reason this time and watched as Kašović's head came up and his back tensed in anticipation. Garret's eyes flicked toward the man's hands and he saw the assassin's finger twitch lightly on the trigger—not enough to pull it, but just enough to remind the digit of what its job would ultimately be.

Only that wasn't going to happen.

Garret was thirty feet away when he saw Kašović realize that something wasn't quite right. No one, not Kit or anyone else, had emerged from the parking area to walk the path to the front door—the path that would lead her right into his crosshairs. Kašović drew back from his scope just enough to look with his naked eye, though Garret knew this movement was more of an instinctive move than anything else, since the visibility hadn't improved that much. Whatever Kašović could see through his scope would be much clearer than anything he would be able to see without it. Although, Garret conceded to himself, what the man could see through his scope was somewhat limited in range—the narrow site wouldn't be able to show Kašović what was going on anywhere else other than what could be seen through the tiny hole.

Silently, Garret swung his rifle up. This was the moment of truth. The moment he could—the moment he *would*—bring an end to everything that was happening to Kit. And then Kašović swung around, moving faster than any man of his years ought to.

Before Garret had a chance to bring his rifle to the ready, he was in Kašović's crosshairs.

They both froze in that tableau. Garret didn't even bother to look toward the house to see if he could make out Caleb. But rather, he kept his eyes locked on Kašović, on those ice-blue eyes that had already tried not once, but twice, to kill Kit.

"If you kill me, you'll never find her," Garret said, his hands in front of him, still gripping his rifle.

"And I'm supposed to believe that if I *don't* kill you, you'll tell me where she is," Kašović countered.

Garret didn't answer.

A hint of a knowing smile lifted Kašović's lips. "So we're at a bit of an impasse, aren't we?" he said, his Serbian accent tinged with the hint of a South American inflection.

Garret inclined his head.

"It turns out, I don't much like impasses," Kašović said.

Garret heard the words but before he had time to react, he heard a shot. Searing pain lanced through his chest and the last thing he remembered before everything went black was the icy sharpness of the snow burning into his cheek as he collapsed.

• • •

Kit paused, then glanced behind her. Well, if anyone looked with anything more than a passing glance, they'd see her tracks. She had tried to cover them as best as she could using the technique Garret had taught her, but it wasn't as easy as swishing a branch over her footprints. Thankfully, the snow, and now ice, was still falling, which helped camouflage her trail a bit.

She pulled her phone out of her pocket to look at the time just as a text message from Garret came in. She let out sigh of relief reading that their backup had arrived as planned. She didn't really know what that meant, or what the specifics of the actual plan were, but at least she knew Caleb and Garret weren't alone.

It had taken her fifteen minutes to get to the cave—well,

almost to the cave. She could see the angled birch tree that marked its entrance even though she wasn't quite there yet. She sighed and admitted to herself that she'd been lollygagging. She potentially had hours to wait for Garret; it was easier to waste some of that time walking to their meeting spot than getting there fast and sitting with nothing to do but stare at the walls and think about all the things that could be happening. All the things that could go wrong.

Of course, Garret could also be coming along at any moment. She knew the rough workings of his plan to sneak up on Kašović, but she didn't know—and Garret couldn't tell her—how he was going to do that or how long that could take. She hoped not long; she hoped Garret would come along within the next thirty minutes. But she was also trying not to get her hopes up too high.

Her breath fogged in front of her as she sighed and turned back toward the cave. To her left, a branch cracked under the weight of the weather and she startled, then turned to watch the limb crash down in a big puff of snow and ice. Momentarily distracted, she nearly stumbled over her own feet when she caught a glimpse of movement—*human* movement—just beyond the settling branch.

For one fleeting second, she was frozen, her mind refusing to comprehend what she'd seen. Then adrenaline exploded through her system. Her heart launched itself into her throat and any chill she'd been experiencing from the freezing temperatures was now a thing of the past. Sweat gathered on her neck and her breaths came fast and furious.

She cursed herself for taking so long to get to the cave—if she hadn't been needlessly wasting time, she'd already be safe inside. But now, as it was, she was pretty sure she didn't want to go in there. She didn't know who was in the woods with her, but she knew it wasn't her brother or Garret—they would have called out to her, or at least texted her a message. And leading someone she didn't know into a place with only one entrance and one exit wasn't something she was dumb enough to do, not even with all the panic coursing through her system.

Forcing herself to take a deep breath and slow down, she stood as still as she could. She was still somewhat in the forest; she hadn't yet made it to the clearing they'd designated as their meeting place. Maybe she was still hidden. Maybe whoever was out there hadn't seen her.

And just who was out there?

Of course her first thought was Kašović. But as the seconds ticked by, her gut was telling her what her mind wouldn't accept quite yet. It *couldn't* be Kašović. She knew her brother had his eyes on the man and that if Kašović had started heading in her direction, either Caleb or Garret would have let her know. There was always the possibility that Kašović had gotten to her brother, but the possibility that he'd gotten to *both* Garret and Caleb before either could send her some signal didn't seem possible.

But even her slow recognition of the logic didn't entirely ease her mind. There was still *someone* there, and she had no idea who. It could be the backup that Garret had texted her about. But he hadn't said anything about them being anywhere near the cave. And while she supposed it could be a neighbor who hadn't seen her so hadn't bothered to say hello, she wasn't quite ready to buy that. Mostly because the movement she'd seen had been swift and sure—not those of someone out for a leisurely winter walk in the forest or of someone trying to take cover from an unexpected ice storm.

Slowly, she inched her way toward the trunk of a large tree. Its diameter was enough to hide her if someone was watching from the other side, but it wasn't so large as to provide much more cover than that. Still, the solid wood against her back provided an unexpected sense of support.

Casting her eyes into the forest around her, she willed herself to see more than just the falling snow and ice. Within a few seconds, she could make out the lines of other trees more easily, leafless bushes crushed under the weight of the winter, and even the rocky shore of the lake off in the distance.

What she couldn't see was any sign of a human presence.

Taking more comfort from the tree than she knew she should,

she waited—silent and unmoving. Slowly, the cold began to penetrate her clothing and her body grew chilled after the initial adrenaline rush. And still, she heard nothing. Saw nothing.

Kit shivered in her coat and began to wonder if maybe she hadn't seen what she thought she'd seen. Perhaps all she'd seen was another branch falling in an unusual way, or snow being thrown as it was knocked about by the falling limb. A few more minutes of silence passed, and she knew she had to do something. The cold was seeping through to her bones, and the snow and ice mix had turned sharply to ice alone—or, as she thought when one pelted her in the face, ice daggers.

She thought about trying to text Caleb or Garret, but didn't want to disturb them if they were in the middle of something. And so, standing there on her own, she accepted that she'd have to make her own plan. Pushing away from the shelter of the tree, Kit turned toward the cave.

She'd taken six steps when a man appeared out of the storm before her. She stumbled backward; the shock was so great that she had a fleeting thought she might actually be having a heart attack. But then she heard the report of a rifle off in the distance and everything coalesced into one crystal clear moment.

Knowing it probably wasn't her only option, but it was likely her best, she spun and ran.

Right into the arms of another man.

On instinct, she scrambled back, fighting to get out of the second man's grip. But in the snow and ice, her feet found no purchase. Finally, she twisted away and, sucking in a deep breath, she prepared to scream and run. But the man grabbed ahold of her jacket from behind just as her boot landed on a patch of packed ice.

As her feet left the ground and she started to fall backward, she knew she'd just made what would likely end up being the biggest mistake of her life. When her head slammed into something hard under the thick snow and pain shot through her body, a crushing sense of having failed Garret was her last thought before her mind faded into darkness.

CHAPTER 20

GARRET FELT THE SNOW AND ice melting against the heat of his cheek as he lay on his side. He hadn't been out long, probably not more than the few seconds it took to get over the shock of having been shot. But still, he didn't open his eyes.

Taking a moment to assess the situation, he reminded himself that this was all part of the plan. Well, getting shot wasn't exactly part of the plan, but getting Kašović to use him to find Kit was because it was the only way they could think to get Kašović moving toward the meeting spot along the route they'd mapped out for their backup.

The plan wasn't airtight, but the only thing that made Garret and Caleb and Drew so sure about it was that Kašović was predictable. Kašović was very, very good at his job, but like many leaders of the old-school military regimes, there was an order to everything and everything had an order.

Garret had counted on that order. He'd counted on being caught, counted on Kašović trying to *convince* him to reveal Kit's location. And he was counting on Kašović to believe that, after some show of force on Kašović's part—albeit somewhat more forcible that Garret had anticipated—Garret would be more interested in saving his own skin than protecting Kit.

The subtle warmth of another body invaded Garret's space and he knew, without looking, that Kašović was standing over him, assessing the damage. Garret had no doubt that Kašović had hit exactly where he'd aimed—Garret's right shoulder. Painful enough to make a point, but not dangerous enough to cause death. At least not immediate death.

Still, it hurt like hell.

"You should open your eyes," came Kašović's voice.

Garret debated for a moment, just to piss Kašović off, but then decided to comply, figuring the man probably wasn't above getting a kick in or maybe even another shot.

Garret rolled to his back and lifted his lids. Kašović stood over him, rifle in hand, appearing casual and almost careless, but Garret knew better. He noticed his cell phone in Kašović's hand—he must have been out a little longer than he'd initially thought, since he hadn't felt the man go through his pockets.

"The code?" Kašović said, holding up the device.

Garret smirked and let out a small laugh that jarred his shoulder; his smirk quickly turned into a grimace. "I don't think so."

"I could shoot you again."

Garret eyed him before answering. "You could, but you'd run the risk of making me pass out from the blood loss, and then you'd never have the time to figure out how to get into my phone and find her before she's long gone."

Kašović's expression was completely blank—not vapid-blank, but calculating-blank. Sociopath-blank.

"Then we are at an impasse again. And I believe you know my feelings on impasses," Kašović said, still watching Garret.

Garret paused for a long moment before speaking again, but it was more for effect than for any other reason. "I'll take you to her," he finally said.

A muscle in Kašović's cheek ticked, the only indication that he'd heard the offer. Then he inclined his head. "Why would you do that? You don't expect me to believe that you'll simply lead me to her."

Garret let out another chuckle. Pushing himself into a sitting position with his left arm, he began to shake the snow from his body. Kašović stepped back but made no other move to raise his rifle.

"No, I don't expect you to believe that," Garret said. "But the truth is, I know where she is and you don't. If I don't tell you, you'll shoot me. If I tell you, you'll shoot me *and* shoot her. But if I take you to her, at least I buy myself some time to figure out the best way to send you to hell."

Slowly, he got his legs under him, and not without effort, raised himself to a standing position. He'd been divested of his own rifle—where it was he couldn't say, but it wasn't anywhere visible. He also noted that his jacket was open. The bad news was that meant Kašović had his holstered gun as well. The good news was that the cold that had flooded through the opening had worked to numb the pain in his shoulder a bit.

"There's a trap," Kašović said, taking another step back but not moving too far away. "Clearly you have someone helping you," he said with a nod toward the cabin, toward the car parked there.

Garret wagged his head as he tried to brush the ice off his chest and get his jacket zipped. "Maybe, but you don't have many options either. If I take you to her, I buy time to think about how to get rid of your sorry ass and you buy time to figure out whether or not it really is a trap, and if it is, how to get away without becoming a casualty."

Kašović seemed to think this over for a long moment, or at least that's what Garret thought might be going on. Getting a good read on a sociopath wasn't exactly a cake walk.

"Call her," Kašović said, tossing Garret's phone back to him. "Have her meet us at the cabin," he ordered.

Garret could have caught the phone—he was pretty good with his left hand, but opted to fumble and let it drop to the ground. Reaching down, he double-checked his ankle holster. Surprisingly, the gun was still there. Then again, it was more tucked into his boot than strapped to his ankle, which made it harder to find—but harder to reach, too.

Straightening up, he ignored Kašović's order and slid the phone into his pocket. Turning away, he started to walk. It was a gamble and when he heard Kašović raise his rifle, all the hairs on his neck stood on end. He might die in the next few moments, but if he did, at least he knew Kit would be safe because he also knew Caleb was out there watching. He believed the plan was a good one and he had no intention of dying. But like he'd already told himself, getting into the mind of a sociopath wasn't exactly easy.

• • •

Kit came to wakefulness with the same kind of shock as being dunked in a bucket of ice—abruptly, completely, and not at all comfortably. Her eyes, now open, took in her location—lying on her side, covered with a blanket, on the floor of the cave. Her head ached like it was about to implode.

Something vibrating on the floor of the enclosure made her head pound even more. It was a sound that seemed to echo off the walls, but was probably quieter than when her phone went off in her purse. Her eyes followed the noise and it was then that she spotted the two men toward the opening of the cave. One of the men, who sat with his knees propped up and his back resting against one of the walls, picked up the phone and read the message before keying something back in. The other man was on his knees examining what looked to be a rifle about half as tall as she was. The man who had the phone said something quietly to the other man, who glanced up at his companion and gave a quick nod.

The light from outside was casting their faces into shadows; from where she lay, she couldn't really tell their ages. They were dressed in winter clothing, clothing Kit recognized as that of the two men she'd encountered in the woods before blacking out, though their white jackets lay beside them on the cave floor.

She frowned. She never fainted. Then she remembered the struggle and then her fall. As the memory came back, her stomach roiled in fear. Who were these men? And what did they want with her?

Eyeing them, she wondered if they were in league with Kašović—if they were, they might be waiting for him to join them in the cave. At the thought of what three men could do to her, it was no longer just her stomach that protested.

"Miss Forrester, if you are awake, you are welcome to join us," the man leaning against the wall said without even looking in her direction. The other man, however, did. And when he turned, she could see that he was young, about her age, maybe a few years older. His face was set and serious, but not unkind. Again, she frowned in confusion.

A small smile touched the man's mouth. "I'm Zoran Delic and this is my father, Ivo," he said with a nod to the other man.

Delic, why did that name sound familiar? Kit plowed through her memory as she brought her legs underneath her and sat up. Her head spun for a moment, but that discomfort was quickly replaced by another—a violent shiver that racked her body. She grabbed the blanket and wrapped it around her, feeling a little bit like a kid.

Delic! And then she knew exactly what was going on.

"Kašović killed your family," she blurted out without thinking, remembering the conversation she'd overheard Drew, Caleb, and Garret having in her apartment shortly after they'd learned that Kašović had been hired to kill her.

The older man looked away, but Zoran answered. "Yes, ours and many others."

Kit met Zoran's gaze and saw not just sorrow and anger for his own loss, but compassion for the many others who had experienced the same.

"I'm so sorry," she mumbled, feeling horribly inadequate. Zoran dipped his head in acknowledgement and went back to examining his rifle.

A few moments later, the phone buzzed again and the elder Delic responded. Sliding it into his pocket this time, he said something to Zoran that Kit couldn't hear. Zoran nodded, held out a hand to his father, and helped him up. It was the signal Kit needed to remind her of just what was going on.

"Drew sent you, didn't he?" she asked, remembering what Garret had said to her before dropping her off.

Zoran nodded. "Your brother and Cantona actually requested our involvement. Drew organized it," he said, helping his dad get into his coat and outfitted in some kind of gear Kit didn't recognize. "I've worked with your brother and Cantona a few times over the years—I'm an Army Ranger now—and when they realized what was going on, they asked Drew to bring me and my father in."

"Do you know Ian MacAllister?" she asked before she could stop herself. Then rolled her eyes at herself.

Zoran gave a sharp nod. "I heard he settled in New York. You know him?"

He seemed to be humoring her. And she was okay with that. "He did. We live in the same area; his wife is a good friend of mine. *He's* a good friend of mine. His son is adorable."

Zoran gave another smile at that, then went back to getting ready. For what, she didn't know. Not exactly.

She watched the men in silence. Zoran checked one last thing on his father's gear, then stepped back. Both men shared a look that, even from where she was sitting, needed no interpretation. Then the older man gave his son a quick hug and walked out of the cave. She watched the cave opening for a long moment after he had disappeared and, just as she was about to look away, he reappeared. Stopping three feet into the enclosure, he paused and looked at her.

"I am sorry, Miss Forrester, that Kašović has you in his sights. I know it must be a trying time for you. But I thank your brother and your friend for contacting my son and giving us this opportunity to see that justice is done." With that he turned again and walked away.

Kit didn't expect him to return again, so she switched her gaze to Zoran. She thought about asking just what kind of justice was going to be done, but decided she'd rather not know. And it appeared Zoran didn't wish to speak about it either.

"In a few minutes, I'll leave too. Shortly after that, Cantona will bring Kašović here. He says you trust him."

It wasn't really a question, but Kit nodded. "But why is Garret bringing him here?" The thought of being in a confined space with no escape when Kašović arrived didn't sound all that great.

Zoran inclined his head. "We, my father and I, had hoped to get here sooner and then, yes, we could have taken care of him without bringing him anywhere near you. We could have taken care of him where he was lying in wait outside the cabin," he responded to her unspoken concern. "But with time being short and the weather being what it is, we had to move onto our alternate plan."

"Which is to bring him here?" Kit asked.

Zoran dipped his head. "Not so much specifically *here*," he said, indicating the cave. "But moving toward here. Your brother and Cantona are keeping him occupied by moving him toward this cave to give my father and me time to get into position."

"But?" Kit pressed, because she'd heard a "but" in his statement, even if he hadn't said it.

"But my father and I weren't able to get here or gear up as quickly as we had originally anticipated," he answered.

"So that means Garret will be leading Kašović closer to here, closer to me, than you all had planned in order to give you and your father time to set up." Kit stated.

Zoran nodded. Then he hesitated, his hand paused on his weapon. His head fell a fraction and his eyes closed. For a moment, Kit wondered if he was praying.

But then his head came up and his eyes, grim with the history of his family and his people, locked onto hers. "You have no idea what being here today means to my father and me. Your brother and Cantona could have taken care of Kašović on their own today. But not only did they request our involvement, they have delayed the capture and orchestrated the events so that my father and I can be there, can be the ones to do it."

Kit watched as Zoran blinked several times then looked away.

She said nothing as he took a few minutes to regain his composure. When he was ready, he turned to face her again. "It means more than you can know to be here today, and you have our eternal gratitude for letting us be a part of it."

In all her years, the closest she'd ever come to hearing the kind of emotion she heard in Zoran's voice were the voices of her characters in her own head when she wrote. And that depth of emotion wasn't something she had adequate words to respond to, so she simply nodded. He held her gaze for a moment, then gave her a small nod in return and went back to his task.

"Are you going to be okay?" Zoran asked after a moment, gesturing with his head to the blanket she still held around her.

She shrugged off his concern. "I'm just cold. And feeling a little disoriented. I fell, right?" she asked, wincing as she felt a knot on the back of her head—a knot that would explain her headache.

To his credit, Zoran looked a little chagrined. "Yes, we didn't want you to scream and give Kašović an idea of your location so we tried to subdue you, perhaps a little too forcefully, and you slipped," he said.

She noticed he didn't say he was sorry for it. "Well," she said on an exhale, "if it matters, I think my disorientation has more to do with this whole situation than with any minor head injury. I mean, really, what's a little concussion amongst friends?"

At that, Zoran barked out a laugh. "You'll do fine, Kit," he said, still chuckling.

"Yeah, I know. I'll be fine. I'm always fine. But may I ask something before you go?" she said quickly, because he looked to be doing a final check of his clothing and gear. "I'm glad you're here, but why didn't I know you were coming? I mean, Garret told me backup was coming, but he never mentioned you and your father," she added.

Zoran zipped up his jacket and turned to face her. "Drew contacted my unit as soon as Caleb asked him to, but I was deployed, well, somewhere it wasn't easy to get back from. It took a little while for the message to get to me and then for me to get out and back to the States. Your brother and Cantona might not have known until a short while ago that we were indeed going to be here. And by then, my guess is Cantona's mind was occupied with things other than making sure you knew the names of his backup—backup I'm fairly certain he thought you'd have no cause to even meet." He paused and gave her one last assessing look. "But we're here now and I can promise you that whatever happens next, all this will be over in the next thirty minutes," he added.

That sounded nice. "Promise?" Kit asked with a smile.

Zoran shot her a smile back. "Promise," he said.

And then he was gone. Leaving her to sit in silence and wait. And wait.

For what felt like the longest time, Kit heard nothing but the pinging sound of the ice storm still waging outside the cave. She tried her best not to let her mind wander to everything that *could* happen, so she grabbed hold of every random thought thread that dared traipse through her mind. She wondered how Vivi, Ian, and baby Jeffery were doing, and if there were fires in this kind of weather and, if so, if David was working. Chances were Jesse was at home making dinner, as were Matty and Dash. She knew they were all anxious for her to be back in Windsor—not, of course, as anxious as she was—and she looked forward to sitting down to one of Matty's amazing meals or curling up on the couch to catch up with Jesse.

It didn't come as a complete shock when she realized that Garret was a part of all these daydreams. He was with her in Matty and Dash's kitchen, he was having a beer with David while she and Jesse talked, and he and Ian, well, they could go off into the woods and relive their covert ops days. Actually, that thought did make her smile because she *could* imagine them having a rousing game of paintball in the woods around her home while she and Vivi enjoyed a glass of wine or two.

She shifted in her blanket, still smiling at the image of the guys playing paintball, then froze. Cocking her ear toward the entrance of the cave, she strained to hear what she'd just thought she'd heard. Garret.

And there. There it was again. She couldn't hear his words, but the wind had picked up his voice and carried it toward her. Relief washed through her at knowing that at least he was fine enough to be talking. To be coming to her.

Dropping the blanket, she approached the cave entrance but didn't step out. Zoran's voice echoed in her mind, his order telling her to trust Garret and do what he said. Thanks to the Ranger, she now had a better idea of what was going to happen, though she still didn't know the specifics of how they would capture Kašović. But she had full faith in Garret and Caleb, and Zoran's quiet confidence had given her a surety she now took refuge in. And since Garret hadn't told her to come out, she wasn't going to set foot outside of that cave.

But that didn't mean she couldn't inch closer to its opening. Especially not now that she could tell from his voice the direction he was coming from and could even catch a few of his words. The cave was already difficult to see into from the direction she knew Garret was coming from, and if she kept to one side, no one would be able to see her at all unless they walked straight into the opening.

"So, do you have a plan yet, Kašović?" she heard Garret say.

What? Kašović was *with* him? Her throat choked up as she felt the blood pound through her body. Every bit of assurance she'd just felt fled as panic crawled over her skin. She'd heard what Zoran had said about Garret getting Kašović closer to the cave, but she had assumed that meant Garret was creating a trail for Kašović to *follow*. She hadn't imagined that Garret would be walking *with* him.

"No, seriously, Kašović," Garret said now. "I'm just curious, because we're almost there and, well, I *do* have a plan."

Kit could hear them making their way closer to where she hid and Garret was making no effort to quiet his arrival. Which gave her pause. He was *always* quiet, even when he wasn't trying to be quiet. But now, by his standards, he was crashing through the woods like an elephant.

Giving her a warning.

As soon as the thought entered her mind, she knew that was exactly what he was doing. Giving her some time to prepare for their arrival, to prepare for the fact that Kašović was with him, to prepare for whatever came next. Unbidden, a smile touched her lips. Even despite what was going on, despite the fact that he was walking through the woods with a killer—an armed killer, no doubt—he was thinking of her.

Abruptly, the sounds came to a halt and she knew without looking that Garret and Kašović had reached the clearing in front of the cave.

She thought she heard someone say, "Where is she?" but the voice was gruff and muffled and she couldn't be certain.

"Kit, honey, why don't you come out?" Garret said. His tone was light, but she could hear now what she hadn't been able to hear before—an underlying anxiety that laced his every word.

"Where is she?" the voice repeated.

"Kit, remember what we talked about in the car? It's time to come out," Garret said.

Kit sucked in a breath. They'd talked about trust in the car. It seemed to be the topic of the day and this seemed to be the biggest test. Stepping into sight of the man who had been hired to kill her was only possible when she also accepted the fact that if she didn't, Kašović would most likely kill Garret. He hadn't said as much, but now, knowing they were together, it didn't take a genius to figure out what was likely to happen if she didn't do as Garret said.

And so she did. Tentatively, she approached the edge of the cave's opening, then took a single step out. Blinking away the ice that hit her face and gathered on her eyelashes, her heart nearly stopped when her gaze landed on Garret.

It was a miracle she was breathing at all. Garret stood about thirty feet before her with a gun pressed to his head and blood staining his right shoulder. His eyes met hers and he seemed to be apologizing, but for what she couldn't fathom. If anyone should be feeling sorry about the situation, it was her. She was the one Kašović wanted.

Switching her eyes to the man in question, she met his empty stare. He was older than she'd expected and, vacant stare notwithstanding, looked more like an elderly grandfather than a killer. But then again, just because he was one, didn't mean he couldn't be both.

"There you are, my dear," Kašović said.

And then everything happened at once.

Kašović grabbed Garret's shoulder and, using the pain there to weaken him, dropped him to the ground. As he raised his rifle, Kit realized that Kašović planned to kill Garret first *then* kill her. Even in the split second it took for her to understand this, she knew it was the best plan, because if Kašović killed her first, Garret would never let him survive.

As Garret grunted and rolled over on the ground, she screamed a warning. Frantically, she looked around for something to distract Kašović as his finger closed around the trigger. Finding nothing, no way to stop him, she did the only thing she could think of doing, and that was to run toward him. She'd taken two steps when she heard the shot.

Much to her shock, Kašović dropped.

CHAPTER 21

UNABLE TO COMPREHEND WHAT HAD just happened, Kit slid to a halt. Garret, on the other hand, rolled over and kicked Kašović's gun out of reach. She felt like she was watching everything from a distance—or in a movie—but within seconds, Garret was at her side.

"Kit, are you okay?" he asked. "Kit?" he repeated when she didn't immediately answer.

Her eyes were glued to Kašović, and even though in the back of her mind she knew there were three other shooters out there—Zoran, Ivo, and her brother—there didn't seem to be any blood on their target. And there should be blood, right? She should be able to see it pooling in the snow, staining it with his hatred and sins. But there was nothing.

"Kit?" Garret slipped his hands inside the hood of her jacket and forced her face toward his. Almost unwillingly, her eyes sought his.

"There's no blood?" she asked, her eyes going back to Kašović. And then panic shot through her system again. "There's no blood, Garret! He isn't dead, we can't be standing here—"

"Hey." He cut her off gently, trying to get her attention, even as she struggled against him.

They couldn't be there, she thought. If Kašović wasn't dead, they were still in danger.

"He's as good as, Kit. Trust me. Can you hear me?"

Slowly the words penetrated her fear, and though she wasn't calm, she felt the first inkling of curiosity. Her inner struggle must have been apparent because she could see Garret's shoulders drop just a hair when she looked back into his eyes.

His shoulder. "Oh my god, Garret. Your shoulder. What happened to you?" she demanded as she stepped back and tried examining him through the thick layers of clothing.

"He got shot," said Caleb, as he made his way over the top of the cave down to the clearing to join them. "Stupid bloody bastard," he added, coming to stop beside her. She looked at her brother, then back at Garret. She knew what had happened, but she didn't *know* what had happened, and between the fear and the adrenaline, she was having a hard time sorting it out.

"That wasn't part of the plan, Cantona," Caleb said.

Garret shrugged his left shoulder. "It hurts like hell, but it's not gonna kill me."

Kit blinked at that statement. Then almost slapped him. She wasn't one for hitting, but his casual treatment of the situation roused her anger, swift and strong.

"Whoa there, Kit," Caleb said, taking a step back. "He's fine. Trust me, he's fine."

Kit glared at her brother. "*Trust me,*" she mimicked. "Everyone keeps telling me to trust them today."

"And see, it has worked out," Zoran said, approaching them from the woods. Ivo came toward the scene from the opposite direction, but rather than walk toward them, he walked toward Kašović.

Kašović.

"What happened to him?" Kit managed to ask with a nod toward the assassin.

"Heavy duty tranquilizer," Zoran said, surprising the hell out of her.

"I thought, well, I," she let her words trail off, not wanting to say that she had assumed they would kill Kašović.

"I know, you thought we were going kill him," Zoran supplied. "And it was tempting, but aside from the fact that the Army might frown on that, there are many families—too many—that deserve to know the fate of Kašović. They deserve to know he will be brought to justice. If we'd taken care of it here, they would never have that closure. There would always be questions."

It made sense, but still, it didn't. She turned her questioning eyes to Garret, who answered her unspoken question. "Ivo and Zoran are going to escort Kašović to the International Criminal Court where he'll stand trial for crimes against humanity. Everyone he has hurt will be able to stand witness."

Kit glanced at the body, still lying in the snow. A sudden rush of tears threatened to come cascading down her cheeks. Blinking rapidly, she turned to Zoran. "Thank you," she said. "Not just for this, but for what you're doing for everyone else who's been hurt by that man. Both you and your father are amazing."

He seemed somewhat embarrassed by her words and mumbled a few things before turning to make his way over to his dad. Once Zoran joined Ivo, the father and son proceeded to search Kašović and then truss him up.

Kit watched in silence as they lifted the bound man, then Zoran put him in a fireman's hold. Kašović was by no means small, but the young soldier lifted him easily. He was like her brother, Kit realized. And Garret. Maybe not quite like them, since Zoran was part of the Army, but they were definitely of the same breed, physically and mentally.

Ivo and Zoran turned toward the three of them; Ivo lifted a hand in farewell and Zoran gave a small salute. She returned their gestures with a small wave of her own, but Caleb and Garret only nodded. When the two men and their prisoner disappeared into the trees, she looked back to Garret.

Relief washed over her. It was over. Well, except for Garret's shoulder.

"Caleb?" she said.

Seeming to know where her mind was, he pulled out his phone and began making a call.

Leaving the arrangements for medical care to her brother, she looked at Garret, really looked at him, for the first time in what felt like ages. A tentative smile played on his lips as his blue eyes fixed on her.

She felt an answering response of her own. A little smile that, of its own accord, turned into a big grin. "We did it, didn't we?" she asked.

He gave her a big smile and held out his good arm to her, beckoning her. "Yeah, we did. I never had any doubt, but yes, we did it."

She stepped close to his side, being sure to stay well clear of his injury. She wanted to sink her fingers into his hair and pull him down for a long kiss, but the practicalities of winter got in the way. Through the bulk of their clothing—jackets, scarves, and hats—not to mention Garret's shoulder, all she managed to do was place a quick kiss on his jaw.

"Okay, kids, let's go," Caleb said, interrupting their moment. "Drew sent some people for Ivo and Zoran, and the car they came in is parked about a half mile from here. It's not as close as I would like, but it's closer than the car back at the cabin."

As best she could, Kit took Garret's hand as they started to follow Caleb through the snow and ice. "Drew sent people?" she asked.

"Yes, Zoran and Ivo will be transported with Kašović to Burlington by van where a plane will be waiting for them. In a couple of hours, Kašović will be airborne and on his way to The Hague."

"What about their stuff?" she asked. It was still raining ice, but it had let up a bit. The sky, though still a solid bank of clouds, was lightening up a little bit too.

In front of her, Caleb lifted a shoulder at her question. "They have what they need, the rest I'll come back for tomorrow."

With Kašović in their custody, Kit knew her brother's statement to be the truth.

CHAPTER 22

GARRET SANK HIS FINGERS INTO Kit's hair and tilted her head up to look at him. "I'll be back tomorrow night," he said.

They were standing in the entryway of her home, his bag by his side. She smiled at his pronouncement; he always made sure now that she knew where he was going and when he'd be back. At the sight of her happiness, a wave of pleasure rippled through him. Even if he'd wanted to, he couldn't have stopped himself from lowering his lips to hers.

It had been five weeks since their time in Vermont. Kašović was standing trial—the survivors of his cruelty had let out a collective cry for justice when he'd been handed over. And he and Kit had finally been able to start living the life they'd both wanted together without anything hanging over their heads.

"Do you have the key to the apartment?" she asked when he pulled away from her. She pulled him back to her for another kiss when he nodded.

"Drive safely," she said, lifting her lips for one last kiss he had no interest in denying her.

As he climbed into his car and made his way down the drive, he glanced back at the house. It was mid-April and leaves were just thinking about making an appearance on the many trees that dotted the landscape of Kit's property. It was that time of year that fell between the drab browns and grays of late winter and the vibrant greens of early spring. It held both the memory of the passing season and the promise of new life. As he turned onto the road, he let himself smile at the thought. The seasons were mimicking his and Kit's relationship. Or maybe it was the other way around. Either way, a little bit of summer would be a good thing.

• • •

As Kit watched Garret's car disappear down the driveway, she picked up her cup of tea and made her way toward her office. After everything that had happened in the past few months, she was reveling in the quiet of work, life, and exploring her relationship with Garret. It had been easier than she had anticipated, sharing her space—emotional and physical—with Garret. And though she knew they were still in the fledgling stages, and she still worried every now and then that he would regret having left his other job, she felt good about where they were and what they were doing.

Sitting down at her desk to start her morning, Kit pulled up her e-mail and saw a note from her friend Carly. Kit and Garret had spent some time with Matty and Dash, Vivi and Ian, and Jesse and David, but much to her dismay, she hadn't seen much of Carly. Not that it was either of their faults. Carly, as the acting deputy chief of police to an understaffed department, was busier than ever—far busier than she wanted to be, judging by the note Kit was reading. And though Kit had been working steadily on her book, as well as getting used to having Garret in her life, she still felt a bit guilty about not taking time to see Carly.

On a whim, Kit shot off a quick reply to her friend to ask if she might be around to grab some dinner together that night. Kit didn't really expect Carly to be available on such short notice, but within a few minutes, she had a response. Carly was open for dinner, but didn't want to go home, shower, change, and get dressed up to go back out again.

Kit smiled. There were days when she didn't even get out of her pajamas, so she completely understood Carly's desire to just chill when she got off of work. Making a unilateral decision, Kit sent another response saying she'd pick up some food and be over at Carly's place at seven p.m. Carly sent her a smiley face as a confirmation.

After forcing herself to take her computer offline so she could focus on her writing without distractions, Kit went to work. Several hours later, she sat back, stretched her arms over her head, and looked at the last few words she'd written. They sucked. And she knew it. But she also knew enough to know when to let it go. They would still be there tomorrow, and until the story went to print she could, and would, change them.

She set her computer to reconnect to Wi-Fi, then she headed to the kitchen to grab a snack and another cup of tea. Returning to her seat, she noted an e-mail from a prestigious local liberal arts college. She'd been offered an honorary doctorate at another school and wondered if this e-mail was regarding another such honor. But much to her surprise, the college had actually written to ask if she would teach a seminar during the upcoming fall semester.

She knew her name was well known amongst the literati and, given that her first novel had won so much acclaim at its debut when she'd been only twenty-two, she'd been dubbed a bit of a wunderkind. And when her second and third books had topped several critic's favorite-reads lists, as well as several best-seller lists, she'd laid her foundation as one of the country's most promising literary talents.

But sometimes it seemed like the person who won the awards and received the accolades was someone else—as if that part of her life was one she watched or read about but didn't really participate in. But the college wanted *her*. She'd have to be herself and connect with students, and not just in a "have you read this book" kind of way, but in a way that could enrich both their lives and hers.

Her fingers drummed over the keyboard as she considered the opportunity she'd been presented. She didn't know if she would like teaching, and she didn't know if teaching would impact her writing, or if it did, if it would be in a positive or negative way. On the other hand, one of the key lessons Marco had taught her was that in order to write about life, she had to live one. Sitting all day in her pajamas in her home office didn't really qualify.

Who knew whether she'd like the experience or not, but the idea of doing something new appealed to her and, lately, doing new things had been working out for her. With a smile, she typed out a quick response to the college. She didn't explicitly accept the offer, but she did express an interest and ask for a meeting.

After going through the rest of her e-mail and handling a bit of social media, she glanced at the clock. If she wanted to get to Carly's by seven and pick up dinner before that, she needed to get going. Actually, truth be told, she had time, but she wanted to go to her favorite grocery store that was about forty-five minutes away. It had all the stuff she could want for dinner, but it had the added bonus of giving her some time in the car, winding through back country roads—one of her favorite pastimes.

At six forty-five, Kit put her car in park in the parking lot outside Carly's apartment building, killed the engine, and pulled out her notebook. As she'd hoped, during her drive, those last few lines she hadn't liked in her book had worked themselves out in her head and now she wanted to make sure to record her ideas. After scribbling down the changes, she flipped the notebook shut, grabbed her purse and the bags of food she'd bought, and made her way toward Carly's door.

Climbing the outside stairs to Carly's second-floor apartment, Kit sidestepped a few remaining ice patches visible in the dim lighting and wondered idly whether Carly hired someone to help her with snow and ice removal in the winter or if she did it herself, since Kit knew the owner of her building was less than reliable. Knowing Carly, Kit thought she probably did it herself. Even in the dead of morning or the dark of winter nights.

"You made it," Carly said with a smile as she opened the door and ushered Kit in.

"Did you doubt me?" Kit asked as she made her way through the small apartment to the kitchen.

"Not really, but I knew you were working on your book earlier and I know how Matty can forget her own name sometimes when she's so wrapped up in writing," Carly answered, rifling through the bag Kit had placed on the counter.

"Ooh, you went all the way to Giovanni's?" Carly asked, pulling out a roasted chicken. "Not that I'm complaining," she added as she pulled out a container of green beans roasted with garlic and sundried tomatoes.

"I needed to plot," Kit answered.

Carly's eyes came up, even as she set a container of mashed potatoes down. "Did it work?"

Kit smiled at her friend's acceptance of her plotting techniques. "It did. But then I also wanted one of these," she said, popping the top on the little white box she'd brought in.

"Is that . . .?" Carly asked.

Kit leaned down, inhaled deeply, then smiled. "It is. Salted caramel cheesecake." She pushed the box over and Carly eyed it as though she might just start with dessert.

"I thought they stopped making these," Carly said, giving into temptation a tiny bit by dipping her finger into the caramel that topped the cheesecake.

"Mostly they have. The woman who makes them only comes up this way a few times a year and she'll make them when she's here." Kit replied, rifling in the drawer where she knew Carly kept a corkscrew.

"And how did you know they had them now?"

Kit flashed her friend a grin as she opened a bottle of white wine. "I have my sources."

Carly laughed. "That cute kid, what was his name? Jacob— yes, that was it. He tells you, doesn't he?" She accepted a glass of wine from Kit as she pulled out some plates.

"I *did* help him with his MFA application. He'll be starting in the fall," Kit pointed out good-naturedly.

"Ha, I would have written his application *for him* if I'd known what kind of inside-Giovanni's info it could have gotten me," Carly said.

"Thankfully, he didn't need that much help. He's a very talented writer. I wouldn't be surprised if we see his name in print in a few years," Kit added as they dished up their food and took a seat at Carly's small dining table.

"So, how are you?" Kit asked just before popping some chicken into her mouth.

Carly shrugged, "Okay, busy."

Kit frowned as she chewed. None of her friends were really the type to complain, but Carly was always the most reticent. The less she said, the more stressed out she probably was. But Kit knew she'd never just come out and say it.

"How's Marcus?" Kit asked instead, changing tactics.

Again, Carly shrugged. "It's slow going. He's frustrated and angry, then feels guilty because he thinks he shouldn't be feeling any of those things." Carly paused, then rolled her eyes. "Of course, *he* won't tell you any of this. He doesn't talk about it at all. But I know him well enough to know what's going through his mind."

"Is he still in rehab?" Kit asked, taking a sip of wine.

Carly nodded and finished a bite of her dinner before answering. "He is. Three times a week. His knee and hip are still giving him some trouble. The skin graft is healing well, though."

"When will he come back to Windsor?" Kit asked, feeling sympathy for him.

Carly's lips flattened for a moment, then just as fast, her face relaxed. "I don't know. His rehab should be done in the next month or so. But honestly, I think he's a bit scared to come back. Not scared to be in the same area where the bomb went off or anything like that, but scared about how people will react to him being back. The last thing he wants is anyone's pity, and because everyone in town knows what happened, I think it makes him sick to think about people stopping him all the time to ask how he's doing.

"I also think he might still be too angry to come back. He's feeling a lot of things he doesn't think he should be feeling, considering he was part of the team that saved Jesse and her son. He doesn't know what to do with those emotions, so it's just easier not to face them."

Kit sat back and mulled over what Carly had just said. If Carly was right in her assessment of what Marcus was thinking, she didn't agree with Marcus's feelings. They lived in a small town and, yes, everyone knew what had happened, but it wouldn't be pity Marcus would receive from people, it would be genuine concern. Still, he was a young man who'd had his body nearly destroyed in a town he'd sworn to protect. Kit felt nothing but concern and affection for him, but she could see how he might misinterpret people's reactions and chafe against the proximity of people in their small town.

"And so it's easier to stay in Albany and be the anonymous guy with a limp?" Kit asked.

Carly nodded. "His physical therapist is up there, and with the administrative work that Ian arranged for him to take on for the Albany PD while he's on leave, it made sense for him to get an apartment there. At least until he's ready to come back here."

"Do you think he'll ever be ready? And how are you holding up?"

Carly wagged her head in indecision. "I think he'll be ready to come back soon. Or maybe I just *hope* that he will be."

"Is it that bad?"

Her friend took a long sip from her wineglass before answering. "It's actually not *that* bad. It would be easier if Vic were around to handle some of the more administrative tasks."

"Is he still leaving everything to you?" Kit asked.

Carly hesitated, then nodded. "Not everything, but a lot of things. Don't get me wrong, I'm learning a ton about the administration of law enforcement, and it's actually kind of interesting."

"But?"

"But it would be nice not to have to do it all while also still running patrols, handling calls, managing accidents, and all the other stuff I have to do as a duty officer."

"And I imagine it might be kind of nice to have someone *help* you learn everything rather than just leave you to figure it out?"

Carly nodded. "Anyway," she said, laying her napkin on the

table and reaching for Kit's now-empty dinner plate. "I shouldn't complain. It's a small town, crime isn't that high, and I haven't been in this job for all that long. It's a good opportunity and it's not as though I have a lot of extra-curricular activities to occupy my time."

Kit was about to point out that what Carly was going through could only be considered a good opportunity if she had plans to stay in law enforcement—something Kit wasn't altogether sure was the case.

"Dessert time," Carly said, cutting off anything Kit might have wanted to say. "Coffee? Tea?"

"More wine," Kit answered with a grin. "I've only had one glass and if I stay and gossip for a while, I should be just fine to drive after one more."

Carly laughed and began cutting obscenely large pieces of cheesecake. "I actually have the morning off tomorrow. My first half day off in nine days, so you can stay as late as you like."

And stay she did. Not too late, but it was close to midnight when she made her way out of Carly's apartment. Having caught up on all sorts of topics—from friends to the town's current events—Kit was smiling as she made her way down the stairs to the parking lot, keeping a wary eye open for any leftover ice. The weather was starting to warm up a bit during the day, but winter hadn't yet loosened its grip entirely.

"You're letting all the cold air in, Carly. Close the door," Kit said as she paused at the bottom of the stairs and turned to see her friend standing in the doorway of her apartment waiting for her to reach her car. "I'm fine, Officer," Kit insisted. Finally, she heard Carly grumble something and shut her door.

Turning back toward her car, Kit began to pick her way across the gravel lot, then paused as a train whistled in the night. A gust of cold air buffeted her body; she hunched her shoulders and continued on. This was the time of winter she didn't like. The in-between time when everything just looked brown and dead.

Shaking her head at her macabre thoughts, she imagined her

warm bed and big, picture windows and picked up her pace. To her right, she heard a shuffle of gravel being kicked up and her head jerked up in surprise. Peering into the darkened corners of the parking lot, Kit told herself to get a grip. It was probably a cat and she was just letting her imagination get to her.

Gripping her keys, she made it to her car, unlocked the doors, and popped the trunk. Carly had insisted that she take some leftovers and after she placed them in the back and shut the trunk, she glanced around one more time and let out a small sigh of relief when she saw no one; nothing out of the ordinary.

Pulling her scarf and jacket tighter across her body, she made her way toward the driver's door. She was so focused on getting into the warmth and safety of her car that she never saw the man—or the knife—coming.

CHAPTER 23

"You'll finally be gone, bitch," Kit heard a voice say as she felt a strong arm grip her from behind and something slash across her throat. Pain seared its way through her body even as adrenaline shot through every fiber of her being. Stunned, she dropped to the ground near the door, her hand going automatically to her neck.

She didn't have time to think; she only knew she was in a dark parking lot and someone was attacking her. Ignoring the pain at her throat, she rolled over to see the man who had assaulted her. He was standing over her, wearing a ski mask, and holding a knife. A knife with blood on it. Hers.

That thought registered and it was all she needed to catapult her out of her stunned state.

She screamed.

For a moment, he seemed just as surprised as she was to hear her voice tear through the quiet winter night. Then he was on her.

But she was ready for him. Or as ready as she could ever be to fend off a man with a knife.

She kicked out at him and wrenched away as he came down on top of her. Rolling onto her hands and knees, she felt the tip of the knife hit her upper arm as she scrambled toward the back of her car, out of the shadows, and toward the open part of the parking lot. Fumbling for anything to help her, she scraped up some gravel and threw it over her shoulder into what she hoped was the man's face. He had a mask on, but his eyes were exposed, and judging by his sudden blast of curse words, she figured she'd at least made some contact.

Distantly, she recognized her name being called. She thought it was Carly, was pretty sure it was Carly, but didn't have time to confirm or to answer her.

As she clawed her way toward the back of her car, the man caught her foot with his free hand and tried to drag her back into the shadows. She felt a burst of panic when she realized that, unlike her bulky winter coat, her jeans would prove to be little help in stopping a knife. And no sooner had the thought entered her mind than she felt something slice across her calf. Instinctively, she recoiled, trying to pull her injured leg toward her chest, but he held firm. Struggling and knowing she didn't have much time, she reached one more time for a handful of gravel and threw it at her assailant. She didn't hold much hope that it would stop him, or even stall him, but she had to try something as she started to crawl once again toward the lit part of the parking lot where Carly would be able to see her.

And then, suddenly, he was gone.

Just like that.

She didn't stop to question where he was or what he was doing. She only knew that his death grip on her leg was gone. She shot forward, still crawling on her belly, until she finally reached the end of her car. When no hand reached for her and no knife found its way into her body, she paused and turned around.

He was gone. Just simply gone.

"Kit!" Carly called.

Dazed, Kit looked toward her friend's apartment and noted absently that Carly was standing three steps up from the parking lot, her gun in hand.

"Kit! Are you okay?" Carly called again.

Kit reached for the bumper of her car, steading herself as she tried to pull herself upright. Adrenaline was still coursing through her body, but the pain was starting to scream and claw at her.

"I'm here," she choked out. It hurt to talk and she coughed in response. Tears shot to her eyes and she gritted her teeth against the pain. Taking a few deep breaths, she pulled herself all the way up, keeping her weight off her injured leg.

"Kit." At the alarm in Carly's voice, panic lanced through Kit one more time as she took a few steps toward her friend. Her friend who was vigilantly scanning the parking lot. Her friend with the gun.

"I've called the police. Backup will be here in a minute," Carly was saying soothingly as she slowly made her way toward Kit. "I'm coming to you, Kit. Just hold on one sec for me, can you do that?"

Kit took a few more steps away from her car toward Carly, toward the safety of Carly's apartment, then stopped and nodded. Her friend was doing her best to make sure whoever had attacked her wasn't still around; she was making sure they were both safe. Because they needed to be safe before Carly could put her gun away and help her.

She felt exposed standing in the parking lot and her body was shaking so much she considered taking the few steps back toward her car just so she could lean on the trunk to keep herself from collapsing. But the sounds of the sirens in the distance gave her some courage; she locked her knees and waited for Carly to give her the all clear.

"Talk to me, Kit," Carly said as she made her way quickly around the parking lot. "Are you okay?"

Kit could feel the blood streaming down her calf and her blood dampened jacket clinging to her arm. She tried to talk again, but then just decided to nod. Which was a joke because she wasn't okay. And she knew Carly knew that. But Kit needed that connection, that human connection to someone safe, and Carly seemed to know that too. Carly kept talking as she swept the rest of the parking lot. It felt as if it took ages, but Kit knew that, in reality, it probably took less than a minute. Still, she was glad when she saw her friend lower her gun and start to come toward her.

Relief hit her like a ton of bricks and Kit sank to the ground. The pain, the fear, the anger, and the shame of being caught unaware choked her injured throat. She didn't want to cry because she knew it would hurt. But knowing it would hurt, and why, made the tears come even faster.

"It's okay, Kit. I have you," Carly was saying. Kit was dimly aware of Carly checking her over, cataloging her injuries. When she started to remove the scarf from around Kit's neck, Kit shrank back and closed her eyes against the flood of tears the pain commanded.

"Try to relax, Kit. I won't touch the scarf again. Just lay back. The police and EMTs will be here any second now." Kit felt her head being lowered down onto her friend's lap, and like a child, she curled up and soaked in the reassuring feel of Carly. Shutting down her thoughts about what had just happened, Kit focused on trying to control the pain that was battering through her body. It wasn't easy, but after a few beats, she got her breathing under control and found that, as long as she inhaled and exhaled steadily and shallowly, the pain roared through her body rather than pierced through it.

She was so focused on her own breath and willing herself to release some of the tension she'd been feeling that she nearly shot up when she felt the muscles in Carly's thighs tense beneath her.

"Oh shit," she heard Carly say as her friend abruptly pulled away.

Confused Kit opened her eyes.

To the sight of a car headed right for them.

Kit registered the sound of the tires on the gravel, the feel of Carly's arms coming under her own, and the tug and pull of her own body being dragged.

And then everything stopped.

CHAPTER 24

GARRET FELT THE ROUGH WEAVE of the hospital blanket dig into his forehead. Ignoring it and focusing on the smoothness of Kit's skin, he rubbed a thumb over the back of her hand, then tightened his grip.

There was nothing. No response.

Blinking back his frustration and terror, he raised his head. Caleb sat sprawled in a chair on the other side of Kit's hospital bed. His pose was deceptively casual, but he was staring at his sister's face in much the same way he had been since he and Garret had arrived over twenty hours ago.

Kit was in a coma. And they didn't know when she'd come out of it.

Garret stroked the back of her hand again. He supposed that's the way it was with comas, that doctors never really knew when, or if, a patient would come out of one. He'd heard that before, but it had never carried as much meaning as it did now.

His eyes shifted to the monitors. Her heart rate was steady, and the rest of her vitals were as strong as could be expected. The machine beeped in the same slow rhythm as the device that pumped air into her lungs.

He never should have left. Or rather, he never should have let Drew handle Maria Costello and Louis Ramon. If he'd taken matters into his own hands like he'd wanted to when they'd first learned of Costello's involvement, none of this would ever have happened.

Guilt seared through his gut, swift and brutal. They'd been so intent on bringing Kašović in that he'd let himself get sloppy. He'd let loose ends unravel further. Unravel enough to wrap themselves around Kit and drag her back into the abyss.

"Jesus," he said under his breath, not really knowing if it was a curse or a prayer.

"There's nothing you could have done," Caleb said. At Caleb's tone, Garret looked over at him again. Caleb's voice was often flat, devoid of all emotion, but this was different. For the first time since Garret had started working with Caleb, he heard *emptiness* in Caleb's voice. And the guilt just kept coming.

"I shouldn't have let Drew and his team handle Maria Costello and her son," Garret said.

"I could have gone down and handled it myself. But I didn't," Caleb countered.

"I have more contacts in that family than you do."

"I have plenty of contacts. You were trying to start a life with her. You did what you should have done—you stayed with her. You committed yourself to making a new life work."

"And look at what good that did," Garret said, loosening the grip he had on Kit's hand that he now realized had grown tight.

"I should have gone," Caleb insisted.

For a long moment, Garret said nothing and just observed his partner and friend. Caleb's face was pale and scruffy—hell, both their faces were, after having sat at Kit's side since they'd arrived. And though Caleb was preternaturally still, Garret knew his mind was working. But for once, he'd bet his friend's mind wasn't focused on solving a problem or planning a mission. No, Garret would bet Caleb was reliving every memory he had of Kit. And probably feeling his own wave of guilt—for having left her with their father, for not having been a bigger part of her life, for not having stopped Louis Ramon. Because that was who had done this to Kit.

Carly, who had saved Kit's life by dragging her just far enough out of the path of the oncoming car that it had hit her hips and legs rather than her chest and head, had escaped significant injury and walked away with a couple of bruised ribs and a broken wrist.

She'd also gotten a good look at the driver. And had confirmed that it was Louis Ramon.

How Louis had gotten into the country, Garret didn't know and didn't care. But he had. And he'd done this to Kit. And Garret could have stopped him.

Garret opened his mouth to confess to Caleb why this was his fault. And why he could have stopped it. But before he had the opportunity, the door slid open and Drew walked in carrying coffee. He'd arrived eight hours earlier, and though outwardly, he didn't look as rumpled as Garret and Caleb, Garret could see it in his eyes. Drew's eyes didn't bother to hide his distress and, yes, his guilt. There seemed to be a lot of that going around.

Garret continued to hold Kit's hand in one of his as he accepted the coffee with the other. Caleb took a cup but let it hang in his fingers. Drew leaned against the wall and all three just simply watched her, lost in their own feelings; fearing to hope, but hoping nonetheless.

"We have to do something," Caleb finally said. "We can't just let this happen."

"Maria Costello assures me she had no idea her son was going to do this," Drew said.

"And I give a damn what Maria Costello says, why?" Caleb bit out.

Not taking his eyes off Kit, Drew shrugged. "I'm just saying."

"And you believe her?" Garret asked.

Drew tipped his head in a noncommittal gesture. "Maybe, but it doesn't matter if she knew, it only matters what she does now. I just wanted tell you both."

"Meaning you don't want one of us to go down and have a chat with her until you have a better idea of what her next step might be," Garret said, not bothering to keep the bite out of his tone.

"She's useful to us now that this thing with Kašović is over," Drew commented. However, Garret noted a blasé tone in the agent's voice, as if Drew were toeing the company line but didn't really give a damn if something happened to make Maria Costello pay for what had happened.

"I'm—" Again, Garret was cut off as the door slid open.

This time, it was Carly who stepped into the room. She was wearing jeans, work boots, and a big sweater. Her wrist was in a cast and when she came into the room, Garret could see that she was moving gingerly.

Her eyes bounced between the three men, landed on Kit for a long moment, then returned to Garret.

"How is she?" Carly asked.

He lifted a shoulder. "No change."

Carly bit her lip and Garret knew she was experiencing the same thing they all were: guilt. Jesus, the room was so filled with it that he wondered if it might become visible, like a thick fog filling the room.

Drew cleared his throat, causing Garret to glance at him. The agent raised an eyebrow in response.

"Carly Drummond, this is Drew Carmichael, a friend of Kit's. Drew, this is Carly Drummond, the Deputy Chief of Police in Windsor and also Kit's friend." Garret made the introduction. "Carly's the one who saw the attack and pulled Kit out of the way."

Carly turned to face Drew. She had to look up to meet his gaze, and though she gave him a nod of acknowledgement, she didn't bother to hold her hand out. And neither did he.

"How are you?" Garret asked.

Carly shrugged. "Fine, a little sore, but fine."

He'd bet she was more than just a little sore. But he had to respect her attitude.

"You broke your wrist?" Drew asked.

Again, she turned to face him, then nodded.

"And bruised a few ribs," Caleb added.

"Was it a bad break?" Drew asked.

Carly looked between Caleb and Drew then shook her head. "It's fine," she answered, turning back to look at Kit.

"Any news at all?" she asked Garret.

"No, the doctor is supposed to come by any minute now. Any update on Louis Ramon?" he asked.

She bobbed her head then gestured with her eyes toward Drew in a silent question.

Garret glanced at Drew who was watching Carly, though she was turned mostly away from him so his view was primarily of her back.

"Drew knows all about Louis Ramon. He was with us when we discovered who he was and why he was after Kit," Garret supplied. He didn't say anything about Drew being with the CIA, more out of habit than as an attempt to keep it from her.

At this explanation, Carly looked at Drew with an expression of curiosity, then turned back to Garret.

"The car he used was found off the Taconic Parkway yesterday, hidden off on one of the side roads. It's up at the state lab. Vivi and Dr. Buckley, the head of the lab, are going over it now. We think he must have picked up another car, or had someone meet him, since there aren't a lot of places he could get to easily from where he dumped the car."

"No trains, buses, or anything like that?" Caleb asked.

Carly shook her head. "No, there's a train station in the area, but it's several miles from where the car was found and my colleagues down in that county already ran through all the video footage at the train station. He hasn't shown up on any of it since the time of the attack. Of course, they have someone posted there now, just in case, but nothing yet."

"I don't think Louis Ramon is the kind of kid who would be interested in taking the train. He'd probably have someone waiting for him," Drew offered.

Carly studied him for a moment, then nodded. "Yes, we think so too. The car he was driving when he went after Kit was stolen from a family in Millbrook. The family has a summer house up there, but occasionally visit in the winter, so they have a beater car they keep in the garage for the snow."

"Millbrook seems more his style," Drew agreed, commenting

on the affluent community. Garret watched Carly examine Drew's face again. He could almost sense the questions forming in her mind about just who this man was and why he seemed to so comfortably jump into asking questions and making observations about a police investigation.

"There are way too many people in here," a voice said as the door opened yet again and the doctor strode in. She was tall, thin, and had straight black hair cut into a short bob. With her knee-high black boots, leather studded belt looped through a pair of jeans, and nose ring, she was not what Garret had expected of a critical care doctor, but he'd grown to appreciate her candor and unusual style.

When no one moved, she paused and gave the room a quick assessment. Garret suspected it was also an efficient assessment. Dr. Lila Rose did not seem the type to dawdle.

"You and you," she said, pointing to Drew and Carly, "need to leave. Mr. Cantona or Mr. Forrester can share whatever they feel comfortable sharing with you after I examine Kit and have a chat with them about where we are."

With an economy of words, she made her point and then stared at them until they both made to leave.

"Garret?" Carly said as she paused at the door.

"I'll call you when we're done. You too, Carmichael," he added, knowing Drew would want the same. Drew gave a quick nod, then ushered Carly out the door. As it closed behind them, Garret turned to Dr. Rose, who was already going through Kit's chart. Dr. Rose had been on rotation when Kit was brought up from the ER after the emergency surgery she'd undergone. Judging by the current time, Garret figured she must have gone off shift and come back on.

Without a word, Dr. Rose put the chart back and went to check each machine. Once she was done with that, she pulled out her tablet device, typed in a few things, then stood at the foot of Kit's bed and read. Garret didn't have to look to know that Caleb was watching her too—both of them watching closely for any change in expression that might give away what she was thinking.

After a few minutes, Garret realized just how intently he was observing her. She had the kind of face that was not devoid of animation; in fact, several movements crossed her face. She frowned at one thing, cocked her head to the side at something else, and gave a little "huh" at yet another. But despite all that, it was nearly impossible to tell what she was thinking. He couldn't tell what that frown meant or if the "huh" was good or bad.

He turned a questioning look to Caleb, and it didn't take long for Caleb to meet his gaze with his own questioning look. Dr. Rose was young—too young to have done anything other than go straight through college, medical school, and residency, but if he didn't know any better, Garret would have thought she'd been a part of *their* world at some point in time.

"Well, gentlemen," she said as she turned her tablet off and lowered it. "Her brain functions are good, solid. And her vitals also look good for the state she's in. There's no internal bleeding, but I'm going to order another CAT scan this afternoon to be sure there isn't a slow leak in her brain that might not have been picked up yesterday. For what her body went through, she's responding well. The next fifteen hours or so will tell us more."

Garret wanted more. He wanted Dr. Rose to tell them Kit would be okay. He wanted to hear her say that her experience led her to believe that Kit would pull through this just fine. He opened his mouth to ask her if these things were true, but then shut it. Judging by the way she was standing there, weight on one leg, holding his gaze, he knew he wasn't going to get any more out of her. And definitely not any false promises.

He narrowed his eyes and pursed his lips but said nothing. She seemed to acknowledge his effort when she gave a curt nod, then turned to leave the room. "I'll have the nurse schedule the CAT scan. Once that's done, I'll have a look at it and come back to talk to you."

Garret nodded. Dr. Rose's gaze went to Caleb for a brief

moment, but Caleb didn't seem to notice as his attention was back on Kit. Then she turned back toward the hall and left. The door snicked shut behind her.

"She's an interesting doctor, don't you think?" Garret asked for no particular reason.

Caleb's eyes flicked to his, but he said nothing.

The sounds of the machines filled the room for several minutes as Garret began to feel the post-doctor visit letdown—with every visit, he hoped for new news, for good news; and after each visit, it took a moment to sink in—to accept that he still hadn't heard what he so wanted to hear.

In the silence, Garret felt each beat of his heart sync with the beep of the machines. Her breathing became his, and with every shared breath, every shared heartbeat, he poured all his hope into her. Hope for her recovery, hope that she would soon breathe on her own, hope that she would soon open her eyes and smile. And hope that she would forgive him for what he was about to do.

Breaking his connection to her was one of the hardest things he would ever do. He'd thought walking away from her that day in Vermont was hard, but this was harder. *That* had been part of a plan they were both in on. What he was about to do next was something he'd never talked about with her before and something he knew would hurt her. He knew it would help in the end, and he knew Kit would be able to see that too. But, as he placed one last kiss on her palm and gave her hand one last squeeze, he hoped that she would understand *why* he was doing what he was about to do and not just that it had needed to be done.

Straightening in his seat, Garret rose. His legs were stiff from sitting so long, but he ignored the throbbing sensation as he let go of Kit's hand and stepped back. His gaze lingered on her face for a long moment, and he hoped that soon he'd be able to see her golden eyes laughing again. Then he turned to Caleb.

"I'm going to take care of this," he said, wishing his voice sounded more confident than fatigued.

Caleb sat up and slowly, deliberately put his coffee cup down. "If you know the best way to take care of this, then let me do it."

Garret wished like hell it was that simple. He shook his head. "It's a long story, but you can't do it. You can't go in my place."

"Like hell," Caleb bit back.

Garret held up a hand. "It's not because you're not capable."

Caleb's eyes narrowed.

"It's," Garret paused, debating how much to tell his partner. Finally, he took a deep breath and let it out. "Do you remember two years ago when we had that stretch of R & R that lasted about six weeks?"

Caleb nodded. It had been their longest stretch between jobs since they'd started working together and not something either was likely to forget. Garret would never forget it, since he'd had no rest or relaxation at all.

"You remember when, back when we first figured out who was behind everything that was happening to Kit, I said I could take care of it?" He didn't wait for Caleb to nod, he just continued. "I have connections in the Salazar family. Not the kind of connections we usually make in our line of work, but, well," again he paused, debating about how much to say.

"Spill it, Cantona," Caleb all but ordered.

"I'm not sure if you know this, but after Maria Costello's birth, Emmanuel Salazar was forced to break it off with Olivia Costello, her mother, in order to marry a woman his brother had selected for him. His intended bride was Rosa Louise Dias. Rosa had four sons by Emmanuel, and though Esteban is still the titular head of the cartel, everyone knows it's Emmanuel's sons who run it, since Esteban had no children of his own, or none he wanted to bring into the business."

"Yeah, so?" Caleb interjected.

"Like Emmanuel, before Rosa was forced to marry Emmanuel, she was in love with someone else. It was young love; they were maybe seventeen at the time."

"Get to the point, Cantona," Caleb snapped, no doubt sensing the tension in Garret's own voice.

"The man she was in love with was my father, Antonio Cantona."

Caleb blinked. "What the fuck?" he said finally.

"From a young age, Rosa had already been marked by Esteban, Emmanuel's brother, as Emmanuel's bride. When the Salazar family threatened to kill both my father and Rosa if they didn't break it off, my father left Colombia to save her life. He fled to Louisiana, where *his* father was from and where he met my mother. They married and had me and my sister, but he never forgot his first love or how he'd been treated. I'm sure I don't have to tell you what that kind of bitterness can do to a man—the best day of my life was when my mom said she was leaving him, and she moved us to Baton Rouge with her to stay with her sister."

"And your father? And what does that have to do with what's going on now?"

"When Emmanuel Salazar died, my dad found his way back to Rosa. By then, she was the matriarch of the family. She wasn't involved in it, per se, but because she had given birth to its entire next generation, she held the kind of power that isn't common for a woman to hold in that line of business."

"And?"

"And she and my father picked up their relationship again. They had a daughter. Her name is Consuela and she's seventeen."

"What about your father?"

Garret shrugged. "I never saw him again after he left Louisiana, but he died five years ago. By then I was already in this line of business. I guess he kept tabs on me because Rosa knew who I was and what I did."

"So?"

"So when Consuela was fifteen, she was kidnapped. Rosa came to me asking for help finding her." Garret could barely believe he was talking about this. There were lots of secrets in his world, and the line between good and evil was never very clear. But even so, he knew that helping one of the most powerful figures of a ruthless cartel was not something he wanted to put on his resume. Even though he'd done it to save an innocent fifteen-year-old girl.

"What the hell?"

"Rosa knew it was likely someone in one of the rival cartels who had taken her daughter."

"Why didn't she sic her sons on it?"

"Aside from the fact that her sons don't really acknowledge Consuela, she didn't want to start a war. If she went to her own family and her sons went after the group who had Consuela, she was certain no one would survive. She knows what her sons do, and though I've never asked, I'm pretty sure she's not living the life she would have wanted for herself. But even so, she doesn't want any of her children to die."

"And so she asked you."

"And so she asked me," Garret repeated.

"And I assume you found the girl?"

Garret nodded and walked toward the window. The day was cloudy and with the snow mostly melted into gray heaps of ice and no signs of spring life visible from where he stood, everything looked tired and heavy.

"I did," he said, answering Caleb's question. "I found her. She'd been roughed up a bit, but not sexually assaulted. They'd kept her in a room with a bed and she'd been mostly treated decently—at least decently enough not to cause too much damage to her psyche."

"And the reason for it? Did the other family want to start a war?"

Garret shook his head. "It was more complicated than that. They were looking for a way to get to Rosa's oldest son. They wanted his attention to negotiate distribution channels. He hadn't been taking them seriously, and they figured if they kidnapped his sister he'd have to talk to them."

Caleb blinked. "Uh, did they forget who they were dealing with? Why on earth would they think Rosa's son would *talk* to his sister's kidnapper?"

Garret shrugged. "It was an elaborate plan with Consuela being held somewhere else, and they would only get her back if Rosa's son agreed to meet, yada, yada, yada . . ." Garret's voice trailed off.

Normally, he'd agree with Caleb, but given what he'd learned while working on the situation, it was actually the kind of plan that was just foolhardy enough to work.

"And so you have an in with Rosa Salazar."

"And so I have an in with Rosa Salazar," he repeated. "Especially since her daughter is my half-sister."

Caleb let out a low whistle. "No wonder you never mentioned this. I'm pretty sure your security clearance would change if this were general knowledge."

"I'm pretty sure my *life* would change if this became general knowledge." Because the truth was, as much as the government might question him, it would be nothing compared to what the Salazar family might do if they found out they had "family" who knew the kinds of things Garret knew. He had no doubt they would stop at nothing to use his position and knowledge for their own purposes.

"So what's your plan?" Caleb asked. Garret wasn't sure whether or not to be pleased with the assurance he heard in Caleb's voice.

Garret sighed. "I'm going to go to Mexico, where Rosa now lives, and talk to her. She will talk to her sons, and her sons will talk to Louis Ramon."

"Talk?"

"Or something like that," Garret said as he shoved his hands into his pockets and turned back to the room. Instantly, his eyes fell on Kit.

"You're going to leave," Caleb said, starting to give voice to Garret's biggest fear.

"I have to."

"You'll be leaving her."

Garret nodded.

"Without telling her where you're going or what you're doing or when you'll be back."

"I can't tell her anything right now, and it's not something I want to put in writing."

"You'll be doing exactly what you promised you wouldn't do. You'd be doing exactly what both my father and I did to her."

Garret's jaw clenched. "I'm doing it to help her. To keep her from being killed."

"That was my reason too," Caleb said quietly.

Garret moved his eyes to his friend. "Tell her. If she wakes up while I'm gone, tell her. Please."

Caleb was silent for a good long moment. Garret didn't doubt Caleb would do as he asked. But he knew Caleb had just as much doubt as he did as to whether or not it would make a difference. Because the fact of the matter was, he *was* leaving her. He was doing what he'd promised her wouldn't. And though he'd like to think that, had she been awake, he would have told her, a small part of him wondered if that was true. A small part of him still thought he'd do exactly what he was doing now, leave her without an explanation, because what he was going to do wasn't something he really wanted her to know—not the actual details and not what it said about him.

Finally, Caleb nodded.

Garret let out a long breath he hadn't realized he'd been holding. "Thank you."

Caleb nodded again and held his gaze for moment before turning back to his sister. Garret knew when he'd been dismissed and started for the door.

"Cantona," Caleb's voice stopped him as him just as he was about to close the door behind him. "Come back," his partner said.

Garret nodded, closed the door, and walked away.

CHAPTER 25

Dimly, Kit heard a persistent beep echoing through the fog in her mind. It didn't have the same romantic sound, but some tendril of something in her mind followed it like it was a fog horn. Only it was calling to her, not warning her away.

As her mind grabbed hold of the methodical sound, she was pulled from a place so deep and dark that she wouldn't call it sleep. And slowly, as the beeping became louder and crisper, her other senses awoke as well.

Her body was laid out flat. She was neither warm nor cold, though she could feel the weight of what she thought might be blankets covering her. She felt pleasantly heavy and sluggish, the way one did when just waking in the morning after a deep sleep. But the recognition of something pressing against her nostrils jolted her to a full wakefulness.

She flinched and her eyes flew open. The square pattern of a ceiling was visible for a moment and then her sight was filled with Caleb's face. She blinked a few times, and in a sudden rush of fear, she tried to claw the oxygen tube from her nose.

She didn't understand why Caleb was stopping her, why he was holding her hands, gripping them tightly in his own. And it took more than a moment for his soothing words to sink in. She still wasn't sure what was going on, but Caleb was with her. He wasn't gone. He hadn't left her.

She let out a breath. He hadn't left her.

Her eyes scanned the room—a hospital room. There was an oxygen machine beside her and an IV tube that ran from a bag down to her arm. There was another machine with a tangle of wires snaking out of it, and as she followed their path with her eyes, she became aware of the feel of the adhesive that was binding the opposite ends of those wires to her chest.

She took a deep breath and felt pain lancing through her chest. Caleb muttered something about it being all right, that he'd called the nurse. He still held her hands in his.

He hadn't left.

Slowly, as though her own mind was fighting it, she realized what was missing.

Kit turned her face toward her brother. "Garret?" was all she managed to whisper.

She didn't need to hear what Caleb said to know Garret wasn't simply out getting coffee. Caleb's eyes told her everything she needed to know.

A different kind of pain settled like a weight on her chest. She closed her eyes against it and drifted back to the blackness.

He'd left her.

CHAPTER 26

ONE WEEK LATER, GARRET STEPPED into the entryway of Kit's kitchen, closing the door softly behind him. It was early morning, the sun barely coming up; Kit should be sleeping safely in her bed. But as he stood there, he could all but feel the emptiness of the house. For a moment, he just leaned against the door, closed his eyes, and prayed Kit would give him the chance to explain. Because even though he'd given Caleb the go-ahead to tell her where he was going and why, that wasn't the kind of explanation that would be important to her—not now.

"She's gone," came Caleb's voice from the kitchen.

Not bothering to take off his boots, Garret stepped into the kitchen. Caleb was sitting at the kitchen island drinking coffee. He looked like shit.

Garret paused.

Caleb took another sip of his coffee, never taking his eyes from Garret. He had a scruffy week's worth of growth on his beard; his eyes were bloodshot, his face gaunt and drawn.

"Do you know where she is?" Garret asked.

Caleb shook his head.

"How was she when she left?"

"Physically?" Caleb clarified.

Garret nodded.

"Battered, bruised, beaten up, but no lasting damage. Her hip was sore and she was walking with crutches when she left the hospital, but no more head trauma or broken bones, and the knife wounds were healing."

"And when did she walk out of the hospital?" Garret almost didn't want to know the answer to that. In the dark recesses of his mind, there was a little part of him that had hoped she'd have had to stay bedridden until he got home. Because then she'd be forced to listen to him.

"They kept her another four days. She got out three days ago."

Garret swallowed. He'd intentionally not kept in touch with Caleb after he left because Garret hadn't trusted himself to stay and do what he'd needed to do if he'd known that Kit was coming home without him. "Three days? And you don't know where she is?"

The thing with Kit was that she could go anywhere. With friends like Drew and Dani, disappearing could be incredibly easy if she really wanted to.

Again, Caleb shook his head.

"She just packed and left?" Great, she really could be anywhere.

Caleb shrugged. "She said she needed some time." Not to recover from her injuries was left unsaid. Garret felt the bile churning in his stomach.

"And you haven't looked for her?" Garret could hardly believe that. Not the Caleb he knew.

But Caleb gave him a long, hard look. "I think she's had enough of the men in her life testing her trust. She asked me to let her go, not to follow her or look into her whereabouts. I thought it was the least I could do."

Garret felt the accusation lance through his chest. He knew in his heart Kit understood that neither he nor Caleb were anything like her father in the results of their actions. But the cold, unvarnished truth was that, in the actions themselves, they were very much alike. Coming and going as they saw fit, leaving with no notice, going places they wouldn't divulge, coming back only when the job—whatever it may be—was done.

Distantly, Garret noticed his hand was shaking. Taking a deep breath, he willed himself to stay calm. "Did she say *anything* else?" he asked.

Again, Caleb lifted a shoulder as he took another sip of coffee.

"She said something about needing to heal and just giving herself the space to do that."

Garret blinked, the fog starting to lift. "She said that? Those words, about needing to heal?"

As if sensing the shift in Garret's focus, Caleb put his coffee down with a soft thunk on the granite countertop. "Yes."

Garret turned for the door.

"Cantona?" Caleb's voice called him back.

Garret turned, "I know where she is and I'm going to be with her. Hopefully, I can also convince her that I'm worth being with, but at the very least, I want her to know exactly why I did what I did so that she doesn't carry my betrayal with her for the rest of her life. She doesn't deserve that."

And not that there had been any doubt, but it was in that moment that Garret realized just what Kit meant to him. When her healing and her happiness became far more important to him than getting what he wanted.

CHAPTER 27

GARRET PULLED HIS SMALL RENTAL car into a spot that was barely bigger than the car itself and killed the engine. He eyed the cobblestone "street" that was no wider than an alley and glanced at the buildings jutting up almost directly from the street itself. The muted colors stood in stark contrast to the blue sea he knew lay down the hill from this tiny village just west of the Cinque Terre in Italy.

He could drive no farther into the town, as cars were prevented from doing so. He assumed at some point that hadn't been the case. But with tourism came traffic, and cars not suited to the tiny roads, and drivers even less suited. So, at some point, the town must have just decided not to allow any traffic into its center. But it was a small town; walking wouldn't take long.

He'd called in some favors and spent his flight from New York to Rome studying a map of the area. He was parked on the east side of the village; Marco Baresi's villa lay on the west side, down closer to the water. The aerial photos showed a three-tiered building that stepped down the hillside, with abundant patios and outdoor space, along with a set of stairs down to the ocean. It was one of the larger homes in the area, though not quite large enough to be considered ostentatious.

Having caught the red-eye out of New York, Garret had bought a first-class ticket that allowed him to catch a little sleep during the nine-hour flight. But given that he'd also just flown up to New York from South America the day before, he was travel weary and in need of some coffee before confronting Kit. A little reconnaissance wouldn't hurt either.

It was close to noon and the small town was as bustling as he imagined it got when not in tourist season. It was early spring and, unlike Windsor where spring was only just starting to claw its way from under the blanket of winter, the weather here was about as perfect as could be. The flowers were in bloom and people were out and about.

He made his way toward Baresi's villa. Walking past the author's non-descript but charming gate that led into the court-yard of the house, Garret found a café one block away. Ordering an espresso and a small pastry, he took a seat in the window and watched. He didn't expect Kit or Marco to come out of the gate, but he felt the need to lie in wait for just a little while. Or maybe he was just delaying.

He sighed, finished off the last of the pastry, downed his espresso, and rose. Three minutes later, he was ringing the bell on the gate, his heart pounding in his ears.

An older woman answered, her gray hair pulled back into a bun. She was tall, thin, and wearing slacks and a blouse. Garret didn't know how he knew, but there was no doubt in his mind that she was the housekeeper of, and gatekeeper to, Marco Baresi's sanctuary.

"*Buongiorno*," he said.

Rather than answer, she inclined her head.

"Is Kit here?" he asked, reverting to English.

She tilted her head and studied him.

"I'm Garret—"

"I know who you are," she said in English that was only slightly accented. Her words gave him some semblance of hope, after all. If this person knew him, Kit must have said something.

"You're expecting me, then?" he asked.

A ghost of a smile played on her lips. "I'm not sure if 'expecting' is the right word," she countered.

Not sure what to make of that statement, Garret opted to take the reins in hand and asked, "May I come in?"

Her brown eyes never moved from his face. After ten seconds that felt like an eternity, she gave a single nod and stepped back from the gate. Not wanting to give her the opportunity to change her mind, he quickly stepped through the thick wooden gate and into a lush courtyard.

"I'm Imelda." She offered her name but not her hand in a measured greeting. Garret nodded in response.

"Come, follow me."

And Garret did. With every step through the colorful courtyard and into a stunning room, his heart beat a little faster. It didn't help that this floor of the villa sat on top of the cliff and the big, picture windows—windows that looked out onto the Italian Mediterranean—gave it the appearance of being about to tumble into the sea below. Of course, Garret knew from the maps he had studied that there were two levels below them, but from this vantage point, it was hard to tell.

Glancing around the room, both hoping and fearing he'd see Kit, he took in his surroundings. After a quick perusal, it was clear to Garret that this top floor was the "public" floor. Not that Baresi opened his house to the public, but if he held parties or hosted an event, this was the space where he would do it. Most of the area consisted of one large room banked with six-foot windows, maximizing the view of the bay below. But to his left stood another, smaller room where perhaps Marco wrote or held business meetings, and behind it looked to be a kitchen—not a full kitchen, but the kind of kitchen that a caterer could use to prepare food and drinks.

To his right was a staircase with a wrought iron railing that led down, and it was down these stairs that Imelda led Garret. And just as the purpose of the top floor was obvious, it was equally as clear upon entering this middle level of the villa that he had entered the private sanctuary of one of the world's literary geniuses. Books were strewn everywhere—on the floor, on the large dining table that sat in the middle of the room, and on the coffee table near the sofa to his left. There were even books on the counters in the kitchen—a kitchen that looked as though it was used for everyday cooking—that lay to his right.

There were big sliding doors that led out onto a terrace built on the roof of the floor below, and from where he stood, he could see a large round table, four chairs, and strings of overhead lighting. Potted plants were everywhere, containing flowers of all colors and sizes in bloom. It was the perfect place for a romantic dinner. Garret clenched his jaw and began to look in earnest for Kit.

If the maps he had seen were accurate, and he had no reason to think otherwise, beyond the wall to his left was a hallway that led to two bedrooms. Also to his left was another stairwell that led down to the lowest level of the house.

Following Imelda down, Garret held a not-so-fleeting thought about descending into hell. But then, when they hit the landing, all thoughts of hell vanished—or at least suspended themselves. The views were breathtaking. It was hard for him to imagine better vistas than what he'd seen from the top floor, but where the top floor was meant to awe a visitor, the views from this floor were meant to enchant.

This being the only level with earth outside, its doors led to a small patch of grass and a garden that Garret could only call whimsical. From where he stood, he could see narrow paths leading who-knew-where, arbors thick with hanging flowers, and benches scattered about. Being built on the cliff, it wasn't a huge area, but it was filled with the same kind of sensual expression as Baresi's novels—the kind of place that made one want to ask questions rather than seek answers.

"So, you've come."

Caught up in the view, Garret hadn't even noticed the author himself sitting at a desk on the far side of the room. He willed his eyes away from the landscape to peer at Marco. Never in his life had he met Italians as non-expressive as Imelda and Marco. Finally, unsure what to think or do, Garret simply nodded.

Still holding a sheaf of paper in one hand and pen in the other, Marco regarded him for a long moment. Then he sighed and rose.

"Thank you, Imelda," he said, dismissing his gatekeeper. Without a word, the woman turned and disappeared up the stairs.

"Can I get you a drink?" Marco asked, walking toward a small refrigerator and pulling out a bottle of sparkling water.

Garret shook his head. "I'd like to see Kit," he said.

Marco gave a small laugh as he poured himself a drink. Making a small toasting gesture, he answered, "I'm sure you would." As Marco took a sip, Garret waited.

Finally, Marco spoke again. "You hurt her." Coming from a man who knew how to use words like no one else of his generation, the short, concise statement said more than just those three words. And again, as he had with Caleb, Garret felt the weight of guilt take his breath away.

"I know," he managed to say. "How is she?"

Marco gave a shrug. "Physically? She is healing. Emotionally, it's hard for even me to say. You took care of what you left to take care of, did you not?"

The flash of worry he saw in Marco's eyes gave him some hope. Obviously, Caleb had told Kit why he had left—as Garret had asked him to do—and Kit had told Marco. It didn't surprise him at all. In fact, he wondered if he might eventually have an ally in the author. The man cared deeply for her, of that there was no doubt, and Garret knew Marco would no more want something bad to happen to her than Garret would.

Garret nodded. "Two days ago, Louis Ramon was found dead outside a popular club in Bali where he'd been visiting some friends. It was a club known for its drug scene. Poor Louis stepped outside to try some of the best cocaine Indonesia had to offer and overdosed on a nearly 100 percent pure sample."

Marco shook his head. "Drugs. A bit clichéd, but effective, nonetheless."

"Marco, I made it to the bottom and back!" Kit's happy voice suddenly filled the air.

Garret spun toward the garden in time to see the top of her auburn head appear at the edge of the cliff. With bated breath, he watched as she came into full view, making her way up the stairs that led into the garden from the beach.

As she reached the top, she blew some of her hair out of her face. "Marco? Did you hear me?" she called.

She had most definitely lost weight and he could still see the bruises and cuts on her legs below the skirt she wore, and on her arms, bare in her tank top. The cut at her throat looked to be healing but was still an angry red slash. She looked a bit pale, even though her trek to the bay and back had obviously brought some color to her face.

But she was smiling. And she looked as breathtaking as always.

"Marco?" she called one more time. And then she caught sight of Garret. Her smile faded and her step faltered. But to her credit she never stopped moving toward the house where he and Marco stood.

The top half of the farm door that led into the house from the garden had been left open and as she made her way toward them, she opened the bottom half of the door, then stepped inside. His eyes were glued to hers, but hers seemed to be bouncing every which way. For a split second or two, she would make eye contact with him, then quickly look away. Her eyes would flicker to the floor, then the bookshelves, then back to him.

"Water, my dear?" Marco asked, stepping forward with a glass of water for her—a glass Garret hadn't even seen him pour, he'd been so fixated on Kit.

She murmured a "thank you," glanced at Garret, then took a sip.

"Do you need to sit down?" Garret managed to ask.

Her eyes darted to him and lingered for a moment. He thought she might argue for the sake of arguing, but after a moment, she inclined her head.

"Yes, thank you," she said.

He moved aside as she walked toward the sofa at edge of the

room. As she sat at the far end, she closed her eyes for a second and he could see fatigue wash over her body. The walk to the bay and back must have been her self-prescribed physical therapy, and though she was obviously proud of herself for doing it, there was no doubt it had exhausted her.

A little unsure where to go from there, he cast Marco a look.

"I think you two need to talk," Marco said. He dropped a kiss on Kit's head and made his way up the stairs without another word, leaving them alone.

Rather than sit on the couch with her, Garret took a seat on a well-worn wingback that sat at a ninety-degree angle from where Kit had perched. Bracing his elbows on his knees, he contemplated where to start. And not finding any brilliant answer, he just started.

"Caleb told you where I went?"

For a long moment she said nothing. Her eyes were cast down, focused on her fingers playing with the drops of condensation on her glass. Then she nodded.

"I also read about Louis Ramon in the paper yesterday. About his overdose. Did you have anything to do with that?" she asked.

His gut clenched, but he nodded. "I told Rosa Salazar what was happening—what he'd done to the young ballet dancer and what he'd done to you."

"You had a man killed because of me." It wasn't a question. But stated so baldly, it made him wonder if he and her father weren't so different after all.

"I know Drew told Mossad about him as well, so it's possible that what I told Rosa had nothing to do with what happened to him. But it's also possible that it had everything to do with it." He wasn't going to lie to her about this. Even though he desperately wanted to.

"So, he definitely killed her?" Kit asked.

Garret nodded. That much they knew was true.

"And me? Was there any chance it was anyone other than him who came after me?"

"No, it was him. His blood was collected from you, from

when you fought him, along with DNA that was collected from the car he drove to Windsor. The car that he used to run you over," he added.

Kit was silent for another long moment and he wished like hell he knew what was going on in her head.

"There was no way to extradite him?"

"It wasn't likely. Indonesia has no extradition treaty with the United States. And though it's possible he might have eventually landed in a country where the US *could* have extradited him more easily, the truth is, he knows just enough about his uncle's business that the Salazar cartel would never have allowed it; they would have killed him themselves before the ink was dry on the extradition agreement."

Her fingers tightened on her glass as she closed her eyes and took a deep breath. "I don't know what to think or feel, Garret. I'm trying, I am, but I just don't . . ." Her voice cracked as she stopped.

He reached for her hand, and though she didn't return his grip, she didn't pull away. They sat that way for several minutes, and he gave her time to gather her thoughts. He desperately wanted to ask her how she felt about him. Even more so, he wanted to tell her how he felt about her. However, some tiny but strong, rational part of his brain knew they needed to have this conversation first.

"I don't like it, Garret. I know what he did and I know that what happened to him is probably the best we could hope for—the best the family of the young girl he killed could hope for. But I don't like it."

He didn't either, which was why, he suddenly realized, his new job had come at just the right time. He stood behind everything he'd done in his career, but that didn't mean he had to be the one to keep doing those things.

"But then again, I can hardly judge, can I?" she asked. "I mean, look at what I did to my own father."

He didn't want her going there, but he knew he couldn't stop it. Her father had been a nasty piece of work, and she had most definitely done the world a favor when she'd precipitated his car accident. But taking a life, even when it was justified, had a way of killing the soul just a little bit. Because it was almost as if you were admitting to having no hope—no hope in the justice system, to be sure, but more importantly, no hope in humanity, no hope that good could triumph over evil without becoming just a little bit evil itself. Hope—like life—for people like him and Kit, was a frail thing. And if it shattered, there was no knowing just what would remain.

"Kit," he said, rubbing his thumb over her palm.

She looked up, held his gaze for the first time since she'd come into the room, and asked, "You love me, don't you?"

He wasn't sure where her question had come from, but he was sure of his answer. "Yes, very much."

"And if something happened like what happened last week, would you leave again?"

He wanted to say no. He wanted to assure her that he would never leave her again. But he'd done that. He'd said all those things to her and then left anyway. And so he told her the truth.

"Leaving you was the hardest thing I have ever done. Not because of what I was leaving you to do, but because I knew what it would mean to you that I did. I'd promised you I wouldn't do that anymore and I broke that promise. But if it happened again? I don't know, Kit." He'd had a reason—a good reason—why he'd left and they both knew it. But still, he'd made a promise to her and broken it.

He paused, took a deep breath, then continued. "I had a choice. Someone was trying to kill you. Someone who had already killed another woman. Someone who had already successfully tracked you down, attacked you, and *nearly* killed you. I knew who that someone was and I knew how to stop him. My choice was to stay and wonder every day while you were in that hospital if he was going to try to kill you again. Wonder if one day soon he would succeed. Or I could break your heart by breaking a promise to you and stop him. I made a choice to break a promise to you to ensure your safety and the safety of other women who came into his life. I don't like that I had to do it, but I don't regret it, Kit."

She looked at him with a thoughtful expression on her face. He tried not to get too excited by the fact that he was beginning to be able to read her again.

"I'm sorry, Garret," she said.

The comment came as such a surprise that he drew back and frowned. "For what?"

She leaned forward, pulled their joined hands onto her lap, and wrapped her other hand around them. "I'm sorry that was the choice you had to make. Please don't misunderstand—I'm still not sure how I feel about everything that happened. But I do know that the choice you had to make, between breaking a promise to someone you love and living indefinitely in fear that she'd be killed, isn't one anyone should have to make."

He had not thought of it that way, because in his mind there was no *real* choice. Oh, there was a choice, per se, but there was no way he would have been able to live with himself, or her, if he hadn't done everything he could to protect her. He hadn't lied when he'd said that walking away that day, leaving her lying in the hospital, was the hardest thing he'd ever done. But he'd *had* to do it. Even if it had meant she would never let him into his life again. At least she'd have a life to choose whom to let into. And that was what had mattered to him.

"I'm sorry too, Kit. I wish it could have happened differently. I wish it was something we could have talked about. I wish—"

She cut him off. "But it wasn't different and we couldn't have talked. It was what it was, Garret. What are we going to do from here?"

At her words, at her use of the word "we," the grip on his heart that had held him so tightly for the past week eased. They may not be okay, and they most definitely weren't going to go back to the happy-new-couple phase they'd been in before, but wherever it was they were going, they were going together.

He shook his head. "I don't know, Kit, but maybe it's something we can figure out together?"

For the first time in what felt like ages, he saw her smile at him.

"I don't know either, Garret. But maybe we could go to your place in Mexico for a little while. Maybe find some of the humanity we've both lost over the years. And then afterward, we can figure it out together."

ACKNOWLEDGMENTS

THIS IS THE FOURTH BOOK in the Windsor Series and my fifth in publication. Through all of them, I have had an editor that I feel lucky to continue to work with. So, Julie, thanks for sticking with me, even when you've had to patiently remind me like six hundred times that when I'm writing about a female, "blonde" is spelled with an "e" (and I won't say anything about when you have to remind me about which perspective I'm supposed to be writing from at any given time). My new beta reader, John Kurtze, also provided invaluable feedback—I know he'll notice some of the changes he suggested in this version.

My mountain movers continue to be a source of inspiration and joy; without them life wouldn't be nearly as fun. Of course, they are also the ones who assured me that I didn't need a graphic sex scene in this book, so you know who to go to if you disagree. Also, my ladies on the Eastside—Sarah, Jere, and Lisa—distance will never make a difference.

And last but not least, I want to acknowledge and thank my family for supporting me in the many, many ways they do, such as feeding me, making me laugh, buying me whiskey, promoting my books to their friends as well as random strangers, and just enjoying this journey we call life with me (not necessarily in that order).

Keep reading for a preview of Tamsen Schultz's upcoming book,

AN INARTICULATE SEA
WINDSOR SERIES BOOK 5

Rules. Everyone has them and everyone lives by them. Sometimes they're our own and sometimes they are someone else's. But when Deputy Chief of Police Carly Drummond finds a woman tortured, killed, and dumped in her town, she's forced to play by rules she doesn't understand that were put in place by someone she doesn't know. If she doesn't, life in Windsor—life as she knows it—could experience a sea change no one is prepared for.

Order. Drew Carmichael is man who likes order. He doesn't just like it, he requires it—it's the only reason he's been able to lead the double life he's been living for almost twenty years. But when he can't pull himself away from the secrets, uncertainties, and dangers swirling around Carly, his orderly life takes a dive and he finds himself swimming in waters he's never before encountered.

Chaos. Control is what Drew and Carly both want—control over their futures, over their growing feelings for each other, and most of all, over the situation that is threatening to throw their lives into chaos. But it is within this chaos that the opportunity to set a new course, to find a new horizon, can be found. If only they can stem the tide of the coming storm.

CHAPTER ONE

"IT SHOULD BE YOU," CARLY Drummond said to her partner, Marcus Brown, as they climbed out of their newly issued police SUV.

"Actually, it should be Ian," Marcus countered calmly. He was right, of course. But his logic did nothing to assuage her agitation, as unfounded as it might be.

Roughly, she zipped her jacket against the chill of the fall morning and started toward the door of her friend's home.

It had been just over a year since Marcus had been seriously injured in a near-fatal incident. And twelve months since Carly had been appointed to his former position of deputy chief of police. Three months ago, after being deemed fit for duty, Marcus had come back to work. Two months ago, she had requested that Vic Ballard, Windsor's chief of police, reinstate Marcus as deputy chief of police, but he'd refused and, much to her irritation, left her in charge. Two days ago, she'd had to miss most of a big fall leaf-peeping party she'd been looking forward to for months—a fundraiser thrown by two of her friends, Kit Forrester and Garret Cantona, to help raise money for one of the orphanages they supported—because, once again, duty had called. And to top it all off, just twenty minutes ago, Carly had received a call from Ian McAllister, the county sheriff and her good friend and mentor, telling her that some of Kit's lingering houseguests had found a dead body.

Yes, a dead body.

The last year had not been easy for her—and this day wasn't shaping up to be much better.

As Carly reached Kit and Garret's front door, Marcus came up alongside her and she paused to scan the area. Technically, the house was in county territory, so Marcus was right in that Ian, as sheriff, should be the one leading the investigation. But he'd been tied up with a multi-car accident in the southern-most part of the county, so he'd called in a favor—a favor she couldn't have turned down even if she'd wanted to.

"It will be fine," Marcus said.

"Says the man who has significantly more experience than I have," she retorted as she rang the bell.

She wasn't actually too concerned about whatever would come next; she was good at her job, had a solid—if small—team, and decent relationships with the assisting agencies. But she was tired—not physically, but mentally—from the last year.

"I've been out of the game for over a year. If anyone is rusty, it's me," Marcus countered.

Just when she was about to point out that, since he had been an MP before becoming a police officer, he still had her beat when it came to the number of investigations he'd been a part of, the door swung open to reveal a striking blonde woman whom Carly recognized from the fundraiser. But because she hadn't been able to stay very long, she hadn't been introduced to any of the guests, including this one.

"I'm Carly Drummond, Deputy Chief of Police," she said, holding out her hand.

The woman smiled then opened the door wider. "Dani Fuller, please call me Dani," she replied, then added, "I think you knew already that Kit and Garret left for Rwanda yesterday." She tried extending her hand somewhat out to the side to accommodate her exceptionally large, rounded belly. Something resembling shock must have shown in Carly's expression because Dani laughed. "I'm having twins, I'm actually only six months along, so you don't have to worry about me going into labor any minute, despite appearances to the contrary."

Only moments into the investigation and already she'd lost her "cop face." Taking a deep breath, Carly pulled on her metaphorical "big girl panties" and straightened her shoulders.

"Congratulations," she said. "This is Officer Marcus Brown. Dispatch reported a call about a possible body?"

"There's no 'possible' about it," came a voice from behind Dani. A voice Carly remembered more easily than she ought to. *This Monday morning just keeps getting better*, she thought.

Drew Carmichael's tall, lean frame appeared behind Dani's shoulders. He was tugging on leather gloves while his knee-length black jacket hung open, revealing a button-down shirt that was just about the same blue as his eyes and a pair of dark gray wool slacks. She'd met him a handful of times before: four or five times while investigating an attack on Kit that had happened outside Carly's old apartment, and then again, several months later in New York City, when she and Kit had gone out for a girls' night and run into him out on a date.

Hailing from a wealthy family that ran several businesses out of a New York City headquarters, Drew was a man who wore his wealth and power as comfortably as an old pair of jeans—although he didn't seem like the type who would actually *wear* an old pair of jeans.

But despite his sophistication, he had an odd sort of edge Carly hadn't quite figured out. Back when Kit had been assaulted, he'd inserted himself into the investigation like he'd had every right to be there. That alone wasn't a surprise, given his personality, but what *had* surprised her was that he'd seemed to know what he was talking about. And she had yet to puzzle out why a businessman from New York would have understood the intricacies of a criminal investigation.

"Deputy Chief Drummond." As he spoke, he gave a curt nod in her direction; then his eyes darted to Marcus.

"Mr. Carmichael." Carly responded with her own nod. "This

is Officer Marcus Brown. I assume you're the one who called it in?" A fact that didn't bode well. Before knowing Drew was involved, she'd held some hope that the "body" would turn out to be nothing more than an animal decomposed beyond easy recognition. Now, that thin thread of hope vanished, because if there was one thing she'd learned from her interactions with Drew, it was that if he bothered to make an assertion, it was only because it was true.

"Call me Drew," he all but ordered. He'd issued the same command several times before, but so far, she hadn't quite brought herself to follow it. "And no, it wasn't me. It was Ty, Dani's husband, who called. He and I were out for a morning walk when we saw her. He stayed with the body; I came back to show you the way."

Her eyes bounced to Dani, who seemed concerned about the situation, but surprisingly calm at the fact that her husband was out somewhere sitting with a dead body. Carly had a moment's reflection on the fact that Kit had some interesting friends.

Dani smiled. "My husband was a Navy SEAL and also a detective with Portland Vice for several years. While finding a body on a hike, especially here in Windsor, isn't exactly what he would have expected from his morning, he's not going to fall apart—and he also won't contaminate your scene." She added the last part with a small emphasis.

Carly felt a flush of embarrassment because contamination of her crime scene was exactly what she'd been worried about, and it hadn't been very charitable of her to be thinking that way. As a human being, she should have been at least a little concerned about Ty Fuller and his state of mind. Internally, she sighed.

"Thank you," she said to Dani before turning her gaze back to Drew, who was watching her with a look of patience that, to her mind, bordered on condescension. "Can you give us a rough idea of where the body is? The medical examiner will be coming along soon, as will the state police, and we'll need to give them a location."

"We followed that path there," he said, still standing behind

Dani in the open doorway as he pointed to a trail that led east, away from Kit's driveway. "I didn't have my GPS, so I can't give you a specific location, but we found her not far from a dirt road about twenty to twenty-five minutes up that trail."

Carly turned to Marcus. "Churchkill Road, do you think?"

Marcus's eyes went to the path and, after a moment, he nodded. "Probably. Lancaster Road is the main road that goes back into those hills, but Churchkill forks off and follows the ridge when Lancaster turns east. I'm pretty sure the fork happens before that trail comes out," he said.

"Were there any distinguishing landmarks on the road that you can remember?" Carly asked Drew.

He seemed to give the question some consideration before answering. "There weren't any houses nearby, but when I made my way to the road there was a bend not far to the north of the trail, and from there I could see a farm down in the valley. It had a large yellowish house and two big brown barns."

"The Kirby place," she confirmed. The Kirby family had been providing local beef to the Hudson Valley for generations; their farm was well known.

"Churchkill Road it is," Marcus said.

"Why don't you take the SUV and wait down where County 17 meets Lancaster Road?" she asked Marcus. "When the State Patrol and Vivi get there, you can lead them up Lancaster to Churchkill. By then, I should have reached the site and will be able to give an exact location."

Marcus agreed and she handed him the keys.

"Is it just this trail here I should take, Mr. Carmichael, or did you turn off at any point?" Carly gestured to the path that clearly started between two trees but was quickly engulfed in forest and greenery.

"Call me Drew. And I'll show you the way. As for you," he said, stepping through the doorway and turning to Dani. "You need to lie down and put your feet up. Ty will have my head if he finds out you've been running around while he's been gone."

"I wouldn't mind seeing that," Dani retorted with a grin.

Drew let out a long-suffering sigh. "Dani."

Dani let out her own sigh. "Fine, *Dad*," she said with obvious sarcasm. Then she turned to Carly and Marcus. "It was nice to meet you, Deputy Chief Drummond, Officer Brown. I wish it had been under better circumstances."

Carly smiled, somewhat intrigued by the interchange between these two guests of Kit's. Their age difference didn't appear to be more than a few years, but she hadn't missed the paternal tone of concern in Drew's voice when he'd issued his order to Dani. The obvious and easy affection between the two surprised her since she'd only ever seen him as cool and efficient.

Brushing the thought away, Carly stepped back to let him pass by, then she and Marcus followed him onto the driveway as Dani shut the door behind them. Her partner veered off to the SUV, as she and Drew continued toward the woods. She paused while Marcus backed out, then lifted a hand to him as he pulled out of the driveway. He answered with a small wave of his own before turning around the side of the house and out of sight, leaving her alone with the enigmatic Drew in the silence of the fall morning.

She exhaled into the clean, crisp morning air. The fall, with its cool nights and mornings, had settled in like a familiar blanket over the Hudson Valley. And with the drop in temperatures, the trees had turned the colors of fire; the hills were lit with reds, yellows, and brilliant oranges that contrasted sharply against a pale blue sky.

It was a beautiful day to find a body.

"Shall we?" he gestured toward the trail.

Carly nodded and preceded him into the woods without a word. They walked for several minutes in a silence punctuated by the sound of their feet landing on the dry ground and the occasional call of a bird or rustle of an autumn breeze through the dying leaves. As they walked, Carly turned her thoughts to what might lay ahead.

She *hoped* what Drew had come upon was simply the result

of a tragic accident. Crime in Windsor, with a few exceptions, was primarily made up of thefts or an occasional assault. Even so, she harbored no illusions about the Hudson Valley. Crime happened everywhere, even amongst the rolling hills and hay fields of her county. Still, she wanted to believe that the people she served and protected wouldn't violate their own community by committing murder. At least she hoped they wouldn't.

With this thought in mind, she took a deep breath, inhaling the comforting scents of fall as they began to climb the slight slope toward the ridge of the hill. It did not escape her notice that, even in hoping for the best, "the best" would still be a dead body.

"Churchkill?" Drew asked from behind her.

Coming seemingly out of nowhere, his word interrupted her thoughts and she wondered if she'd missed something he'd said earlier. When she paused and turned toward him to ask, she caught him by surprise. He nearly walked into her, but pulled up abruptly and stopped just short; then he stepped back a few inches to put some space between them.

"Churchkill," he repeated, presumably at her questioning look. "It's an unusual name, but I've noticed a lot of towns and roads in this area have the word 'kill' in them. I know there were a lot of revolutionaries around here back in the 1700s, but they couldn't have been *that* bloodthirsty."

That actually made Carly smile: his certainty in the morals of their founding fathers. She shook her head as she turned around and started walking up the trail again.

"No, they weren't. Or not any more so than they needed to be, I would imagine. Before the revolution, in the early 1700s, the area was settled heavily by the Dutch." As she spoke, the trail started a brief but steep ascent. Vain as she was, she tipped her hat to Murphy and his laws and accepted that she was going to be huffing and puffing as she talked. She'd either sound like a phone-sex operator or an out-of-shape cop, and after a fleeting moment's consideration, she thought it would be significantly more embarrassing to be thought of as the latter.

"And?" he prompted.

"The word 'kill' is the equivalent of 'creek' in Dutch, or in the Dutch language of the time." She unzipped her jacket then tucked an errant curl behind her ear as they continued. Thankfully, she could see the end of the rise ahead and she knew it would level out after that. "Churchkill Road ends at the Kirby farm now, but back in the day, it continued on and into one of the local hamlets. There's a church there, and at the edge of the church's property is a creek. It's a popular swimming and picnicking area today—and it was back then too."

"And because the road was the road that took people to the church creek, it became Churchkill Road," he concluded.

"Most likely, yes," she agreed.

"And you said the church is still there?" he asked as they started down the now-level path.

"It is. The whole hamlet is still there, but you can't reach it from this side anymore. There's a county road, a paved one, that will take you to it now."

They walked another minute in silence before he surprised her with another question.

"You love this area, don't you?"

Again, Carly came to a halt—this time at the personal nature of the question—and turned around. From where they stood, she could see the gentle roll of the hills, green fields cut out of the woods, and trees rioting with color.

She must have paused long enough because, beside her, Drew turned too.

"What's not to love?" she asked, not bothering to hide the wistfulness in her voice. Dotted with old farms and new gardens, the county stretched out before them, peaceful and inviting. She could see the old clock tower in town peeking through the trees miles away. In a few hours, she knew she'd hear the siren at the volunteer fire department echoing through the valley as it did every day at noon. The Kirby farm produced fresh local beef, the Zucchini Patch the most sought after fruits and vegetables, and, this time of year, The Apple Barn had apple cider donuts that were, well, not quite worth killing for, but definitely worth the thirty-minute drive. It was a place so achingly beautiful in so many ways—a place that felt very nearly enchanted at times—that she still had a difficult time absorbing the fact that she lived there. That she was a part of it.

And, as if to give voice to that difficulty, a familiar, uncomfortable feeling began to creep into her mind as she stood there taking it all in. Her chest began to tighten and her heartbeat thudded in her ears as the old recognizable panic set in, reminding her that no matter how much she felt like she belonged there, it could all be taken from her in an instant.

Abruptly, she turned and started back up the trail.

"It is lovely," Drew said, as he followed her.

Carly let out a little breath. "Yes, it is," she agreed, because that was what he would expect her to say.

She turned her attention back to their more immediate surroundings and several more minutes passed as they continued their walk. At one point, she stumbled over a tree root, and as she felt the pull of her uniform across her body, she also became uncomfortably aware of just how poorly police uniforms fit. Of course, a flattering fit wasn't the point and she knew she shouldn't even be thinking about it. But having someone so immaculately put together breezing along behind her wasn't putting her in the most charitable, or reasonable, of moods.

"Is it much farther?" she asked.

"Just around the bend," Drew answered with a gesture to their right.

Knowing how close they were to the scene sharpened her focus, making her more alert and aware of everything around her. Despite her doubts about her personal life and wardrobe, Carly *was* confident about her job. It was the one area of her life in which she felt completely and utterly competent. The certainty she felt concerning her professional life was like a security web that held the rest of her life together.

"Drew?" a male voice called from their right.

"Yes, it's us," Drew answered as they rounded the bend.

Carly stopped to take in the scene before acknowledging the other man.

The trail continued on to her right, but her eyes were drawn to the hill that rose sharply in front of her. She knew if she forged ahead, Churchkill Road lay less than two-hundred yards up the rise. But between where she stood and where the road ran, the land was uneven and littered with the leaves of past seasons. It was also dotted with enough trees to cast the area into a shadowed darkness, with sunlight managing to filter through the few spaces made by branches that had already shed their leaves.

Covered in leaves and debris and lying about three quarters of the way between the road and where Carly stood was the body of a woman. A body that looked as if it had rolled down the hill and come to an awkward and final stop.

She lay mostly on her stomach, but with the pitch of the hill, she'd rolled slightly onto her side, giving Carly a view of her back. The woman was wearing a dark rose-colored lightweight knit sweater that was covered in bits of leaves and small twigs, both of which were also tangled in her long, dark brown hair, which fell across her back and the ground behind her.

Though Carly could not see her face, there was no question in her mind that she was looking at the form of a woman. With the discernable dip of her waist and curve of her hip, the woman's body lay much like Carly's own did when she reclined on her side. Also, one of the woman's arms was thrown over her head, leaving a delicate, feminine hand in view. Those details, along with her hair and her petite feet—feet that were bare—left Carly with no doubt that Drew had been right when he'd first referred to the body as "her."

Moving her focus from the body back to the area around it, Carly scanned the hillside. It wasn't a bad spot for a body dump, and though she would need to wait for Vivi, the medical examiner, to make the official call and then for all the evidence to come in, it was pretty obvious to her that that was exactly what this spot was—a body dump. Whoever the woman was, Carly knew she hadn't died there, not given what she was—and wasn't—wearing. Which led her to believe that she probably hadn't died naturally, either. There was something reckless in the way the woman had been left, something that spoke of a careless disregard for human life.

"Carly?"

Turning to look at Drew, she caught a look of concern on his face.

"Yes?" she responded, wary of what he might be concerned about. There was, of course, the body to be apprehensive about, but it was also possible that he was wondering why she was just standing there—apparently doing nothing. Maybe he was even considering whether or not she had the ability to do the job at hand. It was a lot to read into a single word, but between being a woman in a male-dominated profession, and a younger woman at that, she almost couldn't blame him. Almost.

"You let out a big sigh, everything okay?"

She frowned. She hadn't remembered sighing. Then again, she'd been caught up in cataloging the scene.

"Other than her," Carly said with a small gesture of her head toward the woman, "everything is fine. I was just thinking that this scene isn't going to be the easiest to process."

"No, I doubt it is," came a response, this time from the man at Drew's side—presumably Dani Fuller's husband, Ty.

Carly switched her gaze from Drew to Ty. Both men had moved off to the side, well away from the body and the scene she and her team would need to comb through. Unlike Drew, with his lanky, sophisticated appearance, Ty Fuller came across as down-to-earth and *real* to her, or maybe just more like the men she was used to seeing where she lived. He was tall, almost as tall as Drew, and built more solidly—exactly what she would expect from a former SEAL—and definitely differently than Drew, whose physique looked like a swimmer's. Ty had dark hair and dark eyes, and in his jeans, boots, and leather jacket, he could have been any town's working man.

"You must be Ty Fuller," she said, walking forward to shake his hand.

"Call me Ty, please," he said before casting Drew a quick look.

"Ty, this is Deputy Chief Carly Drummond." Drew performed the introductions.

"Nice to meet you," Ty said. "I saw you briefly at the fundraiser, which would have been a more pleasant place to meet, but . . ." He stopped talking and shrugged in a gesture of "what can you do?"

"I was there but on duty and got called away about ten minutes after I arrived. I know Kit was happy you were all able to come. Now, I don't mean to be rude, but I need to radio my partner where we are, then I'd like to ask you a few questions. Both of you," she added.

The two men smiled politely as she stepped a short distance away to make her call to Marcus. She'd noted her GPS position when they'd arrived and relayed the information to him. She also gave him a quick debrief on the scene and asked him to warn the support vehicles to stay to the center of the road. Churchkill Road was a dead end—whoever had brought that body there would have had to turn around somewhere. They'd look for tire impressions at the two spots where the dirt road widened enough to turn a vehicle around between where the body had been dumped and the Kirby farm. But she didn't want to rule out getting any additional impression matches from the road coming in. It wasn't likely they'd find much, but she'd rather play it safe and preserve as much of the road as possible.

When she turned back, Drew and Ty were both leaning against the trunk of a large fallen tree. Ty had his hands tucked into his jacket pockets and Drew's arms were crossed. Both were silent and seemed lost in thought.

"I know this isn't all together new to you," she said to Ty with another gesture toward the woman behind them. "But it must have come as a surprise this morning. Can you tell me everything that happened, including whether or not you touched anything?"

Carly almost smiled when Ty answered the last part first, as adept as his wife in knowing what was foremost on her mind. "We came around the bend and saw her. Drew stayed back, but I approached from there," he said, pointing out the path he'd taken from the trail to the body, "and felt for a pulse. I didn't move the body in the process as I was able to reach her artery by reaching into the gap created by the arm that's raised over her head and her neck. When it was clear she wasn't alive, and she was cold to the touch, I backed out the way I came and have pretty much been standing here ever since."

She glanced at the body then turned back to the men. "Thank you," she said, acknowledging their caution. "I'll let the evidence teams know. And now, can you tell me what happened?"

"At the risk of sounding cliché," Drew spoke before Ty had a chance, "there isn't much to tell. We were on a morning walk, the same walk we've been doing since we got here three days ago, and we came around the bend and saw her. Ty then checked to see if there were any signs of life, and when there weren't, he placed the call to the police and I went back to meet you."

Again, it struck Carly as curious that Drew seemed so matter-of-fact about coming across a dead body. There was no horror, no panic, nothing to indicate that finding the body of a woman was anything other than a minor blip in his day. Maybe corporate America was more cutthroat than she thought.

"Did you see anything else or maybe hear anything? A car or vehicle on the road?" she pressed.

Both men shook their heads. Which wasn't a surprise. There were only three other properties this far up Churchkill Road before it dead-ended at the Kirby farm. Two of those were weekend homes and the third was empty and for sale; it was not a high-traffic kind of road.

"And about what time did you find her?" As the question came out of her mouth, she realized that perhaps she should be more circumspect. It was the right question to ask, of course, but was it possible they hadn't just "found" her but put her there, too? Her gut said no, but her intellect knew she'd also have to pursue that line of questioning.

"About eight thirty or so, right before we called," Ty answered.

"And if you're wondering," Drew spoke, "we were all at Kit's house last night, all five of us, all night. She has an alarm system that tracks when doors or windows are opened. Feel free to check it."

"Five of you?" she asked.

"Ty, Dani, my brother, Jason, and his wife, Sam, who also happens to be Dani's sister, and myself, of course," he answered. Succinct and efficient as always.

Carly didn't miss the assessing look Ty gave his friend.

"It's interesting that you would offer that information," Carly commented.

"It was going to be your next question, wasn't it?" Drew countered.

She cocked her head. "It was. But in my experience, most people are surprised when asked to provide their whereabouts or an alibi. Have you been through something like this before?"

A ghost of a smile touched his lips at her not-so-subtle inquiry into his past. "Not this specifically, but I've been involved in more than my fair share of investigations."

She held his gaze as she let his enigmatic statement sift through her brain. She briefly considered asking several of the follow-up questions that popped into her mind, but just as quickly, she dismissed the strategy. The truth was, she no more thought he was involved than she was; and somehow, instinctively, she knew that if she pressed him, she'd get nothing other than more oblique answers until she was frustrated and, potentially, flustered. And she had no intention of letting either of these men put her on the defensive. She gave a curt nod and let it go for the time being.

"Thank you, both. Now, if you'll excuse me, I hear some vehicles on the road and suspect the support team is arriving. I'm going to go up and meet them. You're both welcome to head back to Kit's; if we need anything more, we know where to find you."

She didn't wait for a response from the two men, though she didn't anticipate either of them leaving for a good long while. Making her way up the hill, she stepped onto the road just as Marcus came into sight in the police SUV. Standing off to the side, she watched as he pulled up, followed by Vivi in the medical examiner van, Ian in his sheriff's truck, and two state trooper vans carrying the evidence response team.

When everyone had gathered around her, she gave them the details of the situation. She looked to Ian to put a plan into place—partly because he was the senior officer, but mostly because he loved his plans. But Ian simply stared back at her, making it clear that he expected her, the responding officer and deputy chief, to make the decisions. She knew it was Ian's way of mentoring her, of encouraging her to grow professionally—something he'd been doing since they'd first met—and that she should be grateful for the opportunity, but as it was, she felt more resigned than anything else as she issued orders and delegated tasks.

Having sent Marcus down the road to check the two areas where a car was most likely to have turned around, Carly watched Vivi and her assistant, Daniel Westerbrook, make their way down to the body, careful of where they tread.

"Everything okay?" Ian asked, coming up beside her.

She lifted a shoulder. "Yes, fine. I mean other than that poor woman, of course."

"Of course," Ian murmured in agreement. Carly was aware of the evidence collection team starting their work. They were always a buzz of activity—a systematic buzz, but a buzz nonetheless. However, even as they moved around the scene—taking pictures, placing markers, and making notes—she and Ian watched Vivi and Daniel.

"It's hard to believe he's the governor's son, isn't it?" Ian asked, speaking of Daniel.

She let out a little laugh, "I would say yes, but after seeing how hard he worked on that first case we worked together, it's hard to see him as anything other than a dedicated forensic anthropologist." Carly didn't need to go into detail about just which case she was referring to—it was one neither she nor Ian would ever forget. A serial killer had landed in Windsor and set his sights on Vivi. It was also the case that had brought Vivi and Ian, now married with a one-year-old son, together over two years ago.

"This should be your case, you know," she said after a short silence.

"And I'll be the officer of record, but there's no reason you can't lead the charge. After all, that's what good managers do, right? Manage down," he asked with a grin.

Carly all but rolled her eyes at him. He wasn't doing this to manage down, he was doing this because he thought it would be a good opportunity for her. And even though she wasn't entirely happy about embracing the opportunity, she knew he was right. Glancing at her former boss, she found herself wishing, not for the first time, that Ian hadn't left the Windsor Police department after his short stint as their deputy chief of police, the position she now held. Of course, she knew why he'd made the move and become the county sheriff, and she honestly believed it was the best move for him, but still, she missed having his daily guidance and support.

"Fine," she said with a small laugh. "Why don't you go manage the evidence team then? I'm going to join your wife at the body. Whoever she is, I hope we can figure out what happened to her, and quickly." She paused for a moment, letting the sounds of the scene filter through her mind. "No one deserves to be treated that way," she added quietly.

"It does speak of carelessness and maybe even some depravity," Ian replied.

And that was the part that really got to her: the thought of such depravity in Windsor. She knew that with 7,000 people, they would have their fair share of good and bad. But for the most part, crimes committed by *residents* of Windsor were pretty minor. And there was some measure of comfort in that knowledge.

But even as she approached the body and caught a few of Vivi's words as they were faithfully documented by Daniel, she knew that comfort was an illusion. Crime, even murder, could happen anywhere people lived. And today, it just happened to have landed on her doorstep.

"Rough time of death appears to be somewhere between eight and ten p.m. last night," Vivi reported without preamble as soon as Carly came to a stop a few feet from the body. "Female, obviously," she continued. "No ID in the pockets I can reach. Hard to say age without a closer examination, but judging by her hands and what I can see of her face, I'd say well into her forties. I won't know cause of the death until we get her back to the lab for an autopsy, but I can tell you now, it wasn't a natural death."

After working with Vivi for more than two years, Carly knew she shouldn't be surprised by what the medical examiner could determine so quickly with so little information, but she was. Of course, she'd suspected it wasn't a natural death, but to hear Vivi pronounce it was entirely different.

"How do you know?" Carly asked.

Vivi glanced up, ignoring the crime scene tech who was busy snapping pictures of the body, the flash going off at regular intervals in the tree-shaded area.

"See here and here?" Vivi asked, pointing to an area on the woman's jeans and another on her sweater. At first Carly saw nothing, but as she looked closer, she saw small spots of dark discoloration.

"I see the spots, but what are they?"

"Blood," Vivi pronounced as she sat back on her heels. "There are several areas like that on her clothing, areas where blood has seeped through, staining the fabric."

Carly was silent for a long moment, as was Vivi. No doubt, they were both wondering just what Vivi would find when she removed the victim's clothing back at the lab.

"How many areas?' Carly asked.

"Seven, so far," Daniel answered. "And we haven't turned the body yet."

"Any idea what caused them?"

Vivi shook her head. "And I don't want to lift her sweater to look while we're out here in the woods, I'd rather do that back at the lab."

"Of course," Carly murmured. "Are you almost ready to turn the body?" she asked, wanting to get a look at the face of the woman they were all focused on.

"I need a few more minutes and then we'll be ready," Vivi answered.

Carly watched Vivi and Daniel turn their attention back to the woman, then took a few steps up toward the road and caught sight of Ian talking with one of the evidence techs. With a wave, she got his attention, then gestured for him to join her with Vivi and Daniel.

Once he had made his way to her side, she spoke. "Vivi is going to turn her in a minute, and I want you here to see if you recognize her. There hasn't been any obvious identification found yet."

His head bobbed once in response.

Even though, in recent years, she'd been living in Windsor longer than Ian—she'd moved to the area five years earlier, and he'd only returned from the Army about two years after that—Ian had grown up in the small town and knew quite a few more people than she did, or at least he could recognize more than she could.

When Vivi and Daniel indicated that they were ready, Carly watched them brace the body. Taking care not to disturb anything more than necessary, the pair rotated the woman until she lay prone on her back.

Unexpectedly, Carly experienced a moment of hesitation. She didn't want to see the woman's face, she didn't want to know if it was someone from the community who had been tortured and killed—at least not yet, not until she'd had a moment to really brace herself for that option. And so her eyes went first to the woman's feet then slowly traveled up her legs. Now that she knew what to look for, she could see more signs of bleeding through the light blue denim of the jeans. Tracing her gaze upward, the rose-colored sweater had been hiked up enough to reveal a thin strip of flesh at the woman's waist, but it also looked like parts of the knit top were stuck to the victim's skin—perhaps from dried blood—leaving the general shape of the garment skewed.

It was when her eyes caught on a thin gold chain around the victim's neck that Carly's hesitation turned swiftly into a sense of foreboding that settled surely on her shoulders. For reasons she didn't understand, her instincts warred with her intellect for a moment and all she wanted was to be away. Far away.

"Carly?" Ian asked at her side.

Using him as a reprieve, she looked away from the scene and at her former boss. "Yes?"

"Do you recognize her? I don't. Vivi?" he added.

Carly turned her attention to Vivi, who was shaking her head.

"No ID that we can find, either," Daniel said having concluded his preliminary search of the jeans pockets.

Knowing she had to swallow the irrational fear that had gripped her, Carly took a deep breath. And looked down.

Years ago, when an infection had developed after she'd had her wisdom teeth extracted, a dentist had prescribed a painkiller and she would never forget the moment when it had kicked in. She'd been beyond grateful for the pain relief, but as the medication had washed through her body, she'd felt a disconcerting numbness spread from the top of her head down to her toes. She knew there were people who liked that feeling, but to Carly it had felt like the life, *her* life, was being drained from her own body, leaving nothing behind but a confused, emotionless empty shell. And that wasn't something she'd ever wanted to experience again.

But now, looking down at the face of the woman who had mostly likely been killed, then dumped, not ten miles from where Carly lived and worked, she had that exact same feeling.

Seconds passed, or maybe it had been minutes, when she

became dimly aware of Vivi's voice saying her name—once, then a second time. Then she felt Ian's hand on her shoulder. That touch, that solid, real touch, a touch that was meant for comfort, was just the reminder she needed. A reminder that there were special protocols she had to follow now—protocols that had nothing to do with processing the crime scene. No, the rules and procedures that came flooding back to her were ones that no one around her could know about.

She took a deep breath and pushed the fear crowding her brain back into the shadows.

"Yeah?" she answered, stepping away and looking at him.

"Do you know her?"

Carly glanced at the face again, then frowned. "No, she doesn't look familiar to me," she forced herself to answer. She didn't spare a glance for Vivi, knowing the trained forensic psychologist would pick up more than anyone else.

She let her gaze linger on the woman long enough to appear as if she was giving what she saw before her some consideration. "Can you tell us anything else, Vivi?" she asked. And only when she was sure Vivi had turned her attention back to the body did Carly look at her friend.

"No—no more than what we already know, but I can add that her face seems to confirm my original impression that she is well into her forties."

As Vivi spoke, movement to Carly's left caught her attention and she looked up to find Drew and Ty still leaning against the fallen trunk. Ty's eyes were on the body and she had little doubt that, as an ex-vice cop, he was probably asking himself all the questions cops ask—who, what, why, when, etc.

But not Drew. Drew wasn't looking at the body. No, he was watching her—as if the dead body at her feet were of no consequence and his only interest was in her. She held his gaze, wondering if he'd seen her reaction to the woman's face. Wondering if he thought that the sight of a body had been a shock to her relatively inexperienced eyes.

But his face held no judgment. No, as he stood there, still leaning against the trunk with his arms crossed, he looked to be calmly assessing her. When he continued to watch, she gave him a small, dismissive smile then simply turned and walked away. She felt his eyes following her, or perhaps it was her imagination, but as she moved away from the scene, she pushed his image from her mind.

Climbing up the hill, she tamped down her initial shock. Halfway to the top, she stopped to answer a crime scene tech's question, then directed another tech to take some extra photos of an area by the side of the road that looked slightly more disturbed than the rest. Before she'd even set foot on the road, she'd slipped back into her role as deputy chief of police.

Up by the vehicles, she paused for a moment and watched the activity. It was easier to focus on the tasks at hand than face what she knew she would ultimately need to face. She forced back a wave of sadness; now was not the time or the place. She knew that if she let the sorrow even so much as crack open a door it would leave an opening for the fear, panic, and utter confusion Carly knew was hovering in the far reaches of her brain, clamoring to be heard.

"Hey, Carly," Marcus said as he approached her, carrying a tire cast he'd presumably taken from one of the turn-out areas she'd sent him to scout. "I got one impression, but who knows if it will turn into anything useful. I hear the victim was cut up pretty badly, or it appears that way. One of the techs mentioned it to me on my way back. Any ID?"

She looked at Marcus, newly back on the job, almost back to his old self. She didn't want him here. But then again, she didn't want him anywhere else. He was the one person who would know exactly what it meant when she told him what she was about to tell him.

"Carly?"

She turned her gaze back to the primary scene. From where she stood, she could see the tops of heads—Vivi's, Daniel's, and

Ian's—along with those of a few techs moving around the hillside. A brisk autumn breeze touched her face and lifted her hair; the sun now hung high in the sky.

It was a beautiful day to find a body.

"It's Marguerite," she said.

Printed in the USA
CPSIA information can be obtained
at www.ICGtesting.com
JSHW031707140824
68134JS00038B/3569